"Out of the truck!" Laura yelled, grabbing the camera for no other reason than not wanting to lose another one. Chris was already fumbling with her door handle and had fallen out when Laura reached down to grab her hand, pulling the smaller woman up and forward as they ran furiously to the relative safety of the culvert. Scrambling into the opening, they settled on their knees looking back at the world behind them as all hell broke loose. Laura punched the record trigger on the camera, looking into the viewfinder just long enough to make sure that there was an image framed beyond the opening. Without pausing for thought, she reached out an arm and pulled Chris to her, settling the other woman against her side and yelled in the reporter's ear, "Don't let go!"

Chris shuddered against the suction of the wind and held on to Laura for dear life. She could feel the assault of water, grit and other debris against the exposed skin of her face and hands. The wind howled like a jet at takeoff, deafening in its intensity. She squeezed her eyes shut tighter if that was possible, and just when she thought that she couldn't stand it anymore, the fury turned off, like a faucet, leaving unnatural quiet behind.

Laura became conscious of her own ragged breathing in the eerie silence that followed and realizing that she was still holding Chris in an iron grip, she dropped her arms. Concerned, she lifted the smaller woman's chin and looked into green eyes for a clue as to what to do next. *Ah, hell. Go directly to jail, do not pass go, do not collect two hundred dollars.*

She found the mouth under hers softer than she expected, and for the first time in as long as she could remember, Laura wished for a little more expertise in the area of kissing, not certain that she was even doing it right, but enjoying the texture and the taste. She pulled back, gently letting go of Chris' lower lip and swallowed, preparing herself for whatever was going to happen next.

Chris blinked, not certain that the kiss had even really happened, and wanting much more. Then the implications crashed down and she couldn't begin to keep up with all the questions tripping through her mind. She cleared her throat nervously. "Cat's out of the bag?"

"Oh, yeah."

**Other books by**

## Justice House Publishing

**Accidental Love**
BL Miller

**The Deal**
Maggie Ryan

**Of Drag Kings and the Wheel of Fate**
Susan Smith

**Hurricane Watch**
Melissa Good

**Josie & Rebecca:**
**The Western Chronicles**
BL Miller & Vada Foster

**Lucifer Rising**
Sharon Bowers

**Redemption**
Susanne Beck

**Tropical Storm**
Melissa Good

# The Deal

by

Maggie Ryan

**Justice House Publishing, Inc.**
Tacoma, Washington, USA
www.justicehouse.com

THE DEAL



Cover art by BF Reed

Book Design by R Paterson



This is printed on acid-free paper.
The typeface is Times New Roman, 10 point.

ISBN 0-9677687-7-2

March 2001

2 3 4 5 6 7 8 9

PRINTED IN AMERICA

## Acknowledgments

*Lisa said, "Of course you can do this." And so I did, but not without her help. Thanks for being my best good friend.*

## A Note from the Author

About the TV business… The United States is divided up into about 210 TV markets. New York is number 1, Los Angeles is number 2, Chicago is 3, and so on. This novel takes place in a medium market at 61. That actual market is Richmond, VA, but I just inserted a fictional place because it's my universe. Any similarities to on-air personnel, reporters, or management at any TV station in any market are purely coincidental.

*For Jennifer*

*"Couldn't you have just kicked him in the nuts?"*

*I'm gonna lose my job.*

*I'm probably not going to work in TV ever again.*

*And I'm gonna be sued.*

She sat in her office with the door closed and the lights off. Four TV monitors were on across the room, lighting her face with their flickering. Her long dark hair gleamed with blue highlights from the various network late shows as she stared dully into space. The monitors were always on; *god forbid some other station across town would cut in and we not know about it*, she thought.

Sighing, she thumped her forehead down on the desk. She could still hear some activity going on in the newsroom, though most everyone had left after the 10 o'clock newscast. The overnight crew didn't really get cranking until after midnight. *Well*, she thought, *if I'm going to make a clean getaway, now's the time to do it.*

Shit.

With that, Laura Kasdan gathered up her briefcase and her box of belongings and left her office. You never brought more into a TV station than you could carry out in one box, running. Someone had told her that years ago, and after today she understood the sentiment.

*Deep breath, open the door, and just walk*, she told herself. Laura strode purposefully across the newsroom, turned, and looked back, noticing the fresh bloodstain on the carpet. *Cleaning that will probably be coming out of my successor's budget*, she thought. *Noses do bleed profusely, don't they?*

And with that, she walked down the hall and out of the building.

The General Manager of KDAL had two problems. One was his News Director, and the other was his news anchor, Roger MacNamara. Roger was the number one on-air personality in Dallas. He spoke with authority, and his journalistic integrity was unimpeachable. He was Walter Cronkite and Edward R. Murrow all rolled into one.

At least that's what market research told the suits at Corporate. Dark-haired with just a bit of silver on the temples, carefully colored every two weeks, and chiseled features, he oozed sincerity...*well, when you can fake that, you've got it made*, the GM thought. Roger was also a prima donna who hit the sauce pretty hard and was a lawsuit waiting to happen.

Laura Kasdan was the best News Director he'd ever worked with, and he'd worked with some good ones. She didn't take any crap or any excuses, and she'd gotten them back to number one on all the prime time newscasts. He pinched the bridge of his nose and grimaced. Two years ago, when Laura Kasdan had been named as the News Director, everyone in the building had been shocked. She had the rep though, the GM thought as he drummed his fingers on the open personnel file in front of him. KDAL needed some fresh blood, and boy, did they get it.

There was opposition in the newsroom, of course. Just how did Corporate justify handing over the news operation of their flagship station in a top five market to a twenty-eight year-old whiz kid?

But Kaz had done everything they'd asked of her. She'd trimmed the fat, streamlined the organization, and delivered the numbers. The ratings were everything they'd hoped for and a little bit more. The reporters and photogs, always an unruly bunch even in the best circumstances, were brought in line. And they'd finally gotten the right teams of on-air talent together.

Everything was going so smoothly, something was bound to screw up.

*Then Roger had to go and grab her ass*, the GM fumed. According to witnesses, Laura asked him to remove his hand.

He didn't...and all hell broke loose.

Laura spun around and punched him in the nose. *Punched is really too mild a word for what she did to his nose. Socked, slugged, splattered, flattened...whatever, 'ol Rog is gonna be off the air for a while. Thank god it wasn't sweeps, but it's still a public relations nightmare.*

*So there it is...I want to keep 'em both, but that's not gonna happen*, the General Manager thought as he picked up the receiver and punched in a phone number. *I bet Corporate already knows*, he smiled wryly.

They did.

It was a forty-five minute commute from the station to Grapevine where she lived, and even though it was March it was warm enough to have the windows open as she drove her Jeep down I-635. Laura had the music up really loud, partly because of the wind noise and partly so she wouldn't have to think about Roger and her job.

She'd been spoiling for a fight after a day of a million and one frustrations. Stories had fallen apart and the reporters couldn't seem to get a firm hold on the stories that were working. The newscasts had seemed incomplete. Not a good news day, she mused, running her hand through her hair as it blew in the wind.

There was still a lot of traffic on the interstate, especially for a Thursday night. Laura changed lanes to get ready for her exit. *Well*, she thought, *you can put it out of your mind for only so long. There's going to be hell to pay, on so many levels. You could go to work for a news consulting firm. You could teach the part on what not to do when dealing with talent.*

The guard at the gate waved the Jeep through and Laura continued around the tree-lined street until she got to her house, opened the garage door with the remote, and pulled the Jeep inside next to the gleaming chrome of a Triumph motorcycle. She picked up her briefcase, shoved it into the box, and then carried it all inside, dropping the load just inside the door. Laura spared a glance toward her answering machine, noting that there were twenty-eight messages waiting. She unclipped her pager from her waistband and tossed it on the counter by the phone, making her way from the living room to the master bedroom and into the bathroom where she started the shower.

She stripped efficiently, tossed her clothes in the hamper, and stepped into the shower stall. After wetting her hair, she leaned back against the wall and slowly slid down until she was sitting with her chin on her knees with the water pounding the top of her head. *Oh god, what have I done?*

She stayed like that until there was no hot water left. When it ran cold, she figured there was no point in it anymore and she stepped out of the stall and grabbed a towel, dripping water all over the bathroom floor. After slipping on an oversized t-shirt and boxer shorts, she began combing out her hair, looking into the mirror at tired blue eyes, ignoring the phone as it began to ring, figuring the machine would pick it up.

"Laura, this is Don Farmer at Corporate. We need to talk. Uh, you've put us in a hell of a position, and we need to talk about how this is gonna shake down. Give me a call in the morning…probably not a good idea to go to the station tomorrow…"

*No shit*, Laura thought as she listened to the machine echo eerily through the house.

"Anyway, I wanted to let you know that you still have some options…We're not ready to cut you loose, so just hang tight…call me."

Laura walked back to the kitchen where the answering machine was. There were twenty-nine messages now, and she deleted them all. She'd call Don in the morning, but there wasn't anyone else she wanted to talk to, or explain to.

Options. Laura snorted. All her choicest options disappeared when she plowed her fist into Roger's face. She crawled into bed, switched off the light and rolled onto her side, hugging a pillow to her chest. *Oh, come on, you have options…You can take some time off and play some golf.* She yawned, the fifteen-hour day catching up with her. *Brood about it in the morning*, she told herself.

And Laura Kasdan closed her eyes on the worst day of her thirty year-old life.

The alarm didn't go off and for a minute, just a minute, Laura thought she'd overslept. The clock read seven-fifteen, and Laura rolled over with a concerted effort to prolong her sleep. *Don's not going to have his butt into his office until nine Atlanta time*, she thought, *so go back to sleep.*

Except that her mind was off and running, making her stomach churn.

No point, Laura sighed after a few minutes, so she sat up and threw the covers off and ambled into the kitchen, rubbing her neck absently. *Staring into the refrigerator is not going to make food appear*, she told herself, *you have to buy it once in a while*. She grabbed a Coke, popped it open and took a big gulp, feeling it burn all the way down. *Ah, the breakfast of champions*, Laura thought as the phone rang.

"Kaz, it's Brian," the General Manager said. "Pick up the phone, I know you're there. I called the pro shop and they said you hadn't called for a tee time yet and I know it's too early for you to get a hold of your lawyer."

Laura picked up. "All right, what's going on."

"Jesus, Kaz, I left about 20 messages on your machine last night, could you have at least given me a sign that you made it home okay?"

"I made it home okay. How's Roger's nose?"

"Roger needs a plastic surgeon and he's gonna be off the air for a bit. God knows how we'll file the insurance claim. Couldn't you have just kicked him in the nuts?"

"I'm not sure he had any to kick."

"Very funny," Brian said. "Both of you are in a shitload of trouble; I called Don Farmer last night, he already knew everything."

"I know, I had a message to call him this morning," Laura told him.

"Well, forget that, my friend, he's on his way here. He called last night when you weren't answering your phone or your beeper…"

"I turned it off."

"…and said he'd be on the 10am Delta from Atlanta. So get dressed and get to DFW, pick him up, and do what you have to do to save your career."

"Roger grabbed me, and I have to save *my* career?"

"You know you can't fuck with the talent, Kaz, they're like race-horses: when they're running good they're money in the bank. News Directors pale next to a thirty share."

"I got you that thirty share!"

"I guess it comes down to this: You're young, you can still make it to the network if you want, but if you make waves, if you sue, you commit career suicide. Roger wins anyway. You are three years away from your vested stock plan. Can you swallow your pride and stay in this corporation for three years for half a million dollars?" Brian took a breath. "If you can walk away from that, then walk. But otherwise, get to DFW and pick up the head of News Operations at the largest employee-owned media conglomerate in the country and do what you have to do to save your career!"

"Brian, you know I'm out already…I'll miss you."

"Yeah, me too. I hope you end up someplace nice. If you never punch anyone ever again, you might even get your own station." He paused. "I'm sorry…maybe the deal won't be too bad."

"You're right, I'd better get going."

"One thing, Kaz…be careful what you agree to. Don't let them back you into a corner—or hang you out to dry."

"Later, Brian." She hung up and padded back to the bedroom to get dressed.

There wasn't much that frightened Laura Kasdan; she worked in an environment that was hostile at best and outright confrontational at worst. But driving to DFW was tantamount to taking your life in your hands and it always made her nervous. Traffic around the airport was miserable on this Friday morning, and she resigned herself to a good long walk from the parking area to the Delta terminal. She stepped out of the Jeep and felt the wind gust around her, blowing her khaki pants against her legs. She shrugged into a jacket over her red polo shirt and started walking, not looking forward to the encounter with Don. As she entered the terminal, she moved her sunglasses to the top of her head and inhaled, smelling that strange airport smell that brought with it the promise of journeys ending and beginning.

She checked the monitors on the way down the concourse, noting that the flight was on time, and made her way through security, dumping her keys into the dish that the agent held out for her and reaching for her pager. Then she remembered that she'd left it on the counter, turned off, her one last tangible contact with the newsroom that had been her life for the past two years.

She stepped through the metal detector, picked up her keys, and continued on to the gate, getting there just as the passengers were arriving through the long plastic hallway connected to the plane. She waited with her arms crossed until she spotted the tall, stocky blond man carrying an oversized briefcase and then she moved toward him.

Don spotted her immediately and smiled, "Kaz," he said, "good to see you, wish it was under better circumstances."

"Likewise, Don," she answered. "Did you check anything?"

"No, I'm just here to see you and then I'm gone. I've gotten us a meeting room; let's see if we can find out where it is." He stepped up to the check in booth, inquired after the location, then they both started back down the concourse.

They followed the signs and turned down a narrow hallway, past a small office where a woman at a desk looked up and smiled at them. "I reserved a conference room, William-Simon Communications," Don informed the woman.

"Yes, Mr. Farmer," she answered. "Room three, just down the hall; your lunch is ready as you requested." Laura and Don made their way to the room; Don opened the door and Laura stepped inside. Don followed, closing the door behind him.

"Well, Kaz," Don said as he pulled up a chair, "this is a supreme cluster fuck. What the hell were you thinking?"

"Wasn't thinking anything. He grabbed my butt and I slugged him." She reached up and plucked the Ray Bans off the top of her head and tossed them on the table. "I have grounds for a lawsuit, so does he. You want him back on the air, and that's sort of impossible if I'm running the newsroom. So unless you've become the hiring and firing fairy, I can only assume that you've come to cut a deal." She paused and leaned forward. "So, what's the deal?"

Icy blue eyes narrowed at him across the table and Don took stock of the woman seated there. Well, you couldn't fault Roger's taste; she was beautiful, that dark hair and those incredible eyes set in that perfectly proportioned face. She'd never be anchor material; no one would buy the news from looks like those. But in a business where everyone wanted to be on the air, she'd been an exception. Just a little while as a reporter, and then she'd turned into one hell of a producer. Now, regardless of her age, she was the best news director in the company and he'd be damned if someone else was going to snatch her up.

"Brief and to the point as always, Kaz," Don answered. "All right, you get to be News Director at another station, your salary and benefits stay the same. Roger is reprimanded and retires in three years, you come back to Dallas and run the show. How's that?"

"Which station?" Laura asked in a low, dangerous voice.

"WBFC in Burkett Falls." Don inwardly winced, waiting for the reaction.

"Burkett! Jesus, what is that, a number sixty something market?" She stood up shouting. "From top ten to Bum Fuck Egypt. I should have killed Roger—at least I could've stayed in Texas!"

"Look—it's just three years, Kaz, and when you get back, you run the show in Dallas...not just the News Department, the station. You'll be the GM." Don waited for the implications to sink in.

"What about Brian?" she asked quietly.

"Brian's going to be a Regional Manager in three years; he'll be over 15 stations, probably including Dallas." Don waited a moment. "You're on the same track, you know, if you don't hit anyone else." She was considering it, and he knew he was close.

*Be careful, Laura*, she told herself, and tipped her head back as she weighed her options. It was incredibly tempting to just tell Don, no how, no way, take your medium market pissant station and shove it where the sun don't shine. But no...*remember the plan, Laura,* she told herself. Three years was all she needed in the company, even if it was in exile from Texas.

"You need an answer today, right?" Don nodded. "One thing: I have Cowboy season tickets and I'm not giving them up. Get me to Dallas for the games and you have a deal." Laura smiled.

"Awww, they're not even a good team anymore." Don said.

Laura actually snarled, "Otherwise I go shopping—I start here in town, and I will make it my goddamned mission in life to see that KDAL never sees a thirty share again."

"You don't have to be nasty, we've got airline trade," Don smiled.

"You were pretty sure of yourself there, Don," Laura returned with a lopsided smirk.

"I won't fight if I can't win, Kaz. Learn from that." He pulled a file out of his briefcase, passed it to her and checked his watch. "Did you park in the short term lot?"

"No, long term." She smiled at him and lifted one eyebrow. "I always plan for most situations. Learn from that." Don gave a little snort and tossed two airline tickets on the table. "We have tickets for the 12:15 flight to Burkett Falls. Art Dement, the GM, is expecting us. You'll arrive back around eight, and unless you just can't imagine going through with this, you'll have the weekend to start planning your move."

"What, no golf?" Laura said, half joking, then sobered. "What if Mr. Dement doesn't want me for a News Director?"

"It's not his choice anymore," Don said, standing. "He needs help and I'm gonna drop six feet of blue-eyed help on his station and watch what happens." Both of them looked back at the plate of sandwiches in the middle of the table that neither one of them had touched. They looked at each other, shrugged, sat back down, and started on the sandwiches. It sure beat airline peanuts.

The flight was uneventful and Laura wiggled her jaw a little to ease the uncomfortable pressure that had built up in her ears in the pressurized cabin. The closed in space made her a little antsy as they taxied to the gate, and as soon as the flight attendant opened the door, she and Don stepped out into the aisle and moved forward with the rest of the crowd off of the plane.

Coming through the gate, Don spotted who he was looking for and gave a brief wave. Laura followed him over to a middle-aged man with salt and pepper hair and a beard. Don performed the introductions and Laura offered a hand to the General Manager of WBFC.

"I've heard a lot about you, Ms. Kasdan," he said smoothly, shaking her hand with a firm, dry grip. Blue eyes looked into his ordinary brown ones. For a moment, he was aware of an incredible surge of power and charisma, then it was gone. He blinked. "We didn't think we'd see a candidate for our news director's job with your kind of…qualifications." Laura raised an eyebrow. *So that's how it's going to be*, she thought.

"I didn't think I'd be applying," she answered sweetly. He laughed a bit nervously.

"C'mon, the car's out front, we'll go to the station and take a look around." The three of them went down an escalator, past the rental car counters and out the automatic sliding glass doors where a gold Lexus waited. *How cliché*, Laura thought. *I'd like to meet a GM who didn't drive a Lexus*. She flipped her dark hair back over her shoulder and smirked at Don as she opened up the front passenger door and slid into the seat, pulling her Ray Bans out of her jacket pocket and putting them on.

Art got in and started the car, pulling it smoothly away from the curb. He stole a glance at Laura's profile. He wasn't sure what he expected, but the beautiful woman sitting next to him was not it. This might not be such a bad deal after all. "So you went to UT? Great to win that national championship last year, huh?"

"Um…I went to Texas, not Tennessee." Laura rolled her eyes, glad of the sunglasses and hearing Don's low laugh coming from the back seat.

"Oh, right. I just saw UT on the stuff that Corporate sent last night, and I assumed…"

"S'alright," she drawled, "An honest mistake." She shifted in her seat and looked at him. "Tell me about your news operation."

"Right. We do a Noon, Five, Six, and Ten, Monday through Friday, and a Morning Show from five-thirty to seven during the week and from eight to nine on the weekends. Then a Five or Six on the weekends, depending on network, plus a Ten O'Clock newscast." He smiled over at her. "We do more news than anyone else in the market."

"How many people?" Laura asked.

"Sixty in the newsroom, that doesn't include part timers. They're a good bunch but they don't have much direction. The Managing Editor is young and a little on the explosive side, but he's been running things since our news director left." He took a breath. "We're not major market, Ms. Kasdan, but we have a clue about how to do news."

"Call me Kaz," Laura said. "What about live?"

"We've got two live trucks in town and one up at the Jacksonville bureau, that's about 50 miles north of Burkett, and part of our DMA. No satellite truck," his eyes met Don's in the rearview mirror, "…yet, but our competitor has one that they went in halfsies with their network for. Two of the trucks are scheduled to be replaced this year. There are ten news vehicles, none older than two years, and we just replaced all the newsroom computers with Pentium III processors. We're using Associated Press as our service and we subscribe to CNN. What else do you need?"

"What's your on-air talent situation?"

"All the on-air guys are under contract right now. No one's up for renewal until October, except for the noon anchor. I know that makes November sweeps a little tricky if you were to make any changes, but if you're gonna change, we'll want to wait 'til after May anyway." Art looked at Laura for a minute and continued. "The last few books have been disasters for us. We're losing huge chunks of our audience to the guys across town, and revenue from first quarter has sucked. I need... We need a really good May book. Here we are."

They pulled into a small lot in front of a square brick building. The landscaping was tasteful, and a four-color logo looked down from one corner proclaiming: Action News 8 –Where the News Comes First. Laura blew out a short breath. *There really are too many clichés in this freaking business*, she thought.

The lobby had a red clay tile floor that had been waxed and buffed until it gleamed, with the requisite on-air talent portraits decorating the walls. The receptionist smiled and buzzed the three of them through a set of double doors that opened up into an area filled with desk cubicles and offices with actual doors. "This is Sales," Art gestured, "and the business offices. My office is at the end of the hall. News and Production are upstairs and they overlook the studio." He led them to a black metal staircase and started up while Don and Laura followed close behind. The relative quiet was broken as soon as Art pushed open the glass door at the top of the stairs and the full pandemonium of a busy newsroom on a Friday afternoon spilled out.

Danny Rendally had the desk at the very back corner of the newsroom for a reason. He was the most senior reporter and as others had left, he took over desks that slowly moved him back to the prime office position. His desk sat facing the door so he could observe everything in the newsroom, all the comings and goings plus the added bonus protection of knowing that if some nutcase came through the door with a gun, upset about something they'd reported, he wouldn't be the primary target. It had happened before in other markets. Paranoia had worked very well for Danny and he wasn't about to change.

So he was paying attention when the GM came through the door with a guy he recognized as a corporate suit, and a tall, dark-haired woman who didn't look like Corporate at all. She was casually dressed for one thing, her jacket pushed up past her elbows, wearing khakis and a polo shirt. Plus, she actually *looked* at the newsroom. When her blue eyes finished their sweep and fastened on him, he swallowed nervously as it all clicked into place.

The Kazmanian Devil.

Well, that's what some of the reporters from Dallas called her after she'd given a seminar at RTNDA, the News Director's convention last year. *Laura Kasdan in Burkett Falls*, he thought as the threesome went into the News Director's office. *What the hell is going on?* He turned and reached for his phone.

Don closed the door and slipped his hands into his pockets, regarding Laura and Art soberly. "So," he said, "is this going to work?"

Laura half smiled and said "News is news, I could do worse." She cocked her head at Art and asked, "What do you want from my end?"

"I want a first rate news operation that I don't have to be concerned with." He looked at Don before continuing, "I was always in Sales, never had much to do with news except sell with the numbers they gave me. If the numbers are good and you stay within your budget, I'll stay out of your hair. Is that what you wanted to hear?"

Laura wasn't sure if Art was asking her or Don that question. "Alright, I can start in a week," she drawled. "Next Monday good enough?"

"Sure," he answered. "Just one thing, though…Why did you hit Roger MacNamara?"

Laura's eyes became ice chips as they narrowed and bored into his. "He grabbed me…and I don't like to be touched," she said in a low rumble. Art barely resisted swallowing and stepping back.

Don looked at Laura and concealed a laugh. "Okay then, make the announcement." *This is gonna be good*, he thought.

"Hey Mitch, it's Danny Rendally at WBFC in Burkett Falls. How're things in Big D?" Danny was doodling on a legal pad because that's what he always did when he was on the phone. He listened to the other reporter's answer and then came right to the point. "Listen, Mitch, Don Farmer, the Head of News Operations, just strolled into our newsroom with Laura Kasdan in tow… Tell me something, have you misplaced your news director?"

He listened to a detailed explanation of the previous day's events with his mouth slightly ajar and he stopped doodling. *Holy shit, no one's going to believe this.* It wasn't hard to put two and two together. "That's what I needed to know. Hmm? Yeah, yeah, I'll let you know as soon as I know something."

Rendally practically vaulted over his desk to get to the assignment editor's desk where two reporters were standing. He started laughing. "You're not gonna believe this…I think Laura Kasdan is going to be our new news director…"

Just then the door opened on the News Director's Office, cutting him off, and he turned to see the Corporate Guy, the GM, and the woman who was surely going to make his life a living hell.

The GM cleared his throat and waved at Rendally. "Go round up the news staff, we'll have a little meeting here." The reporter bolted down the hall. *Man, oh man*, he thought as he poked his head into the edit bays to call everyone to the meeting.

Once everyone was assembled, Art began, speaking over the background noise of police scanners and ringing phones. "I have an announcement to make. We have a News Director. This is Laura Kasdan. She's been at KDAL in Dallas for the last two years and…" a bit of a pause, "It's great to have her here. Laura, anything you'd like to add?"

Laura gave a humorless half smile, letting her eyes sweep around the room. Speculative looks and frank curiosity met her gaze. "You can call me Kaz," she said, giving them permission *not* to use her first name. "And I'm damn glad to be here," she said through slightly clenched teeth.

One of the men, who looked to be thirtyish, stepped forward and offered a hand. "I'm Keith Roberts, the Managing Editor. I've…heard some good things about you, hope you like it here." *Ah*, she thought, *so this is Mr.Young and Explosive*. She shook the offered hand and started to say something when she was interrupted by a woman's insistent voice.

"We've got some bad news, some good news and some weird news of the, um, Chris Hanson variety…what do you want to hear first, Keith?" The woman had been manning the scanners and seemed to have a phone surgically attached to her ear, so Laura assumed that this was the assignment editor. She raised an eyebrow questioningly. Keith turned and asked, "What happened?"

She answered, her words spilling out in a mad rush. "A truck jackknifed on I-20 and the traffic is backed up forever, the good news is that we sent Chris to do that story on the construction and the traffic tie-ups, so we got some video."

Keith rolled his eyes, "And the weird part?"

"Well, Chris was driving because Jody was shooting video of the traffic and the truck was actually *in front* of them when it skidded, and well, Jody got it on tape." The staff in the newsroom started talking at once, but Laura still heard Keith take a deep breath and ask, "Then what happened?"

The newsroom suddenly got very quiet as the occupants suddenly heard the question. Laura tilted her head, very much aware of the undercurrents in the room. It was like they were holding their collective breath or something.

"Well, the truck clipped the front of the news unit and Chris went into a spin, then into the median and, uh, crashed into those barrels full of water that they put around those big poles on the interstate to keep you from killing yourself if you were to, like, hit one."

"Are they alright?" Keith asked. The assignment editor nodded her head so hard that her bangs bobbed up and down. "They're fine, except that Chris split her lip when she hit the steering wheel. The really neat part is we got it all on tape, the truck skidding, hitting the car, the car spinning then crashing through those barrels and everything," she finished, out of breath. The room was absolutely quiet until the GM started to laugh, shaking his head.

"That's a hell of a story," Don Farmer said. Art kept laughing and turned to Laura and raised his eyebrows and said, "Welcome to WBFC. You just had an introduction to the main reason our last news director ran out of here screaming."

"So that's THE Chris Hanson?" Don asked, and Art nodded. "She makes the bullet list at least once a week," Don told Laura, referring to the list that each department had to turn in to corporate weekly, outlining what was going on. "Yeah, that's Chris. Well, if we're done here, can I interest you two in an early supper before you have to catch your plane?"

Laura was busy looking at the assignment board, a flow chart of how the day's stories were making their way to their respective newscasts. She checked her watch and turned to the managing editor, who was watching her closely. "You'll go live from that accident at five, won't you?" she asked.

"Yeah, if I can get the truck out there in time." He looked past her and said to one of the photographers sitting over on a desk. "Bobby, get Live 2 over to the I-20 exit at Johnson Road for a live shot at five, and take Rendally with you in case Chris looks too bad to go on the air."

"Good deal," Laura said, "I'll go too."

"What about dinner, and your flight?" Don inquired.

She shrugged. "I'll get a later flight. Thanks for the job. Later, Art." And she followed the cameraman and the reporter out the door.

The Head of News Operations and the General Manager left the newsroom in silence, opening the glass door and starting down the stairs. "Do you honestly think she's going to work out here?" Art asked Don. "This isn't Dallas."

Don thought for a second and said, "It doesn't really matter. She can help you while she's here, and you know what she'd lose if she took a walk." He smiled. "The ball's in her court now. It should be pretty interesting anyway. Just enjoy the ride."

*Like I have a choice*, the GM thought.

The live truck was old and it smelled bad, the tall woman noted as she climbed into the passenger seat. The reporter blinked as he realized he wasn't going to ride shotgun, then opened the sliding door and got in the back. Laura looked around with interest. The beta tape decks in the rack looked pretty new, and the rest of the truck showed only a few signs of abuse. She felt a shudder as the engine came to life and started rolling. They pulled through the gate and out into the street heading north to the interstate.

"So, how long have you been here?" she asked. That was always a safe place to start since TV people loved to talk about where they'd been and where they wanted to be. Rendally answered first, pretty much as Laura expected. Seven years, came from the ABC affiliate in Columbus, graduated from Ole Miss, and so on. Bobby said he'd only been a photographer for about a year. Laura filed the information away for later.

"I've met Mitch Carstairs…he was one of yours at KDAL wasn't he?" Rendally remarked pointedly.

Was. Laura smiled slowly and looked over her shoulder at the reporter. "You didn't waste any time making that phone call, Mr. Rendally." She flipped her hair back over her shoulder and settled back into her seat. *Here we go.*

"Is any of it true?"

"What?"

"The part about slugging the anchor?"

An eyebrow arched. "What do *you* think?"

A pause. "I think I'm probably safer changing the subject."

"Oooh, good choice," Laura drawled. She turned and looked right at the reporter, letting her blue eyes emphasize her point. "For the record—you bet I belted him. As for the rest of it…" she shrugged, put on her sunglasses and said, "Believe what you want."

Rendally just nodded and Bobby concentrated on his driving. As they approached the exit, Laura could see that the traffic had come to a standstill on the other side of the interstate. The wrecked eighteen-wheeler lay on its side. Bobby steered the live truck over to the left shoulder, passing the rubberneckers staring at the mess. A Ford Taurus with a Channel 8 logo rested drunkenly next to a pole surrounded by the broken remains of plastic safety barrels. There were police cars and fire trucks everywhere and a small crowd was gathered nearby.

"I think we've found them," the cameraman said as he pulled into the grassy median.

Christine Hanson licked the cut on her lip carefully, tasting blood and wincing a bit as it stung. *If I didn't have bad luck, I'd have no luck at all*, she thought. The police officers were hovering; one had given her a handkerchief to wipe the blood off of her mouth. Now he was hitting on her. She sighed. That was the problem with being on the air; everyone thought they knew you personally.

One of the officers gestured, "Hey, your people are here." Chris looked up to see one of the live trucks pulling into the grassy center section of the interstate. She looked over to where Jody, her cameraman, was setting up the camera and tripod. He'd seen the truck too, and started walking toward her.

"Cavalry's here," he said shortly as he reached her. "Who's that?" he asked as a tall, dark-haired woman climbed out of the front seat of the live truck and walked toward them with long, ground-eating strides.

"I don't know," Chris answered as she and Jody started making their way over to the truck. "What's Rendally doing here?"

"Hey Chris," Rendally said as they met, "You look like hell."

"A little makeup, I'll be fine." Her green eyes sparkled in the afternoon sun.

"Brought a surprise for ya, Chrissy," he said, using her hated nickname. "Meet our News Director, Laura Kasdan."

The first thought that crossed Chris Hanson's mind was that she had seen eyes like that only once before but she couldn't remember where. Clear blue and piercing. The second thought was that she was looking way up into them. *God, she's tall.* Dark, rich hair framed those startling eyes and her clothes were worn with a casual elegance. Chris realized she was staring and gave herself a mental shake. *This is your new boss*, she told herself, *act like you have a clue.*

"Hi, I'm Christine Hanson." She stuck out her hand and felt it enveloped by a somewhat larger hand in a warm, firm, almost familiar grip.

*That portrait in the lobby doesn't do her justice*, Laura thought. The camera hadn't captured the playfulness and intelligence that sparkled in the green eyes. Her blond hair was cut short on the sides and longer and fluffier on the top, a good on-air look, Laura thought idly. And there was something else she couldn't quite put her finger on, something…comforting? *Where the hell did that come from*?

"Laura Kasdan," she said, forgetting to add the automatic "Call me Kaz." She smiled a bit as she broke contact and turned to the photographer. Jody introduced himself and the two cameramen left to start pulling cables and setting up for the live shot. Rendally, left behind, regarded the two women.

"Do you really want her to do the live shot?" he asked Laura. "She looks a little shaken up."

"You're not doing my story," Chris told him emphatically.

"She was there, she does it, busted lip and all," Laura answered, a little pleased at the competition between the two. "A little makeup, she'll be fine." She repeated the reporter's words, then turned and started walking toward one of the fire trucks parked near the wrecked eighteen-wheeler. The reporters watched her leave.

"You are not gonna believe all the shit I've heard about Miz Kasdan," Rendally said in a low voice.

"I don't get it, where'd she come from?"

"Dallas, KDAL," Rendally answered. "She was the News Director there."

"A little young for it, what the hell is she doing here?" Chris asked.

"She fucked up," he answered simply. "This is where you'll end up if you ever punch an anchor."

"She hit an anchor? Damn!" Chris started to laugh as Jody walked up and handed over her IFB and makeup kit. "Let's get this set up, we're getting close to news time. Where do you want me, Jody?" she asked the cameraman as she put on the earpiece, opened her makeup, and began the business of making herself presentable to a million viewers.

Laura heard the whispers as soon as they thought she was out of earshot. She knew that news people were about the worst when it came to gossip. After all, they made their living ferreting out information and spreading it around to anyone who would listen. And it was a good story. Really. If she hadn't been so personally involved she'd be talking about it too.

She walked up to the man she guessed was in charge, introduced herself as being with Channel 8, and arranged for him to comment during the live shot. That accomplished, she made her way back to the live truck where Rendally was sitting glumly in the front seat.

"Hey, Captain Wallace is gonna give us some time during the live shot, why don't you get him set up." She glanced at her watch. "You've got about fifteen minutes before we go on."

The sandy-haired reporter took off and Laura looked into the van where Jody was editing his video. She watched him for a while as Bobby positioned the mast for the best signal back to the station. Chris was pacing next to the truck, going over what she planned to say, gesturing and flipping through her notebook, stopping and starting, and organizing the pace of her tale. Laura smiled. This should be interesting.

The time evaporated, and all the players moved into position. Chris did her mic check, fiddled with the earpiece of her IFB, squared her shoulders and took a deep breath. Sell it, sell it, sell it, she told herself as she looked into the lens, heard her cue for the tease, and the words began to flow.

"Traffic was already slow because of the construction on I-20, but this accident brought it to a standstill. You'll see exclusive footage of this eighteen wheeler spin out of control, tonight on Action 8 News Live at Five."

"'Bout 30 seconds, then you're back on, Chris." The producer's voice said in her ear.

Laura watched the show open roll in the monitor inside the truck… anchors were up full on the screen…toss to Chris and she was on. The young blonde reporter projected lots of energy, was precise in her telling, and very, very credible. As Chris told the story of the accident and got a quick comment from the Captain, Laura grew more impressed by the second. *I've been in major markets that didn't have reporter talent half this good,* she thought. *Well, bright spots are where you find them.* She listened as Chris tossed it back to the anchor, answered a question, and then waited to be told she was clear. A very professional performance, split lip and all, Laura thought.

Chris blew out the breath she'd been holding and asked the producer if they were coming back to her again during the show. She got a very definite "maybe" in her ear, then looked up at the woman who'd been watching her carefully during her stand up. "They'll probably come back for a traffic update toward the end of the 'cast," she answered the raised eyebrow from the dark haired woman. "Do we need to stay for the 6 O'Clock show?"

"Yeah," Laura answered, "unless something happens and Keith needs the live truck. Good job, by the way…considering."

"Oh," the reporter looked startled, and touched her lip gingerly. "I forgot about that." There were a hundred questions she wanted to ask Laura Kasdan, and now seemed as good a time as any, but for the first time in her life, she had no idea how to begin. *Weird*, she thought.

Laura crossed her arms and leaned back against the live truck, watching the cameramen putter with the cables. *They're uncomfortable*, she thought. *Nothing like a new boss looking over your shoulder to give you the jitters. Rendally's just pouting*. Chris had walked over to one of the officers, probably to ask about traffic control. Laura always forgot how much she hated waiting around a news scene until she had to visit one. Life was more hectic in the newsroom where you had to balance more than one crisis at a time.

It could be worse, the tall woman thought. It could have been market number 199 and somewhere up north. At least Burkett Falls was only about three hundred miles from Dallas. She sighed as Jody gestured to Chris that it was almost time to set up for the wrap and tease the 6 o'clock show.

Watching the reporter come to life in front of the camera again, Laura thought, *Yep, it could be a lot worse.*

It was after seven by the time they got back to the station. Laura expected Art Dement to be waiting, and she was not disappointed. White carpet and dark cherry furniture decorated the General Manager's office along with the ever-present monitors. *Ah,* thought Laura sarcastically, *another surprise. Just once couldn't the furniture be oak?*

"How'd it go?" he asked her as she sat down in a chair in front of his desk.

"Not too bad. Chris is pretty good, Jody runs a mean live truck, and Rendally is shopping for a larger market."

"They're always shopping for a larger market," the GM answered.

"Yeah, but I've seen his demo tape. He sent it to me in Dallas." She laughed softly at the look on Art's face, leaned back and with eyes half closed said, "Remember that everyone will eventually meet everyone else who works in TV. Mr. Rendally just met me sooner rather than later."

"So—is this gonna work?" Art asked.

"Sure it is." *It has to,* she thought. "You'll get what you want and I'll get what I want. It's a good deal all the way around."

"I don't want a hot-head News Director who makes the newsroom into a combat zone. No using the anchors as punching bags."

Laura gave a humorless laugh. "No, the newsroom will run like a well-oiled machine. Trust me."

It was Art's turn to lift an eyebrow. "Uh huh…Well, you've got a week to get ready. Here." He handed her a binder, a sheaf of papers, and three Nielsen rating books. "You'll need these, your budget, paperwork, and the last February, May, and November ratings. Don changed your flight to 8:30, so you can still make it home by midnight."

Laura opened one of the rating books and looked up. "What's the story on Christine Hanson?"

"Chris?" The man actually started to snicker. "She's…well…she's a fabulous reporter, it's just that…things happen around Chris. She has this huge loyal following…did I tell you she anchors the Noon News? Anyway she's wrecked half a dozen cars…"

"Seven after today."

"Okay, seven…but it's always some great story, so…what do you do?" He spread his hands in a gesture of futility. "I wish I could tell you that today was the exception rather than the rule," he laughed again, "but I can't."

"If she anchors, she's got a contract, right?"

"Yes, but it's up in June."

"Then we need to get her signed, because you don't let someone with that kind of on-air presence and that kind of luck just walk out of here," Laura said, standing. "And someone else will get her if we don't." *I would have*.

"Luck?" the GM asked.

"Yeah, 'cause when the shit hits the fan, at least you know you'll have someone close by. I'll get someone in the newsroom to drop me at the airport." She gave a thin smile. "I'll see you a week from Monday. I'll let you know my schedule as soon as I can."

"I am...looking forward to having you here...Kaz," Art said standing, "I just wish circumstances were...better."

Laura shrugged. "There's a reason for everything, I guess."

"And for wrecking yet another news vehicle, we, the All Powerful Producers of Action 8 News, do hereby put another notch on the desk of our erstwhile reporter, Christine Hanson...hoping that next time she'll take out the car with the busted air conditioner." Applause followed the Six O'Clock producer's announcement. Chris hid her face in her hands as Rendally put another hash mark on the side of her desk, bringing the total to seven.

"Could I have picked a worse time to crack up another car?" she asked with a slightly hysterical laugh. "Got the Head of News Operations in town, new boss, the whole package." Chris shut down her computer and threw her notebook into an open drawer.

"Yeah, I'd say you've done enough damage for one day, but hey, there's always Monday," Rendally answered as he picked up his jacket and prepared to leave. "So, Chris are they real or fake?"

"What? You're disgusting!"

"I meant her eyes. God, you're easy. Is she wearing contacts?"

Chris pondered the question and shook her head. "No, colored contacts give you dead eyes. Those were definitely not..."

"Ah, the ice woman cometh," he interrupted, spotting Laura as she walked through the door.

"I need a ride to the airport, anyone headed that way?" she asked the cluster of people still left in the newsroom.

"Uh, sure...I'll give you a lift," Chris volunteered.

"Kiss-up," Rendally whispered and she gave him a little shove.

"Sure you don't mind?" the taller woman asked.

"Not if you don't mind getting in a car with me…no, really, I'm an excellent driver." Groans came from around the newsroom. "I am. Stuff just…happens. C'mon," the blonde reporter said as she led the way out of the newsroom.

Once they got to the parking lot, Chris made her way over to where a dark red Volvo sedan was parked. Laura lifted an eyebrow and said, "Probably a pretty good choice for you."

"Very funny…that's not even original."

Laura smirked as she opened the door and got in. Chris was quiet as she started the car and drove out of the parking lot, but she couldn't stay that way forever. "So, when do you start?" she asked, looking over at Laura.

"I'll be back in the office a week from Monday." She gave a sideways glance at the reporter. "Try not to destroy anything while I'm gone."

Chris just laughed. "So it's back to Dallas to pack up and move, hmm? Do you know where you'll be staying yet?"

"Not yet."

Chris just went on, "This'll be a big change from Dallas, I bet. What's the smallest market you've been in?"

"I was in Austin for a bit."

"That doesn't count, it's only one market size larger than us…a real Texan, huh?" she looked over and smiled.

Laura didn't really mind the chatter from the younger woman, which was a little strange since personal questions usually drove her insane, but Chris was so good-natured it didn't bother her, so she just listened, answering briefly if at all. It was kind of nice.

They arrived at the terminal and Laura squashed a slight feeling of disappointment. She could see the Delta counter just inside the glass front where Chris parked the Volvo.

"Thanks for the ride," she said getting out of the car. "I'll see you in about a week." She tucked the binder under her arm, turned and shut the door.

"Have a good flight, Laura," Chris said softly, watching her go inside. The car was oddly quiet without the other woman's presence. Everything she'd heard about Laura Kasdan today had seemed so much larger than life, and Chris wasn't sure how she was going to fit into their little corner of the world. And despite the speculation in the newsroom, Chris was certain that Laura Kasdan knew exactly what she was doing and what she was getting into.

What an interesting puzzle, she thought. Chris was a reporter, and there was nothing she liked better than puzzles.

* * * *

What a day, Laura thought closing the binder and leaning back in her seat. She checked her watch. Yeah, she'd be home before midnight, but just barely.

*You idiot. One minute of uncontrolled anger and your whole life is turned upside down.* She blew out a breath and closed her eyes tiredly. There were a million things to do, and she had no idea where to start.

*Stop it. Sell the house, make the move, that's all there is to it.* Ruthlessly, she squashed any self-pity she might have been feeling. *Three years, that's all; remember the plan.* With that thought firmly in mind, she slept for the rest of the flight.

# Welcome to the Newsroom

*"TV people are a foul-mouthed lot."*

Laura lay on her back and watched the first light of Monday break through the slats of the mini blinds in her bedroom. She'd been awake for a couple of hours, unable to sleep and unwilling to get up. A busy week of moving and settling in had taken its toll and her nerves were shot to hell. Sunday night she finally walked away from the chaos of her new apartment and went to a driving range to hit golf balls until the manager turned off the lights and she was forced to leave.

She looked over at her clock for what seemed like the hundredth time. The digital numbers had not progressed at all since the last time. *C'mon Kaz, quit putting it off...just get up.* With a groan, she sat up and swung her legs over the side of the bed, standing and stretching as she made her way to the bathroom.

At least the shower had decent pressure, she thought after climbing out of the tub and slicking her hair back. She absently grabbed a towel and just blotted some of the water off of her sleek form, letting a goodly amount drip onto the floor on her way back to the bedroom.

What to wear, what to wear, Laura pondered, looking into her closet and thinking that she should have gone to the dry cleaners. Too late now, she thought with a shrug, settling on a pair of black cotton pants, white silk shirt and basic linen jacket. *Take the Jeep today*, she thought...*no need to freak them out just yet.*

No, Laura amended, *wear the boots and take the bike. Let 'em see what they're getting. Besides it'll be...fun.*

She dressed quickly, listening to Morning Edition on the radio, then stamped her feet into black cowboy boots. After locking the door she clattered down the concrete steps to the ground level of her apartment where her bike was covered with a tarp. Laura stowed it in the Jeep, then swung her leg over the Triumph Thunderbird. After donning her helmet and zipping a battered leather jacket closed over the linen one, she brought the motorcycle to life, feeling a familiar surge of adrenaline.

*If there's a god in heaven*, she thought, *he's got a bike like this*.

It was a good idea to ride this morning, she thought. It helped to strip away all the distractions and focus on the pure mental and physical aspects of getting from one point to another. By the time she got to the station parking lot, she was in total control.

She parked near the base of the stairs leading to the back door of the newsroom. Another good thing about the bike, she mused, there's always a good parking place close to the door. There were already a couple of employees standing outside in the designated smoking area, puffing away and watching her with idle interest. She took off the helmet, shook her hair free and started up the stairs, oblivious to the looks she was getting.

The newsroom was just beginning to stir as Laura entered and made her way to the managing editor's desk. "Do you have the key?" she asked, jerking her thumb toward her office.

"Yeah, sure," Keith answered, rummaging around in the top drawer, locating it and handing it to her. She motioned for him to follow and unlocked the door, unprepared for the sight that greeted her.

Videotapes and FedEx packages covered every flat surface in the office; only the floor was spared. There were six chairs and a low table in front of the desk and all were completely obscured by the stacks and stacks of packages. "What the hell is this?" the News Director asked.

Keith scratched the back of his neck. "I guess your reputation precedes you. We put a little blurb about you on the website, one of the trade magazines put it on their site, and by Wednesday the packages started coming in. They're from reporters, videographers, anchors, and you even got some resumes from producers."

"Keith, you seem like a bright guy, what does this look like to you?" She turned to look at him.

Chris was right, he thought, they weren't colored contacts. "It looks like…" He paused and answered very carefully, "Someone thinks you're going to clean house, and a whole buncha people want to work for you."

"Are we short some bodies?"

"No," Keith replied, "we've got a full count right now unless…you *are* planning to…or we have a mass exodus…or something," he trailed off.

"Then get rid of 'em…all of 'em," Laura said firmly, gesturing at the piles of tapes.

"You sure?"

"Yeah, we go with what we've got for the time being." She made her way behind the desk and put down her helmet. "Morning meeting starts at nine, right?"

"Right, and you've got a department head meeting at ten."

"Good, then let's go over the schedules now. I have some questions about the stuff you sent me last week."

Chris walked into the newsroom ten minutes before the morning meeting. It wouldn't do to antagonize the new News Director, and, judging from the number of others in the newsroom on time, she knew she wasn't the only one who felt that way. It had been a pretty good morning so far, a trip to the "Y" for an early workout and on to the bagel shop for breakfast. She smoothed down the collar of her forest green blazer, put her briefcase next to her desk, and logged on to the Associated Press server to check the updates.

The usual stuff, she thought, scrolling down and making notes to arm herself for the meeting where the reporters and producers would pitch their story ideas. An early encounter at the gym had resulted in a tip, which meant she wouldn't go into the meeting empty-handed. Sometimes it got ugly since everyone had a different opinion as to what was newsworthy, and what stories or features had clear viewer benefit. The reporters would then be assigned their stories and the newscasts would start to take shape.

It always amazed Chris that it ever came together at all. Sometimes a newscast showed every indication of being a train wreck, and those were the ones that went well. Others were smooth sailing from the beginning, and, piece by piece, they self-destructed on the air.

Oh, the joys of live TV.

Chris checked the clock, picked up her notebook, and entered the News Director's office where four other reporters were already gathered. She took a seat next to the door and started flipping through her notes, sneaking a glance at her new boss. Laura Kasdan was frowning at her computer screen as the news staff filed in. Keith took the chair closest to the desk and Rendally plopped down next to him. Everyone was quietly fidgeting, and Chris fought back the urge to laugh.

"Okay," Laura spoke up, "I've met some of you already. I'm still getting a feel for the station and the newsroom, so bear with me. What do we have today…let's start over here." She gestured to the right side of the room where one of the producers was standing.

It was like planning for battle, the dark-haired woman thought. You sent your troops out to gather the information, put together a plan, and lay siege to the airwaves with newscasts at five, six and ten. Sometimes you dominated the competition, beating them soundly on coverage, and sometimes they did the same to you. It was all about winning. If your reporters and producers fought hard, protected their sources, and dug enough so that they were never surprised by what floated to the surface, then they won that battle, that day.

String those battles together during a ratings book and you gave the sales staff numbers to sell, down the hall and at corporate.

Laura listened carefully as they went around the room, asking questions and getting mostly good answers. When it was Chris's turn, blue eyes fixed on green. *Okay, impress me*, the news director thought.

"Last night we covered a drive-by shooting at Northside Mall. One of the security guards was shot in the hand. This morning, Mark Norton, the Information Officer for the Burkett PD, told me that the wound was caused by a weapon less than a foot away from the guard's hand when it was fired." The blonde reporter gave a wry smile. "Which means it didn't happen the way he told the police."

"Did Mark say what he thought happened?" Rendally asked.

"He said he thought the guard was messing with his gun and shot himself. Anyway, they're going to charge him with filing a false police report, but probably not 'til this afternoon, so we should be able to break it on the noon'cast," Chris finished.

"What about Channel 4? They go on at 11:30," Laura inquired.

"Mark won't tell if they don't ask; they burned him a few months ago, so he's not willing to do them any favors."

"Alright, we can short-form it for noon, and make it a package for the five focusing on…the forensic technique that tipped the guard's hand…so to speak." Laura favored the reporter with a half smile before continuing around the room.

After hitting the checks and follow-up list, the reporters were given their final assignments and the meeting was over. "Chris, I need to see you for just a minute," the news director said. The reporter turned to face Laura, eyebrows raised questioningly. "Go ahead and shut the door."

"Is this about the car? If you want to make it condition of my employment that I can't drive station vehicles, I'll understand, but really…"

"No, this isn't about the car, though maybe it would be better if you didn't drive them for a while."

"…it doesn't matter because they wreck even if I'm just a passenger." Earnest green eyes looked into amused blue ones.

Odd, Laura thought, people made such a big deal out of blue eyes, but Chris's were the more unusual color. Grass green with flecks of gold, they gave away everything the blonde woman was thinking and feeling. In this business it didn't pay to be that open.

"Your contract is up in June, and we'd like to get you taken care of before we go into the May ratings period. We can meet later this week and go over any changes, then you can meet with Art if you've got any concerns."

"Oh." Chris looked startled. "Then I guess you're not gonna fire me right away."

"Well, not right away. Wreck another car and we'll talk." Laura hid a smile. The younger woman was as transparent as glass, so she tried to dig a little on another subject. "When did Mark Norton tell you about the forensics on last night's shooting?"

"We work out at the same gym, so I usually see him in the mornings," Chris told her.

"Okay," Laura dismissed her. "Better get to work." She turned her attention back to her computer screen, but couldn't help flicking a glance to the window out to the newsroom, watching the reporter go to her desk and pick up the phone.

*Admit it, you were looking forward to seeing her again. You're comfortable around her and that surprises you.* She sighed and turned back to the computer, looking through the schedule that Keith had mailed to her when she was interrupted by…

"Well, I always knew that 'I'm God and you're not' attitude was going to get you into trouble but I never thought it'd land you here."

Laura looked up, surprised.

"If it isn't Laura-Kasdan-call-me-Kaz right here in MY station running the news department in a godforsaken sixty-one market." The intruder slammed the door.

A delighted smile spread across the news director's face as she leaned back in her chair. "Lisa Tyler, what the hell are you doing here? I thought you were in Houston."

"I was, then I left…God, it's good to see you." Lisa was much shorter than Laura, with light brown hair and eyes the color of whiskey. "I heard about what happened in Dallas; I'm really sorry."

"You know, you're the first one who's told me that and meant it." Laura brightened. "So, what are you doing here?"

"I'm the production manager…don't laugh, and I direct your Six O'Clock newscast, so be nice."

"I wasn't going to laugh, but here?" Laura asked.

"Just another Texan in exile. No, it's really better. The money's not as good but it's cheaper to live here." Lisa picked a chair close to Laura's desk and sat down. "Besides, that major market pressure will grind you down, then one day you just…snap."

"I didn't just snap, I self-destructed. You never let me get away with anything." Laura smiled wryly. The two women had been on the golf team together at UT. Lisa was a big hitter off the tee with an erratic short game and no desire to practice it. After graduation, they both went to work for the same station in Austin. Lisa had stayed in production and Laura had immersed herself in news.

"With your temper, it was bound to happen sooner or later." Lisa regarded the News Director thoughtfully and crossed her legs at the ankles. "Coulda been worse…you could have ended up in Yakima or something."

"Nah, you'd have to actually kill an anchor to end up in Yakima," Laura replied. "Are you going to the department head meeting?"

"Yes. Oddly enough, I qualify as a department head. Freaky, isn't it?"

Laura met the other managers and they slogged through the meeting. Her overall impression was that this was a pretty smooth running station, very profitable and with few personnel issues. The one problem was the news department. Jerry Nelson, the previous News Director, had walked out two months earlier, leaving the newsroom in chaos.

Not that chaos was unusual in a newsroom.

They wanted it organized, streamlined, and, of course, sellable. Lisa explained all of this on their way down the hall. So what else is new, she thought, looking down the table and listening to the drone of the sales manager as he described how April was pacing compared to last year. She looked over to where Lisa was trying her best to look interested and failing miserably.

The sales manager finally finished his spiel and Art dismissed them all except for Laura, who stayed where she was, leaning back in her chair.

"So, how's it going?"

"Well, it's quite a change," she answered.

"Yeah, there are a few problems back there, but that makes for some interesting opportunities." The general manager stroked his beard.

"To tell you the truth, Art, I don't really believe it when someone tells me that problems are opportunities. Opportunities are good, problems are bad…any idiot should be able to tell the difference." Laura didn't take her eyes off her boss as she smiled. "When do I get my new live trucks?"

Art stuck out his chin and said firmly, "That's out of my hands, we're on Corporate's timetable now." He let Laura sit in silence for a minute. "As for the news department…I believe in letting my managers manage their departments. I don't really want to be involved in the day-to-day operations. I will stay out of your hair as long as your department performs the way it should. I am not a journalist, but I know that compelling news sells. Just give me the numbers and I'll sell it."

"Okay…so lemme go manage." She stood up and walked to the door, pausing with her hand on the knob. "As for compelling news, be careful what you ask for—it has a tendency to bite you on the ass."

Laura closed the door behind her and went on a mission to find some caffeine. Eventually, she found the break room, complete with the requisite vending machines. A glass door opened onto a good-sized brick patio dotted with picnic tables.

She fed quarters to one of the machines and punched her selection, listening to the sound of the canned drink as it tumbled down. Retrieving the Coke, she started back down the hall and ran into Keith. Laura raised her eyebrows in inquiry.

"A bunch of city employees have just been arrested. They're charging them with payroll fraud, the Mayor's gonna have a news conference, and we can probably go live at noon."

"Okay, get Rendally over there to do the live shot." And they both went back to the noise and pandemonium of the newsroom.

Chris finished putting on her makeup and fitted the IFB in her ear, clipping the cord to the back of her collar and letting the plug trail behind her. She really liked anchoring the noon newscast because it meant that she still had a good part of the day to work on her story. She had a good one today and an exclusive for her 'cast, so she was in a very good mood as she walked down the hall to the studio.

As always, the bright lights made her eyes water until she got used to them. Chris took her seat, sitting on the tail of her jacket to give her shoulders a good line. Turning, she plugged in the IFB, bringing to life the sounds of the control room.

"Hey Chris, just letting you know that Kaz is in here watching." The producer's voice sounded tinny in her ear. "Try not to screw up." Chris just smiled as she shuffled through the scripts, knowing that while the producer's comments could only be heard by the crew wearing headsets and IFBs, anything she said could be heard by everyone in the booth.

"Okay folks," the director's deep voice cut in, "Chris, we'll come out to you on camera one, toss to the live tease, then weather on two…we're one minute out."

Chris clicked her pen and checked the clock. *Hurry up and wait.* She smiled at the camera and tried not to think about the news director in the control room. Well, at least the crew wouldn't be cutting up.

"Standby, coming to you in five...four…three…two…one…cue her."

It looked easier than it actually was. Read from the teleprompter and comprehend it, chat coherently, and obey the instructions coming from the IFB. Chris was good at it; she maintained the flow of the newscast, her cadence and rhythm set the pace, and it was up to the director and producer to make the content match her timing.

Laura leaned back against the wall in the control room. Standing next to the audio board, she could watch everyone and follow the newscast on the monitors. She wished there was an extra headset so she could hear the producer and made a mental note to check with Engineering about providing one.

Laura was more impressed with the blonde reporter every time she saw her on camera. Whatever that quality was that made you like and trust someone immediately, Chris Hanson had it in abundance, she thought, listening to her chat with the weatherman.

The content was good, the 'cast was clean. The News Director waited for the five and six o'clock promos to be shot, then left the control room, striding back to the newsroom and meeting Chris as she came up the stairs from the studio. "Nice job," she told her.

"Thanks." Green eyes smiled. "Who's making the lunch run today? I'm starving."

"You're always starving." This from Keith as he walked up. "Pitt Grill today…you want the usual?"

"Sounds good, K Bob." Chris said, unclipping her IFB and rolling it up. "Grilled cheese and tater tots."

"Don't call me that. Anything for you, Kaz?"

"Uh, no." Laura answered. "K Bob? Oh…Keith Roberts." Keith looked uncomfortable and she smiled broadly. "Fine, you won't hear it from me." She headed for her office, went in and shut the door.

Keith was shocked to discover his mouth was dry and all she'd done was smile at him. Chris snapped her fingers under his nose and he blinked, looking down at the shorter woman.

"Earth to Keith…stop it, you're practically drooling."

"She's…she's not what I was expecting," he stammered.

"Yeah, but it's early days," she answered. "You coming to Mainstreet tonight? We're doing happy hour." Chris was referring to the bar and grill up the street.

If anyone else but Chris had asked him, he would have turned the invitation down flat. It was hard enough being a supervisor without socializing with the staff after hours. But this was Chris, and he really liked talking with her, so he shrugged. "Maybe, we'll see." She smiled and he went to call in the lunch order.

Laura closed her office door and went to her desk, pulled out the phone book, opened the yellow pages and looked under golf courses, finding the listing she was looking for. Burkett Falls may be smaller than she was used to, but there was a mighty fine golf course in town. She dialed the number, expelling a breath as she waited.

"Northridge Country Club," a voice answered.

"Yes, I was wondering if you could tell me about your membership requirements." She waited while she was transferred. "Member services, this is Linda."

"Hello, my name is Laura Kasdan, and I was wondering about your membership requirements."

"Well, Ms. Kasdan, this is a very exclusive club, we would want to set up an interview…"

"I'm a member of a club that's in the Southern Association of Country Clubs. Would it be possible to transfer that membership since Northridge is also a member of that organization?"

"Yes, the membership itself could transfer, but you would still have to be interviewed and pay the initiation fee."

Laura forced down the urge to scream. "I understand that. How soon could I be interviewed?"

"You're in luck, Ms. Kasdan. There is a reception tonight to examine a few other possible members; you are welcome to join them. Cocktails are at seven-thirty." The woman asked a few more questions and finally the phone conversation was over. With that out of the way, she opened up a small black book, found a number, and punched it in with a smile.

"Oak Hills, this is Charles."

"Charles, it's Kaz. How the hell are you?"

"I've been waiting to hear from you. Are you ready yet?" He asked the question almost wistfully.

"Almost, Charles. I'm gonna try to qualify for the Open at the sectional in Austin on May 18$^{th}$. I need a caddy…"

"I'm there," he answered simply.

"Uh, I'll still be an amateur, Charles. If I qualify, you might do better with someone who'd be in the money, so this doesn't mean you'd have to work the Open for me." She waited.

"If you're in the Open, I'm on your bag, for as long as you want me there. Damn Kaz, when you turn pro, I'll be there too."

"Someday, Charles." *I needed that.* "It's in Austin, at Pierremont Country Club…Fly or drive?"

"Drive," he answered.

"I'll fly in, I'm not in Dallas anymore," Laura told him.

"No shit, I heard. Tell me when you see me."

"I'll be in touch," she told him and hung up. So, she was committed now. She looked down at the confirmation letter from the USGA. Three years ago she had an automatic invitation to the Open, then things went to hell in a handbasket. *Not this time*, Laura thought, *this move to Burkett is just an inconvenience. It'll make it interesting, but it won't make a difference.*

She hated giving up her membership in Dallas, but she just couldn't afford two clubs. The initiation fee for Northridge was going to be pricey, too. Laura hated the bullshit country club scene anyway, understanding that it was a means to an end. If you wanted to play competitive golf, you just put up with it.

*Three years, Charles. Then I can support myself on tour. I can kiss news goodbye and the crap that comes with it.* She looked out the window that covered most of one wall in her office and out into the newsroom. *Never say yes when you want to scream no, especially if you're making a promise.* She turned to her desk and sighed. There were purchase orders to sign and schedules to fix, all before the afternoon meeting.

It had been a pretty slow news day, Chris thought as she ordered a beer from the bar and turned to look at the room. She spotted a table with a couple of the photogs and gave a little wave. The bartender handed her the Corona and she snagged a slice of lime and shoved it into the bottle. Walking to the table, she noticed that Rendally had joined them. "You're a married man, shouldn't you be at home?" she asked.

"Just one drink and I'm gone," he said, waving toward a waitress.

"So, what's the latest gossip?" Chris asked him, propping her chin on her hand.

"Well, Day One of the Kasdan regime went smoothly enough—she didn't punch anyone." The waitress brought his beer and he took a sip. "There was a bit of an altercation with Lisa Tyler this morning in her office. Don't know what that was about."

"Nah, that was just for show. They've known each other for a while. Lisa was telling me about it this afternoon. Any other good stuff?"

"No, except that Randy is leaving to go to Cleveland," he said, referring to one of the photographers.

Chris made a face. “Ugh, Cleveland.”

“C’mon, it’s a nice move for him into a bigger market. You could move too, bigger than Cleveland if you wanted.”

The blonde reporter shook her head. “No, I like the South, I like the weather. Besides, I’ll probably renew my contract anyway. You don’t get the chance to work with someone like Laura Kasdan in a market this size very often. I’m telling you, Rendally, this could be really good for us.”

Jason, one of the photographers, spoke up, “I’m with you, Chris. She could move us into bigger and better things. When she goes, and she will, she might take some of us with her. I want a network job, man. I’m not slaving away at an affiliate for the rest of my life.”

“Oh yeah, she’s your ticket to the network all right. Didja know her old man was David Kasdan, the reporter who was killed in Bosnia a few years ago? She could probably be a producer at any of the networks just like that.” He snapped his fingers. “So why isn’t she?”

Chris shrugged. “Who knows? Not everyone wants to work for a network.” She thought for a minute and remembered seeing the footage of David Kasdan’s death played over and over again. Of course there was a disclaimer, telling parents not to let their children see the gruesome scene, and some photographer won an award for outstanding coverage. She felt a wave of sympathy for the News Director and shook her head. “That’s gotta be tough, watching your dad die like that.”

“Yeah, well, it certainly explains a lot.” Rendally finished his beer. “I’m outta here, see you all tomorrow.” He threw a dollar on the table for a tip and left as Jody and Keith came in laughing.

“Hey Keith,” Jason greeted the stocky man, and cut his eyes at Chris, guessing that she had invited the supervisor. She just winked at the photographer and made room for them at the table. More of the newsroom staff came in and it wasn’t long before they were the loudest table in the place. Keith thawed a bit, even telling some humorous stories.

Eventually the group at the table began to thin until it was just Chris and Keith. He looked at Chris and smiled. “Thanks for inviting me…it was fun.”

“S’okay. You were fun too. You don’t have to be a supervisor all the time.”

“Are you okay to drive?”

“I only had one,” she answered. “How ’bout you?”

“Yeah, I’m fine.” He paused. “Listen, I’m not gossiping, really, but what do you think is going on? I’m talking about corporate-wise. What is she doing here?”

*Ah, so that’s what this is.* Chris listened closely.

"I mean, they gave the News Director job to her in Dallas when she was twenty-eight…I'm twenty-nine…this isn't major market, we're sixty-one. I guess that sounds shallow," he finished.

"Keith, I think you need to look at this from a business point of view. They couldn't keep her in Dallas, she's probably a shareholder, and News Directors are hard to come by. Plus, she could have sued the pants off that anchor, and boy, that's a public relations nightmare." Chris took a breath. "Look, she's not here forever and I know it's hard to be patient, but come on, Keith, you'll be a News Director." She stood up. "I think you do a good job. We were talking before you came in. Most of us think that this is a good opportunity to work for someone who can help our careers. Did you know her dad was David Kasdan?"

"No shit," he said softly.

"Yeah, well, I need to go." She shouldered her briefcase. "You'll get where you want to go. See you tomorrow."

She walked the block back to the station and unlocked the Volvo, tossed in the briefcase and climbed in. It wasn't a long drive to her house, a modest patio home in a quiet subdivision. She took pride in the tiny immaculate yard with its neat flowerbeds and carefully pruned shrubs. Walking in, she tossed down her keys on a small table near the door and smiled at her cat stretching in greeting. "Hello, Biggio." She scratched him under the chin. "Were you good today?"

Humming, she went into the kitchen and poured dry cat food into the dish on the floor. After changing into shorts and a T-shirt, she retrieved a bottle of water from the fridge, turned on the living room TV and smiled happily. Monday night baseball—what could be better? Pondering the day's events, Chris curled up on the couch with an afghan and her water and settled in for the evening. The newsroom had been busy the week before digging up information on the enigmatic News Director. Now that they'd seen her in action, it wasn't such a mystery as to why she'd been so successful at such a young age.

Still, as the details filtered in, the bigger mystery to the young reporter was why she was so fascinated by the older woman. It wasn't just the professional competence, or the quiet confidence; there was a pull there, a familiarity that reached beyond brief acquaintance.

Chris yawned and stroked the cat laying on the armrest. There were worse things than hitching your future to a can't-miss opportunity like Laura Kasdan.

---

Laura barely made it to the club before eight. She stopped to go over some problems with the 6 o'clock 'cast with Kate, the producer, so she was late getting home, then had to change for the reception-slash-cocktail party-slash-interview. She chose a simple black sleeveless dress and tossed a dark blue silk blazer over it, twisted her hair into a knot at her neck, and dusted on some makeup. She grabbed some ridiculously high heels, hoping that she wouldn't twist an ankle, and ran down the stairs to get in the Jeep.

When she pulled into the circular drive, the valet opened the door of her Jeep and stared as she stepped out, towering over him by several inches. Laura took the ticket from his hand in exchange for her keys and walked to the front door of the clubhouse. The chandelier in the foyer cast a golden light and bright reflections on the wooden floor, automatically making everything much more formal. She gave her name to an attendant at the door and was ushered into a much more intimate room where several people were gathered into little groups, sipping their drinks.

A petite brunette excused herself from one of the groups and made her way over to where Laura stood. "Hello, I'm Linda Marsh," she introduced herself. "You must be Laura Kasdan. Can I get you something to drink?"

Laura smiled. "White wine would be fine." The membership rep left and returned an instant later with a glass. Laura tasted it appreciatively. "This is nice." The smaller woman tittered something meaningless and then began the introductions. *My social skills on display...too bad I don't have any,* Laura thought.

She made the rounds, showing a little charm, and finally Linda left her with the last group. She dubbed them the Banker, the Lawyer, and the Pretty Boy.

"So, Miz Kasdan, what do you do for a living?" This from the Banker.

"I'm the News Director at Channel 8," she replied.

The Lawyer raised an eyebrow. "We tried to get Art Dement interested in joining a few years ago, but he doesn't play golf or tennis." He paused, letting his eyes drift over her. "What's your game? And is there a Mr. Kasdan?"

"Oh, I play golf." Laura gave him a half smile, meeting his eyes and narrowing hers.

"I know you..." the Pretty Boy said. "Laura Kasdan: the U.S. Amateur Champion...'95, '96, right?" He shook her hand enthusiastically. "Peter Davis, Club Pro. Your mom was Amateur Champ too...Oh this is cool, are you joining?"

"Trying to," she replied, giving him a warmer smile and ignoring the Banker and the Lawyer.

"Well, come on, have you met the club president?" He pulled her away from the two dour men.

"The large gentleman over there? Yeah, we met." Laura had gotten the impression that he wasn't interested in a single woman trying to join his exclusive club.

"Let's reintroduce you, and this time let's include your credentials." Peter smiled at her. "This'll be fun."

He was right, it was. The portly gentleman practically fell over himself trying to make up for his earlier slight once Peter filled in the details. Now she was being treated like royalty, except there wasn't a discount on the seven thousand dollar initiation fee. After she was assured that her membership would be accepted, Laura followed Peter on a tour of the facilities.

It was a warm night, and eventually the two ended up outside near the green on the ninth hole. Laura leaned against a low stone wall and looked down toward the tee and the lake that edged the left side. They talked about some of the courses they had played and found some common ground in their love of the game.

"You wanna play Saturday?" the pro asked.

"Sure," Laura said, "the earlier the better, but I walk—no cart."

"Then it'll have to be *really* early. How about six forty-five?"

"Can I warm up at six?"

"I'll be here," Peter said. "You want the same time on Sunday?"

"Yes, you might as well make it a regular thing." Laura smiled. "It's been a pleasure, Peter. I'll see you Saturday."

"Likewise, Laura." He took her hand.

"Call me Kaz," she said easily, disengaging his hold with the ease of long practice.

Walking to the front of the clubhouse, she gave the valet her ticket and waited for her Jeep. Peter held the door open for her and she got in gracefully despite the height of the vehicle. As she drove off she reached up, pulled the pins out, and shook her hair free, running her hand through the dark length. *It's over*, she thought. *I have a place to play, and a tee time for Saturday, there's a hot tub and a masseuse on staff. It's pricey, but it's worth it.*

She looked at the clock on the metal dashboard of the Jeep. Nine-forty; she could be in bed by ten. Not too bad for a first day. Laura laughed softly and turned up the radio, feeling really good for the first time since she hit that idiot Roger. She unzipped the window, letting the wind blow her hair free…and started to sing.

"Yeah, that'll be fine." The engineer handed Laura the headset connected to a jack on the wall behind the audio board. She adjusted the size and put it on. "Test…can you hear me?"

"It's working," Lisa said from her seat at the switcher as she removed her headset. "Your producers are not going to be thrilled about this and neither will the rest of the crew."

The dark haired woman lifted an eyebrow. "Whatever. This way, I'm in the loop, and you won't be such a potty mouth either." Lisa was the only person she knew who could say the word "shit" with six syllables.

"It'd take more than you listening in to clean up my language. Besides, you're one to talk…TV people are a foul-mouthed lot."

It was Thursday, and with the exception of a few incidents, the week was going pretty smoothly. Laura was sure that the honeymoon was about over. She was going to have to sit down with their lead male anchor and have a little chat this afternoon and knew that it wasn't going to be pleasant.

"Thanks, Richard," she told the engineer who had rigged the setup.

"Oh, this was easy. Now I've got to figure out what's wrong with Live 2. Any word on when we can look for those new trucks?"

An exasperated sigh. "As I was told, so shall I tell you: we're on Corporate's timetable now."

"Yeah, great," he said as he left the booth. Laura hung up the headset and walked over to where Lisa was working on graphics for the newscast. The technical director punched up effects on the board with speed and precision, swinging from the effects generator, or ADO, then back to the character generator, to type up font.

All the graphics, font, and over-the-shoulder boxes had to be built before the newscast. In addition to having to direct the talent as to what camera to look into, the director had to match graphics and font to the stories, direct the camera operators, listen to what the producer was adding and subtracting from the newscast, and roll tape. They used five tape machines for a newscast, and one member of the crew had the sole responsibility of rotating the tapes in and out of the machines and keeping the director informed of what tape was where.

Every newscast was different and had its own set of problems. But when it was over, it was over. There was no going back to fix things that went wrong. It took a quick-thinking problem solver with a short memory of past mistakes to direct news live, and Lisa excelled at it.

"So you left Houston for this guy…" Laura prodded, sitting at the producer's station.

"No, I'd already decided I didn't want to stay there when I met Trey. We'd been dating about six months when he was transferred." She turned to write on her clipboard before continuing, "Then I called corporate personnel to see about a job in this market. WBFC had an opening, so here I am." She looked into the blue eyes regarding her seriously. "This is a good fit for me…I don't regret leaving Houston at all," she shrugged, "except I miss the baseball."

"So what's Trey like?"

"Ah…that's a little tricky. He's…well, he's an Aggie."

Laura howled with laugher. "Oh, that's great! Miss Longhorn fanatic-all-Aggies-are-scum. I bet Thanksgiving is a real joy at your house," she said, referring to the annual UT–Texas A & M game.

"It's worse than that…he played football for 'em. Stop laughing!" Lisa threw a wad of paper at the other woman who batted it away. "You can meet him if you come to Mainstreet for happy hour tomorrow night."

"Oh, I wouldn't miss it." Laura checked her watch. "Gotta go…meeting with talent. I'll probably sit in on the six, oh, and try to work up some new swearing combinations. I've missed that."

Laura was on the phone in her office when Chris tapped on the door. "No, you can have the footage if you pay for it. We're not in the business of helping out rival networks." The dark-haired woman waved the reporter in while she finished the conversation. "I doubt that I will ever need a favor from you guys…No, thank *you.*" She slammed the phone down. "Sorry 'bout that. Go on, sit down." Laura took a packet out of her desk drawer and handed it to Chris. "This is our contract proposal. I'd like to go over it, you can have your lawyer check it out, then if you want to negotiate any changes, Art and I will get with you and hammer them out. You can bring your lawyer to that meeting if you so desire."

Chris opened up the packet and started reading. For the most part, it read like the one she had signed previously, but with a few changes. Her eyes widened as she looked up. "Six O'Clock?"

Laura smiled slightly. *Here's where we find out about your ego, kid.* "We feel that Tracy is not as strong with Tom as you could be on the Six. Tracy also has two children and has asked to work an earlier shift. She would be moved to Noon and you would be teamed with Tom. Ray and Michelle would still do the Five and Ten."

"But what about reporting?"

"You'd come in an hour later, and work your assignment same as always. The only difference is that you probably couldn't do as much live reporting, since it would be tough to get you back in time for the newscast if, say, you were live on the Five." Laura studied Chris, waiting.

The reporter flipped to the back of the contract where compensation was discussed, and swallowed at the number she read there.

"That's a thirty percent increase with a guarantee of a ten percent increase every year for the remaining two years of the contact," Laura said matter-of-factly.

"Three years? Art doesn't do anything longer than two years." She continued reading, looking for one item in particular. Not finding it, Chris flipped through the contract again. "There's not an out if I get an offer from a top ten market?"

"No, there's not."

"Why?"

"We want you for three years." Laura chose her words carefully. "You could be the franchise anchor in this market and if that's the case, you'll be compensated for it. But we want all of your attention for three years—no shopping around, no rumors about you leaving, and no News Director from a big market looking to take you away." *Like I would have if I'd known you were here.*

Chris looked doubtful, which to Laura was a good thing. Anchors were funny; they usually had huge egos wrapped in the thinnest of shells. How something so enormous could bruise so easily was a mystery to her. They exposed themselves to a million viewers and risked possible humiliation with every broadcast, yet sometimes they acted with the reason of a three year-old. The things that made them good on the air were the same qualities that made them hell to work with.

"Okay, so what's this?" Chris pointed to one paragraph in the contract. "This wasn't here on the last one I signed."

"That's new. William-Simon is including a full disclosure clause in all their talent contracts from now on." This was something that the lawyers were screaming about, and it probably wouldn't hold up in court, but it hadn't been tested yet. Laura went on, "Basically it says that if you do something…if you indulge in any kind of behavior which might damage the credibility of the station, you'd better tell your supervisor before it becomes a problem. You had a morals clause in your last contract, right?" Chris nodded. "It's kind of the same thing."

"This won't hold up in court," the reporter said, earning a half smile from Laura. *It's not like we're dealing with idiots here*, Laura thought, *they look at issues like this everyday.*

"All right, Laura…"

"Kaz."

"…tell me why, besides thirty percent and the Six O'Clock, I should stick around here for three years, when you obviously think I'm good enough to look elsewhere."

Ah, there it was. Laura gave a lopsided grin. "Oh, you're good Chris, but I can make you better."

The smile caught Chris off guard, and so did the comment. *It's a good thing she doesn't do that very often; it's blinding.* Chris swallowed and tried to compose herself by flipping to the back of the contract. She looked up once more and took a pen out of the holder on Laura's desk. She signed her name quickly to the bottom of the page, dated it, and slid it across the desk to the dark-haired woman.

"Sure you don't want a lawyer to see that?" Laura asked, a little surprised at the reporter's lack of caution.

"Nah, my sister's a lawyer and she can break anything on paper, so I'm not worried."

"Chris, you will be giving up a significant amount of privacy. The Six is a lot more high profile than Noon. You'll be more of a celebrity than you are now, and small town celebrity has all kinds of problems attached," Laura said seriously. "Maybe you should think about this."

"No," the reporter shook her head, "This is the road I'm on; I'll stick to it."

"Then I guess congratulations are in order. The ratings book starts on April 28th, you'll start doing the Six on April 26th. I'll make the announcement on Monday. If you could keep this to yourself'til then, I'd appreciate it." Laura offered her hand to Chris and the younger woman took it, letting out a breath.

"I would've signed it anyway, even without the promotion and the raise."

"Now you tell me." Laura pointed to the newsroom. "Story. Go work on it." Before Chris could leave, Keith knocked once and opened the door.

"Sorry to interrupt, but we've got a train derailment outside of town. The live truck's on its way, but we need a reporter on the scene. Jason can take Chris over."

"No. Let Jason finish editing the package he's working on; I'll get her over there. Gimme an extra camera and I'll shoot," she said, striding out of the office with Chris and Keith in her wake. "Chris, get the directions from Janie. Keith, help me load up."

Laura snagged the keys to the four-wheel drive news unit and helped Keith stow the camera in the back, adding batteries and tape. When Chris came out and got in on the passenger side, Laura cranked it up and they headed out of the parking lot.

She followed Chris's directions until the traffic backed up behind a roadblock. Guessing that this was close to the accident, Laura pulled around and drove on the shoulder until she reached the sawhorses and saw the sheriff's deputy motion for her to stop.

"Your other truck is about a quarter of a mile down this road," he said, gesturing at the turn. "Sheriff says y'all can go in, but be careful."

"Is there a Hazardous Materials crew on the way?" Chris asked, leaning over.

"Miz Hanson," the deputy touched his hat. "Tankers were empty, so no Haz Mats. It's just a hell of a mess."

The tracks ran parallel to the road, and after a moment she could see the live truck and the tumbled tanker cars. Pulling up behind a fire truck, she cut the engine and they both jumped out. Laura got the camera and followed the reporter through the maze of vehicles parked on the road until they reached Jody, who was standing beside Live 1 a scant fifty yards from the wreckage.

"Are you feeding this?" Laura pointed at the camera.

"Yeah, Keith said he was rolling tape at the station, just in case we want to do a cut in, they'll have some B roll."

Laura nodded. "Chris, you wanna…" she stopped looking at a slight shimmer above the derailed cars. It's not that hot. She twisted to look down the road, hoping to see heat rising from the asphalt. There wasn't any.

Chris stopped at the look on the News Director's face. "What?"

"Fumes! Let's go, now!" Laura grabbed the reporter's arm and pulled. "Jody! Leave it! Come on!" The photographer ran to catch up, reaching to grab the camera that Laura was still carrying. They had almost made it to the other side of the road when the world exploded at their backs.

Laura was thrown forward against Chris, and, wrapping her arms around the reporter, she twisted, taking the full force of their fall on her right side. Jody was blown off his feet, his photographer's instincts making him roll to protect the camera.

Chris saw the ground rushing up to meet her, but the impact wasn't as forceful as it should have been, and she vaguely registered the protective shield provided by the taller woman. The reporter lay there, blinking in shock and wondering why she didn't feel frightened.

For a moment, none of them moved, ears ringing from the blast, then survival instincts kicked in. Laura got them both up and nearly tossed them to the relative safety of the deep muddy ditch on the other side of the road. "Is everyone all right?" she panted, falling down next to Chris. The pain in her back was excruciating and she clenched her jaw.

"Sonofabitch, the live truck!" Jody swore, looking back.

Laura rolled her head to look back. Sure enough, Live 1 was a goner. She gave a weak laugh. "Guess we'll be getting that new truck sooner than Corporate thought."

"It's not my fault!" Chris protested, struggling to get a look, then collapsing back next to Laura. "Oh shit, it's bad."

"We need to get out of here. C'mon, along the ditch, stay low. Jody, is that camera working?"

"Yeah, I think so."

"Just keep it rolling. We'll try to get back to the Blazer." Laura helped Chris up, and still crouching they made their way along the ditch. Jody stood long enough to get some footage of the burning wreckage and then followed. When Laura thought that they had gone far enough, the three of them emerged from the ditch into total chaos. "Keep shooting!" she told the cameraman as firemen and police officers swarmed over the scene.

Chris spotted the Blazer and they started towards it, but before they got there, a sheriff's deputy intercepted them. "You can't be here!" he yelled over the din.

"That's my live truck your empty tankers just blew to hell! I'm here until we find out what happened," Laura said, trapping him with angry eyes. "You guys said it was safe." With that, she brushed past him toward the Blazer with Chris following behind. Opening the door, she grabbed the cell phone and hit the automatic dial for the station. Keith answered immediately.

"Tell me you were rolling on that, because getting the tape out of the camera is out of the question." Laura didn't bother to identify herself.

"Jesus Christ, are you okay? Yeah, we got it all, what the hell happened?"

Chris just stood there halfway listening to the one-sided conversation. She guessed she should find Jody and do some sort of standup, but she just couldn't find the will. It's just shock, the reasonable part of her brain told herself, it's perfectly normal. She looked back at Laura with wide green eyes.

"Gotta go Keith, I'm leaving this line open…Oh shit!" Laura barely caught Chris as she slid into a dead faint.

"It's okay, I've got you," she said, easing the reporter down and propping her up on the tire. She left Chris to rummage through the front seat of the Blazer, coming up with a first aid kit, a rag, and a bottle of water. Laura quickly soaked the rag with water, sat down next to the reporter, and pulled Chris into her lap. Gently, she placed the cloth on her forehead and wished for some help. *Oh, this is just great. The live truck is gone, and the franchise anchor you just signed to a multi-year contract is passed out cold. Don't say it! It can always get worse.*

Slowly, Chris came to, swallowing and blinking, feeling the heat of the pavement against the back of her legs. Laura's concerned face shifted into focus and she looked up at her boss, mumbling the first thing that came to mind.

"You have the most amazing eyes."

One eyebrow went up and Laura gave a half smile. "I get that a lot," she said dryly, then, more gently, "What happened?"

Chris rubbed the towel on her forehead. "Dunno, guess I just checked out to evaluate the situation." She looked around at the running figures, too occupied to pay any attention to the two of them. "Where's Jody?"

As if on cue, the short photographer appeared, carrying the camera. He took in the sight of the two of them against the tire without comment and crouched down. "It's almost out, the fire I mean. What do you want to do now?"

"Oh, shit." Laura struggled to her feet and stumbled around the Blazer's open door to grab the cell phone. "Keith…"

"Kaz! What the hell is going on?"

"Sorry, listen, is someone else on their way out here?"

"Yeah, Bobby and Terence left here right after it blew. Are you coming in?"

"As soon as we can…I think Chris and Jody are in shock…" She lifted the back of her jacket to press a hand to her left side and stopped when she felt the sticky goo; swallowing, she looked down to see her hand covered with blood.

*Oh, great,* she thought, wiping her hand on the corner of her dark jacket out of the sight of Chris and Jody. *And it just keeps getting better,* was the added thought as she caught sight of the Channel 4 live truck pulling in.

"Keith, Channel 4 is here. Cut into programming now, Chris'll do it on this phone. It's the best we can do."

"Okay, I'm transferring you to the control room."

Laura pulled the phone over to where Chris and Jody were sitting while she waited for the connection. "Chris, are you good to do a phoner on what happened? We're gonna do a cut-in before they can." She pointed at the other station's truck.

"Those sons of bitches! They are not getting MY story," Chris practically snarled.

"Good girl," said Laura, handing her the phone. "Jody, did you shoot the live truck burning?"

"Yeah, I figured we'd need it for the insurance anyway," he shrugged. "Not much left but it's about out now."

"Are you okay to shoot Chris's standup? 'Cause we need one before we can get out of here." She gave him an encouraging smile.

"Sure, what about Chris?"

"I'll hold her up if I have to."

"I heard that," the blond reporter said. "We're about ready for the phoner. Jody, wanna grab the little TV out of the truck? You can watch…be careful with the sound."

Jody dug the TV out of the back and set it down away from the reporter to avoid any audio feedback. He adjusted the rabbit ears until he got a clear picture. It was an inexpensive but efficient way to keep track of what was on the air when the reporters didn't have the live truck.

Laura turned back to Chris, who was sitting against the tire with her legs stretched out, her suit ruined, knees bloodied, and hose shredded. But she had a notebook out, scribbling. Laura crouched down next to the reporter, clenching her jaw against the pain in her back. "Just be as clear as you can and tell what happened…do the eyewitness thing, and let the pictures carry it. Terence and Bobby will be here in a bit; they can dig out the details, okay?"

Chris smiled at the dark-haired woman. "You said you could make me better."

"Yeah, but I wasn't trying to get you blown up." Laura got to her feet, proud that she only staggered a little, and went to the back of the truck just as the Special Report graphic came on.

"This is Tom Olson with an Action News 8 Special Report. A train has derailed on Highway 28 just south of Burkett Falls. Originally, it was thought that the tankers were empty and posed no threat, but we have some rather remarkable video to show you."

Laura and Jody leaned in to look. Except for the tumbled tankers, it was peaceful. The image was recent enough that Laura could remember the details sharply. Without warning, there was a puff of smoke and then a huge fireball erupted right into the camera, blowing the picture into electronic snow.

They ran it again. Laura put her hands in her pockets so she could control their shaking and looked over at Jody. The photographer was breathing in and out rapidly on the verge of hyperventilating. Tom Olson was giving the details, and then Chris was answering questions over the phone.

*We were so lucky! How on god's green earth did we survive that?*

Without a word, Jody turned and went to the other side of the Blazer. Laura glanced back at Chris to check how she was, then followed the cameraman.

Jody was on his knees, his body convulsing with dry heaves. There wasn't anything she could do for him, so she waited until his stomach quit rebelling at what his mind said almost happened.

"Sorry," he mumbled. "Guess we were pretty lucky."

"Yeah," Laura answered. "How's your wrist?"

"How did you…" he winced as she lifted his left arm from the elbow.

"Call it a hunch." She swore softly. "Christ, Jody, it's probably broken. How were you shooting with that?"

"Just used it for focusing." He saw her eyes look past him and he turned around. Terence and Bobby were making their way through the clutter toward them.

"Not much longer...c'mon." She helped Jody stand and get into the back seat of the Blazer. "We're gonna get you to the emergency room," she told him, as the new reporter and his cameraman reached her side. "Glad you could make it."

Laura turned to Terence. "Get Chris's notes. She should be about done with the phoner. Bobby, help me get this packed up."

Terence protested, "Get the EMS guys over here…" and stopped abruptly when the blue eyes of the News Director swung over to burn into his.

"We're already part of this story. In a few hours every news organization in the country is going to have video of our live truck burning to the ground. I will not give them…" she jerked her head in the direction of the Channel 4 truck, "…the satisfaction of rolling tape on some EMS guy taking care of one of us." She put the camera in the case and shut the tailgate. "Bobby, get set up to shoot a standup with Chris. Terence, pretend you're a reporter and start asking some questions."

Laura walked to where Chris was sitting and the reporter handed back the cell phone. "I guess it's standup time."

"Yeah, Bobby's gonna shoot it. Let me get you up."

"Oh great, it's one of the Kathys." It was a running joke that Channel 4 had not one, but three reporters named Kathy. This one was a petite brunette with a prediliction toward cattiness, and she came over just as Laura pulled Chris to her feet.

"Well, Chrissy, busy day for you, hmm?" Kathy looked at Laura. "New photog? Bit of an amazon, isn't she?"

"No, new boss," Chris answered. "Laura Kasdan, Kathy Warner."

The petite reporter turned her 100-watt capped-tooth smile on the News Director, hoping to cover her mistake. "So, you're the great Laura Kasdan. It is a pleasure to meet you. I sent a tape to you in Dallas."

"I don't remember, I get so many. You'll have to excuse us…we have a story," she said, leading Chris away and ignoring the stare that followed them.

Chris tried to concentrate on what she was going to say instead of how cool it was to get a jab in at Kathy, but she was having difficulty focusing on any one thought. Snickering, she let her boss pull her forward. *One thing at a time...you might try to walk without staggering first,* she told herself.

"Look, lean on me. I'll walk you over so Bobby can get our dearly departed live truck in his shot."

"Whatever you say." Looking at the News Director, the reporter tried to control the energy moving through her. Rationally, she could explain it as just an adrenaline rush in a stressful situation, but there was also the charge she was feeling from being with Laura in the middle of a situation that a storyteller lives for.

*Organize,* Chris told herself. *Break it down into three separate thoughts, then elaborate on each one. Train derails...Supposed to be empty...Boom.* She stumbled a bit, but Laura was there, helping her along. *Tell the story, keep it simple.* The reporter ran her free hand through her hair and started speaking softly, backing up and going forward, choosing, shifting, and discarding words as she tried to make the last half hour into a coherent report.

Laura just listened as she offered steady support, stopping when they got to the place where Bobby had set up the camera, close enough to see the charred remains of the live truck. Whatever else, they had some kick ass video.

"Can you do this?" Laura looked into green eyes.

"In my sleep," the reporter told her. Laura went to stand behind the camera with a slight smile. It had been rough on the reporter, but she seemed to be holding up pretty well. Bobby handed Chris the stick mic and went back to roll the tape, and the standup was underway.

They did four takes, each saying basically the same thing, with just a few subtle differences. Chris also cut a promo, which could run a few times before the news to help drive viewers to the coverage of the derailment. After all, they had an exclusive, and a crispy live truck should be worth something.

Laura took the tape from the photographer and labeled it. "Bobby, we'll get this to the station. You and Terence get onto Captain Wallace and find out why they thought there wasn't any danger of the tank cars blowing. We're gone...Jody's got to get to a hospital."

"What's wrong with Jody?" Chris asked.

"I think his wrist is broken. Let's go." Chris was moving a little better and didn't need help walking. "Probably need to get you checked out too."

"No, I'm fine, just a little shaky." She looked at her watch. "God, it's only 2:30...seems like we've been here for hours."

"Well, it was all pretty bang-bang...literally. Get in." Laura opened the Blazer door for Chris. "What's the closest hospital?"

"That'd be St. Joseph's, you know, the guys who sponsor our Tower Cam."

"Right. Always good to give a client some business. Hang on." Sitting and holding the steering wheel was definitely better than walking.

The pain in Laura's back was becoming unbearable. Twisting to look before reversing the Blazer, she ground her teeth together. Not much longer.

"Chris, call Keith and tell him to meet us at St. Joe's emergency room...better tell him to let Phyllis know we're gonna have some workman's comp claims," Laura said, referring to the business manager. "Jody, you doing all right back there?"

"Just peachy," he mumbled.

"Keith, it's Chris. We're on our way to the emergency room at St. Joseph's...yeah, send someone to pick up the tapes. Tell Phyllis we're going so she can get the workman's comp claims in."

"Almost there," Laura said as they pulled to a stop close to the front. She pushed open the door and practically fell out of the vehicle groaning. It was agony to move now. Using a hand to brace against the truck, she straightened.

"What is that?" Chris asked, pointing at the driver's seat, green eyes wide.

"That would be blood," Laura said between clenched teeth, "a lot of it. So it would be real good if we could get inside before I pass out."

"Shit! Why didn't you say something? Jody, go on in." Chris came around to Laura's side and took hold of her arm, lifting the back of her dark blue jacket. Some of the drying blood had stiffened the cloth and the blonde woman inhaled sharply when she saw the gaping wound on the lower part of her boss's back. "Oh for Christ's sake! Were you and Jody trying to out-tough each other? I've never seen anything so stupid..."

"Your concern is touching," came the dry response. "Could we just get inside? The sooner I get some really strong painkillers, the better."

"Lean on me, it's okay...We could have left right after it happened, we didn't have to stay and shoot."

"Yes, we did," Laura swallowed in pain as the automatic doors swished open to admit them "It was our story, and when you establish ownership of the story, you never turn it loose."

One of the benefits of being a local news celebrity was that sometimes you got really good service. Laura watched with some amusement as Chris worked the staff, oozing charm to get her co-workers taken care of as soon as possible. Before she knew it, Laura was in a curtained cubicle laying face down on a bed waiting for a doctor to examine her. She heard the door open, and Chris was pulling up a chair, her eyes level with Laura's as she settled in to wait with her boss.

"Hey, the doctor's going to be here in just a minute."

"The nurse just left. I asked for morphine but she just laughed. How's Jody?"

"They're putting a cast on his wrist. I guess he's going to be edit boy for a while, since he can't really shoot." The reporter crossed her arms. "So why didn't one of you say something? I mean…you were hurt and Jody should have been screaming."

Laura gave a wry half smile and plucked at the sheet covering the mattress. "I don't get to go out on stories much anymore. You do." She shifted a little wincing at the pain. "You should know by now that there's an incredible adrenaline kick. That's all it was."

"Oh, I get my fair share of adrenaline."

"Given what usually happens to you on a story, I bet you do."

Just then the nurse bustled in, followed by a doctor in scrubs. "So here's the rest of the Channel 8 wrecking crew. Hi, I'm Dr. Reeves." He smiled down at Chris. "It's nice to meet you Miss Hanson, I watch you every day at noon." Laura rolled her eyes. The talent always got the attention.

"I'm really hurting here, Doc. You and Chris can talk later."

He laughed, lifting the cloth that covered her wound and turning to the nurse for the gloves she held out. "You've got a pretty good sized hole here, Miz Kasdan…let's get it cleaned out, then we'll stitch you up." He picked up a needle and a vial. "Now, this is probably going to burn a bit going in…"

"You're a liar, it burns A LOT," Laura hissed, grabbing hold of the edge of the bed.

"We'll wait a minute for that area to deaden." The doctor dropped the needle into the sharp object container. "Is all this going to be on the news tonight?"

"Boy, I hope so. Otherwise we wasted a perfectly good afternoon." Chris sat down in front of Laura again. "Sorry, I don't have a bullet for you to bite on, but you can squeeze my hand if you promise not to break any bones."

The doctor was cleaning the injury now and Chris could see Laura's eyes darken with the pain. Without waiting for permission, she took the one of the older woman's hands in her own, looking down at strong long fingers. "Hey, what's this?"

"What."

"Your right hand is tanned and the left is really white."

"Oh. Golf glove."

"Golf? That's right, you won some tournament once. I read it in your bio. I thought maybe softball or something."

"Used to play softball, don't have much time anymore," Laura mumbled, squeezing Chris's hand a bit. They were interrupted by the sound of metal hitting a tray.

"You picked up a piece of shrapnel here and you worked it in pretty good. Sorry it took so long to get it out. This is about clean, now we're going to stitch it up. You okay there?" the doctor asked.

Laura could feel herself begin to panic. Shrapnel? "Wha…What kind of damage to my back?"

"Well, I don't think there was any serious damage but you're going to be sore for a while."

"For how long?"

"Probably for a week or so." The doctor started stitching.

"Can I play golf this weekend?"

"That's not a good idea." He could almost hear teeth grinding and he stopped for a moment. "Hey, it's just a game."

Doctors, she thought with venom. "Let me rephrase the question: if I play golf this weekend, will I permanently injure myself?"

"Well, no, but…"

"Thank you."

"It could slow your recovery."

"I'm a quick healer." Laura looked up at Chris. "You okay?" she asked, suddenly very tired.

"Sure."

"Good, 'cause you're gonna have to do a debrief at five."

Chris gave a short laugh. "You never stop thinking about it do you? There's a life outside of news, you know."

"I know, and I'd get to it if the news didn't keep interrupting." She put her head down on the mattress, feeling the rough sheet on her forehead, and trying not to think about her back.

"You mentioned softball…do you still play?" Chris asked, trying to distract her, "Because we have a media league here, you know, all the TV stations, newspaper, and radio guys get together to play on Sundays. It's co-ed and a lot of fun…you ought to come out and at least cheer us on."

"Do you play?"

"Yep, second base." Green eyes crinkled merrily. "Ah, you don't believe me. Let me tell you, I hold my own."

"Let me guess," Laura said dryly. "You wear eye black."

"Sure. They think I'm real cute right up 'til the time I turn two." Chris turned her head as the door opened and Keith walked in followed by Jody, his arm in a cast.

"I've got the tape, what's next?" Keith asked, blinking at the amount of smooth feminine skin exposed on the News Director's back. Laura ignored the flush creeping up the young man's face.

"Get someone else out to the scene, we need to own this. Get Chris back to the station and get…better yet, Chris are you okay to go back there?"

"Sure."

"Then get a change of clothes and do the debrief from there. Don't try to spare the station any embarrassment, make sure you show the live truck blowing to hell." She paused for a moment and looked back at the doctor. "Are you about finished?"

"Just about."

"Good. Keith, when you get back to the station, tell the Promotions Manager…what's her name? Elly? To get something on the air ASAP that says we pull out all the stops for action news…blah, blah, blah, whatever those promo guys do to make us look good."

"All done," the doctor said, stripping off the gloves. "I'll give you a prescription for a mild painkiller. Just take it easy, okay? Come back in about a week and I'll take the stitches out." He smiled down at Chris. "Nice meeting you, Miz Hanson."

The nurse twitched the tail of Laura's shirt down over the bandaged area, and the patient pushed up and sat on the edge of the gurney, straightening the rest of her clothes. "Anything else you can think of?" she asked Keith.

"We might want to load some of the video up on our web site. I know it's a little sensationalistic…"

"But an exclusive is an exclusive," she smiled. "Good thinking. I'll run Chris by her place for a change of clothes. Did Richard figure out what was wrong with Live 2?"

"He's got it up, but he's not sure how long it will last." Keith opened the door and the four of them started down the hall.

Chris listened as Laura and Keith went over the strategy for the Five and Six newscasts. *They're a perfect team, she thought. Both know exactly what they want to accomplish, and Laura was right, she will make all of us better.* Not to mention the fact that she was pretty good in an emergency. "How does it feel?" she asked Jody.

"I guess it's the edit booth for a while if I can't shoot," the photographer said resignedly. "Just when things were starting to get interesting."

"Yeah, I know what you mean," she chuckled. "At least you got some good stuff for your resume tape."

"Shh, I don't want her to know I'm looking."

"She's not an idiot, Jody. She knows everybody's looking…except me."

"You signed? Aww Chris, we're supposed to get out of here together."

Chris couldn't hold back the grin. It felt good to tell someone. The excitement of the afternoon had taken the edge off her feeling of triumph over the new contract and the new position. "Yeah, I signed…it's a sweet deal."

"C'mon, you two." Laura stood in the doorway. "Jody, are you sure you're alright? Keith can take you home…"

"No way. I'm gonna finish this. I'll edit."

Laura nodded. "Good. I'll meet you back at the station. Go ahead and get Live 2 out there and set up." She and Chris got into the Blazer and followed the other station vehicle out of the parking lot.

"Where to?" Laura asked the reporter. With a minimum of chatter, Chris gave directions to her house, trying to remember what kind of shape it was in. Sometimes she wasn't the tidiest of people, but Chris felt a sense of pride in the little house, and wanted to show it off a bit. Well, at least it looks good from the outside, she thought as Laura pulled into the driveway.

"Nice place," Laura said. "Do you rent?"

"No, it's mine…well, mine and the bank's." Chris unlocked the door and stepped into the cool hallway. "It won't take me any time to change, do you want something to drink?"

"Got any Coke?"

"Should be some in the fridge, help yourself." Chris started for her bedroom, untucking her blouse as she went. "Kitchen's that way."

Opening her closet, the reporter pulled out a pair of navy chinos and tossed them on the bed. Gonna take more than a good dry cleaner to get this suit fixed up, she thought, taking off her skirt. She rummaged in a drawer and found a polo shirt with a Channel 8 Action News logo. That'll work, she told herself, removing the rest of her ruined outfit and trying to get dressed again as quickly as possible.

Laura opened the refrigerator looking for her favorite form of caffeine. *So this is what a well-stocked fridge looks like,* she thought to herself; the kid eats pretty well. The tall woman pushed aside some fruit juice to get to the red and white canned beverage. Closing the door, she looked around the little kitchen before wandering into the living room. It was just a little cluttered; an afghan was spread over the end of the couch and there were books and pieces of mail spread on the coffee table. The room was done in shades of blue and gray, with oak bookcases lining one wall.

Laura smiled wryly as she gulped at her drink, comparing the room to her tiny apartment that was furnished in Early American Dorm, with cinderblock shelves, a battered couch and a recliner. Even when she'd owned the house in Dallas, it hadn't looked this nice.

"All changed, you ready?" Chris said, coming down the hall.

"Yeah, that'll work," Laura said, appraising the younger woman's attire.

"Find the Coke okay?"

"Uh huh, thanks."

Chris locked the door behind them, thinking that getting the woman to open up was like pulling teeth. She tried one more time in the car. "I haven't thanked you yet."

"For what?" Laura started the engine.

"For keeping me…you know…You protected me and you didn't…"

"The explosion pushed me into you, that's all." A flush tinted Laura's skin.

Chris remembered strong arms wrapped around her and a six-foot cushion so she wouldn't slam into the ground. Earnest green eyes looked into blue, and Laura looked away first, uncomfortable.

*She's shy,* Chris thought in wonder, realizing that this woman wasn't the queen bitch they'd all been told about; she pushed everyone because she pushed herself. "Yeah, whatever you say." Chris smiled knowingly. "Thanks."

Laura snorted and concentrated on her driving.

After the six o'clock 'cast, the News Director ordered ten giant pizzas for the newsroom to celebrate the great job that everyone did covering the great train and live truck explosion. The remaining live truck returned and there were high fives all around. Afterwards, Laura stood in her office doorway and watched the staff bestow another hash mark on the side of Chris Hanson's desk to denote the complete destruction of yet another station vehicle, bringing the total to eight. Grimacing, she went to answer the ringing phone, knowing that this time it was Corporate, having already dealt with the General Manager.

"News 8, this is Kaz."

"Well, well, less than a week in town and the shit's already hit the fan."

"Hello, Don, I guess you've already talked to Art."

"Kaz, I sent you to Burkett to clean things up and keep you safe, not to blow the fucking place up."

"Sorry, Don, it's just one of those things. So, when are we gonna get those new live trucks?"

"Dammit, I'm trying to tear you a new asshole here…"

Laura held the phone away from her ear as Don continued his tirade, sorting through the papers on her desk. *What did you expect? Someone has to take the blame.* When his tone indicated he was winding down, she started listening again and eventually he ran out of expletives.

"Look, one of my photographers broke his wrist, I've got a hole in my back, and I'm missing a live truck and a betacam. The damn truck was insured and was gonna have to be replaced anyway. Art and the business manager have already screamed at me. We got some exclusive video, plus some sampling we wouldn't normally get a month out of May sweeps, which is what everyone wants. So unless you're ready to cut me loose, *get off my fucking back!"*

There was silence at the other end for a moment. "How's the camera guy?"

Laura sighed, "He'll be editing for a few weeks, which is just as well since we're short a camera."

"What about you?"

"I'm fine."

"Well, if you need anything, let me know."

"Now that you mention it, two live trucks would be nice."

"Could you lay off on that?" Silence for a moment. "Two weeks. I signed off on it this afternoon."

"Before or after?" Laura winced a little as she put a hand on her back.

"After. You forced our hand again. It won't always work, Kaz." The phone clicked as he hung up.

"I know," she said to herself, understanding that she had just run out of second chances.

At least Jody and Chris were all right, she thought, turning off the computer and closing the door behind her. Tomorrow was Friday and the first week of her new life was almost over. Great, just one hundred and fifty-five more to go.

Chris was determined to wait for her boss to leave to make sure that the older woman was all right, so she waited at the bottom of the stairs enjoying the late spring breeze and the hum of insects. The summer heat would be intolerable in a few months, so she was storing up memories of pleasant weather while she could.

The door opened at the top of the stairs and impatient feet clumped down the steps to where the blond reporter was sitting. Without looking up, she knew who it was, and a briefcase and jacket were laid down on the step next to her.

Laura sat down next to Chris, a little surprised at herself for wanting the company. I'm just tired, that's all. She made the excuse easily. "Big day for you," she said to the younger woman, stretching her long legs out in front and crossing them at the ankles.

"Hmm, yeah. Long day. Good stuff, though. How's your back?"

"I'll live. I looked for Jody, guess he went home."

"His wife picked him up a little while ago."

"What about you?"

Chris shrugged. "I'm just winding down a bit and thinking about how lucky I am."

Laura looked down. "I'm sorry. If I hadn't asked you to keep quiet about your contract for a bit, you'd be out celebrating."

"Probably. But I understand why. Michelle's gonna be pissed that she's not getting the Five, Six, and Ten."

Laura chuckled, "I'm not discussing other the talent's temperament with you. That'd give you an unfair advantage."

"Yeah, but you know I'm right." Chris leaned back laughing. "Um, we all usually meet on Friday nights after the Six at a bar down the street, why don't you join us?"

"Sorry, I'm meeting Lisa Tyler and her boyfriend for drinks."

"Well, I'll probably see you there then. Lisa and Trey always do the Friday night Mainstreet thing."

"The boss showing up at the regular watering hole doesn't bother you?"

"Nah, it'll be a great ice breaker."

Laura was quiet for a minute. "Listen Chris, I'm walking a very thin line here. Lisa is an old friend and socializing with her is not a problem since she is also considered management. But hanging out with the staff would undermine my authority."

Chris turned and narrowed her eyes at the dark haired woman. "Don't you get tired of it?" she asked.

"Tired of what?"

"Building those walls."

"I have no idea what you're talking about."

"No, you wouldn't," Chris sighed. "Look, you came in here with a rep for hard work and driving up the ratings, and if anyone had any doubts, they won't after what happened today. Having a drink with us tomorrow night isn't gonna blow apart your management style."

The reporter thought for a moment that she'd gone too far. Laura Kasdan's temper was also legendary, so she was surprised when the woman gave a short laugh. "Okay, maybe I sounded a little preachy there..." Chris started.

"Just a little," Laura replied, "but you're right, one drink won't hurt anything." She stood up and gathered her briefcase and jacket, smiling down at the younger woman. "We had a good day today; those are few and far between in this business."

"You should do that more often."

"What?"

"Smile." That got Chris a raised eyebrow and another half smirk.

"Whatever would become of my reputation?" Laura drawled.

Green eyes smiled back as Chris held out a hand, silently asking to be pulled to her feet. Laura obliged with a tug and a feeling that she had done this a million times before. It was something she couldn't seem to shake even after she said goodbye to the blond reporter and left for her sterile apartment.

# Thank God It's Friday

*"No one in TV ever goes away, they just change markets."*

Friday was a slow news day, as is often the case after the staff is run ragged on a big story the day before. It would have been totally uneventful if the Six O'Clock show hadn't been a complete meltdown. The tipoff should have come when Chris's IFB didn't work on the live shot, so they used the two-way radio to make contact, which caused even more confusion. Then they lost the signal in the middle of the live report, which meant that Tracy and Tom, the two anchors, had to cover… always a risky move.

"I'm already two minutes short!" the producer wailed.

"Roll VTR 2, dammit, that's the wrong fucking tape!" Lisa punched out of the offending video with a snarl, and spun around to the audio engineer. "Tom sounds like he's in the toilet, can you do something about it at the break, Ron? Camera One, don't move'til I say you're clear! What part of that don't you understand?"

Laura stood against the back wall with her arms crossed, listening as it all fell apart, and knowing that any intervention would just make it worse. So she took off the headset and headed back to her office, where she found the General Manager waiting for her.

"I talked to Don Farmer this afternoon, he says we'll have those live trucks in about two weeks," Art told her, taking a seat in the chair closest to the desk.

"Good, 'cause Live 2 crapped out in the middle of the Six."

Art shook his head. "I'm surprised it lasted this long.

Well, at least we'll be ready to go for May Sweeps...I haven't seen your plan yet."

Laura flipped open the planner on her desk with a frown. "We're going to break down and assign the special reports on Monday, so you'll have the plan on Tuesday. The consultant is coming on Wednesday—that's Dave Franco from Target Research. So, by middle of next week we should be mapped out and ready to go." Laura rubbed her thumb along an eyebrow thoughtfully. "We're one month out, so I'd like to go ahead and announce that Chris is taking over the Six. Any problems with that?"

"Whatever, it's your show, I hope you're right about this." Art stood up and walked to the door. "Yesterday was pretty...interesting. If we were a metered market, it probably would have spiked right off the scale."

Laura gave a wry half smile. "Let's just hope we can carry some of that momentum into May." She caught sight of the Six O'Clock crew filtering into the newsroom, and with a sigh she went out to join them for the post mortem meeting. Accurate, since the sooner they buried this newscast, the better.

Mainstreet Liquid Company was crowded with people rejoicing over the end of the workweek, and the contingent from Channel 8 was doing its best to out-celebrate the other patrons. The music blared as Laura threaded her way through the crowds carrying drinks for Lisa and her boyfriend, the former linebacker from Texas A&M.

"Here y'go," she said, sliding the mugs on to the table. "Next round's on you." Smiling, Laura crunched on the ice in her Coke. "So..." The news director paused awkwardly, wondering what to say next.

"Jesus, Kaz. Your social skills really haven't improved." Lisa started to fold a bar napkin into a tiny square. "You're supposed to start with something like...Trey, how 'bout those Aggies?"

"I don't give a rat's ass about the Aggies, and to pretend otherwise would be insincere."

Trey grinned broadly. "Pretty much what I'd expect, since Longhorns have no manners."

"Oh, I can be civil...at least for Lisa's sake," Laura chuckled. The conversation drifted to other topics, shared acquaintances, restaurants, and since the three of them were Texans, they eventually talked about football.

"Musta been hard to leave those season tickets behind, Kaz." Lisa was still folding things, this time a paper coaster.

"Who said I left 'em behind?"

"You still have Cowboy season tickets?" This from Trey. "Guess you'll fly back for the games, huh?"

"Probably for some of them, then I'll sell the rest." Laura shook her head, "I just couldn't let 'em go…even if the coach is just adequate."

Trey deadpanned, "If only Jerry hadn't fired Jimmy…"

Lisa slapped his arm. "Stop it…he's never coming back."

The couple exchanged the familiar responses affectionately, and Laura looked away, slightly uncomfortable with their intimacy. It's a conversation about football, for Christ's sake. Trey excused himself and headed for the men's room and Lisa turned to the taller woman. "So, what do you think?"

"I think you found a keeper. Is he housebroken?"

"Very funny," Lisa said, leaning in on her elbows and watching the well-built man stop to talk to someone on his way to the back. "It's weird how much you can care for one person." She smiled slightly. "You need someone, Kaz."

"Don't need, don't want," Laura answered, swallowing the last of her Coke. Then she caught sight of a bright blond head bobbing through the crowd and heard an infectious laugh over the music and the babble. "Life is too complicated anyway."

Lisa followed the news director's gaze and heard the laugh. Interesting. She took another swig of her beer and willed the reporter to come over to the table, pleased when she saw Chris head in their direction.

"Lisa T…Where's your hunka hunka burning love?" Chris smiled at her boss even as Laura's brow creased in a frown. "Is this a department head thing or can anyone join in?"

"No, come on." Lisa moved her chair over to make room for the smaller woman. "What'll you have?" she asked, spotting a waitress and waving her over.

"Another Corona, extra lime. How's your back?" She directed the question at Laura.

"Good. Told you I was a quick healer."

"Great, now I can stop feeling guilty." She leaned forward conspiratorially. "Stick with me and you'll never be bored. Hey, Trey, what's going on?" Chris greeted the man easily as he returned to the table and sat down, her green eyes crinkling with her smile.

"Just arguing football with your boss here. Saw you nearly blow yourselves up yesterday; how'd you get so close?" He looked up at the waitress. "N'other couple of Buds, please, ma'am," he requested before turning back to the three women. "Sheriff's guys must have really fucked up."

Laura listened with half an ear as Chris gave an amusing account of yesterday's ordeal, studying the blonde-haired woman and her mannerisms as she gestured to make a point. *She's always comfortable, no self-consciousness, no awkwardness.* Laura smiled slightly as she felt a stab of envy. She had always been taller than anyone in her classes, a bit of an oddity, and it was easier to withdraw and be aloof than to get close to any of the other students; it didn't help that she'd gone to an all-girls Catholic school. Later on in college she'd been too busy. She'd had a lot of acquaintances but no real friends. Lisa had been the exception and only because they started out as roommates.

If Laura was brutally honest with herself, she could admit that she would never have been a good reporter. You have to want to see below the surface and you must be willing to pry. The reluctance to be a reporter led to a job as a producer and then to managing editor. News Director was the next step, and she accomplished it all without ever really getting involved. You just present the facts; it's up to someone else to judge. Just another form of self-preservation: Don't get close to anyone or anything.

But for the first time, Laura Kasdan found herself wanting to get to know someone better, wanting to get below the surface. It was more than a little disturbing. Laura had decided that she would push the feeling away for the time being and take it out later to examine it a little more closely when a shot glass full of golden liquid was placed in front of her.

"Lisa said you drank tequila...it's two-for-one shots on Friday nights." Chris held up the other shot glass and raised an eyebrow in silent challenge. "Here's to change," she toasted, "May we all get what we deserve...if we're lucky, it'll be what we want." Laura picked up her glass and the four of them clinked their drinks together. With a grin, Chris tossed back the liquor, squinting as it went down, then grabbed a slice of lime and bit down on the sour fruit.

Laura picked up another slice of lime and smeared it across the top of her hand. The salt shaker was next. The dry mineral stuck to the dampness and she shook off the excess. Lifting it to her mouth, she licked off the salt, blue-white eyes smiling at the younger woman. Without looking away, Laura swallowed the tequila easily in one gulp, feeling the familiar burn all the way down. Oblivious to Lisa and Trey looking on, she leaned forward, her voice dropping and said, "Chris, I can drink you under the table, so don't start something you can't finish."

Green eyes flashed, and Chris sat up straighter at the challenge. "That sounds suspiciously like a dare."

Lisa rolled her eyes. "Don't, Chris..." Trey waved at the waitress to get her attention, gesturing for two more shots. "You're encouraging them! Stop it!" Lisa scolded, punching her boyfriend in the arm.

Laura felt a tingle in her gut. *Tequila at work. You're making a huge mistake.* For whatever reason, she couldn't look away from the intensity of the other woman's gaze. Again she was struck by the color of Chris's eyes; they were almost grass green even in the dim light of the bar. Lord knew she had been around attractive talent before, good-looking people were a dime a dozen in the television news business…but this was different, she told herself, because Chris was different. Charisma, charm, appeal…whatever, it flowed from the small blond woman in waves. Laura was fascinated and annoyed by it, wishing for something she wasn't quite sure of, and willing to ignore the warning bells going off in the back of her mind. *It's just a game, right?*

*What do you think you're doing?* Chris had her own doubts about where this was going. *You have zero tolerance for alcohol and you've already had two beers, plus, you skipped lunch. You're playing with fire here...never ever overindulge around your boss, remember the rules? Be very, very careful.*

Twin shot glasses arrived, and over Lisa's protests, Chris and Laura repeated the ritual. Her tongue numbed by the liquor, Chris ran it across her teeth, still tasting the tequila and a little of the lime. Feeling a little artificial courage, she decided to try and dig a little information out of the News Director. "So, is it a big deal to win the U.S. Amateur golf thingy?"

Lisa choked on her beer and Laura looked over at her for a second before answering with a half smile. "I thought so at the time."

"And you won it twice?" the reporter continued.

"Yeah."

"So why aren't you, like, playing golf for a living?"

"Yeah, why aren't you playing golf for a living?" Lisa seconded the question.

"Because I already have a job."

"That is a half-assed excuse," Lisa interrupted. Laura raised an eyebrow, waiting for the next shot. The argument was an old one, and the news director could almost predict what was coming next. "You have this fabulous game that you only take out on special occasions, then you pack it up and put it away. We all would have killed for your game…"

"Who would've killed for her game?" Chris asked.

"All of us on the golf team at UT."

"Why?"

Lisa blew out a breath. How do you explain it to a non-golfer? She looked over at Trey, knowing that as an athlete, he understood, then back at Laura…no help there. "Because she's good, really good, and it's such a fucking waste!"

Uncomfortable with the attention, Laura pushed her glass to the center of the table. "Yes, well, if I need a career counselor, I know who to come to. Have a good weekend guys, I've got to go." It was a nice try, she thought, her mouth twisting into a rueful half smile. It always comes back to disappointing someone, doesn't it?

"Laura?"

Blue eyes snapped at the use of her name, and the anger that always seemed to bubble just below the surface rose up to assert itself. "It's Kaz, not Laura, just Kaz, okay?"

"Right." Chris bobbed her head once in understanding and said carefully, "I'm very drunk now, and since it's your fault, could you please take me home?"

"Oh for…" Laura rolled her eyes as Lisa and Trey started to laugh, the tension neatly diffused by the reporter. "How is it my fault? Never mind, can you walk?"

"It's not the walking, it's the standing up."

"Well, come on." With surprising gentleness, Laura helped the smaller woman to her feet, steadying her before reaching for her briefcase.

"Are you all right to drive, Kaz?" Lisa asked with some concern.

"I'm fine," she said shortly, and because she didn't want to be at odds with the other woman she added, "I'll be trying to qualify for the Open in Austin next month…we'll see how it goes."

A smile spread across the other woman's face and she felt Trey squeeze her hand. "Cool," Lisa said, her earlier irritation forgotten. "Be careful driving home."

Chris was disappointed that Laura wasn't on the motorcycle and that she wasn't going to get a ride. Grumbling a little, she accepted help getting into the passenger side of the Jeep and watched as Laura climbed in next to her. "Can we get something to eat? I've really got the munchies."

"I thought you were drunk."

"Yeah, well, I wouldn't be drunk if I had gotten some lunch. You and the tequila took unfair advantage of me."

"Sure we did. Drive-through at Sonic okay?"

"Perfect." Chris leaned back into the seat, looking around at the immaculate vehicle. It was an older Jeep with a metal dashboard and reinforced cloth doors, built before sport utility was supposed to be luxurious. She decided it suited the woman sitting next to her: tough, good-looking, and always dependable. "Do you ever take the top down?"

"Top down and doors off…it's my favorite way to drive it." That was more personal information than she usually gave out in an entire day, and Laura frowned as she pulled into one of the slots at the drive in.

"You're thinking too hard again. Your eyebrows get lower and lower when you do that."

"Excuse me?"

Chris gave a sigh as though explaining something to a child. "It's like 'oops, I gave away too much, how do I take that back?' I'm a reporter, remember? I see that all the time. You could just loosen up…I'm no threat to you." The green eyes were frank and honest. "I promise, you will never have a reason not to trust me."

For a minute she could almost see belief in the clear blue eyes, then it was gone as Laura turned and unzipped the window to reach for the speaker. "Don't make promises you can't keep. What do you want?"

*I want to know what's going on behind those blue eyes, I want you to teach me what you know, and I want to know why you're in a job you so obviously hate. Wanting's a bitch, isn't it?* Chris shook her head slightly; *it's not good to go there,* she thought. "I want a big ol' cheeseburger, a big order of tots and a chocolate shake."

"When you said you had the munchies, you weren't kidding."

"Yeah, it's a severe character flaw." Digging in her briefcase she pulled out some money and handed it to the other woman. Laura took it and answered the squawking speaker. "Two cheeseburgers, a large order of tots, a chocolate shake and a Coke."

"Gotta have your caffeine fix?"

"That would be my severe character flaw." *Don't even get started on character flaws,* Laura's inner voice shot back. *Change the subject to something safe, not something work-related, though.* "Where do you play softball?"

Chris smiled, seeing through the tactic. "This Sunday we play at one thirty. We use a field at Northridge Park, do you know where it is?" At Laura's nod she continued, "You really should come out, it's a lot of fun. You know, we're playing Channel 4, it'd be a good chance for you to meet some of the competition, and their News Director always plays."

"Who's the News Director over there?"

"Lance Barker runs the show."

"Pretty Boy Lance?" Laura laughed unpleasantly. "A word of advice, Chris? No one in TV ever goes away, they just change markets."

"So you know him?"

"Yeah, he was a producer with me in Austin…Lisa knows him, too," she added thoughtfully.

"Anyway, it should be a pretty good game, you should try to make it." Their food arrived and Laura passed the bag and the drinks to Chris as she paid for the order.

"Okay if I eat in your car?"

"Go ahead." A suspicion was starting to form in Laura's mind as she unwrapped her cheeseburger. "Don't eat so fast, you'll throw up."

"Can't help it, I'm starved," Chris wolfed down the burger and started on the tater tots. The younger woman ate with single-minded intensity, not what Laura would have associated with someone who claimed to be smashed.

"You're not really drunk, are you?"

Laura could almost see the laughter in the blond woman's eyes, and Chris answered without apology. "I would never get snockered in front of my boss, but I shouldn't be driving. I just wanted to spend a little time getting to know you away from the office."

"Why?"

"Because I think that you're the best thing that could have happened to us. Understand that we've been beaten down by Jerry Nelson. Nothing we did was ever good enough, smart enough, or aggressive enough. Now here you are. You've got some baggage, sure, but no one doubts that you can run a newsroom. It's only been a week, but there's already a change."

Laura didn't say anything, she just balled up the wrapper and put it in the bag, so Chris went on, "Y'know what's impressed me the most? Not once this week did you say 'That's the way we did it in Dallas.' I waited to hear it, and I never did. Do you have any idea how extraordinary that is?"

A short bitter laugh answered the reporter. "I'm not sure than anything I did in Dallas is worth repeating here." Laura tipped her head back and closed her eyes listening to the sounds of the busy drive in outside the confines of the Jeep, not knowing what else to say.

Chris finished her meal and began stuffing the trash into the bag. "I think you need a friend, that's all." She tried to shrug casually, suddenly a little nervous. "You're in a new place and maybe we could do something...sometime...outside of work." Oh that's just great, she cringed inwardly. *She's smart, she's gorgeous, of course she's not gonna have any trouble making friends.*

Laura started the Jeep and repeated the mantra again and again: *Don't need, don't want.* She put the trash on the tray outside and zipped up the window, still not trusting herself to speak. *Put an end to this, right now.*

"Chris, I don't... It's not that I... Look, I'm the queen bitch of the universe, the Kazmanian Devil, She-Ra Princess of Power, the News

Nazi…yeah, I know all the names." Chris's look of surprise almost made her laugh. "Being friends with me is not healthy, professionally or personally." She didn't look at the reporter, afraid of what she might see, and concentrated on maneuvering the Jeep out of the parking lot and out into the street.

They completed the ride in silence, and for the second time that week, Laura pulled into the driveway of Chris's house. Clearing her throat she turned to the younger woman. "What about your car?"

"It's only a couple of miles to the station. I'll go for a run tomorrow and pick it up." She opened the door and climbed out. "At least you should come out on Sunday and watch us kick some Channel 4 butt. Bring your glove, we can always use an outfielder." With that, she closed the door and walked up the path to the house. Laura waited until she saw her step inside and turn out the porch light, then she threw the stick into reverse, backed out and headed for home.

Chris watched the taillights disappear down the street, disappointed and a little hurt by Laura's reaction. *What difference does it make? It's just a brush off, it's not like you haven't had that happen before, and she's right, you know, it's not a good idea.*

But she couldn't help feeling that it wasn't right. They were supposed to be friends; why else would she have felt that incredible pull when she looked across that interstate median to see the tall dark woman walking toward her? It was like she had been waiting for something or someone and now that all the players were in place, the show could begin.

*Okay, Chris, now you've gone off the deep end. One thing's for sure: life isn't going to be dull around Laura Kasdan.*

*"Nice to know your coverage sucked so bad you were watching us."*

Peter Davis walked down the hill towards the driving range, his metal spikes clacking on the concrete of the cart path. He was running a little late and hoped he hadn't missed all of Laura Kasdan's warm-up. One of the cart boys had told him that she had walked out to the practice tee a little before six, and that everything was ready for her, just like they planned yesterday. Peter hoped all of the day's plans would fall as neatly into place.

There was still a little fog but he could see the tall figure swinging a club loosely and hear the sound of solid contact with the ball. He stepped onto the grass, which muffled the sound of the spikes, and approached from behind, marveling at the clean elegance of her swing. Dressed in a white sleeveless polo shirt and khaki shorts, her skin had the red gold tan that spoke of hours spent in the sun. A tan cap covered the dark hair and a ponytail was pulled through the opening in the back. Stepping up to the slight rise, he noticed that she was barefoot, white feet contrasting with the bronze of her legs. It was a little surprising, and he felt a smile spread involuntarily across his face.

Her concentration broken, Laura stepped back and glanced at the handsome golf pro. "Morning." She ambled over to her bag and picked up a towel, carefully wiping off the club head and then the grip. "Looks like we'll have a pretty good day. A little putting practice and I'll be good to go." She sat down on a plastic chair that one of the cart boys had gotten for her earlier and started to pull on her socks.

"Why practice barefoot?" the pro asked.

"Spikes will give you traction when you're playing, but I've found that if I practice some barefoot, it helps my balance." She clapped the soles of her shoes together a couple of times to remove the grass clippings clumped on them, then slid her feet in, tying double knots.

"No soft spikes?"

"Can't stand 'em," she answered, referring to the plastic spikes that had been developed to save wear and tear on the greens. "If I could wear two inch cleats, I would. With my swing, using soft spikes would probably cost me about two or three strokes a round." Laura hoisted the black nylon golf bag over her right shoulder, bouncing a little to settle it, and they started walking up to the putting green. "Besides, I like the way they sound on pavement."

Dropping the bag on the side of the practice area, Laura unzipped a side pocket and fished out several balls, tossing them to the still wet grass. "Give me about ten minutes. You said you dug up some caddies?" Peter nodded. "Real caddies or just two bodies to hump the bags?"

He smiled in answer. "We do a men's Nike tournament here and these guys are usually part of the caddy pool, so they know what they're doing."

"Well, with everyone going to carts, it's a dying art." Pulling out her putter, she knocked the balls toward the closest hole, then arranged them in a straight line about two feet away. Twirling the putter flexed her wrist, and she leaned over the first of the balls. "It makes me nervous when people watch me practice," she said dryly. "I'll meet you up at the clubhouse."

"Sure," Peter said without taking offense. "I was just curious about the routine."

Six golf balls found their way to the bottom of the cup in rapid succession. Straightening, Laura used the short flag to flip them out and started to arrange them again, this time about four feet from the hole. "It's a new course for me, I don't have a routine yet."

"So it's different every time?"

Laura paused to think about the question. "Yeah, I guess it is. Sometimes I can't wait to just swing the driver and hit it as hard as I can without warming up on the shorter clubs…I know that's a no-no." She putted two balls into the hole. "Other times I just want to hit the course cold…maybe just a little putting first. It depends on my mood, I guess." Four more balls went in, and she retrieved them, throwing them out about twelve feet.

"Okay then. I'll see you in a bit."

Peter got a short grunt in reply, so he left to make sure that the caddies were ready. Reaching the clubhouse, he found the two young men standing outside smoking, both of them with hats pulled low and towels slung over their shoulders. They grinned as he approached. "How's she hitting 'em?" the shorter of the two asked.

"Didn't really see much, but we'll find out soon enough. You guys ready?" At their nods, Peter checked his watch. "Jeremy, why don't you take her bag since you have more experience. That okay with you, Brett?"

"Fine by me. What's she like anyway?"

The scrape of metal spikes on the cart path interrupted them and they turned to see the subject of their discussion walking toward them. Peter hid a smile as he observed the caddies' reaction to the woman. *Not at all what you were expecting, huh, guys?* She set her bag on its end and introduced herself. "I'm Kaz, thanks for coming out."

Jeremy couldn't believe his luck. She didn't look like any lady golfer he'd ever seen, a body to die for, and eyes he couldn't get enough of. He stammered a bit when he told her his name and grinned at Brett's look of envy as he took possession of her bag. It was already worth it to get up early on a Saturday, and he was glad that Peter had talked him into it.

The four of them made their way to the first tee, stopping at the blues, the longer tees that presented the course at its most challenging. Usually only the men with low handicaps hit from there, and Laura expected it from Peter. He apparently didn't expect it from her. He handed her a yardage book and she looked at it briefly before stuffing it in her back pocket.

"Which tees?" he asked.

"These will do."

"Makes it kinda long for a woman, doesn't it?"

She smirked. "Long is not a problem."

One of the caddies coughed to cover a laugh, and Peter waved her up to the box. "Ladies first." Then he stood back, crossing his arms over his chest, ego smugly in place.

Laura stepped up to the marker assessing the hole. *510 yard par 5, slight dogleg right, the turn starts at about 225.* Jeremy handed her the driver and she pulled a ball out of her pocket, leaned over, and teed it up only about an inch. Stepping back, she mentally pictured the flight of the ball and where she wished it to land. Taking a practice swing, she made one adjustment. Finally, she addressed the ball, and in that moment of quiet, Laura was at perfect peace.

Then her swing uncoiled in a perfect balance of power and speed built over years and maintained with hours of long practice, resulting in the ball exploding off the tee to fly down the middle of the fairway, moving slightly from left to right, conquering the dogleg and landing some 275 yards from where it was struck.

"Oh, my god," Jeremy breathed, and Laura smiled with satisfaction. Handing him her club, she gave a low laugh. "Didn't get all of it."

Not to be outdone, Peter stepped up, and after several practice swings he sent a ball in the same direction as Laura's, landing some ten yards behind hers. Hiding his chagrin, he said, "That'll play." Jeremy and Brett shouldered the bags and the four of them started down the fairway, the green of the grass muted by the ground fog which had yet to burn off.

They walked along in silence, both enjoying the early stillness. They arrived at Peter's ball first, and while he was preparing to hit, Laura drank from a water bottle she pulled from her bag. She looked up at the sound of contact; it was a decent shot, but short of the green. He's not getting enough extension, she thought.

Walking up to her ball, she figured she was about 235 yards out. Flipping out the yardage book, she walked forward to where a sprinkler head was marked with 230. Pacing back to the ball she congratulated herself on her accuracy. "Gimme the 3 wood, Jeremy." The caddy was already pulling the club, stripping off the cover and handing it to her. She took aim and swung. This time she got it all, and the ball bounced on the front of the green, finishing its journey about twelve feet below the hole. Pleased, she gave the club back to the caddy, and without looking back at any of the three men she strode toward the green, stripping off the glove as she went and tucking it in the waistband at the back of her shorts.

*Beautiful course, and it suits your game...you can probably get in thirty-six holes today and the same tomorrow. Wait, you told Chris you might go to the softball game.* She stopped, waiting for Peter's chip to the green. "Good shot," she told him as it landed within four feet of the hole. *What's more important, this or softball?*

*This is,* Laura told herself as Jeremy passed her putter over. Marking the ball placement, she flipped it to the caddy to clean. *You didn't promise.* Crouching behind her marker, she checked the line of the putt, looking for any possible break. Thoughtfully, she walked around to check from the other side. *Nice to start off with an eagle if you could. Ahh, you know better than to count your chickens...* She replaced the ball and took a few practice strokes, trying to even out the rhythm of the motion, and finally lined up the putt, imagining its path. A smooth tap sent the ball on its way, but it was too far right, the break never happened, and it stopped less than a foot past the hole. *Time to lay off the caffeine.* With a tight smile, Laura tapped it in for a birdie 4.

Peter nodded, and his eyes narrowed over his own putt. His familiarity with the green worked to his advantage and the ball dove into the cup after a strong confident putt. The birdie put Peter in a better mood and they left the green, caddies scurrying behind them. Writing on her scorecard as she walked, Laura found herself considering the softball game again, and she could almost see the disappointment in the green eyes. *Yeah, she'll be disappointed, so what? She can learn to live with it like the rest of us. But I don't want her to be disappointed.* With an impatient sigh, Laura decided on a compromise. *If you get thirty-six in today, you can come out early for eighteen holes tomorrow, do the softball game, and then hit the driving range…now that sounds like a plan.* With that, Laura shook off the last thoughts that might interfere with her golf game and set her mind to extracting the lowest possible score from the course and beating the club pro in the process.

Christine Hanson loved baseball in all its incarnations: tee ball, little league, slow and fast pitch softball, major and minor league; it didn't matter, she loved them all. Saturday afternoon found her working as the plate umpire in a 13-15 little league scoring fest. The parents were into it as much as the twelve-year-olds, and Chris cheerfully let the comments about her eyesight, or the complete lack thereof, roll off her back.

*God, what are they feeding these kids?* she thought as one boy strolled to the plate. He was as tall as she was and probably outweighed her by twenty pounds. She set her mask and leaned in behind the catcher. The boy swung at the first pitch, popping it up to the outfield, and with a groan of frustration, ran to first base as hard as he could, legs churning beneath him.

The left fielder bobbled the ball and dropped the sure out. By the time he had recovered, two runners had scored and the third was on his way home. The play at the plate wasn't even close, and the Auto Mart Red Sox had a fabulous 16-15 come-from-behind win.

Chris stripped off the cap and mask, running her hand through her hair to fluff it, then left the field. Her bag was stashed behind the fence and she liberated a bottle of Gatorade. After drinking deeply, she wiped her mouth with the back of her hand, enjoying the warmth of the spring afternoon.

"Good job, just one questionable call." Her friend Kate, who also happened to be the producer of the Six O'Clock newscast, joined her at the fence.

"Yeah?"

"Josh was not out at home in the sixth." She crossed her arms indignantly, referring to her nephew.

"I was right on top of it and he was out."

"Well, they won anyway. They're off to Chuck E. Cheese's…I'd rather have splinters shoved under my fingernails than go there. Can I interest you in some Mexican at Lupe's?"

Chris took off the blue button-down shirt that marked her as an official for the parks and recreation department and tossed it into her duffel, leaving her clad in a white T-shirt and navy shorts. "Sure, just let me go to the ladies' room and get cleaned up a bit." Picking up her bag, the two women started walking to the restrooms. Before they reached their destination, a group of teens stopped them. "You're Christine Hanson, I see you on TV!" one of the girls squealed. They surrounded Chris, asking about her job and commenting on her appearance. She rolled her eyes at some of the things they said, and after much ooooing and ahhhing, escaped to the restroom to clean up.

"You handle that so well. I think it'd freak me out," Kate said as Chris went into a stall and shut the door.

"What else can you do? They always say I'm shorter and prettier in person than I am on TV." Laughing, she stripped off the sweaty T-shirt and put on a clean one, then off came the shoes and socks to be replaced by sandals. "Anyway, those kids will be filling out Nielsen diaries someday…A little PR now could go a long way." She buckled her belt and smoothed the front of her shorts. "Besides, it tickles the hell out of me. Ready for chips and salsa?"

"So spill it, Chris." Kate smiled at the other woman. They were in a booth at Lupe's, a popular Mexican restaurant, where the never-ending supply of flour tortillas, chips, and free ice cream made it one of Chris's favorite haunts.

"Spill what?"

"Oh, come on. You can barely sit still you're so wired. You know something, so spill it."

Chris groaned, "Kate, I promised…"

"Ah! So there is something. If I guess, will you tell me?" Kate leaned forward, eyes shining. Movement caught her eye and she sat back. "Man, she didn't waste any time. She's been here what, a week? Look at the guy she's with…what a hunk."

"Who?" Chris turned to look. *Damn! What are the chances? At this point she probably thinks I'm stalking her.* Laura Kasdan and her date were being seated at a table across the restaurant, and Chris had to admit that he was indeed a hunk. *So? A woman like that isn't alone unless she wants to be.*

"Should we go over and say something?" Kate asked.

"Not unless she sees us," Chris answered, hunkering down in the booth.

"I thought you liked her?"

Chris made a face. "I do. It's just…I just seem to babble whenever I'm around her. She gave me a ride home last night, and I think I said too much…" She left the sentence hanging.

"Great. When you screw up, you do it royally."

Their food arrived, distracting them. "Mexican platter for you, Miz Hanson, and chicken fajita salad for you," he said, depositing a huge bowl in front of Kate. "Is there anything else you would like?"

Chris eyed the feast in front of her, taking inventory. "This looks fabulous, Mario. Could I have a side of guacamole too?" She gave her most charming smile to the waiter and he hurried off.

"How can you possibly eat all of that?" Kate shook her head at Chris as she dug into her sensible salad, jealous of the other woman's complete disregard of the calories she was about to consume.

"I exercise like a dog." Chris started in on her chicken enchiladas, the cheese stringing from her fork to the plate. She smiled as she chewed, appreciating the blend of spices, chicken, and peppers. "Besides, I don't have any other vices…I just like to eat." The guacamole arrived, and she added a dollop to one of the tacos on the platter.

Across the room, Laura looked over the menu, deciding on fajitas and a bowl of tortilla soup. She had agreed to have dinner with the golf instructor because the thought of her spartan apartment was suddenly not very appealing. He was trying for more than dinner, though, and she was beginning to regret taking him up on his offer.

"How'd you do on your second round this afternoon?" Peter's question interrupted her train of thought.

"Four under…put one in the lake. I noticed there's a little fungus on a couple of the greens." She ran her thumbs over the calluses in the palms of her hand, thinking that for thirty-six holes, they had held up pretty well.

"Yeah, the grounds crew is really fighting that; it's supposed to be under control." He coated a chip liberally with salsa and bit into it, crunching contentedly. "If that's how you play after a two week layoff, you should have a real chance at the qualifier in Austin."

Laura was pleased with the way she'd played, though a few mental errors and a couple of misses had irritated her. Plus, she knew it was time to get off the caffeine. Boy, that's gonna smart. Work wasn't too stressful; maybe the big market grind had gotten to her. Laura was so busy considering that thought that she almost missed what Peter was saying.

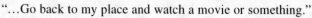

"…Go back to my place and watch a movie or something."

*Damn, damn, damn.* "Ah, sorry, Peter." A rueful smile. "I'm on call this weekend, and I really need to check in at the station."

Peter hid his disappointment. "S'okay, some other time. Will you try for thirty-six tomorrow?" He segued neatly back to the one topic he felt comfortable talking to her about. For someone with those looks, he thought, she had as much warmth as an ice pack. "Jeremy says he's all yours, every weekend for the rest of your life," he said, noting that she had paid more attention to the caddy that day than she had to him.

"He could caddy for a living. He asked for some names and I told him I'd help him make some contacts." She sat back as the waiter flipped out a tray holder and prepared to serve their dinner. The sizzling fajitas reminded her that she was really hungry, and she smiled in anticipation, blue eyes lighting up and fixing on…

Her new Six O'Clock anchor, who was strolling toward her.

"Hey, isn't that Christine Hanson? She's one of yours, isn't she?" One of mine? The waiter finished distributing the plates as Chris and Kate walked up.

"We were on our way out when we saw you," Kate lied, glancing sideways at Chris. Peter scrambled to his feet, motioning to Laura for an introduction.

"Sorry…Chris, Kate, Peter Davis. Peter…this is Chris Hanson and one of my producers, Kate Madison."

Peter turned on the charm. He wasn't getting anywhere with Kaz, and opportunity was knocking. "Won't you join us?" he asked, waving his hand at the table. The opportunity to eat with not one, but three attractive women, was too appealing to pass up.

"Uh, no, thanks." Chris looked at Laura expecting to see annoyance at Peter's obvious flirting, what she got was a wink and an eye roll, which spoke volumes about the way the "date" was progressing. "We've already stuffed ourselves. Nice to meet you, Peter." Giving Kate a gentle shove in the back, they continued down the aisle and out into the lobby.

"Whoa," Chris chuckled. "I don't think that was going very well." She held the door open for Kate and inhaled as the warm spring air greeted them, smelling faintly of freshly mown grass.

Laura unlocked the door to her apartment, tossed her keys on the low table next to the door, and flopped down on the old sofa, letting her hands dangle between her knees. Dinner had gone downhill after Chris and Kate left. Peter really needed someone to stroke his ego, and she wasn't the type. *Just as well, hope it doesn't screw up my weekend tee times.* Laura gave a self-mocking snort. *You are some piece of work. Good-looking guy, he's interested, and all you can think about is how it could mess up your golf game. How shallow can you get?* Her sense of relief at seeing Chris and Kate was all out of proportion. *You're a coward, plain and simple.*

Scrubbing her hand through her bangs, she considered the next day's activities. Golf first, then softball. Now where was her gear? Laura went to the little hall closet and began to rummage through the articles stored there. Ice chests, boxes of books and suitcases were pulled out into the hall as she searched for the red bag that housed her softball equipment. With a cry of triumph, she tugged it free from the confines of the closet. Unzipping it, she checked the contents…two bats and a glove. The glove could use some work, she thought, pounding her hand into the pocket while she walked to the bathroom in search of some baby oil.

The sweet smell of oil filled the enclosed space as Laura worked it into the leather. Satisfied with the way the glove was coated, she put a ball in the pocket and wrapped it securely with a rubber band.

*Isn't that nice…you can break in a baseball glove, regrip your golf clubs, and run a live truck. But you can't flirt and you can't sustain a conversation over dinner. Socially inept, yep, that's me.* She washed the oil off her hands and dropped the glove into the bag. *Another early Saturday night, bath, book, and bed. God, what a life you lead.*

Chris pushed the door of the Volvo closed with her hip and slung the softball duffel over her shoulder, the bat sticking up behind her head. She started down the path that ran along the fence of Northridge Park Field #2, keeping an eye on the game in progress. The team from the Chronicle appeared to be running roughshod over one of the country western radio stations, WKIX. She glanced at her watch; *just past one, should be some of ours here.*

"Hey, K Bob, how're your knees?" Dropping her bag, she clambered up to where he was sitting. A slow smile spread across her face when she saw who was next to him.

Laura Kasdan was leaning back, impossibly long legs stretched out in front and crossed at the ankles, hands laced behind her head. A white tank top showed tanned muscular arms, but Oakley sunglasses covered up the amazing eyes that Chris knew looked out from under the bill of the red Texas Rangers hat that she wore.

"Glad you could make it. No golf today?"

A lazy smile. "Already played, this is my cool down." She sat up, popping the joints in her shoulders.

"Yow, that sounds painful," Keith said, opening his scorer's book. "Okay, Kaz, where can you play? Chris is on second, I'll be on third, Trip'll play first and Rendally will play short. Can you handle right field?"

*Right field, that's where you stick the newbie and hope that it doesn't screw you too bad.* "Sure, wherever." The rest of their team filled up the bleachers, the conversation light and cheerful. Laura watched with a smile as Chris uncapped a tube of eye black and dashed it across her cheeks. "Interesting look for you."

"Don't knock it…I can't wear sunglasses, they get in the way. Besides, this is old school."

"Did you play in college?"

"Yep, fast pitch, though. Thank god for Title IX. I even got an invitation to try out for the '96 Olympic team…wasn't near good enough, but it was a great experience." Chris shrugged away the accomplishment as she double knotted her shoes. "How was your dinner? It didn't look like things were going so well."

"Food was good," Laura wryly commented. "The company was…" she waggled her hand to show that it was so-so. She sighed. *Actually, it was an unmitigated disaster.*

"He seemed nice, you play golf with him?" Laura nodded. "Did you beat him?"

"You bet."

"Well, well. If it isn't the Kazmanian Devil herself, out for a little softball with her motley crew. Well, Kaz, word of your fall from grace was very big in certain circles. How does it feel to give up big D to be a medium market manger with delusions of grandeur?" Laura would have known that voice anywhere. She tilted her head to look up into some old history embodied in the sneering face of the News Director from Channel 4.

"Lance. Wish I could say it's a pleasure…but I can't."

"You can't imagine how much I enjoyed watching your decrepit excuse for a live truck get blown to smithereens…if I were the insurance investigators, I'd look for cause."

"Nice to know your coverage sucked so bad, you were watching us."

Chris ran her tongue across her teeth, watching the exchange as everyone fell silent around them. *This could get interesting.*

"See, what I don't get is why they didn't fire your ass…anybody else pulls that shit, and they're the overnight tape editor in Brownsville. But not you, no, you're still a News Director; like some kind of cat you always land on your feet."

Laura leaned back on her elbows. "Brian didn't look twice at your resume, huh, sport?"

He gave a humorless laugh. "I'll whip your ass this afternoon, then I'll do it again in the May book, just like we did in February. Chris, you're looking nice and blonde today…just get your roots done?"

Keith snarled and jumped up. "Dickhead!" Lance skipped away and headed for the other dugout, his laugh ringing behind him.

"What a prick!" Chris spat at his retreating back.

Laura bent over to pick up her bag. "Yeah, well don't let him get to you…he's just not worth it." Silently figuring if that was the worst poison that came out of Lance's mouth today, they got off lucky. "C'mon, we have a game to play."

"Here," Keith tossed a white mesh jersey to Laura, "Double deuce." Laura smiled at the red and black twenty-two on the back. "Emmitt Smith, thanks."

"Don't mention it. Guess you have some history with Mr. Barker." He opened the gate for her.

"Yeah, we were in Austin together…he thought he should've been the one to get the call to Dallas as an EP. It pissed him off pretty bad, but he was never in the running. He's probably got a pretty nice setup over at 4, and he'll make it to a major market someday, his type always do."

"He's not so hot."

"Don't underestimate him. He is a nasty piece of work." She flashed a hundred-watt smile at the managing editor. "We'll kick his ass today, and take the rest as it comes. Right, Chris?" Knowing that the reporter had heard every word and hoping she had heard the warning as well.

They were the home team, so they took the field, the red clay infield dragged smooth, dust puffing up with the steps of the players as they took their positions. Laura jogged through the bright green grass to the solitude of right field, not expecting to see much action since the majority of the batters would be right-handed and would hit to left field. *Probably a good choice to stick me here.* She had doubts about her arm, and intramural softball seemed a long time ago.

The first out was a grounder fielded cleanly by Rendally and sent over to Trip, the first baseman and one of the weekend sports anchors. Lance was up next and he hit the ball soundly over Keith's head. The leftfielder was ready and got it in to Chris before Lance was committed to second.

That was the end of the friendly softball game. What came next could only be called a war.

"Let's turn two," Keith called, looking for a double play. "One away."

The next man up hit a grounder sharply to Rendally at short, who fired the ball to Chris for the force out at second. Lance accepted that he was out, but the little bitch on second was not going to turn the double play, so he went in for a high slide, aiming his cleats for somewhere on her upper chest. Chris got the ball out of her glove, and had almost released it toward the first baseman when the impact on her collarbone spun her around, knocking her down, and leaving her scrambling for the ball.

"Out at second, safe at first," the umpire decreed.

"You sorry son of a…" Chris hissed, grabbing her shoulder.

"Part of the game, Chrissy. Toughen up." Lance sprung to his feet and jogged to the Channel 4 dugout, part of his mission as goon and chief intimidator accomplished.

"You okay?" Rendally asked, giving her a hand up.

"Yeah, he came in high," she said, wincing as she rubbed the area between her neck and shoulder. "Spiked me."

Keith was getting madder by the minute. This was supposed to be friendly. "One more out and we'll do some damage." A quick glance at the outfield told him that his boss was not taking the attacks on her staff lightly at all. Arms crossed, her stance oozed hostility.

The final out was a pop fly to center, and the side was retired with the only damage being three holes in the second baseman's jersey. Chris was fuming as she flung down her mitt in the dugout. "You could've gotten out of the way, you idiot," berating herself she plopped down on the end of the bench, crossed her arms and glanced over at Laura. "You weren't kidding when you said nasty."

Laura poked her fingers through the chain link fence between the team and the field. Looking out, she started to make plans. *You underestimated me once before, Lance. Bet I can count on you to do it again. Oh, this is too good…you're the pitcher.* A low, evil chuckle started in her throat, and worked its way out as a grin.

Rendally was up first and singled sharply down the third base line. Trip was acting as first base coach, and Chris scooted out of the dugout to coach third. Kurt, the meteorologist/pitcher, batted next and neatly singled as well. That brought up Keith, whose forearms looked like Popeye's as he grasped the toothpick-like bat in ham-sized hands. Lance showed his concern by throwing three straight balls, but Keith's ego would not allow him to be walked in a game of slow pitch, so he swung to miss on the forth pitch.

"Oh, please, Mr. News Director," he taunted, "You're not afraid of me, are you?"

"K Bob, you're an ass."

The dig had its desired effect, and Lance served up a decent pitch, although it was a little low. With a flourish worthy of Mark McGwire, the stocky young man stepped in and swung, solid contact sending the grapefruit-sized ball sailing over the left field fence.

Channel 8 was on top 3-0, and the swing of momentum had them celebrating with high fives and forearm bashes. Trip was up next, then he too was standing on first with a single. There were still no outs when Laura picked up her bat.

Eyes narrowed, she walked to the plate idly twirling the bat to flex her right wrist and shoulder, ready for the duel that was about to take place. She changed hands to give her left equal time, concentrating on the rhythm of the rotation, then stopped the movement, settling into the batter's box and comfortably taking a couple of practice swings.

*It's not the same swing, she reminded herself sternly, don't treat it that way.* One of the Kathys was behind the plate acting as catcher. Acting is right. She was plainly afraid of the ball, which meant that Lance would have to cover home if that's where the play was. She filed the information away and set her mind to the task at hand. *Time to do a little headhunting.*

The first pitch came in low, without the high arch that is the signature of slow-pitch softball. Laura decided that it was adequate for her purposes and lashed out, launching the ball right at the pitcher's head. Lance barely had time to duck and landed face down in the red clay, spewing curses like a fountain. By the time the ball was retrieved, Laura had rounded first with ideas of going to second, and Trip was headed home.

Wisely, they didn't try to stop him by throwing to the Kathy behind the plate, since heaven only knew where the ball would end up. Laura stood at first with a mocking smile as Lance stormed over. "You did that on purpose!"

"Don't be silly. If I'd been trying to hit you, I would have. You had time to duck."

"You asexual frigid bitch..."

"C'mon Lance, let's play," the first baseman tried to calm the irate News Director.

"Hey, Blue," he said to the second base umpire, "You gonna let her get away with that?"

He smirked. "Part of the game...toughen up."

Chris was up next, hoping to cash in on Lance's loss of control. The short reporter presented a small strike zone, so she worked the count to full and Lance into a lather. Finally, she got the pitch she wanted and stroked it down the right field line, past the diving first baseman and into no-man's land next to the fence. Laura never hesitated or looked at the third base coach, she just turned on the burners, past second and around third, barreling toward home.

The ball and Laura arrived at virtually the same time. Lance was blocking the plate, but the throw was high and Laura dove in low, bowling him over as she scrambled to touch home. No tag and she was safe. She heard the umpire say it as she rolled clear of stomping cleats.

"You're a fucking moron! I was blocking the plate!" Lance screamed, a vein bulging at his temple.

"No tag, she's safe."

No one had called time so Chris was still moving around the bases. Lance still had the ball, making no attempt to hold the runner on any base. The other fielders were busy watching their pitcher self-destruct, and by the time it occurred to them that the play was still alive, with a fierce growl, Chris was past third and streaking toward home.

"Lance! She's coming home!"

With a roar Lance launched himself away from the ump and across the plate as Chris executed a perfect slide, or it would have been if Lance hadn't abandoned the softball game in exchange for tackle football. His greater mass stopped her forward motion abruptly in a cloud of dust short of home plate.

"She's out!" The umpire's verdict rang out clearly, and Lance jumped up, slamming the ball to the ground just inches from Chris's head.

"Damn straight the bitch is out!" he bellowed, good sportsmanship forgotten.

"And you're outta this game!" the umpire yelled, jerking his thumb toward the dugout.

"WHAT!" Lance spun to face the ump. "You can't do that! She was out!" Chris scrambled to her feet, and Lance shoved her for good measure.

"Now wait a minute..." Laura started to move forward to get Chris out of the line of fire just in time to see Keith tear out of the dugout and launch himself at the belligerent news director.

At that point it became a free for all, with the rest of the Channel 8 bench joining the fielders from Channel 4 in a pushing, shoving, screaming grudge match. The Kathy was standing to the side with her hands over her mouth, watching the carnage with horrified fascination. Chris had no such inhibition about joining in and was pummeling Lance with all the force she could muster as he and Keith grappled in the dirt.

*Oh, this is just great. And I'm supposed to be the one with the violent temper and no self-control.* Laura blew out a breath and shrugged at the two umpires before she waded in to separate the combatants.

Grabbing Chris by her collar, Laura held the furious woman away from her body while she turned her attention to Lance. With a display of superhuman strength, she plucked Lance from his struggles with Keith and tossed him half way down the third base line to his team's dugout, and roared loud enough to rival the Concorde SST,

"STOP IT RIGHT NOW! OR I WILL BEAT THE LIVING SHIT OUT OF EVERY ONE OF YOU!"

They froze, and the silence was deafening. "Channel 8, get to your dugout! Channel 4, get to yours. NOW!" She was snarling and didn't care, blue eyes were almost white with barely controlled rage, and the players, feeling it, began to move to their respective benches.

Gritting her teeth, Laura turned to the umpires. "Game over? Both teams forfeit?"

"Oh, yeah," came their reply in unison.

"Fine. You wanna tell them?" She waved toward the grumbling group from Channel 4, then gave a lopsided smile. "See you next week." She made her way to their dugout where her sullen team sat with varied degrees of bruising flesh. *My team, for better or worse.* She knelt down in front of Keith, tilting his head to get a better look at his shiner. "Gotta tell ya, you sure know how to show a girl a good time."

"He started it." Keith assigned the blame from his perspective.

"No, I started it, and I shouldn't have. We lose and they lose. Go home and put some ice on it…go on."

"You should see the other guys," Rendally muttered, throwing his glove into his bag.

Standing, she watched them gather their things and file out, everyone but Chris who was slumped in the corner, face buried in her hands. Laura walked over and plopped down next to her, removing her hat and the Oakleys, she leaned over and put her hand on the younger woman's shoulder. *What do I say?* "Chris, It's not the end of the world…jeez, it's just a game that went bad." Shoulders began to shake and Laura was at a total loss, not knowing how to comfort—until Chris moved her hands and Laura could see that she was laughing.

*Laughing!*

Laura sputtered, "You…"

"Oh, come on, you gotta admit, it was priceless! Keith defending our honor, Rendally grabbing that guy by the hair, the hysterical Kathy…god, I wish we had it on tape!" She went into another peal of laughter. "And you! Tossing bodies around like firewood. What'd you have for breakfast, She-Ra, Princess of Power?"

"Me? What about you pounding on Lance? I thought you lost your mind." Laura leaned back with a look of disgust, propping her elbows on the back of the bench while she waited for the laughter to subside. The humor was infectious though, and Laura couldn't hold back a chuckle.

"Okay, I'm much better now," Chris said, wiping her eyes.

"You split your lip again."

"What can I say? I lead with my head."

"That's kinda dangerous for someone in your line of work." Laura leaned forward to touch it lightly with her thumb, blue eyes concerned. Chris smiled ruefully and looked into them, swallowing as her breathing became shallow.

Jerking away to hide her confusion, she faked a pain she didn't feel. "Ouch. Guess some ice would be in order for me too." Uncomfortable with the direction her thoughts were headed, Chris stood and gathered her equipment. *Boss, boss, boss. These are very dangerous waters. Quick, say something witty and charming to diffuse the situation.* "Have you seen my other shoe?" *Wow, now you know why you get the big money.* Looking around briefly, Laura dug it out from under the bench and handed it to her.

"Look, we're just a little ways from my club, we'll go over, get some ice for your lip…Hey, you can even soak in the hot tub while I hit some balls." Laura made the decision and offered the invitation before she had time to think about it. "I'll even throw in dinner at the Grill. What do you say?"

Chris blinked. Yeah, she wanted to go, wanted to be with her, and wanted to get something to eat. *She wouldn't offer if she didn't want to, would she?* "Okay, I have a swimsuit in the car."

"Good, you can just follow me over." They both left the field, the gate clinking shut behind them. "I guess it's too much to hope that this won't get out?"

"What, the game?" At Laura's nod, Chris threw back her head and laughed. "Oh, hell no. The umpires? I guess no one told you that we take turns so we don't have to pay anyone. Those guys are from Channel 12. Everyone in the league probably already knows."

"Which means Art knows."

"I think that's a safe bet."

"Great."

* * * *

Swank.

That was the first word that Chris thought of to describe the clubhouse. Oak floors and a chandelier lent an old fashioned air to the entryway, and even on a Sunday there was a receptionist.

"Good afternoon Miss Kasdan. A guest today?"

"Yes, Marcia, this is Chris Hanson."

"Welcome to Northridge, Miss Hanson, I enjoy watching you at noon. Could you sign in, please?"

"Thanks. They let you watch TV at work?" Chris bent over to sign the guestbook and Laura marveled again at the easy way that the young woman drew people out. By the time they left the front desk, Chris knew Marcia's favorite soap opera, the names of her two children, all about her husband's job, and the special in the Grill for dinner.

"How do you do that?" Laura asked, pushing the door open to the ladies' locker room. "I mean, everyone thinks they know you and they want a part of you. I know other well established on-air personalities that don't handle it as well as you do."

Chris shrugged. "It's like you said: they already know me, I'm already a fixture, so you just connect with a part of their lives. A show or a story I've done usually provides the spark."

"It's going to get worse, you know. When you move to the Six you'll have a bigger audience. I told you before that you'll pay a pretty steep price in the way of privacy."

"It won't bother me the way it would bother you."

"Me?"

"Sure, you're a much more private person than I am. The classic introvert. Whoa, this is nice!"

A wet bar took up one wall of the sitting room, leading to a large carpeted locker area. From there the room opened up into a tiled enclosure where an enormous hot tub bubbled merrily. Past that, there were showers, restrooms, and massage tables.

While Chris poked around, Laura opened her locker and pulled out her clubs and shoes. Swinging the bag over her shoulder, she started for the door. "Chris, there's some ice in the bar, stay in the hot tub as long as you like, and just come down to the driving range when you're ready for dinner."

"You're not gonna soak in the tub?" Chris tried to keep the disappointment out of her voice.

"No, I need the practice. See you in a bit."

Chris watched the door swing shut behind the tall woman. She shook her head at the sudden vacuum that was left behind and chided herself. *Probably just as well.*

Sunday afternoon practice always reminded Laura of her mother, and she smiled as she walked down the slope to the driving range. *Sweetie, you'll never have a game if you don't put in the practice time.* Her mother's Texas accent, thick and low, always made Laura think of hot summer days and hitting bucket after bucket of balls, sometimes until her hands cracked and bled, always trying to find that elusive game her mother spoke so lovingly about. If she closed her eyes, she could almost see the two of them practicing side by side under the watchful eye of her mother's teacher.

Louis was one of the first black teaching pros in the South, and her mother's game was almost solely his creation. Something clicked between the two of them and as far as Laura knew, her mother never took lessons from anyone else, not even from Harvey Penick across town at the trendy Austin Country Club. Louis carried Sarah Kasdan's bag in ten U.S. Amateur Tournaments and five U.S. Opens. So, when it was time to learn, Laura wanted Louis to teach her.

It was Louis who told her it was okay when Arizona State showed no interest in the gangly teenager, that the University of Texas had a fine women's golf team, and she was better off staying in Texas anyway; all the great golfers were from Texas and she should stay close to home.

So Laura went to UT.

Her father had never understood. In a complete reversal of the jock-parent role, it was Sarah who wanted her daughter to be the athlete, and her husband David who had wanted her to be the scholar. She majored in journalism to please him, but it wasn't enough. There wasn't any nobility in golf as a profession, and in the end, she'd made the deal with her father, and bitterly resented both parents for making her choose, always suspecting that she had made the wrong decision but too stubborn to back out of a no-win situation. *Nothing changes. Not seven years ago and not two weeks ago. God, has it only been two weeks?*

Dumping her bag on the ground next to a pyramid of balls, Laura pulled out her seven iron and a glove. Twirling the club absently, she checked to make sure the distance markers were accurate. Twirling faster, she moved it in a figure eight in front of her, rolling her wrist and flexing it. *All Texans can twirl, although this is less baton and more sword.* With a sigh she stopped, thumped the clubhead on the ground, and started drawing the balls to her. *Sweetie, you'll never have a game if…*

Chris lounged in the whirlpool, wishing for a tall glass of iced tea. When the adrenaline high from the brawl wore off, she was a lot sorer than she originally thought. Groaning, she shifted her position, certain that some muscles would be screaming tomorrow.

Monday morning's news meeting was going to be interesting. In addition to the fallout from the game, Laura was going to announce the anchor changes and Chris could finally talk about it to someone other than her family. *Keith and Kate'll be happy, Tom probably won't be, too much change takes the spotlight off of him.* She hadn't really thought about it, but it was a big risk for Laura too. If Chris was a bust, one of their most profitable newscasts was going to lose revenue, and Art would tear the hide off the one who came up with that brilliant idea...*Guess that's why she's the News Director and I'm not.*

*Okay, what have we found out about the enigmatic Miss Kasdan?* Chris ran down a checklist of the things she had learned about the puzzle that was her boss. *She does not like to be called Laura. She drives an older Jeep but belongs to a fabulously expensive country club, where she plays golf very well. She drinks tequila and has the strength of ten men, plus an incredibly high tolerance for pain.* Chris remembered the injury during the live truck episode, and noted that Laura never said another word about it. *And it must've hurt like hell when she started throwing those bodies around. She and Lance Barker have a history, apparently founded on mutual dislike, but Peter, the golf pro looks to be out of the picture.*

With an impatient snort, Chris realized that she didn't know much about the woman at all. But Lisa does. She made a mental note to pick the director's brain about her former roomie, and there was always dinner, even if Laura wasn't much of a talker.

Resolved, Chris got out of the tub, wrapped a towel around herself, and wandered over to the showers to wash the chlorine off of her skin, the cooler water contrasting with the heat of the whirlpool. You're a reporter, you know; just do the research. A trip to the vanity turned up a myriad of moisturizers and lotions. Chris uncapped one bottle and took an experimental sniff, shrugged and began rubbing it onto her legs.

A clean polo shirt and shorts made her feel better, and when she glanced at her watch, she was surprised to see that almost an hour had passed and she was very, very hungry. Stuffing her dirty uniform into her carry bag, she left it next to the locker she thought she'd seen Laura go into earlier. With a last look at her reflection, she headed out of the locker room and out to the reception area. Marcia was happy to give directions to the driving range, and after snagging a mint from the desk, she went to find her boss.

There didn't seem to be too many people around for a Sunday afternoon. A television was on in the bar, and she could hear loud male voices debating the merits of NASCAR racing as the next great American sport. Pushing open the door to the outside, Chris stepped out to the landing that overlooked the 18th green. The honeysuckle was in full bloom, filling the afternoon air with its sweet aroma. She went quickly down the stairs, and started along the path to the practice range as several golf carts buzzed by, their occupants enjoying the last golf of the weekend.

The path rounded a bend and she spotted her quarry. Stepping into the grass, she approached cautiously, not sure about the etiquette in such a situation. Laura was focused only on the ball she was swinging at and the target in front of her, launching ball after ball at the 150-yard marker.

Whootick! as the club made contact and bap as it hit the plastic sign, over and over again. Chris knew it couldn't possibly be as easy as the tall woman made it look, and she couldn't help but smile at the display.

"You ready to get something to eat?" Laura asked, turning to look back at the smaller woman, aware of her the moment she stepped off the cart path.

"Always. So this is what you do on your off time?" Chris approached, noticing the fine sheen of sweat on the smoothly muscled arms and legs. The Oakleys were gone and the blue eyes were relaxed and friendly, not the ice-white of her earlier rage. Interesting, Chris thought, chameleon eyes.

"Pretty much every day if I can."

"Why?"

Laura pondered the question that, for some odd reason, no one had ever asked. "Because the mechanics of my swing have to be maintained through constant repetition."

"Uh huh." Chris said, as though she had a clue what her boss was talking about. "I'm sure that explains the technical reason for practicing everyday, but why dedicate that much time to what is essentially a hobby?"

*It won't always be a hobby.* Laura gave a half smile as she slid the club into the bag, and draped a towel around her neck. "Why umpire little league games on the weekends if you don't have kids?"

"That's different." *How did she know?* Chris wondered.

"Why? I'm good at golf and I love it." A careless shrug. "I'm going to try to qualify for the Open in a few weeks, plus I'd like another shot at the U.S. Amateur." Laura didn't know why, but it was important that Chris understood this one thing about her. "For a number of reasons—WBFC is one of them—I cannot be a full time golfer, so I will compete where I can, when I can."

"Lisa Tyler thinks you should be playing golf for a living."

Laura hoisted the bag to her shoulder. "Lisa and I've had that conversation too many times to count. It's the ritual and the discipline and the patience and the planning. It helps me in every aspect of my life...including running a newsroom. Why do you do the little league umpire thing?"

Chris smiled, green eyes lighting up her face. "Because I love baseball, and I'm good at it."

"There you have it. Let's get some dinner."

The Grill wasn't too crowded and they were quickly shown to a table. Chris was surprised at the number of people who stopped by their table to say something to Laura, and she smiled through a multitude of introductions. *Boy, for someone who's only been in town for a week, she sure knows a lot of people.* "You're kind of a celebrity here, aren't you?" To her surprise, the dark woman blushed.

"Yeah, it's a little freaky sometimes. I think they're having a lottery to see who gets paired with me next weekend when I play."

"So how much do you play?"

"Well, yesterday I played 36 holes, that's two rounds. I played the first with Peter who you met last night, then I picked up two guys after lunch. This morning I played a round with Jim Thompson and Randy Mercer over there. I'll probably try to get nine holes in at least twice this week."

"And you'll practice."

"Yeah, I'll practice."

"That's a lot of golf."

"Not enough if I was doing it for a living."

The waitress interrupted them to take their order. Laura chose chicken, while Chris ordered the special, a marinated ribeye that Marcia recommended, and a large glass of iced tea.

"What, no Coke?"

Laura grimaced, "I'm trying to cut down…the caffeine messes up my putting."

"I see." She sipped her tea, considering. "He called you an asexual frigid bitch."

"Excuse me?" Blue eyes looked startled and just a little angry.

"Lance called you that. Pretty inventive insult for a guy like him, wouldn't you say?" Chris slipped into her curious reporter mode.

"We never really got along."

"That's not just bad blood, Laura, that's poison."

"It's Kaz," she said automatically, continuing their game. "And he wouldn't take no for an answer."

"So then what happened?"

One slim eyebrow raised. "I'm sure, given my reputation, you can fill in the blanks."

Chris leaned back and gave her boss a smirk. "Ah…this is no time to be coy, besides, I have other sources and you're just forcing me to dig deeper until I uncover all of your secrets."

Laura returned the smirk. "Dig away. You'll just find a bad-tempered News Director with a whole lotta enemies." She sipped at her water, crunching the crushed ice with her front teeth. "What about you? You're from Nashville, hmm? Probably the youngest child because you seem used to getting your way. Yeah a big family, and they spoiled you rotten."

Chris laughed. "Oh, you're right on all counts. I have four brothers and a sister, Mom's a teacher and Dad's an electrician. I'm the youngest and you're absolutely right, I was spoiled rotten."

"Are you close?"

"Yeah, we still are, and it was a nice way to grow up. Do you have any brothers or sisters?"

"Nope. No brothers, no sisters, and both my parents are dead." Laura narrowed her eyes at the reporter, daring her to ask the next question. *You started this,* she told herself.

It was the opening Chris had been waiting for and she took advantage of it, saying gently, "I remember your father giving a lecture when I was in school…are you a lot like him?"

It wasn't at all what Laura expected. *You're supposed to ask how he died, or how I felt seeing his brains splattered all over the ground again and again on every network feed for a week!* She could feel her mouth go a little slack and a tightness in her chest that made it next to impossible to breathe. She swallowed hard and clenched her jaw against the pain of remembering.

"I have his eyes." It was out before she could stop herself. Looking down, Laura started to rearrange the silverware around her napkin. Chris didn't say anything, she just waited. "And his height." She gave a bitter laugh. "Certainly not his patience or persistence."

They were interrupted by dinner and after serving them the waitress beat a hasty retreat, feeling the tension pouring from the dark woman. Laura had completely lost her appetite, the succulent chicken no longer having any appeal. That was not the case with Chris, who eyed her steak appreciatively and dug in with relish. "Did you get along?"

"Not terribly well." Laura made a decision and pushed her chair away from the table. "As much as I have enjoyed the display of your interview technique, and it is quite impressive, I need some air. Enjoy the rest of your meal, and I'll see you at work tomorrow."

"Wait, I'm sorry, I…"

"No apologies necessary. It was a very…entertaining afternoon." With a mock bow, Laura turned and left the Grill, stopping long enough to sign the chit the waitress offered as she walked by. She went out the back door, past the rows of carts being returned and cleaned after a day of golf. Spotting her bag at the drop, Laura picked it up and started toward the parking lot and the Jeep. Just go. It was a setup, her opinion doesn't matter. But it did. Cursing herself for all her real and imagined weaknesses, Laura threw the clubs in the back of the Jeep, settling them with a shake. Leaning on the spare tire, she grabbed a fistful of dark bangs and went over the conversation again, trying to figure out where she lost control. *Face it, you were playing a game and you lost...you wanted to see how far she'd go and if you could take it. You can't. And Lance's pet name...jeez, they'd all laugh their asses off if they knew where that came from.*

With one more curse she climbed into the Jeep, the engine coming to life with a twist of her wrist, running as well as it did the day her father brought it home and tossed her the keys. It suits you, he'd said. One spontaneous gift in a lifetime of never-there. Angrily, Laura threw the stick into gear and drove off.

Chris just sat at the table, appalled at her miscalculation. *I pressed too hard, this wasn't a story about public corruption, this was obviously an open wound that wasn't ready for serious probing.* She let out a frustrated breath just as the waitress came up to the table.

"What happened to Miz Kasdan? Didn't she want her dinner?"

"No, we just had a little disagreement. Listen, can you box this up? I'll drop it by her house and it won't go to waste."

"Sure," the waitress replied. "I hope everything'll be all right."

"Yeah," Chris said glumly, "I hope so too."

Laura was sitting on the steps outside her apartment drinking root beer when the dark red Volvo pulled up. Chris climbed out and reached back for the plastic bag that held the go-boxes full of food from the abbreviated dinner. From the base of the stairs she regarded the dark woman looking down at her. "Were you waiting for me to show up?" When all she got was a shrug in return, Chris started up the stairs. "Thought you were laying off the caffeine?"

"Root beer doesn't have any."

"Oh. Listen, I'm..."

"Don't." Laura looked at Chris, and without saying anything else, moved over to make room for her on the step.

"How did you know I'd come?"

A snort. "Because you have stalker tendencies? No, because in a lot of ways you're just like him...pick, pick, pick...until you get what you want. Do they put something in the water at Mizzou?"

"Only if you major in Journalism. Why didn't you go to Missouri? Nope, forget I asked, I'm prying." Chris sat down next to Laura, still holding the plastic bag, and crossed her legs at the ankles.

"You can't help it, it's what you are." She watched as the blonde woman flushed a dull red. "Don't believe I've ever seen you blush before. I didn't go because he wanted me to." She finished her drink and crushed the aluminum can between strong hands with a satisfying crunch. "What else do you want to know?"

"Why the sudden desire to answer my questions?"

"Because you will drive me insane with your need to know. Let's see if I can get you started. My mother was one of the winningest amateur golfers in history and she died of breast cancer a little over three years ago. My father was devastated. He…went to Bosnia right after that. Then…well, you know." Her mouth twisted bitterly. "They fought all the time; you'd never guess that he couldn't live without her."

Chris didn't say anything for a minute, and Laura couldn't begin to guess what was going on in the reporter's head.

"Why are you so angry at him?" The question when it came was soft, and not really meant to intrude. Chris genuinely wanted to understand, and Laura didn't know how to answer.

"A shrink would say that I haven't gotten over my feelings of abandonment."

"My guess is that you were pretty mad at him before he died."

Laura nodded. "I didn't want to be what he wanted me to be. I ended up making all of us, my mother included, pretty miserable. Then they both went and died before I could make it right."

"So there's guilt too."

"Of course there's guilt—I'm Catholic."

Chris laughed a little at that and it eased the tension a bit. "So where do you stand now?"

"I have promises to keep…and miles to go before I sleep." Laura half-smiled as she quoted. "Enough angst for one day. I'm sorry that I ran out on you earlier, didja bring me dinner?"

Chris knew the value of a strategic retreat and allowed her to change the subject as she passed the Styrofoam box containing the chicken dinner. "What have you done to the people at your club? Two of those guys were really mad that I ran you off…they were talking about some kind of drills you were supposed to do together and Marcia would barely speak to me…talk about loyalty."

"And you thought I had no people skills."

"No, I never thought that. No tact maybe…"

"Uh, you are the tactless one, my friend."

*Green eyes narrowed at the casual turn of phrase and Chris smiled thoughtfully. 'My friend.' Well, it's a start.*

*Time to play a little "Spook the Producer."*

The month of April flew by in a blur of planning and preparation for the most brutal of television rating periods, the May Sweeps. Fourth quarter budgets are hung on the numbers earned during season finales and wild stunts, and in the local news business, the participants pray for anything newsworthy. From bad weather to war, nothing brings viewers to the tube like human calamity.

Or new talent.

Laura Kasdan stood with her arms crossed, staring at the news set and the attractive blonde woman sitting in the left anchor chair. The set had gotten a bit of a face-lift over the weekend with new paint and trim. Now it was time to tweak the lights and make sure that the new Six O'Clock anchor looked as good on the new evening set as she had on the noon set. Background changes made subtle differences in skin tones and highlights; the trick was to fix it without changing the light on any of the other anchors.

"How's the back light, Kaz?" Lisa called down from a ladder that held her up to the grid while she narrowed the barn doors on the light in question.

"That's better." Laura squinted at the studio monitor. "It just barely hits her shoulders."

Lisa climbed down the ladder to get a closer look. "It's still a little hot…we can probably take care of that with some diffusion." The Production Manager looked over at Chris thoughtfully, "Chris, are you still good with the teleprompter?"

"It's not too bad," the reporter-turned-anchor answered.

"Are you comfortable?" Laura's deeper tone asked, "Because I think we're almost through here."

Chris blew out a relieved breath. They'd been at it for about an hour, and the lights had begun to get unbearably hot. Chris was a patient woman, but this session was stretching it.

It seemed like it was only a few days ago that Laura announced to the newsroom the anchor changes for the Six, but a whole month had gone by, and Chris had been challenged professionally like never before. She was responsible for four special reports to air during sweeps, and time for anything else had been as scarce as hen's teeth.

Chris didn't know how Laura had done it, but the newsroom was running like a well-oiled machine, and everyone from the photographers to the tape editors knew that this sweeps period was going to be different from any other they had experienced. Everything was mapped out in advance, everyone had his or her assignments, and all was going according to plan.

*At least we all hope it is.* She was nervously aware that Laura Kasdan had staked her reputation on this Nielsen Book, and, for better or worse, Chris's future was tied to the enigmatic News Director's as well.

"All right," Laura nodded, "this is what we'll go with tonight. You happy?" she asked Lisa, who was unfolding a sheet of what looked like gauzy material.

"Hmm? Yeah, this should do the trick. We're good to go, Kaz; Chris, hold on for just a sec." The production manager climbed the ladder and quickly clipped the diffusion filter to the light. "How's that?"

Laura couldn't really tell any difference in the monitor, but guessed that Lisa knew what she was doing. "I thought it looked good before."

"It did." Lisa came down from the ladder. "It looks better now."

"I'm not an *it*." Chris crossed her arms and lifted an eyebrow. "Done yet?"

"You look good. Done." Laura pulled a narrow pad out of a pocket and consulted her list. "That's it, then. Thanks, Lisa." Walking to the double doors, she flipped the pad closed and left the studio.

Chris stretched as she stood up. "So that's how she does it…all those lists. I've never met anyone so organized."

The lights went off as Lisa pulled the faders down. "She's been that way as long as I've known her; just a meticulous planner, I guess." She turned to face the reporter. "So, are you ready?"

"Um, yeah." Chris gave a half smile. "It's finally here…the big show."

"Well, I don't know about that, but it's bigger than Noon."

"Lisa, do you have a minute?" Green eyes were clouded as they looked at the Production Manager.

"I always have time for you, Chris. C'mon, we'll go upstairs."

Lisa's office was on the other side of production control. It wasn't exactly messy, but it looked as though it had been worked in. The most appealing thing about it was the large window, looking out the front of the building, an oddity in a TV station, where, except in the lobby, windows served no purpose.

"I love this office," Chris said, turning to look at the tapes stored neatly on the shelves, "It's the best one in the building."

"I like it," Lisa agreed. "What's up? Close the door." She slid behind her desk, noting that she had e-mail…there was *always* e-mail.

Chris shut the door, but remained standing. "This is awkward, but I really don't know who else to talk to." She brushed nervously at the sleeve of her blazer, trying to decide how to begin. "A few weeks ago I ran into Laura…she was out on a date with that guy she plays golf with, Peter Davis."

"Kaz was out on a date?" Surprise colored Lisa's tone.

"Yeah, anyway, he called me last night…he wants to go out with me." Chris never thought of herself as a nervous person, but she didn't quite know what to do with her hands. She finally stuck them in her pockets.

"And this disturbs you…how? Did you want permission to go out with her golf pro?"

Chris rolled her eyes. "He's not my type, but if Laura's interested in him, shouldn't she know he asked me out?"

"What a jackass…Not you, Peter."

"Yeah." Chris started pacing.

"Kaz doesn't date."

"What do you mean doesn't date?"

Lisa blew out a frustrated breath. "She doesn't date. Not anyone I can remember. Not in school, not in Austin…ever. She never mooned about going out, never had a steady, none of that."

"What about Lance?" Chris was trying not to pry, and losing the battle.

"Lance! Hell no, she didn't date Lance. He tried to cop a feel in one of the editing bays and she kicked him so hard I think his gonads relocated to the back of his throat." Lisa paused for a minute. "Why would you think she and Lance…"

"Ah, something he said," Chris evaded. What Lisa was saying certainly explained a lot, but it also raised more questions.

"He backed off and Kaz went to Dallas…Kaz out on a date?"

"You sound like it's the first sign of Armageddon."

Lisa gave a brief laugh. "It might be."

Chris's mind was racing. *This is weird...what do I do now?* "Would you say that I'm pretty discreet...as far as my love life is concerned?"

Lisa spotted the trap, and she set her own. "Are you asking me if anyone else knows you're gay?"

"How did *you* know?"

"I didn't."

Chris sat down abruptly, tilted her head and looked at the other woman. "Very neatly done."

A wry smile. "You reporters think you know all the tricks. Truth is, I've known for a while, I just needed confirmation. I guess that answers your question, though. Yes, you are discreet."

"Does Kaz know?" As if calling the woman by her impersonal nick-name would make it easier.

Lisa noticed and frowned. "Are you asking in the interest of career preservation, or for personal reasons?"

Chris made a decision and laid her cards on the table. "Both." At this point it was a little late to wonder if she could trust the Production Manager.

"Shit, Chris." Lisa threw a pen down on the desk. "I don't know. Probably not or they wouldn't have signed you to that multi-year deal. We're in the middle of the Bible Belt, you can't just come out...It'd be like committing career *hara kiri.*"

"You're just saying that to make me feel better."

"No, I'm saying it to make me feel better...I may not be your supervisor, but as an officer of the company, I'm bound to inform *my* boss of anything that could prove damaging to the station. All that stuff about hiring without regard to sexual orientation in a very real sense does not apply to on-air talent."

"Relax, nothing's going to change. I just wanted to know if I should tell Laura about Peter."

"Yes. If she's interested, she deserves to know. God, Chris, she doesn't do *anything* social. If she feels something for this guy..."

"I'll tell her." Chris rose and opened the door. "Great." This was starting to look like another Christine Hanson four-star disaster. *Couldn't you just get the normal garden-variety crushes like everyone else?*

Lisa stopped her. "Chris, Kaz is...my friend. Understand that. She is also cold, remote, and driven to torment herself. Professionally speaking, there is no one else I'd rather have running a newsroom, but she hurts people as easily as you charm them. Why on earth would you be attracted to that?"

Why indeed?

"It's the weirdest thing...I've never been so aware of anyone in my life." *When I see her it's as if all the pieces of my soul fall into place. Does she even see me?* Chris gave a half shrug. "Don't worry, no one's gonna get hurt."

Lisa didn't believe that for a minute. *Trey owes me ten bucks.*

Laura took the black metal stairs up to the newsroom two at a time. Just because everything seemed to be taken care of, and all the pieces were falling into place, that wasn't a reason to slow down. Sweeps didn't actually start until Wednesday, but momentum was building, and she wanted all of it to be carried into the book. Details made the difference, and she hoped that that one message stuck in the heads of her staff, even if nothing else did.

She pulled open the glass door and strode through the newsroom. *My newsroom now.* In a lot of ways, this was better than Dallas. One advantage was never having been the number two guy. Here, she came in with authority and no one questioned it. In Dallas, too many people had thought of her as a whiz kid who was promoted faster than she should have been.

Entering her office, she slid behind her desk and clicked open the rundowns for the Five and Six O'Clock 'casts on the AP Server. Kate already had the Six filled in, and Laura dashed off an Express Message about one change, drinking from the ever-present can of carbonated beverage that was supposed to wean her off caffeine. Today it was 7UP, and she grimaced at the overly sweet taste.

Laura growled impatiently at the Five O'Clock rundown. There were still holes, and the producer was having trouble with the flow. *Gotta talk to Rob. He's still not getting it. Oprah's our lead in and this isn't a very woman-friendly show.* She thought for a minute about switching the producers, then dismissed the idea, figuring that she'd rather have her ace producing the Six.

A knock on her open door interrupted her train of thought, and she looked up at someone carrying a large cardboard box. It hit the ground with a thump, revealing Elly Michaels's grinning face.

"You've got mail."

Laura still had no idea how to take the woman who was in charge of on-air promotions and station marketing. She was amazed at some of the topical spots that this unassuming woman produced, and wondered what in the world she was doing in this market. *Face it, the whole station is full of people who could be working in much larger markets. What is it about this place?*

"What's in it?" she asked.

"It's all those shirts you asked me to order; there are some hats and jackets for the photogs too, call 'em a bonus. Just in time for sweeps."

The News Director fished her keys out of a pocket and used one to slit the box open, pulling out one of the polo shirts and examining the logo embroidered on it. "Looks good."

Elly held out a VHS tape, and Laura took it with eyebrows raised. "More spots," Elly said, "Take a look and tell me if anything bugs you."

"The others were great. Especially the new Six O'Clock anchor stuff."

"I live to serve. Oh, I almost forgot." She reached around the doorway and pulled in a long narrow box. "This was in the mailroom so I brought it along."

"Thanks." Laura took it, noting the Austin return address. Elly left as quickly as she came, and Laura swallowed as she again used her keys to slit the tape. When the box fell open, she couldn't help but smile. *Louis.*

The box held a new club and a bundle of golf club grips, bound by a rubber band. *The seven wood you promised me*, she thought as she took off the plastic bag protecting the club head. And a not so subtle reminder that it was time to re-grip. Experimentally, she waggled the club a few times, enjoying the weight and feel. Pleased, she set it carefully against the desk and looked through the packing in the box for a note from the sender. She found it at the bottom and smoothed it out.

*Kaz,*

*This should give you an alternative from about 175-185 yards. Let me know if I need to shorten the shaft. It should be a high shot with very little roll.*

*Charles and I will see you on the 18th. Right now the greens at Pierremont are very slow and sticky, though I expect that will change for the qualifier.*

*Re-grip now, so that you're used to them.*

*Louis*

Laura sighed. She didn't want Louis to get his expectations too high, only to be disappointed. She'd hurt him the most when she walked away after the '96 Amateur, certain that she'd never play golf again. Her mother was dead and her father was dead, and golf was the next victim.

It didn't hurt her career, though. Sixteen-hour days built up the reputation quite nicely, thank you, and when KDAL needed a News Director, she was the cheap and easy answer. William-Simon Communications got a lot for their money, a workaholic with no life or family to speak of outside the station; it was the perfect setup.

Except for that little charity golf tournament.

Brian, the GM, had committed to it, but something had come up and he couldn't make it. So he sent his News Director. Laura told him that she didn't play golf anymore. He told her he didn't want to hear excuses, and to get out there.

So she did, and smoked the field. More than that, she enjoyed it.

The plan was born on that spring afternoon. Five more years and she would be vested in William-Simon; five more years, and she could escape with a cool half million in her pocket, and try her hand at the LPGA tour. It was the perfect solution: she could keep her word to her father—ten years in the news business—and try to play professional golf.

It gave her a new purpose. She bought the house to be close to the club and painstakingly rebuilt her game, digging for the skills that were buried, but not lost. It was all coming together, and for the first time since her mother died, there was a little light in Laura Kasdan's life.

She shook herself out of a daze of remembering. Nothing has changed, she told herself, except that now it's only three years left to go. *You can put up with almost anything for half a million dollars, can't you?* Checking her watch, she noted it was almost news time. Grabbing her notebook, she headed to the control room for the Five O'Clock newscast. *Time to play a little 'Spook the Producer.'*

At fifteen minutes to six, Chris was throwing up in the ladies' room. After only briefly wondering if it was something she ate, she decided that it had to be nerves. Once Chris gave it a name, she could corral it, and control it. Leaning against the cool tile wall, she made up her mind not to be affected by the prospect of humiliating herself in front of a million viewers, and miraculously her stomach halted its heaving.

Chris pushed open the stall, and ran water in the sink to rinse out her mouth. Checking the mirror, she was relieved to see that her makeup was holding firm. *Hell, you need a quart of cold cream to get the crap off.* She pulled a paper towel out of the dispenser to dry her hands, then tossed it into the trash, still checking the mirror. When she heard the door open, Chris didn't have to turn to see who it was; she could tell by the way her spine tingled.

"Are you okay?" It had never occurred to Laura that Chris might be nervous about her debut, but here she was, hiding out in the restroom.

"I'm fine…just swell," came the bright reply. Chris put on the IFB earpiece and started fumbling with the clip.

"Here, let me." Laura plucked it out of the anchor's hand and fastened it to her collar, flipping the plug out so it wouldn't tangle.

"Thanks. Guess it's time." The two of them left the restroom, Chris absently tapping the scripts against her leg as she walked. She glanced at Laura and decided that the taller woman didn't just walk, she prowled.

When they reached the base of the stairs, Laura turned to the smaller woman and gave her an encouraging smile. "I have all the faith in the world in you. Good luck." She surprised herself by giving Chris a quick squeeze on the shoulder before climbing the stairs two at a time.

"Laura?"

"Hmm?" She looked down into green eyes looking up.

"It's gonna be a good 'cast."

"I know." White teeth flashed and the News Director was gone. Chris took a deep breath and pushed through the double doors and into her new role at WBFC.

It was a good show, and to celebrate, Laura passed out the new polo shirts to the staff. It was a good way to make everyone feel like a part of a successful effort. After stashing the remaining shirts in the storage closet for the morning crew, Laura tossed the keys to Keith and went back to her office to gather her things. There was still time to hit the practice range and she was eager to try out the seven wood. *No paperwork tonight,* she promised herself, *just a bucket of balls and maybe a burger later.*

She glanced up at the tap on her door, not surprised to see Chris standing there. "C'mon in." Closing the flap on her briefcase, she switched off the computer monitor and smiled inquiringly at the blond anchor.

"Thanks for…you know, before the show."

"No sweat. Told you you'd be good." Laura knew she was grinning stupidly, but she just couldn't help it. Everything had worked just like she'd hoped, due in no small part to this fabulous young woman. For a minute, Laura let the feeling of doing something right wash over her, even if she hadn't been the one on the air, or the show's producer, it had all worked. The smile faded when it wasn't returned. *Uh oh, problem.*

Chris closed the door slowly, not meeting Laura's eyes, hands nervously thrust into pockets before speaking. "Um…got a call last night," one hand went to the back of her neck. "That guy you were with at Lupe's…"

"Peter."

"Yeah, anyway he asked me out and I just wanted…" Chris looked up as she was interrupted.

"Go out with him." Laura felt her face turn to stone, and she managed a casual shrug. "You're a big girl, you don't need my permission." *Disappointed?* she asked herself. *Learn to live with it.*

"I don't think you understand. I'm not…"

Laura shouldered the briefcase and moved from behind the desk to the door. "Whatever, I don't care one way or the other."

"Wait! I was worried that if you and he were…then you'd be hurt…Ah, nevermind." Frustrated, she turned to wrench open the door, only to be stopped by a hand on her arm. Looking up into carefully shielded blue eyes, she waited.

Laura let go of Chris's arm almost as abruptly as she'd grabbed it, regretting the harshness of her tone. Clearing her throat, she tried to make amends. "It was a one time thing," she explained, "I'm not interested. He's all yours."

Chris gave a humorless laugh. "No, it's not like that. I just wanted you to…I didn't…" She gave an exasperated sigh. "If he was seeing you and he asked me out…what a jerk."

A slight smile flitted across the taller woman's face. "Thanks for the concern, but don't worry about me." It was oddly touching. No one had given thought to her feelings in so long she didn't know what to make of it. *Don't read anything else into it. She was just trying to be…what? Nice?* Laura gestured for Chris to precede her through the door.

Chris stopped at her desk to pick up her things and watched the taller woman leave the newsroom. For every question that was answered about her boss, ten more rose up in its place. She was standing there, lost in thought, when the Six O'Clock producer waved a hand in front of her face. "Hey, you all right?" Kate asked.

"Yeah," she answered with a jerk. "Just daydreaming I guess."

"You did a good job, Chris. Have I told you how glad I am that you're on *my* show?"

"'Bout a million times."

"Make it a million and one then. You wanna get something to eat?"

Kate was a good friend, but Chris didn't want the company right now. "No, I really need to do some shopping…some other time?"

"Sure," came the easy answer. "See ya."

Chris clicked the mouse to shut down her computer and locked her desk drawer, strangely dissatisfied on a day that should have been one of the highlights of her life.

The smell of coffee drifted through the Barnes and Noble bookstore courtesy of the small café located next to the hardcover best-seller section. Chris gave in to the impulse and bought a small cup of coffee with enough stuff in it to make it sweet and creamy. *Why does it always smell much better than it tastes?* Finishing the drink, she tossed the cup in the trash and headed out to the magazine section. She knew it was cheaper to just subscribe to the magazines that she enjoyed, but where was the fun in having them delivered?

Chris picked up the usual *Sports Illustrated, Time, Newsweek,* and a few others, then wandered over to the sports section, not sure what she was in the mood for. Workout and self-help books dominated the aisle, and she took her time looking through the various titles.

One in particular caught her attention and she smiled as she pulled it off the shelf. *Golf for Dummies.* Flipping through it, she noted that it wasn't just about how to play golf, but explained the rules, the etiquette, and some of the finer points of the various tours.

"That one won't help ya much if you wanna learn to play golf."

"Excuse me?"

A middle-aged man pointed to the book in Chris's hand. "You wanna learn how to play?"

Chris gave a little laugh. "No, I just want to know more about it."

"So you're interested in golf?"

She shook her head. "It's more like I'm interested in a golfer."

"Well, that one'll do you." He handed her another one. "Might try this one too."

"Thank you."

"Don't mention it. You're on TV, aren'tcha? You're a lot shorter in person."

Her smile broadened. "I get that a lot." She looked at the two books in her hand and decided to take them both. "Appreciate the help."

"Don't mention it. Tell your weatherman we need some rain. Not that he can do anything about it. Pretty good job if you can be wrong half the time and they still pay you."

Leaving the man to the stacks of books, she went to the checkout and paid for her purchases, wondering what her boss was up to.

*Whoootick!*

Laura sent another ball past the 175-yard marker. It flew on a high trajectory, landing softly with almost no roll. *Just like Louis promised.* She pulled another ball toward her, set up and swung.

*Whoootick!*

It was a warm evening and Laura could feel a trickle of sweat running down her back as she practiced. The bugs were a little thick, too, she thought, brushing a gnat away from her face. She'd been at it for about two hours, and the lights were beginning to bother her so she decided to call it a night. She wiped her face with a towel and took off her hat, shaking down a mane of dark damp hair.

Home and a shower, she thought, remembering that she had a box of macaroni and cheese left in the pantry. Laura sniffed as she picked up her bag, hoping she wasn't coming down with something. The lights in the clubhouse were still on, but she didn't go in, continuing on to the parking lot and her waiting Jeep. The top was down and the doors were off and she remembered telling Chris it was her favorite way to drive. As was becoming all too common, she smiled when she thought about the blonde anchor.

*What are you doing tonight, Chris? Out for a drink with some friends? Bet you're not home eating macaroni and cheese. Snap out of it, Kaz, not like you to wallow in self-pity.*

As she stowed her clubs, Laura heard footsteps behind her and casually glanced over her shoulder. "Evening, Peter. Don't usually see you here this late."

"Saw you walk up; how're you hitting 'em?"

She shrugged noncommittally, "Decently, I guess." Then wondered if she should say anything about his phone call to her anchor. *Ah, what the hell.* Taking a deep breath, Laura stuck her foot into what was, essentially, none of her business: "Chris said you called her."

If Peter was surprised, he didn't show it. "Didn't know she had to ask your permission."

"She doesn't. She just wanted to make sure we weren't…serious or something."

Peter looked a little uncomfortable at that. "Kaz, I love playing golf with you, but you're not…I mean…we don't really work off the course."

"It's okay; I know what you mean." She put her hands in her pockets and leaned against the Jeep. It wasn't as if she felt anything for him, it was just…

"Besides, she said I wasn't her type." He met Laura's eyes slyly.

"Whatever." The discussion was making Laura as uncomfortable as Peter had been. Briefly, she wondered what Chris's type was, then pushed off the Jeep. "See you Saturday?"

"For sure," came the answer. Nodding, Laura got in and drove away.

She found herself taking the long way home, enjoying the late spring evening and the howl of wind through the topless vehicle. Laura didn't even resist the urge to drive down the familiar street, looking for lights at a tidy patio home. Chris's car was sitting outside the garage, and

Laura felt her stomach settle at the sight of a light burning in the window. *Just checking, huh? Great. Now you're doing drive-bys.*

Impatient with herself, Laura gassed the Jeep and took the corner a little faster than she meant to, squealing rubber on her way home.

The first week of sweeps gave way to a much-needed weekend, and Laura invited Lisa and Trey out to the club for a round of golf. Peter rounded out their foursome, and while he and Laura chose to use caddies and walk, the other two opted for a cart.

"Wuss," Laura chided Lisa as she pulled on her glove. "Next thing you know you're hitting from the forward tees."

"I could outdrive you in college, and I'll outdrive you today."

"A pity you still can't putt."

"Couldn't we play at a more civilized hour? Why do you want to get up at the butt-crack of dawn anyway?"

"Ladies, could we get a move on?" Trey grinned and waved them up to the teebox. "Settle it up here."

Lisa had the honor and hit first. Without a practice swing and as advertised, she boomed one down the middle, her slice carving the dogleg and leaving her in perfect position. "I still have it, Kaz…and I don't even practice."

Stepping back, she watched her former roommate tee it up and swing. The athleticism of her college days was still there, but this was a different Kaz, a more controlled, precise, and powerful player, and it showed as she outdrove Lisa by a good ten yards.

The caddies grinned and the men swallowed. It was going to be an interesting morning.

By the time they had reached the eighteenth green, the sky had darkened considerably and large drops of rain were beginning to splatter around them. The weather assured Laura that there would be no afternoon round, and with her teeth grinding in frustration, managed to botch the four-foot birdie putt as she finished with a par.

"Pretty good round, Kaz." Lisa wasn't too disappointed with the way she played, since she still managed to beat Trey by five strokes. "You're playing better than I've ever seen you play, but it's a lot different."

They had decided to clean up and meet in the grill, so the two women were in the locker room changing. "Different how?"

"Not as reckless…more thoughtful. What happened to grip and rip?"

Laura chuckled, "I'm not twenty anymore." She pulled on a watermelon-colored polo shirt and flipped her hair out over the collar. "Besides, a year off made a difference. Louis and I had to make some adjustments."

"A whole year and you didn't play? Jesus, Kaz, what did you do with your time?"

"Worked." There was bitterness in Laura's tone, but she didn't elaborate as she tucked in her shirt. Lisa regarded the other woman somberly, wondering…

"So what's up with you and Peter?"

Laura shook her head slightly, "Nothing, why?"

"Just asking about your love life. Ya look good together, he seems nice…couldn't you just once skip the 'I'm not interested' part of your program and go directly to emotional involvement, do not pass go, do not collect two hundred dollars?"

"He seems more interested in Chris Hanson…"

*Now we're getting somewhere.* "Chris said he wasn't her type." It was out before she could stop it. *Oh shit. Insert foot in mouth and chew vigorously.* Lisa wished she could take it back as blue eyes flew up to meet hers, and she could almost see the wheels turning in the other woman's head.

"Chris has a big mouth." Laura turned to shut the locker door and paced to the sink to wash her hands, glad not to have to look at Lisa. "Nice to know that the newsroom is privy to the details of my social life…or lack thereof." She felt the anger boil up, and something else. "And what exactly would be Chris Hanson's type?" Laura threw the question out in a snarl, not really expecting an answer.

Lisa smirked as she tossed back a reply. "You, actually."

Blue eyes went wide with surprise and she spun around. "Excuse me?"

With a deafening crack of thunder, the storm that had chased them from the course chose that moment to break. The lights flickered for a moment and the locker room was plunged into silent darkness as all power was lost. It was eerily quiet without the hum of the air conditioning or the other mundane sounds of the busy clubhouse.

Laura's voice came out of the inky stillness. "Well, when you make a point, Lisa, you do it with style."

Lisa thought for a minute that it *was* Armageddon.

Laura headed to the station in the driving rain, the wipers barely able to keep up with the volume of water being pounded into the windshield. Severe weather in the middle of sweeps was not an opportunity to be squandered, and the News Director wasted no time in getting the weekend assignment editor to start rounding up some photogs and reporters interested in earning a little overtime cash.

She pulled into a parking place, threw open the door of the Jeep, and raced up the stairs. By the time she was inside, Laura was drenched.

The newsroom was in its weekend mode, quieter and laid back, but Keith was at his desk and on the phone scribbling notes. Laura went in to her office and switched on the lights and all three of the monitors, noting that Kurt, their meteorologist, was on the air with a cut-in and Channel 4 was running an infomercial.

"We've got some problems." Keith walked in with a legal pad and stuck a pencil behind his ear. "Mostly, it's the flooding; the staff is gonna have trouble getting here."

"Lisa's on her way, she'll punch it. Who else is coming?"

"Three photogs and four reporters, Kate's coming, and Janie's here plus two editors, Angela and Reggie."

Laura nodded. "Put Angela and Reggie on the phones and the scanners. See if you can get some of those interns in here; we'll use 'em as runners since we can't use the live trucks in this weather. Any reports of damage yet?"

Keith checked his pad. "Some trees down, but nothing major. Kurt says we haven't seen the worst yet."

Laura reached over and turned up the volume on the monitor airing Kurt's cut-in, frowning when she heard the words "...Doppler indicated tornado. Residents of Braxton, take shelter immediately." Both of them turned to look at the map on the wall. Braxton was northeast of Burkett Falls, and according to the radar, was a mass of red and yellow, signifying the severest of storms.

"Where do you want me?" Chris stood in the door of the New Director's office, dressed in a yellow slicker and black rubber boots dripping on the carpet. "I couldn't drive, so I walked," she explained.

Laura swallowed when her stomach gave an unfamiliar lurch. *I'm not ready for this. Dammit, I'm just getting comfortable around her. Thanks a lot, Lisa.*

Keith looked at Laura. "We could put her on the air with Kurt?"

*Work to the rescue*, Laura thought. "No. Call Tom, get him in here; he can make it, he's got that Suburban. Do we have anyone who can shoot that's here yet?" Keith shook his head. She made the decision quickly, hoping that once it was made she'd feel confident that it was the right one. "All right, that leaves me. I'll be Chris's shooter. We'll go to Braxton, that'll even up reporters with photogs."

"You can shoot?" the reporter questioned. "I mean, I know you were going to when the live truck went boom, but that was just B roll."

"Of course I can shoot. I have many skills besides signing purchase orders."

"Are you sure you wanna do this?" Concern shone in the pale brown eyes of the Managing Editor.

"What? Chase a storm with Chris Hanson? What could possibly happen?" Humor lit the tall woman's features and she glanced at the reporter. *Mark this down Kaz, you're doing something at work for purely personal reasons that have nothing to do with career advancement. If it blows up, remember where it started.* Laura started walking, tossing instructions as she went. "Use the cell phones, the two-ways are gonna be hard to use in this weather. C'mon Chris…Keith, get me some rain gear. The sooner we get there, the sooner we get some stuff on the air."

The Blazer was high enough that the flooded areas didn't bother it, but Laura still had to drive slowly to keep the wake to a minimum. Chris was listening to the portable scanner and making notes on a legal pad balanced on one knee.

"You know this is a little crazy. We don't know what we'll find when we get there."

"Yep," Laura said shortly, "might be nothing, but this is where it's heading." She strained to see through the windshield since the wipers were having little effect. The sky was brightened by the occasional burst of lightning, illuminating sheets of horizontal rain.

They drove in silence broken only by the squawk of the scanner and the static of the two-way radio. Suddenly, Laura skidded the Blazer to a stop on the shoulder that Chris could barely see.

"Godfuckingdamn," Laura breathed. "I gotta get this." Through the window, Chris looked out across a shrub-lined field to see what had grabbed the News Director's attention—and felt the blood drain from her face when she realized what it was.

A funnel cloud was dancing along the ground, maybe a little over a half mile from where they were parked. All the still photos and news video in the world hadn't prepared the reporter for the real entity and the swirling clouds of debris at its base. Chris was startled out of her stupor by the sound of the storm as it invaded the vehicle when Laura opened her door, dragging the plastic-wrapped camera behind her.

Chris scrambled out as well, the rain stinging her face and the wind slapping at the jacket and pants that she wore. "Can I help?" She yelled over the fury of the storm.

"Go ahead and get the tripod. I'll shoot off the shoulder as long as I can." Chris signaled OK to show that she heard and went to the back of the Blazer to get it. The wind made it difficult to get a steady shot, but Laura widened her stance and kept shooting. The twister moved across the field, from right to left, heading in the same direction that they had been: Braxton.

Chris struggled to her side with the tripod and Laura stopped shooting and turned to the reporter, her eyes blue white chips in the stormy light. "Get back to the truck. Call the station and confirm that a tornado is on the ground southwest of Braxton. Stay on as long as you can, get Keith to put you on with a phoner. Go now!" The reporter left, and with one hand Laura flipped open the legs of the tripod and set the camera on it, locking the plate in position. *A little more insurance footage and we'll go,* she told herself.

Chris got through to the weather center without any problems and waited patiently while they set up for the phoner cut in. She rummaged in the back looking for the portable battery-powered TV and dragged it to the front seat. Turning it on, she tuned to the station, pleased that the reception was pretty good. Kurt was on the air and she plugged in the earpiece so that she could hear what he was saying without worrying about audio feedback. The meteorologist tossed to the phoner and Chris started talking, keeping an eye on the tall figure buffeted by winds outside the Blazer.

"I can see the funnel cloud, it's on the ground. If you are anywhere in the vicinity of Braxton, take cover now. I can't see any damage from where we are…I can't really tell how fast it's moving, but it is on the ground and moving toward Braxton." Then the noise of the storm exploded into the cab of the Blazer as the wind caught the door when Laura opened it, pushing the camera and tripod in front of her.

"We need to go *now*. Don't hang up," she ordered as she climbed in and started the engine, pushing the hood of her jacket back. It hadn't helped much; dark hair was plastered to her head and she combed through her bangs with one hand before pulling out on the road.

"Ah, we'll continue to follow the storm and keep you informed…this is Chris Hanson reporting for News 8." She waited until Keith came on the line to tell her she was clear, then handed the cellphone to Laura.

"It's Kaz, what's going on?" She listened as Keith filled in the details. "Do we have any runners yet?" She growled at the negative response. "I'll figure out a way to get this tape to you…we're going to Braxton…Yeah, we'll be careful." Flipping the phone shut, Laura shook her head in frustration. "Two brand new live trucks don't do a damn bit of good if you've got high winds and can't raise the masts. Let's see what's going on in Braxton, then we'll head back."

"Who else is out?" Chris asked, positioning the equipment so it wouldn't shift.

"Maria and Jeff went to North Burkett, the flooding is really bad up there. Rendally and Jason are tagging along with one of the emergency crews, and Terence is our backup, he's on the way with Bobby." Laura drove carefully through the gloom, trying to quash a lingering feeling of anxiety.

Chris flexed her hands nervously. The walls of the Blazer seemed to be closing in and she just wanted out, storm or no storm. She glanced at her boss, noting the twitching muscles in her jaw and smiled just a bit. *I'm not the only one freaking out here.*

The rain had stopped and it was ominously still when they reached the Jaycees sign at the Braxton city limits. They rounded a bend and descended a hill to see the small town spread out in front of them, or what was left of it.

"Oh my god," Chris whispered. The buildings at the edge of town resembled nothing more than a jagged, jumbled scrap heap of lumber and bricks. The smoky haze of destruction had not been washed away by the rain; instead, it hung heavy in the air. Laura pulled over to the side of the road and put the station unit into park.

"Let's switch. You drive, I'll shoot." She opened the door and got out.

"You know what happens when I drive…" Chris warned as they crossed in front of the vehicle.

"Just go slow and we should be pretty safe." Laura set the camera on her shoulder and rolled down the window. "Okay, let's go." They made their way down the main street slowly, surveying the damage and getting it on tape. Emergency crews were beginning to arrive as they made a second pass, and Chris pulled into a lot next to a damaged building.

"I'll find someone who'll talk on camera," Chris said, grabbing the wireless mic. "Anything special you want?"

"See if they had any warning, were there sirens? Stuff like that. Go on, I'm right behind you."

Chris was in her element now, threading through groups of people, gesturing for Laura to set up and shoot one sound bite after another. Her questions were concerned, polite, and probing. The interviewees opened up with vivid descriptions of what they had experienced in the fury of the storm. They even got one man on tape who said that he'd heard the warning on Channel 8 to take cover and that's what saved his life.

"Elly's gonna love that," Laura said, referring to the Promotions Manager. "There's your viewer benefit." They were headed back to the Blazer to switch tape and batteries plus make contact with Keith when a burly man wearing a mesh baseball cap, his weathered face creasing into a smile, stopped them.

"Chris Hanson? I'm Tim Foreman, one of your Storm Watchers." As he introduced himself, Laura smiled, realizing that this man could be the answer to their problems. The Storm Watchers were viewers recruited around the area to call in temperatures and weather conditions. They seemed to be fiercely loyal to the station and often provided news tips as well. "Kurt Denton called me and said that you all were up here, and I wanted to know if there was anything I could do to help you out."

"Pleased to meet you, Mr. Foreman, this is Laura Kasdan, my…photographer." Laura lifted an eyebrow as Chris gave a slight wink. "Did you sustain any damage in the storm?"

"Nope, our house wasn't touched, and we heard the warning, so we were in the cellar…just wanted to know if we could help you folks out."

*Good thinking, Kurt.* Laura spoke up, "Mr. Foreman, could you go to Burkett Falls for us? We're gonna try and follow the storm, but we need to get a tape back to the station."

"Sure, I'd be glad to help. D'you think I could get me one of those Channel 8 coffee cups?" he asked a little wistfully.

Laura gave him a big smile. "We'll make it worth your while."

She boxed the tape with a note to Keith and gave it to the Storm Watcher, who left for his pickup truck, pleased to be a part of the Channel 8 team. Smiling, Laura dialed the station on the cellphone, leaned against the truck and looked up at the stormy sky.

"News 8…Keith."

"Your tape's on the way; tell Kurt he's a smart man—never mind, don't—his head's big enough."

"Kaz, good to hear from you. Braxton's a mess, I hear."

"Pretty much. No reported deaths, though. There's a Storm Watcher by the name of Tim Foreman on his way in with a tape, interviews and stuff. Make sure you give him a shirt, a mug…you know, the whole gift package. Where's the storm going?" Chris came over to where she was standing and raised her eyebrows in question.

"It's kinda stalled just north of where you are. It's a very narrow band, but very intense, moving toward Groveton."

Laura looked over at Chris. "Do you know how to get to Groveton?" The reporter nodded, then turned to follow the News Director's gaze and spotted their backup just pulling in.

"Terence and Bobby are here," she told Keith, "so we're leaving. Remember: continuing coverage, the more pictures the better, okay?"

"You got it."

Flipping the phone shut, she let out a breath and gave a tired smile to Chris. "Ready to go?"

"Lead on." Chris had her second wind and was almost glowing with enthusiasm. *You wanted a storyteller who wasn't afraid to go off prompter,* Laura told herself. *That's what you got.*

"Where do we stand here?" Terence asked as he slammed the door on the other Blazer. He was a little peeved at not being part of the first wave, regardless of the fact that it was his own fault. His handsome features were twisted with impatience as he tapped his reporter's notebook on his thigh. Laura recognized the signs of someone having trouble with her authority, so she forced herself into the cold business mode that she used to strongarm her staff into line.

"Stay here, report on the damage, any injuries or rescues. As soon as it's clear, get Keith to send one of the live trucks. We'll go live at six if we can, but more likely it will be ten. We're heading to Groveton. Get Keith to send a runner for the tape you shoot. Any questions?"

The reporter shook his head, "No."

"Good. I'll see you back at the station." The two women got into their Blazer as the reporter stared balefully after them. Bobby waved as they pulled away and Chris let out a sigh of relief. She'd never liked Terence, and in the hyper-competitive atmosphere of the newsroom, their animosity flared hotly and frequently.

"Not a big Terence fan, hmm?" Laura observed.

Chris sidestepped the question diplomatically, "He's a good reporter."

"No, he's a plumber. That's what we used to call one of those guys that work from nine to six with an hour for lunch. He's got the good shift but he's still pissed off 'cause he's not the number one reporter and he's unwilling to do the work to get there. Come to think of it, it's pretty insulting to plumbers everywhere to call him that."

Chris wasn't used to Laura making speeches, and was a little surprised at the length of the observation. "You come up with some interesting descriptions."

She shrugged. "He is what he is; it's up to him to change."

Chris couldn't resist. "What am I?"

Laura looked over at the smaller blond woman, her green eyes dark in the light of the storm. *Go ahead, answer that one, Kaz.* "Whatever you want to be," she said softly, taking the safe out.

Chris knew it for an evasion and turned to look out the window. Laura took the silence for a minute before apologizing, "I'm sorry, that wasn't fair, you asked me an honest question." She thought about how to answer as she noted the sign marking fifteen miles to Groveton. "You're one of the warmest people on air that I've ever seen. You're a good reporter, but not as cutthroat as Danny Rendally, and you're well liked by the majority of your peers." Laura glanced over to see the reporter looking down at her hands. "What else do you want?"

*You'd be surprised.* Chris clamped down on the thought. "Thanks. So I'm not a plumber?"

"Hell no. It's not in your nature...you'd never do anything half-assed." *And god help me, I'm kinda counting on that.* Laura gave herself a mental shake. *Job at hand, Kaz...Watch where you're going.*

The sky was turning ominous, churning from light to almost black in rippling waves across the horizon. The air fairly crackled with energy, and Laura instinctively slowed the Blazer as it crossed under a concrete bridge. Almost as an afterthought, she searched the landscape looking for shelter, just in case...

The sky in front of them suddenly split open, sending a V-shaped cloud plunging to the earth like a knife, the telltale funnel whipping across road and moving right toward them. Laura spun the Blazer around, coming dangerously close to flipping the vehicle, and headed back the way they had come.

"Hold on!" She wrenched the wheel to the left, heading for a culvert that she'd seen near the bridge. Gravel sprayed as they left the paved surface of the road, and the Blazer slid more than rolled to a stop near the concrete drainage ditch.

"Out of the truck!" Laura yelled, grabbing the camera for no other reason than not wanting to lose another one. Chris was already fumbling with her door handle and had fallen out when Laura reached down to grab her hand, pulling the smaller woman up and forward as they ran furiously to the relative safety of the culvert. Scrambling into the opening, they settled on their knees, looking back at the world behind them as all hell broke loose. Laura punched the record trigger on the camera, looking into the viewfinder just long enough to make sure that there was an image framed beyond the opening. Without pausing for thought, she reached out an arm and pulled Chris to her, settling the other woman against her side, and yelled in the reporter's ear, "Don't let go!"

Chris shuddered against the suction of the wind and held on to Laura for dear life. She could feel the assault of water, grit, and other debris against the exposed skin of her face and hands. The wind howled like a jet at takeoff, deafening in its intensity. She squeezed her eyes shut tighter if that was possible, and just when she thought that she couldn't stand it anymore, the fury turned off like a faucet, leaving unnatural quiet behind.

Laura became conscious of her own ragged breathing in the eerie silence that followed and realizing that she was still holding Chris in an iron grip, she dropped her arms. Concerned, she lifted the smaller woman's chin and looked into green eyes for a clue as to what to do next. *Ah, hell. Go directly to jail, do not pass go, do not collect two hundred dollars.*

She found the mouth under hers softer than she expected, and for the first time in as long as she could remember, Laura wished for a little more expertise in the area of kissing, not certain that she was even doing it right, but enjoying the texture and the taste. She pulled back, gently letting go of Chris's lower lip and swallowed, preparing herself for whatever was going to happen next.

Chris blinked, not certain that the kiss had even really happened, and wanting much more. Then the implications crashed down and she couldn't begin to keep up with all the questions tripping through her mind. She cleared her throat nervously. "Cat's out of the bag?"

"Oh, yeah."

"Who told…"

"Lisa."

Realization dawned. "Wait a minute, *you* kissed me."

"Nothing wrong with your powers of observation." Laura turned away, pushing the camera aside and crawling to the opening of their concrete cave.

"Why?"

"Shouldn't we be trying to get out of here?"

"Answer the question!" Chris grabbed the back of Laura's slicker and pulled, finally getting a reaction when Laura turned around.

"You know, I seem to spend an inordinate amount of time crawling around in ditches with you."

Chris fumed, "You are the most infuriating…"

"Yeah, yeah, I know." Laura peered out at the brightening sky and then pushed her way out into the sodden grass, looking around for the Blazer. *Oh no, not another one.* "Come on." She reached back for Chris who grabbed the camera and let herself be pulled from the culvert and onto her feet.

"Oh shit." Chris could only look resignedly toward the bridge embankment at the station vehicle lying on its side. Then Laura started laughing. "You were driving!" Chris accused her boss.

"It doesn't matter. Apparently you just have to be in the vicinity," Laura answered as she started walking to the truck, squishing through the mud and weeds. When Chris caught up, she automatically took the camera from the reporter and hoisted it up on her shoulder. "By any chance, did you grab the mic?"

"Right here," came the answer.

"Then it's standup time again." Laura fumbled for a minute with the camera controls as she made sure the tape was cued. Speeding through the footage of the tornado while they were in the culvert, she swore softly. "Chris, you gotta see this."

"Hmm?" Looking over Laura's shoulder, she peered into the

viewfinder. Except for a slightly tilted angle, the video was framed pretty well, then she saw the trees in the distance flatten, breaking like so many matchsticks, and their Blazer roll by like a tumbleweed. "Whoa. That could've been us." *She did it again...we could have been killed.*

"Let's do this." The camera was back on Laura's shoulder as she waited for Chris to settle and begin the quick rehearsal of what she was going to say.

"Do I look okay?"

Laura stepped forward, and with just a slight hesitation, she fluffed the reporter's blond hair, her fingers easing the flattened look a bit. "You're fine...let's do a promo, too."

Chris became the storyteller again, slipping into the role of observer as she imparted the details of their ordeal, never once giving any hint of the terror she must have felt...it was more like a great adventure. The standup was brief, and although they did it three times, any of the takes were useable.

"Cool." Laura put the camera down. "Now we need to make some calls."

"Are you sure it's safe?" Chris asked, concerned as she eyed the overturned truck.

"No, but we don't have any choice. I haven't seen any traffic on the road since it hit, and we gotta get back to the station or all this is for nothing."

She opened the back of the Blazer and crawled in, tossing aside equipment until she got to the cellphone. Hoping that it still worked, she dialed the station.

"News 8, this is Keith."

"Do you want the good news or the bad news?"

"Kaz, you could identify yourself, you know. The good news, I guess."

"We've got some kick ass video..."

"The other stuff you shot was great! Must've been scary shooting the twister."

"Then you're gonna love this."

"We were first on the air with damage video. Channel 4 is just trying to keep up. Bad news?"

"Ah, you know the unit we left with?" Laura heard the groan.

"You're kidding. What do you want to do?"

Laura twisted to get a little more comfortable. "I want to get this video to you. Is the live truck in Braxton?"

"On its way."

"Good." She checked her watch. *Three thirty? Seems like it ought to be eight o'clock.* "We're on Highway 61 just north of Braxton. Tell 'em to pick us up first. Oh, and call a wrecker. Was there any damage in

Groveton?"

"No, the storm just turned in on itself and died. They got some rain, but nothing else."

"Then I'll see you when I see you." Laura hung up and crawled out the back again, looking guiltily at Chris as she emerged from the wrecked vehicle. "I'm sorry," she started, "usually the reporter is in charge of a news shoot…I kinda took over."

*That was strange, a News Director apologizing for invading a reporter's territory.* "It's different; you're running the newsroom too."

"The live truck'll pick us up, shouldn't be too long." Uncomfortable, she looked away.

"Thanks."

"For what?" Laura raised an eyebrow.

"For caring about stepping on my toes, and for saving my life…again."

The news director gave a brief laugh. "I just threw you in a ditch…again."

Chris smiled and looked at Laura, her eyes earnest. "Are we going to deal with this?"

Laura knew she wasn't talking about the story and sighed. "How do you want to deal with it? I'm your boss and I was way out of line." She swallowed. "If you want to file a complaint, then go ahead. I have no excuse for what happened…I did it, and I'll pay for it." *Same as always, huh, Kaz?*

"I don't want to file a complaint, I want to know why." Chris *needed* to understand. It was one of the things that made her good at her job; it also explained the warmth of her personality. Knowing that didn't make anything easier.

Laura voiced her thoughts out loud, not realizing it. "Because I wanted to know what it was like."

"What, to kiss a woman? I'm not a freakin' experiment." Chris was angry now, her green eyes snapping.

"No, to kiss someone I wanted to kiss." It was a simple but telling explanation, and Laura gave the half shrug that Chris was beginning to recognize as a sign of hurt dismissed. Then the implication of her words slammed home.

"You've never…"

"No, not really."

"Sex?"

"No."

"You're in your thirties…jeez, Kaz, how…?"

"Suffice to say, I have some intimacy issues and leave it at that."

Laura started picking up the equipment she had tossed out of the Blazer and stacking it in a neat pile, awaiting the arrival of their ride.

Chris stood still, watching and thinking. *Asexual frigid bitch...that's what Lance called her.* Then she said softly, "But you kissed me." Laura said nothing, and Chris knelt down in front of her, the plastic coat crackling as she moved. "Look at me." She noted the darkness of blue eyes determined not to waver. "Where do you want to go from here?"

"I have no idea."

"All right." Chris rubbed her chin thoughtfully. "We can make certain assumptions. There's some mutual attraction, right?" Laura nodded, and Chris continued. "Here's the deal: we'll take it slow, you're in control...you say stop or go."

*Oh shit, not another deal.* After a brief hesitation, Laura nodded again. "It doesn't come into the newsroom."

"Right. It's all up to you."

"That's not fair to you." Laura winced a little at the prospect of someone else giving up that much control.

The blonde reporter fed familiar words back to the source. "Thanks for the concern, but don't worry about me. I think you're worth it." Chris smiled warmly and stood up, holding down a hand for her boss. She pulled the taller woman up easily, feeling a strange sense of role reversal. "You know, I think you're more like your dad than you give yourself credit for."

"Why do you say that?"

"When we were running for cover, you grabbed the camera. I didn't think of it, but I should've. Now we have some great video, and you survived another Chris Hanson story." They spotted the live truck at the same time and started picking up equipment. "You can shoot for me anytime."

"Thanks, I think."

*I've just been kissed senseless by a rank amateur.*



It was Sunday and Laura wasn't playing golf. She'd come home late from the station to a message on her answering machine canceling her tee time due to flooding. *No softball today, either.* So she slept in and decided to use the time to do some maintenance on her gear.

Look sharp, play sharp, her mother used to say. Laura finished twisting off another set of worn down spikes and tossed the shoe to the floor. Looking down, she counted the pairs. *One, two, three, four, five. That's weird, you have one pair of high heels, one pair of everyday loafers, and one pair of black cowboy boots. But you have five pairs of golf shoes. Well, you have to get your priorities straight.* With a sigh, she got out of the chair to look for an old toothbrush and her shoe shine kit.

The CD changer clicked to another track and Mary Chapin-Carpenter was singing about dancing down at the Twist and Shout. Laura hummed along absently as she started on the shoes, wincing at the soreness caused by the previous day's activities. She'd been exhausted after dropping Chris off at her house, but hadn't been able to fall asleep until the wee hours. Awkward with touching the younger woman, but comfortable in her presence, Laura was trying to deal with the contradictions wrapped in a blanket of growing need. *This sucks*, she thought.

Methodically she cleaned, polished, and respiked the shoes, then turned to her clubs, laying them out on the breakfast bar and setting up the vise. She was peeling the old grips off when the smoky sounds of Chris Isaak adamantly denying that he ever wanted to fall in love interrupted her. Pausing, she listened for a minute before snorting impatiently. *Have you ever really paid attention to song lyrics before, Kaz?*

Frustrated by her inability set aside the wash of emotional thought, Laura punched the machine off and switched on the TV. Digging in the couch cushions, she pulled out the remote and began switching through the channels, settling on a Sunday news talk show. One club at a time acquired a brand new grip, and there was something definitely therapeutic about the monotonous task. All she had to do was leave her bag at the pro shop and someone would take care of regripping, but Laura preferred to do it herself.

Laura left the clubs on the breakfast bar to dry and cleaned up the mess spreading from the kitchen to the living room. The stack of newspapers on the table beckoned and she gathered them up, stretching out on the couch to read. Stories about the tornado damage dominated the local paper, but after having been caught in the middle of one, the reports were curiously bland. Her eyes began to droop, and after a few minutes, Laura was sound asleep.

It was late afternoon when her eyes flew open, and she realized she had slept most of the day away. *Guess I needed it*, she thought, stretching languorously and hearing her shoulders pop. Sunset was a couple of hours away, so she made a decision and went to the bedroom closet to get an extra helmet.

Chris spent Sunday cleaning up yard debris from the storm. She helped her new next-door neighbor clear fallen tree limbs from his roof, then drank iced tea on the porch with the newly married man and his wife. It was an easy day of outdoor activity that helped put the happenings of the day before into perspective, but didn't ease the thrumming excitement that still lingered even after a good night's sleep.

Inside the house, Chris opened a beer and started getting her clothes ready for the next workweek. With her ascension to the Six O'Clock anchor position came a new wardrobe, and the consultants had worked up a chart of the colors she could and could not wear, the types of collars that looked best, and even chose the accompanying jewelry. Spontaneous clothing selection was no longer allowed. *Thank god my hair's okay or they would've changed that too.*

She was trying to decide on Thursday's look when she heard the doorbell. Carrying the beer with her down the hall, she could barely make out a figure on the porch through the frosted glass of her front door. Pulling it open, she couldn't help but smile at the fidgeting woman standing there.

"Wanna go for a ride?" Laura was rocking on her heels nervously, and she held out a helmet in invitation. Baggy khaki cargo pants were gathered by a wide black leather belt, and a white tank top showed tanned muscular arms that could easily handle the red and chrome monster parked in the driveway.

Chris decided to tease a bit. "I dunno, is it safe?"

"Sure, and it's the best time of day. When you ride at dusk, you can feel the temperature change from cool to warm back to cool again as you go through the hills." Laura's half smile was shy, but her eyes were relaxed. "It's as good as sex…or at least what I imagine sex is like."

Chris almost stopped breathing. *She really has no idea. How can anyone be so naïve and so seductive at the same time?* "Aahh, okay. Do I need to change?"

"Pants would be good." Laura nodded at Chris's shorts.

"Give me a minute. Come on in. Can I get you something to drink?" Laura followed Chris into the living room.

"No, I'm fine." She stood awkwardly in the middle of the room, still holding the helmets, questioning the wisdom of coming over in the first place. She looked over a cluster of framed photographs, picking out Chris's siblings easily. The images of the laughing family made her smile a little sadly. Laura knew that there were no such pictures of clan Kasdan.

Chris shucked her shorts in record time, yanking a pair of Levis out of the closet. "Have you eaten yet?" she called to the other room.

"No, we can stop somewhere." She turned to see Chris tucking a white sleeveless blouse into faded blue jeans. The smaller woman wore the casual clothes with the same easy style she wore tailored outfits on air. Laura shook herself out of her reverie and handed over one of the helmets. "This might be a little big on you, it's an older one of mine."

They left the house and Chris climbed on the bike behind Laura, settling her feet on the passenger pegs. "Where's the best place for me to hold on?" she asked, wondering why Laura would choose an activity that required such close contact, then realized that she'd answered her own question.

"You can grab hold of my belt, or my waist if you'd rather." She punched the starter and the Triumph rumbled to life. Chris hooked her thumbs in the wide leather band as they jerked forward onto the street, settling in close to the taller woman.

Laura got them out of the city traffic pretty quickly, and soon they were flying down the rolling hills in the piney woods south of town. The storms of the day before left pockets of changing temperatures, and as Chris felt the air slide over her exposed skin, she understood the attraction to what her parents had always considered a dangerous form of transportation.

She breathed in deeply and moved her hands from Laura's belt to circle the other woman's waist, tightening her hold. Conversation was impossible, so she just gave herself up to the sensation of speed and wind and Laura's skill at handling the powerful machine.

They stopped at a country store that was still open and serving roast beef and gravy sandwiches on crusty French bread. Sitting at a picnic table under an awning, Chris devoured the messy meal while Laura looked on with amused eyes.

"Where'd you learn to ride?" she asked between bites.

"Took a class." A careless shrug. "What did you expect?"

"I don't know, something rebellious maybe?" A raised eyebrow told Chris that theory was a stretch.

"So how did you end up in Burkett Falls? You could've gotten a job in Nashville." Laura had decided it was time to turn the tables on the reporter and fill in some of the blanks.

Chris looked thoughtful for a minute. "Nashville is home. It'll always be home, but I didn't want to start in that market. Mostly I just wanted to be on my own."

"No pressure from your parents?"

"I think they knew I wanted to get out, so they let me go. I interned at CNN, and they offered me a job, but you know that's just resume padding since they don't pay worth a damn and they work you like a dog."

"You were at WSB for a bit."

"Yeah, I was still in Atlanta after the CNN gig, and I thought I was hot stuff. Then I found out I'd just be writing stories for anchors who were making seven figures. I didn't see any point in slaving for ten years before I got a chance to do any real reporting, and I started looking. Figured out that a smaller market is the best place to get experience, so I answered an ad in *Electronic Media* for a reporter in Burkett Falls, and here I am." Chris finished her sandwich, wiping her hands on the generous supply of napkins.

"In a few years, you'll be able to go anywhere you want." Laura meant it as a compliment; she wasn't prepared for the frown that crossed the reporter's face.

"Everybody says that, and you're supposed to want to go to a bigger market, but I'm not sure I'd be happy in that grind." She smiled ruefully. "Guess I'm just a small town girl at heart."

"Would you go someplace like Dallas if you had the chance?"

"I don't know." Green eyes looked up in amusement. "Can't go anywhere for three years anyway."

Laura laughed softly, "No one twisted your arm." She stood up, gathering their trash. "We'd better get back; I don't like riding after dark."

Chris skipped the belt this time and wrapped her arms around Laura's waist from the beginning. It was cooler now, and she shivered slightly, tightening her grip and bringing more of her body in contact with the warmth of Laura's back. They took a longer route home to extend the ride, but there was still some light in the sky when they pulled into Chris's driveway. The smaller woman hopped off the bike gracefully and stripped off her helmet, running a hand through her hair. Laura followed suit, feeling it was inappropriate to say goodbye with her head encased in plastic and foam.

"I loved it," Chris said happily. "Can we do it again?"

"Sure. Keep the helmet."

"Cool. See you tomorrow?" The taller woman nodded. "And Laura?"

"It's Kaz."

"You're wrong. It's good, but it's not as good as sex."

At the Monday morning meeting, Laura was wearing the look that Chris recognized as her game face. All the warmth of the weekend had seemingly disappeared, leaving behind a cold stranger impeccably dressed in black pants, cream colored double breasted blazer, and a white silk shirt buttoned all the way to the top. Her eyes were the cold gray of the past Saturday's stormy skies as she went around the room considering story ideas.

"We're in Sweeps, and for every idea you bring in here, you'd better have thought about what's in it for the viewer. If you can't sell it to me, how can you sell it to them?" The only story she showed any warmth to was Rendally's mention of the fire ant epidemic, and that was just good for a kicker, not as a lead. "Chris, you've got your special report on school lunches for the Ten. It's finished, right?"

"They're adding the graphics today."

"What else ya got?"

Chris flipped through her pad, dismissing two ideas outright. "Um, we have two major hospitals here in town, but they share one airlift helicopter. A lot of cities do that; it's not a problem. But here, they only have one pilot…and he works 24-7." She looked up. "He has no relief and he's on call all the time. Since the highest incidences of helicopter accidents occur with medical choppers, I thought it might be interesting to look into this. *Is* it a potentially dangerous situation?"

Laura considered it, rubbing her thumb along her eyebrow thoughtfully. "Okay, can you turn it today?"

"I've got calls in to St. Joe's and Burkett Falls General, so I don't think it'll be a problem."

"All right then. Janie, do the list." They went down the list of checks and follow-ups, and the assignments were given to the remaining staff. The last item on the planner made Janie chuckle a bit and she smiled as she read it. "Kaz has a photo shoot this morning on the riverfront. *City Lights* magazine has named her as one of the twenty most influential people in town. Should be some nice publicity."

The reporters hooted derisively, and Laura twisted her lips into a wry smile. "Look, Lance Barker from 4, Jack Pace from 12, and I tied for ninth place. It's all the News Directors in town; it hardly qualifies as something special."

"Make sure you tell Lance 'hi' for me," Keith said sarcastically.

"Oh, I think he'll be on his best behavior; after all, there will be cameras." She dropped the planner on her desk and looked up. "We done here?" At her dismissal, the reporters and producers filed out, and a tap on her door signaled the arrival of the Promotions Manager.

"Hey, good job on the storm Saturday, we really kicked butt."

"Did you get the promos on?"

"Yeah, got some damn fine proof of performance stuff on pretty quick Saturday night, already got a call from Dave at Target Research. He said we did it right, except for a few things, of course." Elly grinned. "'Cause if we were perfect…"

"We wouldn't need a consultant," Laura finished.

"They really ought to call them 'insultants,' since that's more accurate. Didja remember to dress for the shoot this morning?"

"Yeah," Laura stood up and held out her arms. "This okay?"

"It'll do, but I was hoping for something a little sexier."

"News isn't sexy," came the dry response.

"I'm not doing news, I'm selling it, and as your liar for hire, I don't have to deal with those pesky credibility issues."

Laura chuckled despite herself.

It was windy on the riverfront, and for the hundredth time, Laura wished she'd put her hair up as the dark strands blew around her face. The three News Directors regarded each other with stony silence, standing with arms crossed or hands in pockets, and the photographer was starting to get frustrated.

"C'mon, could you loosen up a bit? It's just a picture, you don't have to be hostile."

Lance snapped the gum he was chewing and bared his teeth. Jack Pace looked over in annoyance. He was a good twenty years older than the other two News Directors and was definitely old school, clad in a dark pinstripe suit with his gray hair combed neatly back. His animosity had more to do with being third in the ratings than any real dislike, as opposed to Laura and Lance, who could barely tolerate their close proximity. The photographer continued to snap away, figuring that *something* had to be useable from this miserable experience.

"Hey, I hear you trashed another car this weekend, Kaz." Lance smirked, trying to bait her as he checked the knot on his tie. "Saw the footage on CNN. Tell me, who was Chris Hanson's lucky shooter?"

Laura just looked away and Jack Pace snorted, "You just wish you had someone as good as Hanson."

Lance sneered. "Just stick to your fifty plus audience, old man, and leave the quality demographics to us."

"Shut up, Lance, what the hell is your problem?"

"Oh, she speaks." Turning to the tall woman, he continued his verbal assault. "How's your May going? Stunts aplenty from what I've seen. Chris is a little young to be carrying the Six, don'tcha think…whose bright idea was that?"

"Got a thing for the little blonde, Barker?" The News Director from 12 couldn't keep out of it. "I heard she beat the crap out of you at a softball game."

Laura smiled tightly and stepped closer to the obnoxious man. "You can say what you want about me, but leave my people out of it."

"Or what?"

She stepped even closer to Lance, and her voice went dangerously low, "If you have to ask, you have a very…short…memory." Laura raised one eyebrow, silently asking how far he wanted to take it, and acknowledging a victory when Lance moved back.

"I think I've got everything I need," the photographer interrupted. "Thanks for your…cooperation."

"Fabulous," Lance said with venom, as he stalked to the parking lot, leaving the others staring after him.

"Miss Kasdan," Jack Pace observed, "Lance is not fond of you."

"That, sir, would be an understatement."

He chuckled wryly and shook his head. "He's not long for this market, nor are you, I suspect. I was an executive producer at KDAL for a while several years ago, and I enjoyed it immensely." He paused thoughtfully. "Would you like to join me for lunch, Miss Kasdan?"

Laura crooked a grin, "I'd like that, and call me Kaz."

Gossip was gossip, and in the media business it never hurt to have a little inside information. Laura's lunch with Jack Pace provided some valuable information, plus a few tidbits about some of the people she had worked with in Dallas. All in all, she was in a good mood as she strolled into the newsroom, happy that most of the reporter's desks were empty since that meant they were out in the field.

Chris was at her desk though, her pale gold head bent over the keyboard of her computer, eyes flicking from her notepad to the screen and lips moving silently as she tried out the words of her story.

"How's it going?" Laura resisted the urge to sit down and opted for keeping a professional distance, noting the addition of another hash mark on the side of her desk. *We're at nine already? Maybe we should try for an even dozen.*

Chris kept typing and didn't even look up. "Good. Wanna take a look?"

"I'll pull it up in my office." Stepping inside her sanctum, she stripped off her jacket and hung it up on the hook behind the door and crossed to her desk, rolling up her sleeves as she went. The file was open, so she couldn't edit it and hit the bar for 'view only' mode. The reporter's writing was crisp and precise without being overly dramatic, a good informative story highlighting the central issues: the pilot's lack of down time and the high occurrences of accidents involving hospital airlift services. She dashed off an express note with her approval and turned to her budget variance reports.

The two-thirty meeting came and went, the newscasts were firmed up, and there was a steady stream of photogs rotating through the edit bays. Laura finished checking stories and turned to the stack of subpoenas and summons served over the last week.

Most of them had to do with accidents and fires that were covered as a matter of course in any given news day, but some were more complicated, asking for details on stories that might prove helpful in civil suits as well as criminal trials. She was making a list of dubs that had to be made and what the station would charge for them when the phone rang. "Newsroom, this is Kaz."

"Art wants to see you and Elly in his office right now." The administrative assistant's voice held a sense of urgency that had Laura frowning as she left the newsroom and headed downstairs to the business offices. She was waved in to the white-carpeted office where the Promotion Manager was already waiting. By the grim look on Elly's face, Laura knew that the news was not good.

"What the fuck is this?" Art pointed a remote at one of the TV/VCRs and a promo started to roll. There was Chris in front of the LifeAir helicopter, doing a standup tease. Art turned up the volume.

*"A chopper like this one can save a lot of lives, maybe even yours...but safety is becoming a real issue when it comes to medical helicopters. Find out why tonight on Action News 8 Live at Five."*

Art looked at Elly. "Did you write this?"

"I approved the copy," the Promotion Manager replied.

Laura shrugged. "What's the problem?"

"The problem is that the CEO of St Joseph's Hospital called when he saw this—you know, the people who sponsor the Tower Cam? He's afraid of a hatchet job on his helicopter service, and I can't say I blame him."

"I read the script, it's not a hatchet job," Laura inserted.

"The damage is done; the promo was irresponsible."

"There was nothing wrong with the promo," Elly said emphatically. "It was a tease, nothing more."

Art was livid. "I don't give a flying fuck, pull the spots and kill the story!"

"Kill the story?" Laura was incredulous. "Why?"

"Because, my thick-headed news director, if St. Joe's pulls the Tower Cam sponsorship, that's ten thousand a month in revenue that I can't afford to give up."

"Art, we have an obligation to report…"

"Elly, could you excuse us?" He waited until she had left and closed the door. "Don't preach to me about what our obligations are! I have an obligation to make budget. If I lose this revenue, I don't see any way to get it back."

"I stand by the story. It needs to be aired." Laura pulled herself to her full height and looked down on the shorter man. "What happened to keeping your nose out of the news end of the building?"

"Listen." Art was quivering with rage. "When they give you that station in Dallas, you can do whatever the fuck you want, but right now, *I say kill the story*." He sucked in a breath and snarled, "Now get out."

Laura turned on her heel and strode to the door only to be stopped by the General Manager's voice. "And Kaz? Don't even think about calling Corporate on this one."

She jerked open the door. "You don't know me at all, do you?" And she slammed it behind her.

Janie had been the assignments editor for over eleven years at Channel 8. She had seen five News Directors, twenty-two producers, and thirty-odd reporters come and go over that span of time. She could feel and predict every hiccup in the newsroom and she knew that something was about to happen when she walked over to Chris's desk and imparted some information that had been passed on from the General Manager's secretary.

"Your story's in trouble, Chris."

The reporter looked up and blinked. "No, it's almost finished, Jody's editing it now."

Keith looked up from his monitor, concerned. "What's the problem?"

Janie elaborated, "Kaz is in Art's office. They're arguing about Chris's story. Apparently, St. Joe's has threatened to pull the Tower Cam sponsorship if it airs."

Puzzled, Chris looked at the Managing Editor, frown lines creasing her forehead. "She wouldn't kill it, would she?"

The door into the newsroom was almost ripped from its hinges as Laura flung it open and walked in. *Uh oh,* Chris thought, recognizing the blue-white rage in her boss's eyes. Laura walked across the room to her office with long angry strides, and as she passed Chris's desk she flung out a command.

"Kill it. The story doesn't air."

The slamming of the door punctuated the directive, followed by the distinct sound of an object shattering as it was hurled against a wall inside the News Director's office.

Elly Michaels's office was large only because it included an editing suite. The large monitors of the computer-based post-production system dominated one entire wall, and videotapes were scattered everywhere. There were no windows and no lights, save for a small halogen lamp in the corner and the flickering from the monitor screens themselves.

"Don't just stand there, c'mon in." Elly directed Kaz without turning around to look, "I'm just finishing up." Her short dark hair stood on end in testimony to the day's frustrations.

While most of the staff was busy with airing the Six O'Clock 'cast, Laura had gone in search of a working copier and had noticed that Elly's door was still open. "How do you work in the dark?"

"Well, it certainly narrows your focus. How do you stand the noise?"

"I close my door."

Elly gave a short laugh. "Rotten day, huh?"

"You too. For what it's worth, the spot was fine."

Elly closed the project she was working on and turned to face Laura. "You know, I used to think that the nicest thing that anyone could say to me was that the promo was better than the story. I exaggerate, I stretch the truth, and I tease, all to drive viewers to the newscasts. Then the one time I get nailed, it's for a promo that wasn't misleading at all."

"This business sucks."

"Yeah, it does. I'm a liar, but he's a pimp." She shut down the computer, switching off the monitors. "Was Chris pissed?"

"Aaahh, I didn't really talk to her."

"Better fix that, don't need another hostile anchor." Elly couldn't resist the pointed barb. "You'd know a lot about that, huh?"

"Don't even go there."

"Can I see you for a minute?" Chris jumped when she heard the low rumble of her boss's voice behind her as she came out of the studio. The blonde anchor had expected the issue of the dead story to be addressed before she went on the air, and was annoyed that it hadn't been.

"Sure." She followed the taller woman up the stairs to the newsroom and into her office. The fragments of a white ceramic coffee mug were strewn across the carpet and Chris could recognize the station's red and black logo on one of the pieces as she turned to shut the door.

Laura's eyebrows lowered thoughtfully as she looked at Chris, debating the best way to begin. This wasn't the first time she'd had to explain a story's untimely demise due to the vagaries of management, but it was the first time that any semblance of personal interest had intruded into that particular chore. "It was a money thing, nothing more." She hoped that the brief explanation would satisfy the reporter, but Laura should've known better.

"A money thing?" Chris was incredulous. "We're talking about lives at stake, and they won't change the way they do things unless someone brings it out into the open."

"Well, for the time being, it won't be us." Laura put on her jacket, sliding into it as Chris continued to fume.

"That's it? How can you be so cold about this? You approved the story!"

Laura slapped her hands down on the desk as her temper snapped for the third time that day. "Didja think I was all powerful and I could change Art's mind when all he's seeing is dollar signs? Get real, Chris. No matter how noble journalism is, television is still a business and the station can't pay the bills if the clients are pissed off."

"You could have…"

"I did everything I could. This is a fight you *cannot* win. Trust me on that."

Chris stood, gritting her teeth furiously, as if she wanted to say something else. She shook her head once to calm herself and looked up Laura, feeling the aggression drain out of her. "All right, what do you want to do?"

"We table it…maybe rework it. It'll hit the air eventually, though probably not in its current form."

The reporter rolled her eyes. "No, us. Do you want to do something tonight?"

Laura stammered, "I'm sorry?" *I just skewered her and she wants to do something tonight?*

"We could go to my house and neck on the couch." The look in Laura's eyes was priceless, and Chris chuckled. "Probably not ready for that."

"No, I'm…not…" Laura bit her lip and grimaced, wondering if this was going to work at all. "You wanna go for a walk?"

"You are not playing golf in the dark." Chris had changed into a pair of soccer shorts and tee shirt, and was standing next to Laura's Jeep holding an eight iron, a wedge, and a putter.

"Nah, it's more like pitch and putt, and there are lights."

"Well, what am I gonna do?"

Laura finished tying her shoes and stood up grinning, showing even white teeth. "You're going to keep me company, and clap politely when I make a good shot. Besides, I promised you dinner later."

The tiny executive golf course had nine short par 3 holes, and was lit up like a football field on a Friday night in Texas. Laura paid the green fee and led Chris to the first tee. More casually than she ever played at the club, Laura tossed a ball to the grass and smirked when she hit it easily to the middle of the green 137 yards away.

"Should I clap now?" Chris took the eight iron as it was handed to her, and the two of them strolled to the green, the hum of insects loud in the twilight. "So, I'm the caddy, right?"

"There's only three clubs, Chris."

"Yeah, but I'm entitled to ten percent of your winnings."

"Someone's been doing their research."

Chris handed over the putter. "Oh, I excel at research." *I'm reading books about golf, for god's sake. I must be head over heels.*

They did the loop in a little less than an hour. Laura smugly thought that this was one of the few times where she got to have her cake and eat it too, a little practice on her short game, and some time with someone who was becoming increasingly important in a life formerly devoid of any emotional entanglements. They laughed, argued and agreed, testing with topics as diverse as movies and the stock market. As they were finishing up, Chris really did clap when the tee shot on nine came within inches of the hole.

"Have you ever had a hole in one?"

"Yep, three of 'em." Laura tapped the ball in and bent over to pull it out of the cup. "Got one the last time I played with my mom."

"Was she good?"

Laura's eyes held a look that Chris could only describe as profound sadness. "She was fabulous, really. In all the years we played, I never beat her. Tied a few times, but she always pulled a rabbit out of her hat. Even with an ace, that last time, she beat me by three strokes." Laura cleared her throat. "She saw me win the '95 Amateur, but the cancer had spread pretty quickly, so…" she trailed off, uncomfortably.

"I'm sorry."

"It's okay, just haven't talked about her in a while." Laura added her score and out of habit, signed and dated the card. "Look, I ended up four under par. Guess that means you're entitled to dinner. What's your pleasure?"

"Mexican at Lupe's?" Green eyes brightened at the mention of food.

"I kinda saw that coming."

Laura hopped out of the doorless Jeep and followed the reporter up to the porch of her house. Chris had forgotten to leave a light on, so it was dark except for the moon and the glow from the streetlight on the corner. "Is this the part where I kiss you goodnight and tell you that I'll call you later?" Laura wasn't too nervous; after all, it was dark, and darkness could hide a multitude of sins. *Or clumsiness.*

"You could do it that way, or I could just kiss you." Chris took one of Laura's hands and laced their fingers together, but didn't step any closer.

"I think I'd like that," came the soft answer.

"You'll have to help me out a bit. It's hell being short." Chris moved closer and slid her other hand lightly up Laura's shoulder to the base of her neck, her knuckles tickled by dark silky hair, and stood on tiptoes to touch her lips to the mouth that smiled slightly down at her. She wasn't prepared for the explosion of longing that curled in her stomach or the white-hot fire that seemed to consume the rest of her body. She reveled in the tentative softening of Laura's lips and reminded herself to go slow.

*It's different from the last one*, Laura thought. *More needy?* She pulled away slowly and Chris looked at her, puzzled.

"I don't know what to do with my hands," Laura whispered.

Chris couldn't hide a smile. "Anything you want."

Laura untangled her fingers from Chris's hand and brought it up to rub her thumb along the smaller woman's jaw. Chris tilted her head into the caress and closed her eyes, willing her tingling flesh to stay that way forever. She brought her hands up to rest on Laura's hips, pleased at the way their bodies fit together, then felt Laura's mouth descend on hers again, this time with a mixture of urgency and curiosity, her tongue exploring lips and mouth gently, softly.

They broke again and Chris slowly opened her eyes to see yet another shade of blue, different from all the others she had seen before. *My god, I'm drowning...*

Laura stepped away, her hands falling to her sides. "I'm...going...now." Her breath hitched and she backed up, nearly tripping down the steps before catching herself. "Tomorrow...okay?"

Chris watched in a stupor as Laura stumbled away to climb into her Jeep and drive off, stalling the engine twice before she reached the corner. *I've just been kissed senseless by a rank amateur.*

By Friday the grind of sweeps was in full swing, and Laura was using every tool in her arsenal to keep the staff focused on the job at hand. They broke a few good stories, and the targeted special reports were generating a lot of interest if the amount of phone calls were any indication. Trouble with one of the new live trucks kept Laura busy with the engineers, and after half a day of running tests on the uncooperative vehicle, she was hot, sweaty and ready for the weekend. The qualifying round for the Open was the following week, and even though the weekend was going to be practice hell, tonight was set aside solely for time with Chris.

She stood in the parking lot, lifting her long hair off the back of her neck to feel what little breeze there was as she waited for Richard to give the word that the truck was fixed. Laura had already had it out with Art about taking Monday and Tuesday off, promising that everything was under control, and still realizing that there wasn't any way to guarantee it. The live trucks were barely a month old and they were still getting the bugs worked out.

"That's everything. You can get one of your photogs to run it out for a test, then it should be good for tonight." Richard closed the side electrical panel and picked up his toolbox, and Laura nodded gratefully.

"Cool, anything special we need to do?"

"Yeah, tell 'em to watch the clearance. These trucks are a little tall to be going to the drive-thru at McDonalds." He let his eyes rove over her tall frame, thinking she was a good-looking woman and too bad he was married.

Another day, another leer, Laura thought as she went back in the building. Funny, it used to bother her more, but lately it just seemed to roll off her back. Pondering the shift in attitude, she opened the newsroom door and realized that something was wrong. Terribly wrong.

Keith and Chris were in the middle of a ferocious argument, the intensity of which had paralyzed nearly everyone in the newsroom. A bluish vein bulged in the forehead of the young man while Chris stood nearly toe-to-toe with him, fury evident in every line of her body. Laura's entrance went unnoticed as they continued to shout.

"What's going on?" Her authoritative tone cut into the fight and they both stopped in mid-bellow and faced her, the silence startling in its intensity.

Keith answered quietly, "The LifeAir Helicopter crashed. All three on board are dead, plus two on the ground. Chris wants…"

"I did the original story, I should be on the scene!"

"…I sent Maria and Jason, they were already out and they can do live at Five and Six, plus Terence has the live from the Clark Trial."

"Tom can solo, I need to be there!" Green eyes were past the point of asking, they pleaded.

Laura stuck out her jaw slightly and shook her head emphatically. "No, Keith's right. I want you on the set."

"We blew it before, Kaz, you can't…"

"I just did. You're too close to it, and if we're doing two live shots, I'd rather have you here." *Don't, Chris. You promised it wouldn't come into the newsroom.*

Awareness of her position and the very public nature of the argument filtered through to Chris and she forced herself to calm. "Fine." Her eyes were still accusing as she turned away and went over to the printer to pick up a script.

"My office, Keith." Laura stalked away.

He followed her inside, pushing the door shut, and started to apologize. "I'm sorry…" He stopped and spread his hands in silent explanation.

"If you learn nothing else from me, Keith, learn this: Never yell at the talent in front of the rest of the staff; nothing good *ever* comes out of it." She sighed and crossed her arms, looking out the window into the newsroom, finding the blonde head bent over her keyboard. "She's still adjusting, Keith. She's not just a reporter anymore, her time in the field is going to get more and more limited, she'll end up doing more public relations crap for the station, and it's not going to be easy."

"Nobody forced her."

Laura nodded. "You're right. Just be patient, okay?" She swallowed against a wash of guilt. Had she pushed Chris into it? *No, she said it was the road she was on. It wasn't my own self-interest, was it?* "And she's thinks this is her fault, Keith, that she could've stopped the accident if we'd aired the story earlier."

"But it's not her fault."

"She won't look at it that way."

Leaning against the wall of the control room, Laura watched the last few minutes of the Six with a feeling of uncertainty, puzzled about something she couldn't quite put a finger on. The 'cast was good, and because Chris had done the background on the story earlier in the week, their coverage of the crash was exceptional. Kate's voice sounded like it was coming from far away as she gave instructions for the wrap. "You've got twenty seconds coming back…we'll close on the downtown Tower Cam."

*Those damn Tower Cams*, Laura thought. *That's what got us into this mess in the first place*. Distracted, she jerked violently at the tap on her shoulder and turned to see the General Manager waving her out of the booth. Silently, she followed him out and down the hall.

They walked past empty cubicles on the way to his office, the sales staff having left early as was their practice on Fridays. After the noise of the control room, the quiet was welcome.

Art waved Laura to a chair, a sure sign that this was an extended meeting, and sat down behind his desk, holding his tie to his chest then smoothing it out. He looked at Laura for a moment and snorted briefly. "We messed up. You can say 'I told you so.'"

"Why? We both have to deal with the fallout." Laura gave a grim smile. "Ever hear that saying? It's only television, it's not brain surgery, and nobody dies…except that this time, they did."

"Would running that story have made a difference?"

Laura thought for a minute. "As a journalist, I have to think so; that's why we do this, after all. The truth is we'll never know." She tapped the arm of her chair absently. "It's a credibility problem…we bowed under the pressure of a sponsor and it looks like we were bought."

"You say 'we.' I made the decision." Art pulled at his lower lip. Laura nodded slowly. "Yes, you did, but I executed it, and that makes me just as responsible."

Art let out a breath. "I'm meeting with the guys from St. Joseph's on Monday. I would've liked for you to be there, is there any way you could postpone…"

"No, I can't. Take Keith, he knows as much about it as I do."

"All right then, get him in here and we'll go over it."

It was after eight o'clock by the time Keith and Laura got out of the General Manager's office, and dinnertime for the nightside crew meant that the newsroom was nearly deserted. After sitting down to send a few more e-mail messages, Laura tried to call Chris at home. Her machine picked up on the second ring, but Laura didn't leave a message. *What would I say anyway? Sorry I reamed you in front of everyone, wanna go out now?* With a sigh, she started to tidy her desk, deciding to bring home some paperwork for the flight to Austin, when the phone rang.

"Kaz, it's Lisa, thank god I caught you. Come down to Mainstreet right now, Chris is drunk off her ass and we can't get her out of here."

"Aw, shit. I'm on my way."

Lisa and Trey met her at the door and pointed to the corner of the bar. The crowd was pretty thin for a Friday night, and she didn't have any problem spotting the miserable, hunched figure separate from the other patrons of the club. Laura nodded at Lisa, indicating that she would take care of Chris, then made her way over. "Can I sit down?" At an absent wave, she pulled a stool over and settled into it, waving the bartender over. "Lemme have a 7UP." Chris tapped her glass to indicate she wanted a refill, and he looked over at Laura. She shook her head and he left, returning with just the one drink, and Chris snorted. "You're the boss," she said bitterly.

"Yeah, I am. Do you think that makes this any easier?"

Chris looked away. "Whatever."

"How much have you had to drink?"

"Not enough, I can still think."

Laura studied the surface of the bar, idly following the whorls of the wood grain. "We sold out, and the truth is, I can't apologize enough for it. I can't even promise that it won't happen again."

"You should've let me finish what I started! It was *my* story."

"No, Chris, that's where you're wrong; it was *our* story. The newsroom acts as a team. You were in the studio, you asked the hard questions, you did the background, and you were the anchor of the story. Just because you weren't on the scene didn't mean that you gave up ownership. It wasn't really yours to begin with."

"You make it sound so reasonable…but that's what you do." Chris gave a humorless laugh and tilted her empty glass. "They shouldn't have died," she said sadly. "If we'd aired the story, they wouldn't have."

"You don't know that, and all the guilt in the world won't change it."

"Yeah, but there we were, ready to take advantage of it…like vultures. Sorry we're not a metered market, we could find out how we did bright and early tomorrow morning." Chris threaded her hands through her hair as if she could strip away the feeling of responsibility. She looked at her boss, her green eyes unreadable in the semidarkness of the bar. "How do you stand it? The need to produce results all the time, no matter what?"

Laura smiled wryly. "They pay me to do it. It's as simple and as complicated as that. Now, have you had enough of this pity party?"

Chris's eyes went a little unfocused as she tried to follow the point that Laura was making. "You make everything so simple professionally…how come you're so messed up personally?"

"Years of practice. C'mon, let's get you home." Laura hopped off the barstool and took hold of Chris's elbow, steadying the smaller woman as she stumbled getting up. "How much have you had?"

"A whole buncha that Absolut vodka stuff. I love the ads, but it doesn't taste very good."

"Maybe it'd be better if you mixed it with something." Laura helped her weave through the tables and out the door. "You'll be sick as a dog in the morning."

"Nope, never hung over. Good genes, I guess. Rats! The Jeep. We never get to ride the motorcycle when I've got a really good buzz."

"Good thing, too, because you'd fall right off, and it'd be quite a show in that skirt. Can you get in or…ah, hell…" Chris turned and fell against Laura, wrapping her arms around the taller woman. "This isn't good."

Chris breathed in the scent of cotton and laundry detergent, with a light tickle of plain deodorant soap. *No perfume, just eau de Kaz.* "What's not good about it? I've finally got you holding me. D'you how long I've been working on that?"

"Could we not do this in the parking lot?" Laura was getting the shakes and she hadn't had anything to drink. The body against hers promised all kind of things she wasn't ready for, and she half pushed, half-lifted Chris into the vehicle. "In the Jeep, there you go." She reached across to buckle the seatbelt, surprised when Chris halted her hand.

"I'm sorry. I guess I stood you up."

"S'all right, you're not the first drunk anchor I've had to take home."

"Oooh, should I be jealous?"

"Not unless you feel that being tossed into the bed of a pickup truck so you won't throw up on the upholstery is a sign of affection." Laura started the Jeep and pulled out of the lot. "If you feel sick, let me know."

Chris closed her eyes and leaned back, suddenly a little queasy. "Which anchor was that?"

"Roger McNamara in Dallas."

It took Chris a minute to place the name. "The guy you slugged?"

"That's the one."

"Hmmm." Chris couldn't concentrate on the subject enough to pursue it any further and she reached over to turn up the radio. "Oh, I like this." Sheryl Crow was singing about her favorite mistake, and Chris joined in...badly. *Thank god it's not a long trip*, Laura thought.

Getting Chris out of the Jeep was a little easier than getting her in, but now that the defenses of Laura's personal space had been breached, the blonde woman was not about to let her boss rebuild the walls, so Laura unlocked the door and went into the house with Chris draped over her.

"Bed for you, I think." Laura gently removed an arm from around her shoulder.

Chris gave a low laugh. "You can come too." She stripped off her blazer, tossing it to the living room floor. Next came the skirt, leaving her clad in only her hose and a pale beige blouse that brushed the tops of her thighs. She reached to grab Laura's hand and began pulling her to the bedroom. "C'mon."

Laura questioned the sanity of following Chris, but couldn't stop. Drawn easily into the seduction, her nerves were shot to the point of no resistance. Stupidly, she stared at the enormous bed in the center of the room while Chris skipped into the bathroom. "Gotta get this makeup off, or I'll have raccoon eyes in the morning." Laura waited, hearing splashing sounds and debating whether or not she should try to escape. Then the bathroom light snapped off and all rational thoughts fled.

Chris was attractive with makeup, but she was beautiful without it. Healthy skin glowed and she smiled, knowing the effect. The hose were gone, so bare legs disappeared into silk blouse that was mostly unbuttoned, and she began a slow walk to the taller woman. "You're still here… guess that means you're staying."

"I guess." Laura's voice was hoarse.

Chris turned and fell on the bed, her arms spread wide, and her feet still on the floor. "I am *so* tired." She yawned, closed her eyes—and fell fast asleep.

Laura stood, waiting for a moment, blinking at the turn of events, realizing that she'd been saved and punished at the same time. For the first time in her life, she understood the allure of a cold shower. With a sigh, she lifted Chris's legs onto the bed and covered her with a blanket.

*Now what?*

Chewing on the inside of her cheek, Laura debated her next course of action. With a calmness that belied the turmoil in her gut, she walked over to the nightstand and picked up the phone. After dialing, she listened to the ringing, then waited for the instructions to finish before leaving a message. "Peter, it's Kaz. I'm…gonna skip the 6:45 tee time and shoot for 11:00. Could you let Jeremy know? Thanks."

*No excuses now.* Without disturbing Chris or getting too close, she stretched out on the bed, sticking one of the pillows behind her head and crossing her legs at the ankles. She briefly wondered if she could even sleep with someone else in the same room, much less the same bed. After only a little while, she relaxed and dropped off, answering that question.

*"Ah, the spirit was willing but the flesh was snot-slinging drunk."*

As Laura eased awake in the stillness of morning, she was conscious of a weight on her chest that didn't move even as she shrugged to dislodge it. Grimacing in irritation, she peeled opened her eyes only to look into narrowed green pools of curiosity that didn't blink at her cool regard. Then the cat licked her chin.

Startled, Laura scrambled to sit up and the cat leapt away lightly. With a jerk, she remembered where she was and turned to look at the woman sharing the bed with her. Chris was awake and lying on her side, head propped up on a hand and regarding her with what could only be described as a smirk. "You snore," Chris teased.

Laura ran her tongue across her teeth, trying to think of an appropriately witty response and drew a total blank, so she opted for the safe standby, "How do you feel?"

Chris squinted a bit, taking stock. "Well, my mouth feels like I've been licking the carpet, but other than that, not too bad." She sat up and stretched, the front of the silk blouse parting to show a significant amount of bare skin and curves, then she dropped her arms. "So we slept together."

"Yeah." Laura pulled her legs up to rest her chin on her knees, leaning her back against the spindles on the head of the bed. "D'you have a spare toothbrush?"

"Probably." The cat reappeared to push its head under Chris's hand, purring at the attention of his owner. "Hey Biggio, you were a good cat this morning…you let me sleep."

"You named your cat after the guy who leads all active

players in being hit by pitches?"

"Best second baseman in the league," she replied absently. "Why'd you stay?"

Laura twitched uncomfortably, "I thought we'd…you were…" she trailed off.

"Ah, the spirit was willing but the flesh was snot-slinging drunk."

"What happened to 'I'd never get snockered in front of my boss?'"

"I didn't. You came looking for me, remember?" Chris's eyes clouded in memory, "I'm sorry, the story got to me, I was angry and I blamed you. Then Lisa and Trey ratted on me."

"Lisa didn't want you to get in trouble." Laura rubbed her chin on her knees. "Do you make a habit of that sort of thing when you get pissed?"

Chris scooted around to sit next to Laura, her back against the headboard. "I wasn't pissed so much as my pride was hurt. You didn't support me."

"I couldn't." The simple answer stood between them like a wall. "Which makes things really, *really* difficult." Laura took a breath as she tried to sort through what she wanted to say, then abruptly gave up. "This isn't gonna work." She threw her legs off the bed and stood up, moving to leave, but Chris anticipated her flight and intercepted Laura at the door.

"Oh, no you don't. I said my pride was hurt because you didn't back me up—I didn't say you were wrong." She pushed the door shut, effectively blocking the only means of escape. "What are you afraid of?"

"Nothing…Everything…This." Blue eyes were dark with confusion.

"Which is it?"

Laura shook her head and went back to the bed. Sitting down on the edge she cracked her knuckles, first on hand and then the other, the noise stark and loud in the quiet. "Just a hunch, but I'm fairly certain that you haven't spent the night with too many thirty year-old virgins."

Chris frowned and nodded, "That's…pretty accurate." She paused. "How does one get to be thirty without…"

"Having sex?" Laura drew a breath through her teeth. "I'd say that the opportunity never presented itself, or that nobody asked, but that'd be a lie." She looked away. "I just didn't have time, then I didn't want to." She blew out an impatient breath. "It wasn't important, I never really socialized and the guys I knew were jerks. The next thing I know I'm thirty and in a drainage ditch, kissing one of my anchors."

"That's a pretty simplified answer."

She looked up, slightly annoyed. "What were you expecting? There was no tragedy, no near rape, no abuse. I was…am...a machine. I played golf, I went to school, I worked my ass off and I was comfortable with it. Now everything's changed and I'm not handling it terribly well."

"What's the problem? You kept your professional head yesterday. I didn't. You'll still be able to run the newsroom the way you always have, 'cause it's not in your nature to do anything half-assed."

Laura laughed a little at that, fidgeted for a second, then asked a question out of the blue. "Does your family know about your…lifestyle?"

Chris sat down next to Laura on the bed, hands clasped between bare knees. "Ah, I guess turnabout is fair play." She grimaced a bit. "Mom knows; she told me not to tell my dad, but I think he knows. My sister guessed, and my brothers…well, they're my brothers…they're kinda dense and I don't think it would ever occur to them."

"How'd your mother take it?"

"She was disappointed…no grandchildren." She lifted her chin. *Go ahead and ask...it matters.* "When we did the contract, would it have made a difference if you'd known?"

Laura was quiet for a moment. "It's a risk, Chris, I won't lie to you." She rubbed her eyebrow the way she always did when she was thinking hard. "Every weatherman I had in Dallas was gay, but it wasn't public knowledge. It's different for a news anchor, especially in a conservative market like this one. I signed you…I would have tried to sign you regardless…but you can't be openly gay."

"Or you'll pull me off the air." It was a statement, not a question.

"Yes."

"That's pretty hypocritical, given the relationship you're fumbling around in."

"We're not talking about me, I'm not a public figure. It's not fair, that's just the way the business is."

Chris nodded slowly in understanding. "So as long as I'm an anchor, I have no chance for an open and aboveboard relationship?"

"I'm sorry. I would have told you if I'd known." Regret colored Laura's tone. "Remember that full disclosure clause in your contract?"

"Yeah?"

"Consider your supervisor notified."

Chris shook her head emphatically. "No, nothing changes." She turned and barely brushed her fingertips against the skin beneath Laura's jaw. "There is no way I could've had an open relationship with you anyway…you're my boss, and that presents all kinds of problems, but I'm willing to risk it. If this doesn't come into the newsroom, and no one knows about us, are you comfortable with that?"

Laura could hardly breathe. "Comfortable is not the word that comes to mind right now."

Chris gave a low chuckle. "Good. But I have to know—is this what *you* want…with me?"

"I wasn't looking for this, and it's a world of complications." Laura looked into sea green eyes and was lost. "But I want it," she managed to get out in a whisper.

A smile lifted the corner of Chris's mouth and with the lightest of pressure she pulled the dark head closer. "I won't hurt you."

*Of course you will.* Laura had time to register the thought before she was sucked into a shivering storm of sensation.

She had to rush to make the eleven o'clock tee time, and had to forego a proper warm-up in the process. Jeremy was waiting at the bag drop and had just crushed out his cigarette when Laura practically threw her clubs at him, her over-heightened emotions making her movements jerky and uncertain. "Bad night?" he asked.

"No, yes, not sure…just got caught up in some…things." The muscle in her jaw twitched and the caddy started to ask a question, then thought better of it. They made their way down to the first tee where the starter was waiting patiently with his clipboard frowning a little in disapproval. Laura pulled on her glove and gave a quick half smile to the threesome that was already waiting with their carts. "Sorry, the time got away from me." The starter gave them the go ahead and her playing partners gave her the courtesy of teeing off first, but things went downhill from there.

It took Laura ten holes to pull herself together, but by then it was too late. Even shooting eight under par on the back nine was not enough to help her break eighty, a horrific omen three days before the U.S. Open Qualifier. Shaking her head at the score card, she tucked it into her bag and looked at Jeremy. "I am *not* going home with that score. Can you do another round?"

"Sure. You wanna check at the shop? I'll get us some water."

Her glove was gummy with perspiration so she threw it into a trashcan on the way up the steps to the pro shop. Pushing open the door, she was startled to see Peter behind the counter, and Laura felt a little uncomfortable when their eyes met. "Hey, Kaz, heard you stunk it up today."

"That would be an understatement. D'you have room for me to go again?"

"You and I could go in ten minutes if that's okay."

Laura picked up a couple of gloves from a rack in the corner and put them on the counter to be added to her account. "Good for me, you gonna walk?"

"I'm playing with you, of course I'll walk." He passed her the ticket to sign. "What happened today? Mercer said you tore it up on the back, but you couldn't buy a shot on the front."

She rubbed her temple and mumbled, "Head wasn't in it, I guess."

Peter looked closely at her, his eyes narrowing speculatively. "You've got three days to get your head in it, or you're just a spectator in the crowd at the Open."

Chris poured a handful of tokens on the ledge next to the coin slot in the batting cage. *Twenty dollars worth oughta do it.* She fed one into the machine and stood back, tugged the bill of her helmet, and waited for the first pitch. With a thunk, a bright orange ball was launched in her direction, and she swatted it easily with the aluminum bat.

"Your hands are gonna be mush." Kate leaned on the fence, watching her friend swing away with an economy of motion she could only envy. She'd run into Chris at the gym and, concerned about the frantic pace of her workout, decided to follow her to the batting cages.

"I just want to hit something." *Again and again and again and again.*

"Who is she? I haven't seen you this bad since Erica."

"This isn't anything like Erica. I was just mad then." *Thunk...Tink!* Chris sent one to the left side of the cage. "You don't know her." *Which is true...in a way.*

"So what happened?"

"Nothing." *Thunk...Tink!*

"Nothing?"

"Well, mostly nothing." *Thunk...Tink!*

After fifteen balls, the machine asked for another token and Chris turned to oblige, the physical activity doing nothing to put what happened earlier out of her mind. *You said it was all up to her, stop or go. You gave up control, so don't bitch about it now.*

She'd pulled Laura down on the bed, resolved to stay distanced enough so that she could stop at any time, knowing that the other woman wasn't ready. But just like before there was no distance, no control, just a surge of raw emotion that washed away any sense of reason. This time there was no storm, no front porch, just the quiet of her bedroom and the intoxicating presence of innocence and smothering need all wrapped up in six feet of wiry muscle.

Hands and lips seemed to be everywhere at once, exposing flesh and covering it again. She remembered thinking that Laura was too thin, her ribs too prominent, before kissing her way lower, her finger tracing a blue vein under white skin.

And when Laura said stop, Chris nearly died.

She'd caught Chris's wrists and twisted away, rolling off the bed and gathering the linen blouse to her chest. Her breathing was ragged as she ran her hands through wild dark hair and paced around the bed, willing herself not to tear open the door and run away. "Can't…Sorry." It was a supremely inadequate explanation.

Chris found strength from some source she'd never tapped before and pulled the remnants of her soul together before answering, "Okay, your call." And she sent Laura away to her golf game or whatever, collapsed against the door, and sobbed in frustration.

*Is she worth it?* Chris dropped the token in the slot, heard the hum of the machine as it started again, and moved back to the batter's box. She felt the answer to her question from the center of her being, remembering a walk in the twilight and laughing blue eyes.

*God yes, if it doesn't kill me first.*

The second round went better than the first, but Laura still forced herself to stay on the practice range until nearly eight o'clock, the swarms of mosquitoes finally sending her to the clubhouse. Under the spray of the shower in the deserted locker room, she allowed herself to think about what had happened in Chris's bedroom.

*I panicked, it's as simple as that. I am not a teenager overrun with hormones, I am a rational thinking adult, and I understand that there are consequences.* It was like riding a roller coaster, she decided. When you go down that first big hill, you reach the point where you don't think you can stand it anymore, then you're snapped out of it when the car zooms up instead of continuing to fall. Except that when she reached that point with Chris…

*I jumped, ran, fled, vamoosed, split, escaped…*Disgusted with herself, Laura got out of the shower and dried off. Catching her reflection in the mirror, she snorted at her appearance. Arms were tanned, legs were tanned, but only to mid thigh, giving testament to a life spent in shorts and sleeveless polo shirts. *A golfer's tan. Gotta say it looks pretty silly.* She finished dressing, donning another pair of khaki shorts and a tee shirt before going to the Grill to grab a bite to eat.

It was after nine when Laura got back to the apartment, and her answering machine blinked urgently as she tossed her keys down beside it. One call was from her realtor in Dallas about the pending sale of the house; another was from Keith asking if she was playing softball on Sunday. Nothing from Chris. Disappointed, she sat down on the couch and clicked on the TV. Too early to go to bed, she told herself.

That lasted about ten minutes before Laura was bored out her mind. The problem with seeing a life outside the confines of the box she'd been living in was that it made her want what she hadn't known she was missing. *I could call her. She might not want to talk. Hell, she's probably not even home.* She picked up the cordless phone and started pacing. *This is good...taking the initiative...acting like a teenager...Hoping that the phone's gonna ring. Emotionally, you're an infant.* Laura punched in the number, deciding that she could just hang up if she wanted to—after she heard Chris's voice, of course.

It rang four times and the machine picked up. Laura listened to the message, smiling at the way Chris treated her answering machine as a voiceover. *Talent...jeez.* The beep caught her by surprise with no opportunity to rehearse. "Um, it's Kaz. Just wondering what you were doing..." There was a crash and fumbling as the receiver was picked up.

"Hey. I was just thinking about you."

"Kinder thoughts than the ones I left you with this morning, I hope."

Chris gave a low chuckle. "A good workout, a cold shower and I was fine."

"Sorry, I..."

"Don't apologize. How was your game?"

Laura grimaced as she turned out the lamp, preferring the anonymity of the dark, even over the phone. "There are no words to describe how awful my game was."

*Good, I'm not the only one who's messed up here.* "Can I take some credit for that?"

"Oh, I think you can." Laura stretched out on the couch, one arm over her head, legs crossed. "What are you doing?"

"I'm in the tub." Chris grinned wickedly. "Shaving my legs. Wanna come over?" She was pleased to hear a sharp intake of breath.

"Aahh, try not to electrocute yourself..."

"You know, this was in that movie *The Truth About Cats and Dogs,* they had this phone sex scene..."

Laura could feel her eyebrows reaching up to her hairline. "I saw that, but we're not having phone sex, we're having an adult conversation."

"With some overtones." Chris put the razor down on the edge of the tub. "You never did this in high school, did you? Just called up your best friend and talked for hours about nothing and everything." There wasn't an answer at the other end of the line, just silence, so Chris changed the subject. "When do you leave?"

"Um, Monday morning. I have a practice round in the afternoon. I'm supposed to meet my swing coach at eleven; his son's caddying for me."

"You have a swing coach? Just like Tiger Woods?" All of Chris's research was paying off. Climbing out of the tub, she put on a terry robe. "Why do you need help with your swing?"

"Well, Louis is really a lot more than that, he'll watch me and point out any inconsistencies, stuff like that. He's also a clubmaker, so he'll want to make sure all my equipment is set up for my game." Shifting to get more comfortable on the sofa, Laura decided that she liked talking to Chris in the dark over the phone, as if escaping from those inquisitive eyes made things easier.

Chris smiled. Without the distraction of Laura's physical presence, she could listen to just the voice and gather information that the other woman wouldn't normally share. The fondness for Louis came through loud and clear. "How long have you known him?"

"All my life. He pretty much taught me how to play."

"What about his son?"

"Charles? We grew up together; he's a teaching pro at a country club in Dallas. He's always been my caddy. I tried to reciprocate and caddy for him once in a Nike Tournament but we almost killed each other."

"Hmm." Chris could see that. Laura would not give up authority easily. "Did you, ah, ever have a crush on him or anything?"

The voice that came over the receiver was dry. "No, he was way too annoying. I guess he was more like a brother. Are you still in the tub?"

"No, I'm in the kitchen looking for something to eat."

"Figures."

"You don't eat enough, Laura, you've lost weight since you've been here. Those khakis you're always wearing are really getting baggy."

"It's Kaz, and I like baggy."

"Uh huh." Chris found a box of fudge bars in the freezer and unwrapped one. "Gonna play softball tomorrow?"

"I really have to practice."

"S'okay, we'll just have to beat *The Chronicle* without the benefit of your glowering presence." Chris's voice was light, but Laura could hear a little disappointment. "Why didn't you just leave for Austin earlier?"

Laura rolled over on her side, tucking the phone in between her neck and shoulder. "This is a blackout month, Chris. Department heads aren't supposed to be out of town during sweeps. Art's already mad that I'm going to be gone for two days, and I gotta admit it makes me nervous too, so *please* be careful while I'm gone."

"Sure, I'll wait 'til you get back before I get into any trouble."

They talked for hours, and Chris roamed through her house, lazily straightening things up and periodically snacking as they bantered back and forth. Getting information out of Laura was like pulling teeth, but the news director was also digging this time, and Chris felt herself blush more than once. *Weird,* she thought, *it must be the voice*... The question, when it came, didn't surprise her, but she wished she could see Laura's eyes when she answered.

"I was a sophomore in college, and pretty sure about my...preferences. It was easier in high school just to go with the flow and I dated a lot of guys, but nothing ever happened.

"Anyway, I was starting on the softball team...boy, that's a bit of a stereotype isn't it? Angie would come to the games and watch. She was sort of a groupie, I guess." Chris was quiet for a minute, remembering that she'd filed the experience away in the part of her brain she reserved for cringe material. Laura's low voice rumbled in her ear, interrupting.

"What happened? I mean...besides that."

"I was just a notch on her belt. Naïve enough to think I was different. It hurt for a bit, then I got over it."

Laura pondered the information, the short answers a dead giveaway of Chris's discomfort with the subject. "What about since then?"

Chris smiled at the other end, hearing an odd note in the other woman's voice. *Is she jealous? Good.* "There've been a few," she evaded. "Nobody for a while though."

"Oh."

Red digital numbers flashed the time and Chris finally noticed. "It's three thirty! We've been talking for six hours." She held the mouthpiece away and yawned. "If you're playing early tomorrow, you'd better get some sleep."

"Guess so." Laura didn't want to stop, but she didn't want to cling, either. "I probably won't see you 'til I get back."

Chris swallowed her disappointment, not wanting to press. "Okay, good luck." Reluctant to hang up, she held the receiver until an insistent tone forced her to cradle it. Sighing, she turned over on her stomach clutched a pillow to her chest, and went through the conversation to find some sign that they were progressing.

It was hot and humid on Sunday, the blue sky stubbornly refusing to supply even a few wisps of clouds to block the sun. The softball game was late starting because the one before it went into extra innings. Chris played like a demon, as though exhausting herself would make a difference when it hadn't the day before. On her third at bat, she walked to the plate, wincing at the condition of her hands and berating herself for spending two hours in the batting cages, when her mouth suddenly went dry. *How does she do that to me?*

Laura was stretched out on the bleachers, leaning on her elbows, a bottle of water swinging from one hand. She smiled when their eyes met and Chris nearly tripped and fell. "Hey," she choked out, "thought you were practicing."

"I'm between rounds and thought I'd watch for a little while."

"Hey Kaz! Wanna play?" Keith called from the dugout.

"Nope, just watching," she answered, then lifted an eyebrow at Chris. "You gonna hit?"

"Oh, yeah." She shook her head as she stepped into the batter's box, then slapped the first pitch down the right field line for a double, scoring Trip and Kurt. Chris did a little hop on the bag and grinned. *You show off*, she thought.

They won the game easily by nine runs, and afterwards Chris, Keith, and Rendally sat with Laura on the bleachers to watch the first part of the next game until the she had to leave for her afternoon round. Chris watched her walk away, thinking that the woman had an endless supply of khaki shorts, and she made them look *really* good.

"Yo, earth to Chris..." Keith snapped his fingers under the blonde reporter's nose. "Wanna get something to eat?"

She took a breath and smiled. *I need the distraction.* "Lead the way."

Laura appreciated the convenience of flying, but she hated it anyway. It wasn't a fear of heights or a fear of falling; rather, it was the invasion of personal space. She wouldn't pay double the fare for first class, so she usually tried for an exit row since they had a little more legroom. Deciding against cluttering her mind with paperwork, Laura left her briefcase at home, leaving her with only a portable CD player to pass the time. Flipping through the disks, most of which had been liberated from Lisa Tyler's collection in college, she chose an old favorite. *Music to go home by.* She closed her eyes and tried to relax.

She was looking forward to being in Austin, even if it was only for two days. *It'll be good to see Louis.* He never passed judgement on anything except her golf game, and since he helped build it, that was his right, especially after she quit in '96. *Make it up to him by qualifying. That would make twelve Opens between Mom and me...that oughta be some kind of record.*

The flight landed, and after what seemed like eons, the doors opened and the passengers were allowed to escape. Laura spotted Charles easily, his six-foot-seven frame dominating the tiny waiting area. He crushed her in a bear hug and lifted her off her feet, oblivious to the staring crowd around them. "You're so skinny, Kaz...you didn't need to lose weight."

She buried her face in his shoulder, realizing that he and Louis were the closest thing to family she had left. "No Coke." She pulled back and smiled. "I gave it up…too much sugar and caffeine."

"That'll do it. Bet you were drinking a twelve-pack a day."

Laura chuckled. "Pretty close. How's your dad?"

"Doing good. He can't wait to see you. Let's get your stuff."

Charles retrieved the hard travel bag that held her golf clubs and led her through the parking lot to a Ford Explorer. "Still got the Jeep?" he asked.

"I'll always have the Jeep," she answered. "What happened to the Z car?"

"All God's children got to grow up. I can haul more stuff in this." Laura hid a smile. *Guess that means he's settling down.*

It was a bit of a drive to Pierremont Country Club, and Laura settled in, listening to Charles's ever-present country & western music. It was strange to hear the large black man sing along to Alan Jackson or Reba McIntire, but it was, after all, Texas. They drove up close to the clubhouse and unloaded, and after agreeing to meet on the practice range, Laura went inside to change. Practice rounds for out-of-towners started after one, and her tee time was for 1:10. That would give her about two hours with Louis.

She changed quickly into navy blue shorts and another white sleeveless polo shirt. Pulling her hair into a ponytail, she threaded it through the opening in the back of her red hat and looked in the mirror at eyes that should not be so nervous for a practice round. The hat was from the last U.S. Amateur that she'd won, and she fervently hoped that there was a little luck left in it.

A warm wind was blowing briskly as she walked to the practice range. *It's always windy here.* Laura could see Charles up on the rise, and when he moved she could see the slightly smaller form of his father.

"Little Kaz! Charles was right, you have lost weight." Louis threw his arms around Laura in a tight embrace, and she who never cried, not even at her parents' funerals, began to sob softly into her teacher's shoulder. It only lasted for a moment, then, appalled at her lack of control, Laura pushed away and dashed at her tears with the back of her hand. "Sorry, Louis. It's been a rough couple of months." She clamped her jaw shut and swallowed, wondering where this inability to maintain control was coming from.

Louis looked at Charles over the top of Laura's head and raised his eyebrows in question, only to be answered by a shrug. "I heard about everything, Kaz. You did what you had to do. I'm not talking about slugging the guy; he had that coming. You stuck with the company and your dad would've been proud." He paused for a second. "Your mom would've laughed. Now c'mon, we have work to do. Let me see your hands."

He grabbed her wrists and turned her hands face up, running his fingers over the calluses, tsskking at one on the middle finger of her right hand. "Still overgripping? It's like shaking hands, firm but not choking. You don't want to overpower the club." Laura had heard the grip speech more times than she could count, and even after all her success it was the one part of her game that Louis still picked on.

Next, they went through all the clubs. Laura hit about five balls with each as Louis made notes on a little pad that he stuffed into his back pocket when he demonstrated what she was doing wrong or what he wanted her to change. The lesson was exhausting and comforting at the same time, but she was glad when they finally called her group to the first tee.

"He's got two other students that are trying to qualify," Charles told her as they walked to the starter. "They practiced Saturday and Sunday 'cause they live here in town."

"Anybody else you know?"

"Becky Martin's here. Y'all were at Texas together, weren't you? She just played a tournament in Austin, almost won."

Laura nodded. "Well, Charles, what kind of score d'you think we need?"

"I think you better just start rolling in the birdies and count 'em up later. Don't even think about the Open. You ain't there yet."

Chris was heating up fettuccine in the microwave when the phone rang, and she answered it, licking the spoon she was using to stir the pasta. "Bet you're eating. Why you're not big as a house is beyond me."

"Well, if it's not my favorite Texan. You know, Keith's right, you could say who you are."

"Why? This makes it more like an obscene phone call."

The microwave beeped and Chris removed her dinner. "You just feel safer over the phone. How'd it go today?"

Laura smiled ruefully at the truth and sat down on the hotel bed, kicking off her shoes. "Good. I've played here before, so that helps. It's hot, though. What happened at work?"

"Oh, it was slow. I did a package on teacher pay raises, then the character generator caught on fire so no supers for the Five, Six or Ten. Lisa tried to kill Richard because he wouldn't sign the purchase order to get the part to fix it and Elly and Rendally got into it over his promo standup and proper use of grammar. All in all, it was pretty normal."

"Sorry I missed it." *What do I say now? I miss you?* The silence was awkward and Laura couldn't fill it, so Chris did. "Everything okay with Louis and Charles?"

"Yeah." Another pause. "I wish I could show you Austin."

"That'd be cool," Chris went along easily. "We were on the phone for six hours the other night, it's okay if you're talked out."

"I'm not, I just…It sounds corny, but I wanted to hear your voice. I wish I'd seen you last night, and I miss you. I didn't think I would."

"Why?" Chris was more than a little intrigued.

"Because I'm home. Austin is as much home as Dallas, and it's strange because I have more of a life in Burkett Falls than I ever had here."

"There's nothing wrong with that. Everyone changes, everyone evolves."

*All God's children got to grow up…it's just taking me longer. Maybe I'll hit my adolescence by the time I'm thirty-five.* Laura laughed and Chris smiled at the sound. "I'm flying in late tomorrow night, so I guess I'll see you Wednesday. Maybe we could do something?"

"You bet." Chris felt the giddiness through the phone line and wondered what was going through Laura's head. "I hope you play well tomorrow. God knows you've worked hard enough."

"It's never enough." Somehow Chris knew that Laura wasn't talking about golf. "I'll see you Wednesday."

The gravel crunched under the tires of the big Buick as Laura maneuvered it along the narrow driveway. Louis had insisted that she borrow his car instead of renting one, overriding her protest that she could afford it. Laura parked under an oak tree and started to walk down a footpath toward a shady corner of the cemetery.

She was still Catholic enough to understand the need to be buried, but practical enough to consider it a waste of real estate. It was quiet except for the ever-present Texas wind swishing through the leaves of the trees, but the sound was comforting. At the bottom of the hill, Laura looked down at the stones that marked the last earthly remains of her parents. *I could've brought flowers.* She was surprised that the bitterness she'd grown accustomed to was fading away. *Three more years, Dad, then I'm free. You were right, I am good at it, though Roger would probably disagree. Gotta qualify for the Open today Mom, it's at Pierremont. I tied you there once, remember?*

Laura stayed a little while longer, enjoying the peace.

"Yeah, okay, thanks." Trip hung up the phone and turned to face Keith and Chris who were standing in the exact same pose, arms crossed and knees locked with eyebrows raised in question. "The USGA will not release the qualifying results until tomorrow…that's when they'll complete the final roster for the Open."

"So unless she calls, we won't know 'til tomorrow?" Keith pulled the pencil from behind his ear. "It's not news unless she qualifies."

"She'll kill you if you put that in a show," Chris observed.

"I just wanna know, don't you?"

"What's the best you've done out here, Kaz?" Charles asked. They were on the tee box of the third hole waiting for the group in front of them to get off the green. It was a longish par 3, 193 yards with a little water on the side. She sorted through her mental list of games played and pulled up the answer. "Six under, and it wasn't a particularly good day." She was already one under par after two holes; a birdie had gone a long way toward making the nervousness vanish.

"Can you do it again?"

The group left the green and Charles handed her a three iron. Her playing partner had bogied the last hole, so Laura had the honor. An easy swing put the ball less than six feet from the pin. "I think I'd better."

Par was 36 on the front nine, and Laura made the turn at four under, well pleased with a 32. With the two most difficult holes on the course behind her, she stopped in the restroom to wash her hands. *Nine more…don't fuck it up,* she told the reflection. Balling the paper towel, she tossed it in the wastebasket on her way out the door. Charles was waiting and they trudged up the path to number ten. "You drinking enough?" he asked.

"Yes, mother." She looked over at him, amused. "You too?"

"I'm just the pack mule, and you never use those big leather staff bags, so I'm happy. You walking at your club?" She nodded. "Got a bagman there?"

"Yeah, he wants some tour work. He's done some Nike, pretty good guy. If you hear that someone's looking, let me know."

"Does he know about us?" Charles gave a mock leer.

"Sure, he's insanely jealous." Her playing partner, Tammy, was already waiting at the tee drinking from a quart bottle of water. Laura put on her game face, and Charles handed her the driver. She bent down to tee up the ball, then stood, twirling the club absently to loosen her wrist, then took a practice swing. Laura was confident now, and the drive showed it. *Probably a good 280 yards.* She gave the club back to the grinning Charles and stood back, feeling the warmth of the sun, and let the pleasure of playing well carry her through the rest of the round.

It was after the Six O'Clock 'cast and the few remaining occupants of the newsroom were sitting around the assignments desk having one of those bizarre conversations that bored groups of overworked people often have. "I'd shave my head for a hundred bucks...hell, I'd shave it for twenty." Jody's confession prompted Keith to jump up and pull out his wallet.

"How 'bout ten? It's not like a nose job, it'll grow back."

The photog snorted, "I have my pride."

Chris laughed from her desk, where she was re-packaging a story for the Ten. It caught Kate's attention and she turned. "How much to run naked through the lobby, Chris?"

"There *isn't* enough money."

"For a thousand bucks, I'd do it," Bobby quipped.

"Who would you sleep with for a thousand bucks?" The staff pondered Kate's question while she elaborated. "Anyone in the newsroom...for a thousand dollars." Bobby and Rendally looked at each other and grinned, replying in unison, "Kaz."

Chris lifted her eyebrows but otherwise gave no sign of interest at the howls of laughter generated by the answer. *You have no idea...*

Tomorrow was a long time to wait to find out if Laura had qualified, and the reporter hoped there would be a message on her machine when she got home. She finished the story, printed the script, and stood up rubbing her neck to work out the kinks. One of the phones rang and Keith picked it up. "Hey! How'd it go?" He covered the mouthpiece and said to Kate, "It's Kaz." Suddenly nervous, Chris put her hands in her pockets, trying to maintain an air of casual indifference as she listened to the one-sided conversation.

"Nope, everything went fine...One of the candidates for the sheriff's race pulled out...No jury for the Bradley trial yet...Uh huh...All vehicles are present and accounted for," Keith grinned at Chris. "No, we can do that tomorrow...You did? Cool...Okay...bye." The Managing Editor hung up the phone and turned around, grinning from ear to ear.

"Eight under par. Kaz is going to the Open."

*"She's a trouble magnet... Dan Rather wishes he had that kind of luck."*

# What Are the Chances?

The pedals on the stationary bike were already spinning at 70rpm, but Chris pushed them even faster, increasing the uncomfortable burn in her thighs. The morning workout was a habit so deeply ingrained that the reporter could no more skip it than she could forget to eat. And since one was the reason for the other, it was probably a good thing that she stuck to the discipline.

It also gave her time to think. Some of her best story ideas came from these morning sessions when her mind was free to wander, or when someone approached her with a tip. The Information Officer for the Burkett Falls PD worked out at the Y, as did the Fire Chief, and her connection to them had proved valuable in the past.

The time expired on the bicycle workout, and she dismounted, wiping the seat and the handgrips with the towel provided. Wednesday was a slow day at the gym as the promises to live a healthier life on Monday gave in to the reality of a busy week, but by Friday it would be crowded again. The incline board was the last part of Chris's workout, the sit ups and crunches her least favorite exercises, and with a sigh she settled into the repetition.

*She's back today.* Chris closed her eyes and conjured up an image of her boss. It had been a while since she'd even thought about entering into another relationship, and even with the stop and go nature of this one, she was enjoying the warmth and the laughter, despite the obvious frustrations.

Chris loved people. She liked talking to them, drawing

them out, and being with them. That said, she could be happy alone as well. There was toughness hidden beneath the layer of spontaneity and charm; it had carried her through the ultra competitive School of Journalism at the University of Missouri, and now it was going to help her get through to Laura Kasdan.

*This is different, it isn't a crush anymore.* It should have made her uneasy. Getting involved with someone at work, or even in the media in the same market, was on her list of things *not* to do, but things hadn't been the same since the live truck blew to hell and took her resolutions with it.

*We're not talking about the "L" word here, are we? Well, there's lust...Haven't been in lust for a while. That would've been Erica...don't go there.* That was another file marked "cringe material."

Finished with the sit-ups, Chris shook out her arms and headed for the locker room to pick up her keys and bag. She went home to shower and change, stopping by the bagel shop on the way. An hour later she was on her way to the station, looking tailored and cool in a soft green skirt and jacket set, an off-white blouse with a Chinese collar completing the outfit. Anchoring meant that there were no more dress down days for her, and she missed wearing jeans to work. She only wore light makeup; the heavy stuff would come later in the day right before she had to go on the set.

Even though she was no longer required to attend the morning meetings, Chris still came anyway, figuring it was a lot better to have a say in the story you were assigned to rather than have one dropped in your lap. Entering the newsroom, Chris played a game with herself to see how long she could keep from looking into the News Director's office for Laura, and felt like she was making real strides when she managed to unlock her desk and turn on the computer before sneaking a peek.

Laura was on the phone when the staff started trickling in for the meeting, one elbow on the desk supporting the hand holding the receiver. Her eyes flicked upward and met Chris's as soon as the reporter cleared the door, a slight smile came and went, and then it was all business and another newsday was underway.

She stood up behind her desk, long fingers barely brushing the blotter, and scowled. "We have a problem. Last night at ten, we reported that one of the women injured in yesterday's three car pileup on I-20 had died. The problem is...she ain't dead." Laura's eyes swept the room and her displeasure was a tangible thing. This was the Kazmanian Devil in full control. "Keith, how did that happen?"

The Managing Editor did his best not to squirm under the scrutiny. "The PIO, Police Information Officer, called last night and said the Coroner confirmed she was dead…It was actually a woman involved in another pileup on Saturday."

"Mark Norton made the mistake?" Her fingers were drumming now.

"No, Mark's on vacation, it was his fill-in."

She nodded once, "Okay, here's what I want: I want a report on exactly what was said by the PIO, what we said on air, what the actual facts are, and how we will air the correction, on my desk by noon."

"Why do you…"

"When Mr. Poteet, the station attorney, comes to you in two years to depose you for the lawsuit that's been filed by this woman's family, are you going to remember?"

"Well…"

"No, you won't. But if I have a copy of the notarized report in my filing cabinet, you won't have to worry and neither will I." Laura dipped her hands into the pockets of her slacks and tilted her head. "We live in a litigious society and every newscast we air makes us vulnerable. A man in Jacksonville is suing us because we reported that he was charged with assault." She shrugged. "No big deal—except we didn't report that he was cleared of the charges."

"What I'm trying to say is that we have to follow up on everything. If it's important enough to report that he was charged, it's important enough to report that he was cleared. It's the ethical thing to do and it protects the station." Then Laura surprised everyone in the room by smiling wryly as she sat down behind the desk. "I'm off my soapbox now. Let's go around the room."

The tension eased considerably as the reporters and producers pitched their stories, and by the time it was Chris's turn they'd had several ideas and a few heated discussions. "I've got a couple of things. There's a rumor of explosions happening at gas pumps when people are using cell phones while they're filling up, something about sparks being generated while the phone is in service. A guy at a gas station who's seen it spark says he'll talk on camera, plus we could talk to some cell phone guys."

Laura crossed her arms and leaned back in her chair as though contemplating the idea, then said in all seriousness, "I think I speak for everyone here, and everyone at Corporate, when I say I don't want you anywhere near that story." The snickers started before turning into full-fledged belly laughs, and the blonde reporter blushed before joining in. Laura waved her had at one of the others, "Maria, why don't you get the information from Chris and check it out. Got anything else?"

"Well, a new government report is out, and did you know that homicide is the second leading cause of death in the workplace?" Chris imparted this information with a puzzled look, "Don't you think that's weird? What about accidents and heart attacks? And homicide is the number one cause of death for women in the workplace."

Keith pulled at his lower lip thoughtfully. "Mostly clerks in convenience and liquor stores right?"

"Mostly," she answered, "but not always. The phrase 'Going Postal' has become part of our vocabulary, and even here, a woman was killed at the Martin Tire Plant when she got into a fight with another employee."

"So what's the angle?" Laura asked.

"We have metal detectors at schools, post offices, and airports, and after the shootings at Columbine, we hear a lot about how to keep our schools safe, but what can businesses do to make sure their employees are safe on the job when the very nature of a business means that you have to be accessible?" Chris paused, waiting for the verdict.

"I like it," said Keith. "We could pack it for the Five and Chris could intro it."

"Sounds good," Laura nodded as they moved on. "The new *Star Wars* movie opens tonight at midnight and they're already lining up at the Cinemark. Rendally, you draw theater duty today. Get me some fanatics in costume, a lightsaber duel would be nice." She checked her notes. "That should do it, people."

"Oh, Kaz?" Keith cleared his throat, and Laura raised her eyebrows in question. "Congratulations on qualifying for the Open." The rest of the staff broke into applause and the tall woman blushed.

"Yeah, well, we still have two weeks of the book to get through before I can even start thinking about it. We can't afford to let up. Second place sucks, and don't let anyone tell you differently." The producers and reporters filed out as Laura picked up an envelope from her desk and opened it. "Kate, Keith, and Chris...Could I see you for a second?" The three stopped and came back into the office. "I've got some tickets to the Star Wars premiere tonight at midnight, thought you might like to go."

Keith's face lit up. "Hey, how'd you get those? They've been sold out for a week."

Laura gave a sheepish half smile. "I'm one of the twenty most influential people in town. I think I can manage a few movie tickets. They're VIP seats, so you don't even have to get there early." She gave out the passes and when Keith and Kate left, Chris lagged behind.

"You, me, Kate, and Keith? That's some group date."

"Lisa and Trey too. I had six total; you don't mind, do you?" Nervous fingers flipped the corner of the remaining ticket. "Besides, it'll give Kate a chance to spend some time with Keith outside the newsroom but without the pressure of an official date."

The reporter's mouth fell open in astonishment. "I would have bet money that you didn't know about that." Kate and Keith's volatile working relationship seemed to be turning into something else, but neither had acknowledged or acted on the obvious attraction.

Laura smirked. "Oh, I know a lot of stuff that goes on out there; I'd be a pretty rotten news director if I didn't keep up. You just think I don't know." She rubbed her chin, nervously unsure of what to say next. "So, I hope that's okay, all of us going."

*Safety in numbers?For both of us.* "Sure, it'll be fun." Chris turned to leave, then stopped. "I'm happy for you about the Open, and I'm really glad you're back." Then she was gone. Laura stood staring at the door, wanting to call her back and knowing that she couldn't.

Chris made some phone calls and set up two interviews before she started to outline where she was taking the story. Jason was her photog and he was taking care of some dubs, waiting on her word to go. Glancing up, she watched Laura leave her office with a sheaf of papers, her black cowboy boots thumping across the floor. Just how did you reconcile the woman who could barely stand to be touched with the person who scrounged up six movie tickets so she could play matchmaker? *Nothing will ever be easy with her, you know that, right?* Taking a deep breath, Chris gathered her notebook and went in search of her cameraman.

"But I have to have those tripods, I can't move them to fourth quarter, I need them now." Arguing capital priorities with the Business Manager was an exercise in frustration since she controlled the purse strings and her decisions were final. "Those cameras are pretty heavy and two of the tripods we're using are liable to collapse at any time. I don't want anyone to get hurt." Laura hoped that by mentioning the possibility of an injury, Phyllis would see things her way. She didn't.

"Kaz, they're moving to fourth quarter. Cheer up, it could've been the script printers; I'm just tired of hearing you bitch about those." Phyllis closed the binder with a snap. "It's a corporate thing, I really don't have that much say in it."

"Well, don't say I didn't warn you." Laura passed over a stack of purchase orders. "Where do we stand on the new camera? I know we filed for the insurance." Jody still wasn't shooting, so they weren't short yet.

"Richard's ordered it, I don't know about delivery." The Business Manager took the forms and arranged them in neat piles on her desk. "Check with him, I haven't seen any paperwork yet."

Ah, the paperwork, Laura fumed. She hated that part of being a manager; the endless reams of faxes, invoices, and urgent messages, not to mention the constant battle to acquire needed equipment and the never-ending meetings. Next to that, dealing with the newsroom was child's play.

She returned to her office and dumped the stack of files on her desk, then opened her top drawer to pull out her copy of the News Department budget. Looking down, Laura caught sight of an envelope and swore softly. With all that had happened Friday, she hadn't had a chance to deposit her paycheck. With a snort, she wished again that William-Simon Communications would move into the twentieth century and go to direct deposit. Oh well, the bank was right across the street from the station and it wouldn't take any time to use the ATM.

*This damn machine is never working, and then the bank wants to charge you for using a real live teller.* Chris resisted the urge to kick the stuffing out of the ATM and resigned herself to waiting in line to cash a check. She left the glass cubicle and went inside the bank proper, groaning inwardly at the crowd already waiting.

Taking her place in line, she fished her checkbook out of her purse and uncapped a pen with her teeth. Her writing was barely legible and she frowned impatiently as she finished filling out the check. A twenty-minute wait for twenty bucks. Now that's high tech. More customers came in and joined the queue. "What's taking so long?" Chris spoke to no one in particular, but the man in front of her turned around. "Don't you hate it when the ATM isn't working?" He grunted disinterestedly but she kept on, "They charge you two dollars for every teller transaction because they say it costs them more, but they won't make sure the stupid machine is working during lunch. I think it's a scam." The man rolled his eyes and faced forward, sticking his hands in the pockets of his windbreaker. *Kinda warm for a jacket,* Chris thought.

"Well, that's just great," Laura muttered as the automatic teller spit her card back and flashed an out of order message. Taking the deposit envelope and the rejected card, she went around the corner and into the bank where she got into line behind a woman she recognized as another station employee. Laura nodded briefly in greeting and settled in to wait, noticing a pale blonde head near the front of the line.

One of the tellers called for the next customer and the man in front of Chris walked over to the counter, his heavy work boots scraping on the tile floor. I'm next, the reporter thought, good-natured patience winning out over frustration. Her attention was drawn back to the counter as voices were raised in some sort of disagreement, then pandemonium ensued.

"Everyone on the floor and nobody gets hurt!" Snatching up a canvas bag, the man in the jacket waved a gun over his head and barked the command. "Now!" Screams and gasps answered him as the crowd of bank customers began to drop to the ground.

Laura rolled her eyes in disbelief as she heard sirens and saw the cop cars pull up outside the glass doors. *What kind of idiot robs a bank at lunchtime three blocks away from a police precinct?*

*It's on the scanners already.* She looked toward the front of the line where she last saw her six o'clock anchor as she started to comply with the gunman's request.

"On the floor! Now!"

Listening to police scanners requires the linguistic skills of an interpreter and the numeric recall of a military codebreaker. The constant squawking had the potential to drive even the most ravenous news hound insane. At Channel 8, the scanners were the domain of the Assignments Editor, and Janie could tell what was going on all over the city while eating, talking on the phone, and riding herd on the reporters simultaneously. It was all stress all the time but she thrived on it.

When the call came asking officers to respond to a possible armed robbery in progress, Janie was all ready to write down the address and send a crew, but she stopped in mid-scrawl, recognizing the address of the bank across the street from the station. "Jason! Terence!" Yelling at the top of her lungs, she scurried down the hall to roust the cameraman and reporter to send them to cover the story unfolding on their doorstep.

Keith shouldered open the back door as he carried in a box full of lunch orders from the deli. "What's going on?" he asked as Janie ran back to her desk.

"Robbery across the street, Jason and Terence are on the way. The silent alarm went off, a teller must've hit it."

Keith slid the box and its contents down on the nearest flat surface. "Chris was going to the bank, you don't think—oh, shit."

"Oh fuck! You set off the alarm!" The agitated gunman spun around frantically trying to figure out a way to get out of the situation with his loot and skin intact. Settling on the only solution he could think of, ingrained from years of watching predictable television, he yanked Chris to her feet with panic driven strength. "I want a car and I want out or I'll kill her, so help me god!"

Chris winced when he jammed the barrel of the gun against her head just behind the ear. If I didn't have bad luck I'd have no luck at all, she thought again, wondering how she was going to get out of this mess. Looking down at the floor crowded with huddled bodies praying not to be noticed, she met the electric blue eyes of her boss and felt a wave of relief so intense she thought her legs would buckle.

*Fix this,* Laura thought. Her mind chased down several possible scenarios, finally landing on the one that stood the best chance of success. *Give him something and keep him talking.* No one else seemed inclined to step up, and that was one of her people in danger. She took a deep breath and called out, "Wait a minute…hey I'm not gonna hurt you. Listen for just a second." The gun swung in her direction and one of the women on the floor whimpered fearfully. "Don't you know who that is?" Laura pointed at Chris. "She's famous…she's on TV."

"Yeah, I seen her, so what?" the gunman snarled.

She eased to her feet slowly so as not to appear threatening. "Look, I run the show over at Channel 8; you know, 'Action News.' I can get a crew over here in no time, put you on the air and you can get whatever you want. Once you control the media, you've got it made." Laura slid a glance to green eyes, trying to convey a message without a word. *Help me out here Chris, sell it to him.* "You've got a card here to play, fella, don't blow it."

The blonde reporter stuttered as she tossed in her two cents worth, "Yeah, she's…she's the boss, she could talk to the cops and get you what you want. The cameras would make sure of it. That way nobody has to get hurt." Chris jerked as the gun was pressed against her neck again. She took a shallow breath, not sure what the News Director was up to, but horrified by the journalistic hustler on display.

"C'mon, c'mon, I'll do it…we need the ratings. Lemme make the call," Laura urged, her eyes glittering maniacally. "They don't know what's going on, they're liable to bust in here and splatter you all over the marble."

"All right! But she does it!" He tightened his grip on Chris's arm, deciding that the petite blonde would be easier to handle than the tall woman with the big mouth. "Tell 'em they better not come in here or I start shooting!"

*Oh hell.* The plan to get Chris out of harm's way hadn't worked. Anxiously, she looked for some kind of edge. He doesn't have enough hands, Laura thought as she watched him push Chris to the counter. The robber was holding on to the money with the same hand he was controlling his hostage with, and waving the gun with the other. "No funny stuff or I'll blow your head off."

Chris was catching on. *Distract and confuse him. He's not the sharpest knife in the drawer.* "D'you want me to call the police first or the TV station?" She was still shaking, but felt like she was taking back control, inch by inch.

"TV…No, the cops first." With only slightly shaking hands Chris dialed the Police Information Office number from memory, wondering what the protocol was in a hostage situation. "Hey Jenny, this is Chris Hanson, listen, I'm inside the Firstbank on Kirby Street…yeah that'd be the one…I'd really appreciate it if you could patch me through to whoever's in charge…I've got the gunman right here. Yeah, same old, same old." There was a long pause, "Mike? Okay." She held out the receiver. "Tell him what you want."

*Good girl, Chris. He has to put something down to talk.* Laura began inching her way forward, stepping around customers who were doing their best to shrink into the floor until she reached one of the posts connected to the red velvet rope designed to keep the customers in an orderly line.

The robber figured out he had a dilemma pretty quickly and snarled, pushing the receiver back at Chris with his gun hand. "Tell him I want them out of the parking lot, now! No cops within fifty yards of this place…And I want a car…tell him I want a car in ten minutes."

"Didja get that, Mike?" Chris listened for a moment. "He wants you to let some of these people go…"

"Fuck no!" he screamed, "Everybody stays! Ten minutes, or I start shooting!" He pushed Chris against the counter as he grabbed the phone with his gun hand and slammed the receiver down. The robber was bordering on hysteria, his head frantically jerking from side to side trying to maintain his dominance over everyone in the bank. Chris tried to ease away, but he grabbed her wrist and pulled back, turning to face the tall dark woman. "Now, she can call your guys," he told Laura. "Tell 'em what I want. Tell 'em the cops better not fuck with me…go on!" Chris picked up the phone again and dialed, her eyes nervously going back to Laura's.

"Keith, ah, it's Chris…could you get a camera over to the Firstbank across the street…There's a robbery in progress and the gunman wants to talk…"

"Chris, thank god! We thought you might be in the bank."

Chris resisted the urge to laugh. "Sorry, I hate to be the one to tell you, but my luck's running true to form and we're about to get an exclusive, so could you send someone over?"

Keith felt a jerk in his gut that was becoming all too familiar when dealing with the blonde reporter. "Oh no…Kaz isn't here, I can't…how…oh Christ."

"Kaz wants you to send someone." Chris put her hand to her forehead. "She's in here, Keith."

"Oh…crap."

"Exactly."

"I'm on my way." Keith hung up the phone and bolted to the door. "Chris and Kaz are in the bank…Get Live 2 out front as fast as you can and get the mast cam cranked up. They are not doing this again without me!" The door closed with a thunk and Janie was left behind as the scanners continued to crackle around her.

"Camera's on its way." Chris set the phone in its cradle, wincing when the gunman shoved her forward in front of him so that he could approach the windows. Using the reporter as a shield, he peeked out and relaxed slightly as the police cars pulled away from the front of the building. "Okay, now we're gettin' somewhere." He turned around, moving away from the windows, waving the gun menacingly. "Everyone stay down...you too!" He pointed it at Laura with a sneer. "Especially you."

*Well, this isn't good.* Laura sank to her knees, her back against the counter. All around her the other hostages were getting restless and the muttering was getting louder. "Ya know," she said, running the risk of irritating the robber into shooting her, "they're probably not gonna let that cameraman come in unless you let some of these folks go, sort of as a sign of good faith."

"You talk too damn much," the man huddled next to Laura hissed. "If you'd shut up, maybe we'd get out of here in one piece."

"Hey, I'm trying to get you out of here."

"Just shut the fuck up!" The gunman trembled with rage, swinging the gun erratically as if he didn't know where to point it. Near the breaking point, he panted in frustration at the situation that had spiraled out of his control. At the end of the counter, the phone began to ring and he started for it, pulling Chris behind him, unwilling to let her go as though she alone would provide him protection, not understanding that she was the reason for what happened next.

It's now or never. As angry feet stomped by where she knelt, Laura snaked out a long arm and grabbed an ankle. Yanking as hard as she could, she sent him sprawling, the gun skittering away from his reaching hands. Scrambling to her feet, Laura tackled him as he tried to stand and chase after the firearm.

What the hell is she doing? Chris stumbled after the gun, kicking it into the corner near the vault. She turned just in time to see Laura stand to pick up a post still attached to a red velvet rope and swing it like a club down on the struggling gunman. "Just stay down and I won't kill you!" He didn't obey, so she swung again. "Don't say I didn't warn you." This time, he lay still. Standing over the man, her chest heaving with exertion, Laura looked up through tangled bangs and smiled crookedly at Chris. "Remind me never to follow you into a bank. Are you okay?"

Oblivious to the others around them, Chris shouted, "Were you trying to get us killed?"

Laura let the post clatter to the floor. "Call Mike or whoever's in charge, tell 'em to get in here." Walking carefully to the corner she bent down and picked up the gun. Flipping the cylinder open she released a short, bitter laugh. "Son of a bitch didn't have any bullets."

There were twenty-eight people in the bank, including the employees, and all of them had to be interviewed by the police. Chris's account was detailed and precise as she formed the skeleton of her story while answering the questions. Resisting the urge to tell the officer, "What she said," Laura told her side of the story in a clipped, even tone that didn't differ from the reporter's version.

Told they could go, Chris stayed behind with Jason to get some interviews and B roll, her story on violence in the workplace coming together in a way that no one had anticipated in the morning meeting. Laura marveled at the transformation. Chris was the quintessential reporter again, doggedly chasing down the details from the others involved. Shaking her head in wonder, Laura and Keith headed back to the station.

"How do we handle this, Kaz?" Following Laura into her office, Keith was still fighting back his disappointment at arriving on the scene too late to do anything but make sure all their bases were covered.

"How does she do that?"

"What?"

"She's like a trouble magnet…Dan Rather wishes he had that kind of luck." Laura sank down into her chair and stared wide-eyed at the Managing Editor. "Everyday is an adventure: cars, live trucks, explosions, tornadoes, bank robberies, you name the disaster, she's there."

"I don't think…"

"Dallas was peaceful compared to this!" She waved a hand emphatically. "I have to remind myself that I wanted it. I wanted a reporter who would be there when the shit hit the fan. I just had no idea that it was gonna happen all the damn time!" The explanation did nothing to ease the worried frustration.

Keith shrugged. "She is what she is." At his words, Laura felt an ache in her chest, unfamiliar and intense. Ah Chris, what have you done to me? She closed her eyes to gather the professionalism that was her stock in trade and clenched her jaw tight before looking up again. "What do we have and what are our options? Get Kate and Rob in here, let's figure out a way to make this work without making it look like something out of the *National Enquirer.*"

Keith took off his glasses and rubbed his eyes. "Are we gonna release your name? I mean, how do we say our News Director beat the living shit out of the alleged gunman without sounding like, well…"

"Don't you think 'beat the living shit' is a little strong?" she sighed. "I know. It would've been a good story, but I had to fuck it up by getting involved. We're supposed to observe, not participate…There's gotta be a way to make it work."

In the end, there wasn't. Channel 4 and 12 both reported that Laura Kasdan tripped and subdued the armed man, and even though it was just a reader and they showed no video, the point was inferred: Channel 8 manufactured their own news. Kate and Rob tried to tone it down, but it was still sensationalistic, great for ratings but lousy for credibility. The other stations also reported that several of the customers caught inside the bank were considering legal action against the bank and Channel 8. All in all, it was a pretty disastrous news day.

*Sometimes you're the windshield, sometimes you're the bug.* Laura hung up her headset in the control room as Chris and Tom were wrapping up their chat out. Both the Five and Six had been painful to watch even though the bank story only took up less than a minute at the top of each 'cast. *Welcome back, Kaz.*

Returning to her office, Laura shut down the computer and loaded up her briefcase before catching sight of the movie pass tucked in the corner of her desk blotter. *Forgot about that.* She had planned for a rare night off from practice to unwind, and the movie seemed like a good idea. Now Laura wasn't so sure.

"You're not getting out of it." Chris walked in, pulling out her earpiece and wrapping the cord around her hand. "This is a once in a lifetime movie opportunity, the ticket stub alone will be worth money to collectors."

Laura looked up, her eyes rueful. "I'm sorry about your story…and I wasn't trying to get you killed."

"I know that." Her green eyes softened. "It all seemed pretty unreal when it was happening. All because of a busted ATM."

"Chris, if anything had happened to you, I…"

"So how do you wanna work this?" Lisa Tyler swept into Laura's office followed by Kate and Keith. "Get something to eat or what?" Unaware that she had interrupted anything, the Production Manager flopped down on a chair, stretching her legs out in front. "We could meet at Denny's at about nine, eat a few Grand Slams and make it to the theater by eleven."

Laura gave herself a mental shake, readjusting her focus. "Sounds like a plan, but could we post mortem this newscast first? I'd like to bury this one."

For Chris, nothing on earth smelled as comfortable as Denny's. The bacon and coffee aroma made her think of Sunday mornings after church and laughing with her family. Remembering what it was like to wait tables for large groups, she wouldn't let the others harass the waitress, instead organizing the order to make it as easy as possible, slapping Keith's hand when he tried to play with the condiments, and refereeing an argument between Lisa, Trey and Kate over which *Star Wars* movie was the best.

"The first one's not the best, but it's the most important." Lisa was emphatic. "*Terminator 2, Jurassic Park, The Abyss*...frankly, all the really big sci-fi blockbusters don't happen unless George Lucas makes that first movie and forms ILM."

Laura was quiet, but not withdrawn, preferring to let the conversation ebb and flow around her, mixing with the clink of glasses and the sounds coming from the kitchen. "You okay?" Chris's voice came from a point close to her ear.

"Fine." Laura felt a hand on her knee and the muscles of her thigh jump at the contact. Chris smiled sweetly and gave a short brisk rub. "Relax, it's just a movie with some friends. Don't get worked up about it."

"How do you do that?" Laura murmured, feeling waves of calm emanating from the smaller woman.

"It's a gift," Chris said, tongue firmly in cheek as her eyes sparkled merrily, and she turned to Kate to ask her about something. Laura studied the blonde woman's profile, watching her laugh with abandon and gesture to make a point. Most of the heavy on-air makeup was gone, making her appear even younger. The casual charisma was overwhelming, thought Laura, you couldn't help being drawn to the laugh or the warmth. *She could have anyone she wants. Anyone at all.*

"So I get to see the lair of the Kazmanian Devil, hmm?" The movie was over and it was close to three o'clock in the morning. Somehow,

Laura found herself inviting Chris over to her apartment. *You were going to do it someday anyway, and at least it's pretty clean right now.* Laura lifted a wry eyebrow as she unlocked the door and pushed it open, gesturing for Chris to go first.

The blonde reporter didn't know what to expect, except to hope for another piece to the puzzle that was the tall dark News Director. A narrow kitchen sported a breakfast bar that opened up to the living room where all kinds of bookshelves lined the walls, filled with newspapers, magazines, books, CDs, and videotapes. A large TV sat next to a stereo rack and a beta deck next to that. A somewhat battered couch and recliner dominated the middle of the room, and a beautiful oak secretary stood sentry against one wall, open with a laptop computer on the desktop. It was an eclectic room that spoke volumes about its occupant.

Laura crossed her arms and watched Chris wander through the small room, as though waiting for judgement to be passed. The smaller woman stopped at the secretary, drawing a finger across the satiny finish of the golden wood. Green eyes looked up into wary blue ones and smiled. "It suits you."

"It's pretty minimalist."

"Oh, I don't know about that, you seem to have everything you need. Can I see the rest?"

Laura flexed her hands nervously. "There's just the bedroom…" she stopped when Chris raised her eyebrows. "Oh hell, come on."

Flipping on the light, Laura stood back as Chris entered. There were more bookcases, more books and tapes and golf clubs everywhere. A nightstand sat next to the bed, a stack of books on top with more on the floor next to it. "No TV in here?"

"I work in television, I don't want to watch it on my off time," came the dry response, "Want something to drink?"

"Sure, do you have some iced tea?" Chris followed Laura out and into the kitchen.

"Just for you." She opened the refrigerator and pulled out two pitchers, setting them on the counter, then retrieving ice and two glasses. Chris settled on a barstool to watch Laura pour, and smiled slightly when their fingers touched as she took the glass of tea.

"What are you drinking?" Chris asked in mock horror as Laura dispensed the purple contents of the other pitcher into her glass.

"Grape Kool-Aid. I know, it looks disgusting."

"Why?"

"Because it's cold, it's sweet, and it doesn't have caffeine. I keep trading one addiction for another."

"Yeah, but Grape Kool-Aid?"

Laura took a long pull, draining half the glass. "Don't knock it 'til you've tried it."

"I'll take your word for it." Chris slid off the barstool and carried her glass into the living room and Laura followed her, switching off the kitchen light, leaving only the dim lamp on next to the sofa. "What are all these tapes? They're not movies."

"Newscasts, stories, shows I produced…News wonk stuff from the days I actually did the journalism thing."

"Did you ever report?" Chris knew it was stupid, but she had forgotten that Laura didn't just start out as a news director.

"Very briefly; I wasn't very good. You can stop the interview any time now."

Chris set her glass down and reached for Laura's hand. "C'mere. I've wanted to do this all day." There was a slight hesitation from the taller woman before Chris wrapped arms around her in a gentle hug and rested her head over Laura's heart. "I was scared today," she confessed. "Stuff happens to me all the time, but I'm never scared. Today I just…"

Laura felt the smaller woman hiccup back a sob and moved her hands across Chris's back. "Shh, I wouldn't have let him hurt you, I swear." She rested her chin on the blonde head, feeling a sense of contentment she was quite sure she'd never known, and wishing it would last forever. *What happened to 'don't need, don't want?'*

Chris gave a light squeeze and pulled back, her eyes glittering in the dim light. "Where to now, Laura?" She dropped her arms almost apologetically. "I'm sorry, no pressure."

"Don't…you're fine. I'm sorry about today. I wish I'd sent you on the damn cell phone story."

"That might've been worse," she chuckled as she sat down on the sofa and looked up. "What else is bothering you?"

Laura closed her eyes briefly. "When I was in Austin I must've thought of a hundred things I wanted to tell you and now I can't think of a single thing. That's not really like me."

It was quite an admission coming from the dark woman, and Chris tilted her head curiously. "There is one thing I wanted to ask you, and I want you to think carefully before you answer, okay?" Laura nodded. "Why are you so much more bothered by idea of making love, than the idea of being gay? It doesn't seem very consistent."

Dark eyebrows furrowed as Laura considered the question. "You always make me out to be more complicated than I actually am. I have no family to approve or disapprove of my choices, and I try not to make assumptions about myself. You're the first person I've ever been interested in…physically, intellectually and all points in between. For me, that makes a label seem pretty insignificant."

"But what about sex?"

"Oh, that." Laura's smile was self-mocking. "Physical intimacy would be the ultimate invasion of privacy, don't you think? And you said so yourself, I'm the classic introvert...add to that workaholic tendencies and an overwhelming need to maintain control, and you have a recipe for...what was that Lance called me? Oh yeah, an asexual frigid bitch."

Chris considered the information carefully and stood up. "It's not an invasion if you invite someone in."

Laura's breath was shallow as Chris moved closer. Pushing aside years of denial, she reached tentatively for the woman she wanted to be with more than anything else in the world. Green eyes never wavered from her own as she asked in a low murmur, "Will you stay?"

Chris closed her eyes, willing strength to come from somewhere that wasn't clawing her with need. "No. I won't." Laura stopped breathing at the apparent rejection and her eyes clouded with confusion. Then Chris went on, her voice low and slowly seductive, "When we make love for the first time, it'll be when we have plenty of time, not when we both have to be at work in five hours." Taking Laura's hand, she kissed the palm, tracing a pattern with her tongue. "You'll feel things you've never felt before, and wonder how you ever lived without it." Chris leaned forward, pushing aside the collar of Laura's blouse, and laid a line of kisses along the prominent collarbone as the taller woman shuddered. "And you'll need me, the way I need you now." One hand skimmed up a muscled arm to caress an angled jaw, softly touching, almost tickling, before sliding around the strong elegant column of Laura's neck and pulling her head down to barely touch lips. "And you'll want me. You'll ache with wanting me."

The kiss was invasive and rough, filled with the promises of sensations to come and doing nothing to disguise the raw emotion felt by the smaller woman. This was not a gentle exploration, but an act of possession, searing in its intensity. Before Laura could react, Chris broke it off, replacing her lips with gentle fingers. Gasping at the absence of contact, at the overload of feeling, Laura opened her mouth but nothing came out.

"Shhh. You were right about the grape Kool-Aid. It kinda grows on you." And with a smirk, Chris left the apartment, closing the door softly behind her, leaving Laura swaying in the middle of the living room.

*Damn, she's good.*

Chris gave the eyebolt a final twist using a screwdriver as a lever through the large hole. Climbing down from the ladder, she looked at the porch swing she was installing and tried to figure out the best way to hang it. It was Saturday, and after spending the morning and most of the afternoon umpiring little league baseball games, the only thing she wanted to do was sit on her porch and sip a beer. Chris had seen the swing when she stopped at Home Depot and couldn't resist it.

"Can I help you with that?" Dave, her neighbor, leaned over the rail and offered his assistance. "It needs to be level;, I'll hold it up while you hook the chains."

"I'd appreciate that. Julie's flower beds look really nice."

"She works hard on 'em." He grunted slightly as he lifted the swing. "This is a nice one, you're really going to enjoy it."

"I think so." Chris set the hooks, climbed down, and stood back squinting to see if it was even.

"Looks good," Dave said, and Chris smiled at the clipped neighbor-speak. "Can I get you a beer? It's the least I can do."

"Nah, gotta get the fire going. Barbecue night." She watched him amble back across the yard, grateful that she got along with the couple next door and wondering if kids were anywhere on the horizon. It was a quiet neighborhood, and Chris was comfortable with her house and the street she lived on. Just two miles from the station, the location was perfect.

Chris heard the phone ring inside the house and she went to answer it, pleased to hear the low voice on the other end and smiling at the jump in her chest. "How'd you play?"

"I putted well…sunk a few long ones. Didja work some good games?"

"No, it was kinda hard today. Some parents were pretty obnoxious…it got ugly."

"I'm sorry. Bet you'd feel better if I brought you something to eat."

"That's a given, what did you have in mind?" Chris opened the fridge and pulled out a beer, twisted the cap off and flipped it into the trash.

"Peter told me about this rib place that's supposed to have real Texas barbecue. I have to go by the station to check the rundowns, but I could pick some up and be at your place in an hour or so."

"Sounds like a plan. See you in a bit." Chris hung up the phone and let out the breath she hadn't realized she was holding. *It'll be great. We'll sit on the swing and eat ribs. I'll get hot and bothered, take an icy cold shower and lay awake all night. Just another Saturday night on the Chris and Kaz Show.*

She was sitting on the swing when the Jeep pulled up an hour and a half later. One leg was tucked under her and the other was propelling her back and forth. The warm day had given way to a cooler dusk, and

Chris inhaled the clean smell of early summer and lawns being watered as she watched the tall woman walk toward her carrying several bags that added to the aroma surrounding the porch.

Watching Laura walk was becoming one of Chris's favorite guilty pastimes. It was a rolling stride that spoke of an unconscious animal grace, and watching the long legs eat up the sidewalk, she tried to decide if it was the motion or the package that made it enjoyable. Both, all of it, everything. Chris smiled as Laura stepped up to the porch, green eyes narrowing speculatively.

"What?" the news director asked with good-humored irritation.

Chris shook her head, grin still in place. "Just looking." The ever-present khaki shorts exposed long tanned legs and well-worn leather sandals, but instead of a polo shirt she wore a crisp button-down dress shirt the color of her eyes, with long sleeves pushed up past her elbows.

"This is new, I like it." Laura lowered her tall frame down on the swing and placed the bags on the porch near her feet. "Wearing white is probably not a good idea when you're gonna eat barbecued ribs."

"Always the practical one." Chris shifted to face Laura, the gauzy white material of her shirt following the movement, falling in waves to baggy white cotton shorts and offering glimpses of pale gold flesh. "What'd you bring me?"

Teasing green eyes fastened on Laura's and the dark woman sucked in air uncertainly. Are we still talking about food? "Uh, potato salad…coleslaw…beans, I think." She felt disconnected from her body, the flooding emotions so unfamiliar that she wondered exactly where she was.

"Cool, I'll get us something to drink." Chris stood up and disappeared into the house, leaving Laura in a haze on the still moving swing. You're a mess, Kaz. Two days of being virtually ignored by the reporter, no phone conversations, and just a casually issued invitation to 'maybe do something on Saturday' had taken its toll. Thirty-six holes of golf had helped, but not much. *She wasn't kidding about aching.*

"I've got root beer…no caffeine, right?" Chris reappeared with a stack of napkins and two brown icy bottles.

"Root beer and ribs, you could almost be a Texan."

"Hey, I'll have you know that thirty Tennesseeans died at the Alamo. We oughta be honorary Texans anyway." She settled down on the swing and started digging in the bags to unwrap the steaming barbecue. "This smells fabulous." Plastic forks were laid out and Chris got to the business of eating. The smaller woman's appetite was legendary at the station, and Laura was constantly amazed at the amount of food she could put away.

"You're not eating," Chris observed, licking some sauce off her thumb.

"Sure I am, my eating habits just pale in comparison." They continued the meal with little conversation, Laura picking at her food, Chris devouring hers.

"It's gonna take a week for me to get this stuff off my hands." She used a napkin to wipe off more sauce and took a sip of root beer. "But it's worth it." Sighing, she wadded up the last of the trash and stuck it in a bag. "What are you doing tomorrow…Oh, lemme guess: golf, golf, and more golf."

"I am nothing if not predictable." Laura's tone was dry. "Sunday means softball for you, I guess."

"Yep, we're playing Channel 12." She put an elbow on the back of the swing and reached for a tendril of dark hair to twist around her finger. "You could come out and play too."

"Maybe." Laura felt the pull and a tingle where Chris's finger brushed. "I uh, have to practice." She could feel her skin flush as the smaller woman leaned in closer. An exotically floral scent tickled her nose and she closed her eyes halfway.

"Why?" Chris asked as she slid questing fingers across a strong jaw and then down the line of Laura's throat.

"Because the mechanics of my swing…have to be…maintained…Oh hell." She gave in to the need to feel Chris's mouth under hers and bowed her head, tracing lips with the tip of her tongue and begging for entry. The taste and feel was becoming more familiar, the wave of heat was not.

*I will not lose control.* Chris battled and held onto a thread of her sanity as a delicious sweetness coursed through her body. *This isn't possible, not from just a kiss.* With an abruptness that made her gasp, it ended, and she was left blinking at blue eyes. "We…What…You are dangerous."

"I'm sorry…" Laura gulped.

*Oh god, not again.* Chris closed her eyes in pain.

"This is kinda public…could we go inside?" Laura was breathing heavily as she stood up and pulled the blonde woman to her feet.

"Inside?" Chris whispered, "Are you sure?"

Laura swallowed. "Oh yeah." Chris searched behind her back and fumbled with the door handle, stumbling over the threshold as she pushed it open. She drew the tall woman inside and enfolded her in another kiss and their bodies crushed together. Her hands moved to broad shoulders, and she felt hands move across her back reaching under the loose shirt to finally come in contact with more intimate flesh.

"Bed?" Chris said against the side of Laura's mouth.

"Now." Laura moved to nibble lightly on the blonde woman's neck. They bumped down the walls of the hall still kissing, hands racing to acquaint themselves with the feel of each other. Breaking apart, Chris gasped as they finally fell through the door of the bedroom.

Somehow they made it to the bed and Chris pushed Laura back against the pillows, stopping the frantic pace with her hands against the tall woman's shoulders. "Slow…we have time."

"I don't know how to…" Embarrassment flickered across Laura's face. "This is all new to me." She gave a shy half smile and Chris felt her heart swell.

"S'okay, we'll just go nice and slow." She leaned down to place a kiss in the hollow of a tanned throat. "As slow as I possibly can." She unbuttoned the top two buttons of Laura's shirt. "For as long as I can." Lips followed the trail of buttons as they were undone down to the edge of the khaki shorts. Chris pushed the fabric aside, exposing creamy white skin that contrasted sharply with the tan of Laura's arms. Chris eased herself up until she covered most of Laura's body with her own and looked down into blazing blue eyes, smiling softly. "What do you want?"

The world moved quickly for Chris as Laura grasped the smaller woman's hips and spun her so that they were lying side by side. For a while, Laura didn't answer. She touched the white fabric of the other woman's blouse, and after looking into green eyes for permission, began to remove it, revealing a golden expanse of smooth skin. "I want you to make me feel…everything."

Chris's nimble hands proceeded to do just that. Clothes were removed and flesh slid against flesh, creating friction that inflamed already heated senses. When Chris slipped her knee between the tall woman's thighs and followed it with an insistent touch, Laura gasped, fighting to breathe. There isn't enough air. A warmth like nothing she'd ever felt before began curling up from the center of her body, and she arched into Chris, her hands grasping a strong back as a blonde head burrowed into her chest.

When her release came, Laura didn't cry out; instead, she fought for control through the blinding explosion of passion, clenching her jaw as shuddering tremors wracked her body. Slowly, the world returned to normal, and as Chris tried to ease back, Laura gave a slight squeeze. "Don't go."

The blonde woman looked down into blue eyes awash in passion and felt a wave of something so intense she almost wept. *She chose me. She could have had anyone on earth, and she chose me.* "I'm not going anywhere," she murmured.

Laura looked up at the ceiling and swallowed. *So this is what all the fuss is about.* Turning back to Chris, she gave her a lopsided smile. "Nobody told me," she whispered as a pleased grin spread across the younger woman's face. A thought suddenly occurred to Laura and her brow creased in consternation. "What about you, I can…"

"Sshhh, it's okay." She kissed Laura's forehead gently, smoothing the dark bangs.

"No, it's not. I want to make you feel too. Show me how." Laura took the initiative, drawing a finger down the center of Chris's abdomen and watched the surface ripple in response. Fascinated, she became more adventurous as Chris played willing instructor to her tentative explorations. The blonde woman was all firm muscle and feminine grace, an even tan covering her body, and the more Laura touched and tasted, the more she wanted to give to Chris.

"Tell me…" Laura ground out, catching Chris's earlobe between her teeth.

"You're…doing…fine…Jesus, Kaz!" Inordinately pleased, Laura felt well manicured nails dig into her back as Chris bucked against her, breath hissing through clenched teeth. Panting slightly, she held the smaller woman until the shaking subsided, feeling a calm wrap around the two of them. Recognizing an unfamiliar peace, she turned and offered up another part of herself to Chris with a smile behind the words. "I guess you can call me Laura."

Chris chuckled lazily. "I kinda like Kaz for special occasions." And she pulled Laura into a slow, deep kiss.

All her appetites sated, Chris wrapped herself around the taller woman, the fingers of one hand still lightly stroking the hollow of Laura's throat. Reaching down, Laura pulled up the comforter to cover them both. Deep, even breathing told her that Chris was close to sleep, and she tightened her hold.

*You are in big trouble. One addiction for another, huh Kaz?*

*"Never carry more into a TV station than you can carry out in one box, running."*

# Aftermath

For such a small woman, Chris managed to take up a good deal of her king-sized bed. Sprawled on her stomach with her arms stretched out, she laid claim to most of the space, leaving just a sliver of room on one side for Laura to sleep on, which was fine, since, once she was asleep, the tall woman didn't move much. Unfamiliar sounds and smells woke Laura as light was beginning to fill the room, and she felt the soft steps of Chris's cat on the foot of the bed, investigating the strange presence in his territory.

She slid out of the bed and, uncomfortable naked, found her shirt and slipped it on before going to the bathroom. Chris watched her leave through slitted eyes, wondering what was next. *Leave or stay, it's up to you. Please stay*. She watched Laura return to stand in the doorway, her hands gripping the frame and hesitating before padding back to the bed to slide under the sheets. Chris smiled when startled blue eyes turned to meet hers. "You stayed," she said softly.

Laura licked her lower lip uncertainly. "I…Good morning."

Chris rolled onto her side and took Laura's hands into her own, lacing their fingers together. "How are you?"

Pausing a moment to take stock, she considered the question. "I feel good."

Chris moved closer and pressed a light kiss on full lips, the rough texture of Laura's shirt scraping on her bare skin as she closed the distance between them. "Oh, I beg to differ…you feel great," she murmured.

Nerves and practicality won out over a sudden jolt of arousal and Laura gave voice to the question that had chased around her brain since she fell asleep with Chris wrapped around her. "Where do we go from here?"

"Do we have to go anywhere? Can't we just stay here all day?" Chris mumbled into a warm shoulder, her fingertips brushing the edge of Laura's ribs underneath the starched shirt.

"That tickles…I have to practice, and you have softball…You're making…it hard to…think." Laura gently stopped a traveling hand and turned, sliding a strong thigh across the lower half of Chris's body. Raising a hand, she rubbed her thumb against the smaller woman's jaw. "So smooth, so beautiful," she whispered. "Can you feel what you're doing to me?"

"Yes." Green eyes glittered like jewels, hiding nothing.

"Good," Laura murmured. "Turnabout is fair play." She bent her head to capture Chris's lips, fastening on the fullness as her hands began to prowl over golden skin. She touched with reverence, from breasts to ribs to hip and lower still, following with lips and mouth eager to taste everything. *It's not enough.* Laura couldn't control the slight shaking in her hands as she moved them from one point to the other, spanning the blonde woman's waist, dipping her thumbs into the well of her navel, and teasing the hollow of her hip. *It'll never be enough.*

Gasping at the sensations running riot, Chris reached for Laura as she moved lower and surged into the other woman, her hands begging for purchase on sinewy arms and shoulders as spasms shook her from head to toe.

Chris fell back on the bed, breathing raggedly as she felt sheets of perspiration peel away from her overheated body. "For a first timer, you're pretty good at this," she managed to get out, closing her eyes because it was too much effort to keep them open.

"Didja think you were the only one who could research?" Laura laid her cheek on a firm abdomen, watching as a few aftershocks trembled across the surface and marveled that she was the one who caused them. "So…I didn't disappoint?"

Chris heard the uncertainty in the low voice, and wondered again at all the contradictions. "God no, Laura." She threaded the fingers of one hand through the dark silky hair that tickled her belly. "It's…" *It's what? Beyond anything you've ever felt before? Tell her that and she's outta here.* "You have no idea what you've done to me," she said with quiet wonder. And with that, Chris realized she was in love, and had been for quite some time.

"No, really…I have to go. My Jeep's been in your driveway all night." Laura wiggled her feet into sandals and stood, tucking her shirt into wrinkled shorts. *I am not running…I just have to think.* "If we're gonna…ah, we need to figure out how…" She stopped, rubbing nervous hands through her hair. "You're not listening."

"Yes I am. What's your Jeep got to do with anything?" Chris sat up against the headboard, pulling the sheet up against the chill from the air conditioner. It was endearing, Chris mused, watching the normally composed News Director fumble around the bedroom gathering clothes and dressing with awkward shyness. This was the same woman who could quell a newsroom argument with just a look, or make Corporate cough up not one, but two brand-new hundred thousand dollar live trucks.

"Goddammit, Chris!" This was a bad sign though, the blonde woman thought. Laura was usually articulate enough not to resort to swearing except when she was *really* disturbed. "I didn't think this through…I should've been more careful." Worried blue eyes finally looked at Chris. "I didn't think about being careful…"

The warm feeling evaporated abruptly. "Don't you dare say you're sorry." Chris scrambled out of the bed grabbing her robe and jamming herself into it angrily.

"No, no, no. I'm not sorry, I just…" Laura looked down at Chris belting the terrycloth around her waist, the hurt obvious in the stiffness of her shoulders. "I never had a private life before. I don't know how to keep one private. If this got out at the station, I couldn't protect you."

"We talked about that."

"No, we glossed over it." Laura rubbed a hand over her forehead, willing the words to make sense. *How do I do this? How do I handle any of this? How do I say I'm scared for her and what could happen?*

"Don't." A smaller hand touched Laura's wrist, stopping the nervous motion. "You're overthinking again. No one's checking my driveway to see who's staying overnight, at least I don't think so. We'll be discreet…necking on the porch in the future is probably out." Chris pulled the tall woman close, laying her head in the hollow of her shoulder, feeling the tension ease ever so slightly as she wrapped her arms around a narrow waist. "But I'm not giving this up. Tell me that you won't either."

Laura closed her eyes, rubbing her chin on the soft gold hair as she felt the worry fade away under the quiet confidence of her lover. *My lover? I never thought I'd have one of those.* "Okay, I won't."

"See, that wasn't hard. Now go play golf, or whatever it is you do when you run off on me."

"I don't..."

"Yes, you do." Chris pushed away regretfully. "I've got some things to take care of before my game." *Time for another trip to the batting cages.* Placing her hand on the small of Laura's back, she propelled her down the hall to the front door. "Whatever you want to do later, I'm up for it, just let me know." She stood on tiptoe to press a feather-light kiss on the taller woman's jaw, promising herself to take out this newfound love and examine it later. Right now, she could only let go.

Standing at the door, Chris watched Laura skip down the steps and stop before spinning around and coming back. "Did you forget something?"

A wicked lopsided smile took up residence on the tall woman's face and Chris raised an eyebrow in question. "I'll blow off golf if you'll skip softball."

"Looks like a rainout to me," Chris drawled.

*Mondays suck.* Chris stood in the middle of a muddy field, her feet encased in rubber boots, staring at a metal pipe contraption that was the subject of her story while Jody tried to shoot it in a way that might be visually compelling. Contaminated wells weren't very compelling unless you had to drink from them, Chris thought, then chided herself for her lack of compassion. She'd gotten two interviews and had enough for a package; she just couldn't work up any enthusiasm.

The rain had come around midnight, starting at about the same time that Laura left the warm confines of the king-sized bed. The steady drizzle matched her unusually somber mood and complemented her troubled thoughts. *Things are different now.* The inherent dangers of a boss/employee relationship mixed with Laura's emotional awakening made Chris nervous. Very nervous.

Beyond a shadow of a doubt, Chris knew what she wanted, all six feet and blue-eyed muscle of it. But getting from point A to point B was going to require more patience than she was sure she possessed. In the morning meeting, the news director had been withdrawn, barely grunting in response to questions from Keith and the producers, hands flexing nervously, never stopping their movement, and she had never once met the blonde reporter's eyes. She'd had time to think, Chris concluded, and now Laura was back behind the walls shoring up her defenses.

Chris tilted her head back to look at the gunmetal gray sky and licked the moisture from her lips as the rain continued to fall. *I'm setting myself up for some kind of hurt. Heartbreaking, soul rending, never get over it kind of hurt.*

"Got it." Jody unlocked the camera from the tripod and held it in one hand while he flipped the legs closed with a jerk. "Here, lemme help," Chris offered, shaking off her pensiveness and taking the camera. It was Jody's first day back as a shooter and the blonde reporter was feeling a little guilty that he'd gotten stuck with such a dog of a story. They started back across the field, the thick red mud squelching around their boots as they made their way back to the gravel road and the news unit parked there. After scraping them off as much as possible, they dumped the boots in the back and climbed in. The two-way radio squawked impatiently and Jody picked up the handset. "Newsroom to unit 2, what's your ETA?"

Jody thumbed the switch, "We're looking at about thirty minutes."

"10-4." The photographer twisted the key in the ignition, but instead of the engine coming to life, there was only the whining grind of a car that refused to start. "Well, this sucks," Jody muttered.

"We need to send a tow out to Gilliam; unit 2 is dead," Janie called across the newsroom to Keith. For a minute there was undisguised panic in the Managing Editor's eyes. "Dead or crashed?"

Laura came out of her office like a shot. "Did someone say crashed?"

"No one said crashed!" Janie shook her head, bangs bobbing from side to side. "Jody can't get it started, we need to send a tow. I'm calling Jimmy Watson; he's close, so it shouldn't take too long."

Nodding with relief, Laura went back to her office, swallowing back a remnant of fear. *This is absurd...it was a friggin' well story. She isn't a child.* Long fingers raked through dark hair as she faced the window that looked out over the studio. *So many changes.* She gave a snort and crossed her arms. It was supposed to get easier, right? When she left the night before, everything was fine. Then the second-guessing started, and, unable to sleep, she paced the apartment obsessing over questions with no easy answers.

*What the hell am I doing?*

*How do I work with her?*

*How do I treat her at work?*

*How will she treat me?*

*How do we keep it private?*

*Will anyone notice?*

*And when can we do it again?*

With a sigh, Laura turned back to her desk. She was supposed to have lunch with Art and the station's lawyers to go over some pending cases and she wanted to be prepared. The timing for this meeting left a lot to be desired since sweeps should have taken priority. *Ah well, I could be out in Gilliam waiting on a tow truck with Chris.* At that moment, it didn't sound too bad.

The tow truck delay meant that it was almost twelve when Chris and Jody got back to the station. Jody ran to cut a VO, raw video for the anchor to voiceover during the noon newscast, and Chris returned to the newsroom, dropping her muddy boots by the door. In a sort of odd lull in the day, Janie was the only staff member around and Chris gave a brief wave as she tossed her things on the desk. Messages were stacked up on her keyboard and she was flipping through them when the News Director's office opened and a nightmare that Chris had hoped she'd never have to experience began to unfold. Looking up, she ground her teeth together, powerless to stop what was coming. *I know that laugh.*

Four people came out of Laura's office, but the reporter had eyes for only two of them. *Old flame, new love...What are the chances? With my luck, pretty good.* The woman smiling at Art Dement was elegance and sophistication wrapped up in a raw silk suit of emerald green. In heels she was almost as tall as Laura, with long shapely legs that went on forever and auburn hair swept smoothly into a knot at the base of an aristocratic neck. Whatever else had burned between them, Erica Lambert made Chris feel short and awkward. She always had.

"Steven, Erica, this is Christine Hanson, one of our Six O'clock anchors." Art was in an expansive, show-off mood, happy to have on-air talent around with which to impress the visitors. "Chris, this is Steven Poteet and Erica Lambert. They take care of the legal matters for the station." The reporter dug up a charming smile and turned it on despite the fact that she could feel every drop of blood draining from her face. *Sell this...Don't give her the satisfaction.* "Steven, it's a pleasure...Erica, nice to see you again." She looked over at the News Director and explained, "I interviewed Ms. Lambert for a story a while back." Erica's beauty was unblemished, but for the first time, Chris could see a hardness that was beginning to take over the looks that were so carefully maintained.

The elegant lawyer turned a mocking smile on Chris, her dark eyes half lidded. "Anchoring certainly agrees with you Chrissy; you look good, though I see you still go stomping around in the mud." She looked pointedly at the dried brown spatters on the legs of the reporter's dark blue slacks.

Chris gave a broad smile, every inch the anchor trying to cover an on-air glitch while she watched her world spin out of control. "Part of the job; besides, what's a little mud? If you'll excuse me, I have a story to deal with. Nice meeting you, Steven." She gathered up her notebook and left the newsroom, avoiding the blue eyes that followed her questioningly, concentrating on getting to the hallway without falling apart.

Laura had never seen Chris so cold before. If she hadn't seen the exchange herself, she would never have believed it. An uncomfortable realization twisted around her gut. *Jeez, Kaz, you are dense. Bet this isn't something you've thought about.* The lawyer turned and regarded her evenly for a second before laughing at something Art said, and Laura knew with bone-deep conviction that this woman was a very dangerous enemy. Almost absently she broke into the conversation. "We have reservations at my club for twelve-thirty, so we should head on over there."

"Yeah, Steven, Kaz has qualified for the U.S. Open in Mississippi next month. It's been quite a boost for sales…an unexpected benefit." Art was showing off again.

"You're quite the athlete, Ms. Kasdan." Erica's tone was smooth but lacking anything that might be called warmth.

"I've worked hard to become so. Art, will we be taking the Lexus?" And she gestured for them to go on down the stairs.

Chris used a damp paper towel to wipe the dry mud off of her pants, acknowledging the bite of humiliation as she brushed the material clean. The door opened and she looked up when Kate came in, then bent back to the task at hand. The producer touched the smaller woman's shoulder apologetically. "When she came in, you and Jody hadn't made it back yet. I would have warned you but I just stepped out for a minute…God, Chris, I'm sorry."

"Shit happens." She tossed the paper towel into the trash and ran water to wash her hands. "I just didn't need to see her," Chris muttered. *Not now.*

"Yeah well, you've got bigger problems if she's gonna be handling the station legal stuff. This is the lawyer who'll be advising them on talent issues. It's a can of worms, Chris. And you're pretty exposed here."

*You have no idea.* Chris grabbed two fistfuls of pale gold hair as she considered the issue. Erica could make things difficult, but only if she could get something out of it. *Because that's the way she works, isn't it? Everybody uses everybody else, right?* "I can't deal with this now; Jody and I have to go out again." She ruffed her hair back into order and straightened her blouse. "Thanks, Kate."

"What are you going to do?"

"Nothing I can do," Chris answered honestly. "We'll see how it plays out."

The one advantage that Laura had was that she'd talked Art into having the lunch at Northridge, and it was more than a little comforting to be on her own turf. Steven Poteet was very entertaining and it was easy to see why he was a successful attorney. He orchestrated the conversation easily, flattering the General Manager and speaking knowledgeably about news and golf. He wasn't as oily as some attorneys she knew, but Laura was certain he could hold his own in a court of law.

As for Erica, there was certain hypnotic charm about the elegant woman. She was at turns seductive, inquiring, amusing, and intelligent with a wry sense of humor that the News Director could have appreciated if she didn't have the sickening feeling that the lawyer and Chris had a history. Jealousy was an emotion as foreign to her as physical desire had been a week ago, and she didn't appreciate expanding the horizons to this new hypersensitized state.

The dishes were cleared after the excellent meal and Steven laid out a folder, painstakingly taking them through the half dozen pending cases and discussing where they stood. It was incredibly boring, and even Laura's powers of concentration were stretched to the breaking point. Eventually everything was discussed, dissected, and covered. Steven packed up his files neatly and gathered the notes that Erica had meticulously taken, placing them into a briefcase before drawing out several cigar tubes. I'm not being exclusive here, ladies, would you like to join us in the cigar bar for a few minutes?"

Laura smirked at the boys' club mentality, but before she could reply, Erica cut in. "If you're going to light up the stinky sticks, I'll pass. What about you, Laura?"

"Call me Kaz, and I think I'll stay here as well." Figuring that this had been the plan all along, she watched as the men went up the stairs, then turned to face the other woman. "Would you care for some coffee? They do a nice cappuccino here."

"I'll take some decaf." Laura motioned the waitress over and watched as she poured from a silver service into Erica's cup, then covered her own to decline. The lawyer sipped the dark liquid and studied the News Director frankly. "You're not at all what I was expecting."

"And what was that?" Laura raised one eyebrow.

"A hot-headed bitch, if you'll pardon me. Your reputation had a lot to do with that, of course. A woman doesn't get to be a news director in a top ten market without cracking a few heads, but I did not expect such a thoughtful planner, or someone so young."

*Where is this going?* Laura smiled tightly. "You're not exactly ancient yourself. How long have you been with Barnes and Poteet?"

"Eight months. It was a good move for me; I have a realistic chance to make partner. What are your plans? I can't see you staying in Burkett Falls forever."

"I'll serve my corporate masters wherever they want me."

Erica nodded, "At least for three years until your ship comes in. I would assume that this is the best offer you could get after Dallas."

Laura remembered in that instant why it wasn't a good idea to play word games with a lawyer. "I don't see why that should concern you at all."

Erica folded her hands and tilted her head. "It concerns me because this is one of my biggest clients. My success is tied to the station's success and, by extension, to yours as well. It's important that you understand that."

"I think you've made yourself clear," came the dry response.

"How well do you know Christine Hanson?"

Laura's expression remained neutral. "I think she's the best reporter/anchor in the market. Certainly the hardest working."

"Mmm." Erica nodded. "Are you aware that she carries some…baggage?" Dark eyes glittered with malicious intent and Laura steeled her own gaze as she recognized the adversarial turn the discussion had taken. *Baggage?* Sitting up straighter, the News Director decided that Erica should have chosen a better word and a better target.

"Baggage?"

"This isn't Dallas, Kaz. It's much more conservative." Her point made, Erica waited for a reaction.

"I see." Laura leaned back in her chair and steepled her fingers. "Let's cut to the chase, shall we? You're the lawyer, let me lay something out for you. Let's say I have a high profile anchor that happens to be gay. As her supervisor and according to her contract, I am already aware of this and it's not a problem as far as I'm concerned. But suppose we yank her off the air for no reason other than small minds, and she brings in a high-powered lawyer to sue the socks off the station for discrimination because the ratings aren't affected at all. Maybe it's even a test case and it generates national media exposure. Do you want to be heading up the team that tries to sort out *that* public relations nightmare?" Laura's eyes went blue-white with controlled rage. "All this is hypothetical, of course. If we're all tied to the station's success, you would do well to let me run the news department and stick to keeping us out of court. How much Willy-Simon stock did you get, anyway, Erica?"

"Oh, very good, Kaz. Corporate was right about you." Another sip of coffee and a smile praising the News Director's perceptiveness. "Definitely a keeper. Is it just the money, or something more? What happens in three years, do you chuck it all to go play golf? What was the deal?"

Laura smiled coldly. "My deal, my concern." She decided to press one more point, allowing the anger to bubble free. "Whatever happened between you and Chris is your own personal business." Erica's dark eyes narrowed. *Bingo,* Laura thought. "If I find that it has any bearing on the way that you conduct business on behalf of the station, I will do everything in my power to see that WBFC terminates its relationship with Barnes and Poteet. Have I made myself clear?"

The lawyer lifted her chin. "Perfectly. You walk a fine line, Ms. Kasdan. Pray you don't stumble."

Laura barely made it back to the station in time to be violently ill, the heaves continuing even after there was nothing left. Bracing her arms against the opposite walls of the stall, she hung there knowing that it wasn't the confrontation, it was the idea that she was enough like Erica to be repulsed by the similarities.

*You told Chris you'd take her off the air, remember? That's just the way the business is. Why didn't you give Chris her options? The only thing that matters is the station, that's why. Erica wants to be a partner, what do you want? Will you really quit in three years if they make you GM in Dallas, or is that the going rate for your soul these days? You took the deal...three years in exile for KDAL. They don't know you have other plans. You're as twisted as she is.*

She straightened shakily and pushed out of the stall, rinsing her hands, face, and mouth with cold water. The stranger that stared back from the mirror bore no likeness to the woman she remembered from Sunday. That Laura Kasdan had been almost giddy, awash in a happiness that hadn't survived past the door of the newsroom. *And that's the real problem isn't it? Now you know what it's like to feel and you miss it when it's gone.* She scrubbed a hand across her face, blowing an impatient breath.

*Chris and Erica...Now that hurts.* Remembering the way the color had drained from the blonde reporter's face, Laura rubbed the heel of her hand along her breastbone as though that could soothe the ache in her chest, and considered the implications, giving free reign to the jealousy that wormed its way up from wherever it had lain dormant for a lifetime. *Everything we did, Chris did with her and probably then some. Erica would know what she was doing...in the same bed...deal with that.* The picture that presented itself was almost enough to make the News Director start heaving again.

*Enough!*

With strength of will born from years of discipline, she shook off the offending emotion. *It's after five, go watch the news, it would be nice if you could contribute to some part of the process today*. Pulling the door open, she left the ladies' room and headed down the hall.

A half-hour newscast is exactly that: one half hour of time that is filled precisely. For those who participate, there is no escape until thirty minutes have passed. Time is measured out story by story, segment by segment, and even the commercial breaks are merely breaths taken before the content runs its course.

Chris rolled her eyes and leaned back in her chair, bored and twitchy. Kurt was doing his weather segment and she had three and a half minutes to simply exist until she was on again, held hostage by the format of the 'cast. Tom was marking his scripts and practicing his facial expressions, tilting his head in silent emphasis and mouthing the words as he went. For a minute Chris thought she might laugh at the absurdity of it all, then the voice in her ear spoke up and she had to focus on getting through the end of the show.

"He's wrapping, Camera Two, you're clear, get a cross shot on Chris, Camera One, gimme a three shot. We're on graphics."

"'Textbooks' is dead, 'animal control' is dead..." Kate read the list of stories dropped for time. "Thirteen and fourteen are dead."

Chat, chat, turn, and read. The rest of the newscast crawled by with no major problems and eventually it went to black and Lisa dismissed the crew, freeing the hostages until they regrouped to do it all again at ten o'clock.

Laura sat through the post-mortem leaning back in her chair, long legs stretched out over one corner of the desk. Her chin rested between the space of her thumb and forefinger, propped up by an elbow on the armrest, but the pose was deceptive since there wasn't a relaxed bone in her body. She kept silent and nodded briefly when the meeting came to an end, content to let them leave while she continued to brood.

"Are you gonna go home, or just think dark thoughts all night?" Chris stood in the doorway hesitantly, briefcase slung over one shoulder. "Must've been some meeting." The office wasn't her first choice as place to clear the air, but it would have to do.

"It was." Laura ran her tongue across her teeth thoughtfully and sighed. "What happened this afternoon?" She picked up a stack of pink paper. "I have three repair requests signed by you and a workman's comp claim from St. Joe's. I was gone for what, five hours? You were busy."

"Ah, those." Chris shrugged ruefully. "I dropped Jody's camera; it's okay though, just a circuit. The board in the audio booth fried while I was cutting my package…that will take a little longer to fix, and I'm real sorry about the live truck, but that one's not my fault."

"The live truck?" Laura forced down another surge of anxiety.

"Um, yeah. Jason scraped part of the microwave dish off on a low overhang at the sheriff's car barn. He should have had enough clearance, but the door to the garage was down a little ways. I signed the repair request because he took Jody to the hospital since I'm not allowed to drive station vehicles."

"Jody went to the hospital?" The pain in her stomach was getting worse.

"We were out getting a standup and there was this bee. I mean, it was just a little sweat bee or something, anyway, I tried to shoo it away but it stung Jody and he's allergic…" she trailed off, running a hand through her hair and grimacing. "Not a particularly good day."

*No, it wasn't.* "You forgot to mention the part about your new girlfriend having lunch with your old girlfriend." Laura was careful not to accuse, just to state a fact, but the clenching muscle in her jaw gave her away.

"Well, there's that too. Sometimes it sucks to be me." Chris could feel the embarrassed heat on her neck and looked away, wondering about the hurt inflicted on both of them.

Her face impassive, Laura drew her long legs off the desk and stood up switching off her computer monitor. Deciding against taking any work home, she left the briefcase in the corner and came out from behind the desk. "Come on over to my place," she said in almost an offhand manner. "I'll fix us something to eat and we'll talk."

Chris could almost see a ray of light on an otherwise bleak landscape. "Pardon my surprise, but you cook?"

"I've been eating for years; someone's gotta do it." Laura followed the blonde woman out of the office and locked the door behind her.

Chris stared into Laura's refrigerator with dumbfounded awe. There wasn't any food at all but every kind of beverage seemed to be represented, except for the red and white cans of her boss's beloved Coke. Bottles, cans, and pitchers of liquid took up every available space on all three shelves. Puzzled, she stole a glance at the woman who was busy sautéing chicken pieces and her mouth twitched into a smile. "Do you have a drinking problem?"

Laura chuckled softly. "Ah, my secret's out. As much golf as I play, I run the risk of dehydration, so I drink a lot. Since I'm off Coke, I'm trying a bunch of other stuff."

"But there's no food in here." Chris took a guess and pulled out a pitcher and congratulated herself on her selection as she poured tea over a glass of ice.

"Hate to tell ya, but you'll die of thirst before you starve to death. Just call me prepared." The chicken sizzled as she stirred it, and Laura turned down the heat. She jerked a little when she felt Chris's chin on her shoulder, peeking over at the selection of food cooking on the stove. "So what are we having?"

"Uh, chicken alfredo. One of two things, no, make that three, counting Kraft Macaroni and Cheese, that I can cook."

"It smells good."

"I haven't poisoned myself yet." She whisked the sauce as it thickened, careful not to let it stick, then pulled it off the burner. As with everything else she did, Laura was efficient in the kitchen. All the dirty utensils were rinsed and placed in the sink as she methodically prepared the meal and cleaned as she went along. The pasta was drained and distributed on two plates, then the chicken, followed by the sauce. "Go ahead and sit down. I've got some bread, too." She set out everything they needed and Chris saw the quiet loner again, spartan even in the way she entertained.

Chris settled onto one of the barstools and picked up a fork. "This is fabulous. Who knew?"

"Who indeed." *When did we become so formal?* Her drink of choice tonight was some kind of bottled lemonade, and Laura shook it before breaking the seal with a pop. Sitting down across from Chris, she took a slice of bread and started eating, but mostly she just pushed the food around on her plate.

Finally, Chris couldn't stand it. "How did you know?" The question was asked quietly and with dread. When blue eyes met hers, the expression was wry. "Let's just say that neither one of you has a poker face and back in my office you didn't correct me."

"Oh," Chris answered, thinking that there was apparently no end to the humiliation the lawyer was going to cause her. "What did she say?"

Laura's smile was tight and humorless. "Well, once the men disappeared into the cigar bar, she outed you and threatened me. I threatened back and we agreed not to be friends. Other than that, she was a delightful woman and a sharp dresser."

Miserable, Chris pushed her plate away and covered her mouth with one hand. "What's next then, am I off the air?"

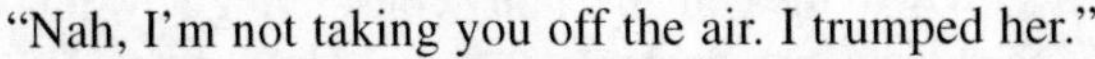

"Nah, I'm not taking you off the air. I trumped her."

"You what? Trumped her?"

"Yeah." With a smug grin, Laura came around to the other side of the bar and pulled Chris to her feet. "I was reminded that a woman does not get to be a news director in a top ten market without cracking some heads, so I started swinging. I laid out a possible scenario that included a lawsuit and lots of bad publicity and other nasty stuff and she backed down. I think she was just trying to make things hard for you. I don't think Steve knows anything or was putting any pressure on since I didn't get a summons from Art." She paused, considering the consequences of what she was about to say next. "Remember when I told you I'd take you off the air? If that ever happens you have options. Legal options. Right now no one knows or cares, so we just maintain the status quo." Laura gently used a thumb to brush the moisture from under Chris's eyes.

"So that's it?"

"We just wait for the book, Chris. We all live and die by those numbers. We'll have the market research done at the end of the month too. If I'm right and we've done our jobs, there won't be anything to worry about."

"And if you're wrong?" Chris tangled a hand in the opening of Laura's shirt before looking up and feeling a catch in her throat when she saw the bitter smile.

"Probably a big management change before November. I'll be gone, Art, Elly, and Mark, the General Sales Manager."

"Just like that?"

"Just like that. Never carry more into a TV station than you can carry out in one box, running." Laura felt the snort of laughter against her shoulder and took a breath. "So, did you love her? No wait, you don't have to answer. That was incredibly presumptuous of me."

"Why is that presumptuous?"

"Because…it's your past, not mine? No. It shouldn't make any difference? No… Because it doesn't matter?" Laura wasn't even aware that she was thinking out loud, then blue eyes snapped emphatically. "Fuck yes it matters." Unable and unwilling to explain any more than that, she gave a half shrug. "Did you?"

Chris smiled, intrigued by the rambling display of the News Director's thought process, then reluctantly pushed away from the comfort of the taller woman's body. Try as she might, the only emotions she could associate with Erica were humiliation and anger, and those paled to insignificance against what she felt for Laura. "No. I never did."

"So…" Her question answered, Laura had no idea what to do next. She leaned against the counter, crossing her arms. "What happened?"

Chris moved slowly to the couch, calmly considering how much to tell. Erica hadn't been just a personal mistake, she'd been a professional mistake as well, and the parallels between then and now were unnerving. *At least you're consistent.* "I was stupid and I got burned." Easing down onto the sofa, she tucked her legs under her. "We had an incident." She paused, pulling at an earlobe nervously. "About nine months ago, a suspect in custody of the Burkett Falls PD was beaten pretty badly. The guy said it was one of the arresting officers, and when they started the investigation, they found one other officer that backed up the suspect's story."

Laura remained silent, wondering what one had to do with the other.

"Jerry had me working the police beat then, so I was doing background checks on the officers involved. I found out some stuff on the cop who was supposed to testify against the officer accused of the beating, and I…" Chris shook her head slightly in bitter memory. "I shot my mouth off to Erica. She gave the information to the head of the officer's defense team, and they got the witness to recant."

Chris raised her eyes and they were filled with self-disgust. "You see, the witness had a kid by his mistress and he was the son-in-law of one of the city councilmen. They told him that if he testified, all of that would come out, so he turned chicken, and the dirty cop walked."

"What about Erica?"

Chris snorted. "Erica got an offer from the firm that handled the cop's defense…Barnes and Poteet." Her lips twitched at Laura's startled expression. "She cut a deal on information I supplied and didn't think there was a problem with it."

Laura couldn't think of a single thing to say.

"She always said everybody uses everybody else and you had to get yours before it was all gone. It would have been sleazy to report about that guy's affair, so we weren't going to say anything. It was just a conversation, with someone I thought I could trust because we were…well, you know…" Chris let out a breath. "So anyway, I don't talk about my stories outside the newsroom anymore."

"God, Chris, I thought it'd be something simple like she dumped you."

That got a short laugh. "Hey, this is me we're talking about. Nothing's ever simple." Laura hadn't moved from her position against the counter, and the distance between them seemed to be growing. Chris looked down, studying a pattern in the carpet. "How freaked out are you about this?"

"Significantly."

"Well, what bothers you the most, the fact that I got a dirty cop off, or that I compromised a story?"

Laura winced, not wanting to sound naïve but knowing she would. "Ah, the fact that you and Erica were…close."

Chris jerked her head up with the realization that Laura wasn't her boss right now, wasn't concerned with a story; she was just a jealous lover, tap-dancing around an uncomfortable subject. "Really?" It was oddly flattering.

Laura dropped her hands, exasperated with herself. "I have no wealth of experience to draw on; I can only rely on what I feel right now." The admission was embarrassing and she cracked her knuckles nervously.

"Would you stop that and sit down?"

Grumbling, Laura complied by dropping her body into the cushions at the far end of the couch and propping her head on a fist. "I don't know what the protocol is for this. If I were honest, I'd say I'm glad one of us knows what we're doing, especially since I reap the benefits of your experience…so to speak. I just didn't want to run into it today." She cocked one eyebrow at Chris. "And she was really smarmy too. I bet that suit costs what I make in a month."

Chris chuckled and pulled herself closer to Laura, sliding in to rest her head between a neck and a strong shoulder. "Kind of a rough day for you."

"Yeah, well, at least I didn't send a photog to the hospital." More content than she'd been all day, Laura stroked the blonde head tucked next to her chin.

"At the risk of sounding like a total slut, let me say that the day after the morning after is always the worst."

"That would be your experience speaking?" Laura could feel Chris laugh against her chest.

"Yeah. Wanna go reap some benefits?"

*"If you play golf the way you make love, no one else stands a chance."*

On Thursday at midnight the May Sweeps period ended with a whimper barely heard by the viewing public. For the larger metered markets, the complete results would be known by the next day. The winners and losers would spend the next few months deciding how to make the numbers work to their advantage, because there was always a spin. For the medium to small markets it would be another week or so before they had the book in their hands. A.C. Nielsen, the God of Television, guarded its power over the ratings system with jealousy and venom, serving up the means for a station's destruction for a hefty subscription fee and on their own time-table.

At least that's what Laura thought.

She'd never had to wait for a book. In Dallas, they kept up with the overnights and could make adjustments as they went along. If something didn't work one night, they could see the numbers and go from there. In a diary market, there were no second chances; viewers returned the diaries at the end of the month and the results came after the game was played. There was no going back.

Laura opened the refrigerator door and let the light brighten the darkened kitchen as she drank from a large bottle of orange juice. Her vigil of the sweeps' passing came more from an inability to sleep than a need to see the ratings period through to the bitter end, and while the sense of relief was welcome, it didn't cure her insomnia. The three-day push to the finish had been hard on everyone in the newsroom, and getting back to her neglected golf game had added to the strain. The Open was a week away and Laura was feeling less than confident.

Too many distractions…okay, just one distraction. Focus had never ever been a problem. Now it seemed as though she had the attention span of a gnat, but it was the neediness that bothered her the most, the craving to be close to the blonde reporter that was giving her fits. *C'mon, you should've expected this, it's all new, it's fabulous and fun and all that stuff, but it can't take over your life…It can't.*

Laura closed the door and felt her way back to the bedroom, flexing her shoulders as she went and feeling the familiar pop. *Overdid it today, I thin*k. She'd gotten up early to practice, practiced at lunch, then hit the range again after work. Laura knew there was a difference between getting in a groove and digging a rut, but she couldn't help feeling that there was something about her swing that wasn't quite right. *You just need to play a round. The walking will help, maybe you could go in a little later in the morning…Keith could handle things for an hour or so, it'll be just what you need.* Having settled on a cure for her restlessness, Laura crawled back into bed, catching a whiff of a floral scent she knew wasn't her own. With a groan, she flopped over on her back, one arm flung over her eyes, and hoped for a little sleep and maybe a dream of holding and being held by someone who was becoming as necessary as air.

Golf.

Chris cursed the game and all who played it, especially demented blue-eyed news directors who could seemingly turn emotions on and off at will. She ground her teeth in frustration as she clicked down the list of stories on the AP wire, her attention divided between the computer and the door of the newsroom. Laura had paged Keith to tell him she'd be in around ten, and it wasn't even nine yet, so there was no point in looking at the door every thirty seconds, but she checked again anyway.

Chris had always known with clear certainty that when she finally fell in love it would be quite a crash, and as far as things went with Laura, the impact was jarring, to say the least.

In the three days since what Chris was starting to call "Erica Monday," Laura had done nothing but ride herd over the newsroom and practice golf. She wasn't cold, she wasn't remote, she was just driven, as though nothing was more important than getting through this one week. For the first time, Chris saw the machine in action and understood how a twenty-eight year old could become a news director in a top market. *I miss her. I understand, but I still miss her. No phone calls, no dinners, just professional interest and support, then off to practice as soon as the Six is finished. The book's over now, does that change anything? Or is everything on hold until she gets back from Mississippi?*

She was gathering her notes for the morning meeting when a stack of magazines tied together in a bundle landed on the floor near her desk and she looked up into the mischievous smile of Danny Rendally. "Hey Chrissy, wanna have some fun?"

It was a good round and Laura had a little swagger back as she took the stairs two at a time up to the newsroom. Her hair was still damp from the hurried shower at the club and she flipped the dark length out as she pulled open the door. It was fairly busy; most of the reporters were on the phone setting up interviews and shoots for the day's stories. Janie was busily filling out the assignment board and as she walked by Keith's desk he handed her the mail. "Morning…good game?"

"Pretty good, needed it," she said laconically, flipping through the envelopes and trade magazines as she continued to her office. "Any problems?"

"Everything's cool so far."

"Great." Still distracted by the mail, she pulled her keys out of her pocket to unlock the door and froze. "What the hell?" Dozens of *City Lights* magazine covers wallpapered the office door and multiple images of three News Directors stared back at her in a weird, faceted, housefly perspective. One eyebrow lifted as she considered the likely suspects. "Mr. Rendally," she called sweetly to the corner of the newsroom, "How long did this take you?" There was a moment of silence and then the laughter started.

The reporter peeked out from behind his computer monitor. "Why do you immediately assume it was me? Anybody else…"

"Anybody else wouldn't have left his tape dispenser behind." Laura picked up the offending desk accessory from the shelf next to the door and tossed it across the room, smirking at his discomfort. "As punishment, you get to take my place at the Harrison School District Career Fair on Monday."

"Aw, come on…not the Career Fair," he said as he came out from behind his desk, "Chris helped…"

"Ooo, a confession and an accomplice. You can both go."

"Rendally, you fink," Chris accused. Laura chuckled softly as she unlocked the door and pushed it open. As she tossed the mail down on her desk it suddenly occurred to her that something like Rendally's little prank would never have happened in Dallas, no one would have dared.

She sat down behind the desk and wondered what had changed. *Me. I've changed.* In Dallas it had been a struggle every day to prove that she was smart enough, good enough, and ruthless enough to run the news operation at KDAL. In Burkett Falls, no one questioned whether she was qualified; they just wanted to see if lightening could strike twice.

"I think it looks good." Elly Michaels stood in the doorway admiring Rendally's handiwork and holding a copy of the magazine. In the photo, the two men were looking into the lens and Laura was on the left, gazing slightly off camera, one hand in a pocket hitching up her unbuttoned blazer on one side. Dark hair blew in strands away from her face, accenting her features. She gave every appearance of being exotically beautiful, aloof and untouchable. "Although Jack looks like he just smelled something really nasty and Lance has that charming sneer, you look really…nice."

Laura snorted in embarrassment. "Well, it's hardly pinup material and it doesn't do us much good the day after sweeps are over."

"Yeah, the timing sucks, but any publicity is good publicity."

"Did you know about the cover?"

"Sure, I saw the proofs." Elly smiled, not unkindly. "Ticked you off, huh?" She nodded at the impassive expression on the News Director's face. "I'd say I'm sorry, but a freebie's a freebie."

"You could've told me."

"I could have." Elly scrubbed her hand through her hair and Laura idly thought it was a little early in the day for it to be standing on end. "But I didn't. If it wasn't against the regulations of the USGA for amateurs, I'd plaster you with our logo next week."

"You checked."

"Of course. The promotion department is an ad agency and the station is my client. My one and only client. I am under no illusions about what will happen to me if the May book sucks." Without apologies or blame, Elly confirmed what Laura already knew, and she nodded in understanding.

"Whatever cranks the numbers, Kaz. It's not like you to forget that." Elly smiled bitterly and passed Keith in the doorway as she left the office.

For a minute, Laura sat motionless as she watched her carefully guarded privacy slip away into the realm of an advertising scheme. Her head was beginning to ache, and she looked up at Keith. "Would you make sure that everyone's here for the two-thirty? We need to do a little post-sweeps staff meeting and we might as well do it now since I'm out next week." Laura threw half the mail in the trash and started sorting through the buildup of paper on her desk. "What else?" she asked Keith since he made no move to leave.

"About next week, the Open…how do we cover that?"

"We don't."

"Oh c'mon, Kaz, Tupelo is only three and a half hours away. You're in the U.S. Open, for god's sake."

Laura dumped more paper into the round file. "Okay, just a blurb in sports."

"If you make a move, we need someone there to cover it." He shifted his weight from one foot to the other.

Laura stopped what she was doing and sighed. "Keith, I probably won't even make the cut…"

They were interrupted by Chris tapping on the door. "Didja ask her?" Laura's eyebrows lowered in irritation. "Ask me what?"

Shift, shift. "Chris had an idea how we could cover it without making you the main event, basically make the Open a follow-up story to her special report on Title IX. We could show how these women have benefited from the increasing number of athletic scholarships offered to women to even out the number offered to their male counterparts…"

Chris picked up the story pitch, "And since the Open will have amateur players from various colleges who are there on scholarships, it seems like a good opportunity." Chris's enthusiasm dulled a little at the look on the News Director's face. "That way, we're already there if something interesting happens…or not," she finished.

Laura leaned back in her chair with a touch of exasperation. "Has it occurred to anyone that this is my vacation we're talking about? It's not a station function and it's not a promotional opportunity. I don't want an entourage and I sure as hell don't want to be put on display."

"Yeah, but if you're there it makes it *our* story, and aren't you always saying that we never give up ownership of a story?" Chris knew she had her and resisted the urge to smirk. Laura regarded the blonde reporter through narrowed eyes, her fingers tapping on the armrests, and figured she'd been cooked in her own juice. Looking away, she blew out an irritated breath. "All right. Keith, set it up for Thursday-Friday, though I don't know where you'll find a hotel rooms for a reporter and a photog at this late date."

Keith did a little victory bounce and fist pump before he turned to leave the office but Laura's voice stopped him. "And Keith? Stay out of my hair…it's my vacation."

"Sure, Kaz." And with a grin he was gone, leaving Chris behind. "Close the door," Laura requested and the reporter complied, returning Laura's gaze evenly, never once breaking eye contact. "Why do you want to do this?" the News Director asked the question softly.

For Chris the answer was easy. "I want to be there with you and for you. Surely that's not so hard to understand." She swallowed against the need to touch the other woman; instead, she slipped her hands into the pockets of her blazer. "Will it bother you if I'm there?"

Laura's mouth was suddenly dry. "I'm…sorry about the last few days. You deserve better than to be ignored."

"Is that what you were doing? I thought you were working your tail off." Chris bit her lower lip and asked again, "Will it bother you if I'm there?"

Laura hesitated for a moment and her brow crinkled thoughtfully. "I'd like for you to see me play. I guess that sounds arrogant."

"You? Arrogant?" The blonde reporter could lift one eyebrow too.

"Sarcasm doesn't become you."

Chris dipped her head and hid a smile. "The deal was that we do this at your speed, and we keep it out of the newsroom. That hasn't changed. I can do the story and not come within fifty yards of you; all you have to do is tell me. Think about it." Chris stepped back to leave knowing it was the only way she could keep from saying too much, but Laura's voice, barely above a whisper, made her stop. "I want you there. More than anything in the world, I want you there." Blue eyes did not waver or hide the unspoken plea from a carefully guarded heart.

Chris sucked in a breath and her lips twitched into a smile. "Cool."

The two-thirty meeting was crowded, but the mood was light and the final firming up of the primetime newscasts was accomplished quickly. Laura nodded at Keith when he finished the rundown for the Six and stood up, clearing her throat. "Well, the book is over and the blackout is lifted. I know a bunch of you are going on vacation next week, I just wanted to get in one last word about…" Laura stopped herself. "Oh hell, I just wanted to say what a good job everyone did. We broke some good stories and dealt with some bad ones. If we don't get some decent numbers, it wasn't from lack of trying."

*She ought to wear jeans more often.* The thought flitted through the back of Chris's mind as she listened to the News Director praise the staff when it suddenly occurred to her that this was the same woman who had ruled KDAL with an iron fist, who had so terrorized a newsroom that they sent a condolence card to WBFC when they found out that this was the new domain of the infamous Laura Kasdan. Puzzled, she looked around at the staff. There was no obvious animosity; in fact, she was certain that, if pressed, most of them would have good things to say about their boss. *Who mistreated whom in Dallas, Laura?*

"The special reports looked good, the series were good, I think we had some strong viewer interest. So we'll take a little break, we won't worry about the July book 'cause nobody looks at those numbers anyway, and we'll be back strong in November." Laura gave a lopsided smile, not sure how to close. "I'm really proud of y'all, and to show my thanks, dinner's on me. We're grilling burgers out on the patio after the Six." Nothing excited a newsroom like free food and the whooping drowned out anything else that Laura wanted to say. The staff began to disperse to assemble the pieces and parts of the Five and Six, and the News Director headed for her office.

"Not so fast, Kaz." Lisa Tyler held up a hand to quiet the newsroom. "We, that is, all of us want to wish you the very best next week." She tossed a package to Laura, who caught it neatly and displayed a plastic bag full of orange University of Texas golf tees. Lisa held out her fist with her forefinger and pinky extended and gave her wrist a waggle in the Longhorn salute, "Hook 'em horns."

Before Laura could open her mouth, Rendally stepped forward with a box. "Just a little token of our affection…really." Laura narrowed her eyes at the reporter and opened the lid with some trepidation, pulling out a Tasmanian Devil golf club head cover…except that the brown tuft on the top of its head had been replaced by a long hank of black hair. "Well," she drawled, "no one ever said you were subtle, Rendally…my very own stuffed mascot."

The reporter blushed slightly. "Tear 'em up, Kaz."

"Pretty nice party." Lisa slid a plastic plate heaped with potato salad and a towering hamburger onto the wooden picnic table and climbed over the bench to sit across from Laura. "We've never done this before. Good idea."

"Yeah, I figured it'd be a good way to end the week." Laura pushed her plate away and for a change most of the food was eaten. They were alone at the table; most of the staff had broken off into splinter groups of five or six.

"Are you ready?"

Laura grimaced nervously. "No."

"Uh huh. You're ready." Lisa poked a fork at her food as she considered how to ferret out the information she was looking for. "So…Chris is going to cover the Open?" She looked up to see a muscle jump in the taller woman's jaw.

"She's doing a follow-up to her special report on Title IX." Laura stilled her hands, waiting and half-afraid of the next question, but Lisa abruptly changed the subject. "I guess this is a lot different from Dallas, Austin too."

Laura relaxed. "You have no idea."

Whiskey-colored eyes narrowed thoughtfully. "You've never let yourself be teased before, you know? You always took everything so seriously."

"So?"

"So what's changed?"

Laura cocked her head to one side and pondered the question. "There's no Roger…I'm not fighting every day to make sure it's done right. I'm not hostile because I don't have to be." *And it makes all the difference in the world, doesn't it?* She gave a short laugh. "Guess it was just that big market grind."

"Hmmm." Lisa looked past Laura's shoulder at the reporters gathered around one of the other tables and her voice dropped to a quiet serious tone. "She watches you, you know. Especially when she thinks no one's looking. She always knows when you're in the booth for the Six and she just lights up on the air, did you know that?" Laura shook her head slowly and Lisa continued, "She's always asking me questions…about you, always digging, and she is relentless. Kaz, what have you gotten yourself into?"

Laura winced, certain that she didn't want to have this conversation. "Could you be more specific?"

"This is so incredibly dangerous, it isn't even funny."

"I know that," Laura snapped in a low voice.

"And it's partly my fault. I had no business pushing…I just never thought you'd…" Lisa stopped at the look on Laura's face, suddenly realizing that her friend had no idea what was happening and was ill-equipped emotionally to deal with it. With a sigh, she shifted arguments, mentally scolding herself for not sticking to the point she wanted to make. "It's not against the rules, you know. The handbook only says intimate relationships are discouraged."

"I am her supervisor, and logic dictates that that kind of relationship is disruptive." Laura tapped on the wooden table for emphasis. "But it's not only that, it's the on-air thing and public perception. I could be the reason she gets yanked. Career-wise, I could probably survive…I'm not sure she could."

"So what's gonna happen?"

Laura dropped her head and spoke so softly that Lisa could barely hear her. "When I'm alone, I can almost talk myself into breaking things off and telling her that it's just not gonna work. I can almost convince myself not to be selfish and put a stop to it before we both get in trouble." Laura paused and lifted dark blue eyes filled with emotion. "But she's the most incredible person I've ever known and she *likes* me. She makes me laugh, and think, and feel. Can you understand what that means to me?"

Lisa nodded, understanding much more than Laura was telling. "For god's sake, be careful, Kaz."

"I will protect her as long as I can. If things…don't work, I'll still protect her." Laura didn't need to see the slight widening of the other woman's eyes to know that Chris was coming up behind her. The shiver running down her spine was notice enough.

"Can I sit here or were you talking about manager stuff that the peons aren't supposed to hear?" Chris put her hand lightly on Laura's shoulder for balance as she stepped over the bench and sat down. The patio was clearing out and they were the only ones left except for the caterers.

"Nope," Lisa said, "we finished talking about manager stuff. I think I'm going home to see if I can talk Trey into a backrub. Kaz, good luck next week, I know you've got the game. See ya, Chris."

They watched her leave and Chris turned to Laura. "Did I chase her away?"

"No, she's just…concerned."

"Us?" Chris inquired.

"Yeah." Laura closed her eyes and inhaled Chris's perfume. "Any plans for tonight?"

"Well, I was thinking that I'd sit on my porch swing until something better came along."

"Oh. I have to make sure the caterers get everything cleaned up. Probably be another hour."

Chris smiled, her eyes crinkling at the corners. "Why don't you bring something to drink since that seems to be your area of expertise right now. Are you playing golf tomorrow?"

"No, I'm a little fried right now, I need a break." Laura hesitated, Lisa's warning still fresh in her mind. "Maybe we should rethink this and…"

"Stop." Chris put one hand out to touch Laura's arm. "I have one day before I have to give you back to the golf gods. I'm not wasting that rethinking." She stood up and slid out from behind the bench. "I'll wait for you," she said, leaving Laura alone with the catering crew and the debris from the celebration.

"Why aren't you sleeping?" Laura felt the breath from Chris's inquiry on her ear, followed by a hand tangling in her hair. The moon shone with a bluish tint through the slats of the blinds and lit the bed where Laura lay on her stomach, chin on her forearm.

"Not tired." Laura still felt the shivers of awareness that the blonde woman seemed to provoke just by her presence.

Chris chuckled. "You should be. We damn near christened every flat surface in the house, horizontal *and* vertical. The word insatiable comes to mind." Chris settled herself across Laura's back, laid her head down between the taller woman's shoulder blades and heard her low hum of embarrassment.

"Guess I got carried away…missed you."

"S'okay," Chris slurred, one hand tracing the muscle of Laura's upper arm as she savored the admission. "I gotta think that if you play golf the way you make love, no one else stands a chance."

Laura peeked over her shoulder and said wryly, "It wasn't just me." The need had been maddening for both of them and Laura wondered if it would ever ease, half-afraid that it would. She filled her lungs, feeling Chris's weight rise and fall with her breath, then twitched when a busy hand found a sensitive spot. "Ah, that's a little sore."

"What? Oh, your live truck scar. That still hurts?" Chris ran her fingertips along the rough edge of skin, unable to make out the detail in the dark. *How 'bout that? Marked you as mine even way back then.* "Maybe you should have a doctor look at it."

"No, it's okay, I think I just bumped it on something when we were…earlier." Laura felt a jolt as her body reacted to the gentle caress, and wondered briefly if it was making up for years of deprivation. Slowly, she rose up on her elbows and turned over on her back. Chris followed the movement, shifted and readjusted until her compact feminine form was draped over Laura's long torso. "You were right, you know," Laura said as she felt soft kisses along her collarbone.

"About what?" The question was murmured against warm skin.

"When you said I'd wonder how I ever lived without it."

Chris laughed seductively and Laura felt the rumble all the way to her feet. "I was trying to be a tease, it was the least I could do." She tucked her head underneath Laura's chin, comfortable with the closeness, and closed her eyes. "What's running through your head, Laura?" she asked in a whisper, not really expecting an answer.

"I love to hear you laugh," came the unexpected reply. "It makes me feel…I don't know…happy is pretty inadequate." Chris felt a shrug and then silence. *It should make you feel loved, you idiot.* Chris bit back one of those laughs and settled for a smile as the body under hers relaxed and Laura drifted off to sleep.

# A Good Walk Spoiled

*"There's nothing unique or different about the people who make it to network, they only pursued the opportunity."*

Heat waves from the expanse of concrete at the Tupelo airport shimmered across the ground, distorting the green edge of the horizon as the jet landed and the tires kicked up twin curls of gray smoke. The terminal was cool, but after four hours of driving Laura was already worn, her white T-shirt was creased and limp, and just the idea of the sweltering heat was enough to exhaust her.

It hadn't been practical for Charles to drive, so he was flying. Laura waited patiently for the passengers to deplane and was finally rewarded by the sight of his tall figure coming through the door. "Kaz! You better've brought the little bag or the heat is gonna kill me humpin' a staff bag." Laura winced against the rib-cracking hug that lifted her off her feet.

"Would I do that to you? It's not the little bag, but it's light. Flight okay?" She smiled as the jitters settled. Familiarity always helped with her nerves. She was just like her mother that way. They started toward the baggage claim and she recognized some of the other golfers gathering up their baggage and clubs. Some of them would have courtesy cars, but most wouldn't. As an amateur who had to qualify, Laura was at the very bottom of the totem pole: no sponsors, no school affiliation, and no USGA title. But the Open was a model of democracy in golf. If the handicap requirement, a 4 for women, was met, and a player could qualify at one of the sectional tournaments, then she could play in the Women's U.S. Open.

There were club bags everywhere in the baggage claim, hard cases and soft cases scattered and stacked all around the conveyor belt. Charles spotted his bags as they came through the flap and picked them up easily, following Laura out and into the heat. "God," he panted as the air conditioning in the doorway warred with the heat and lost. "I was afraid it was going to be *really* hot."

Laura laughed at his discomfort, knowing that they would have a much easier time than some of the others who weren't used to the heat and the humidity. "C'mon, it's worse in Dallas during August."

"Yeah, but you have June and July to get used to it." They crossed the parking lot and Laura opened the back flap of the Jeep, moving her bag and clubs to make room for his. "Is the air working in this thing?" he asked, opening the passenger side and wincing as the vinyl scorched his legs when he sat down.

"Like a charm." She started the engine and turned the blower up full blast. There was a lot of traffic at the airport and it took a few minutes before they were out and on the highway. Laura pulled a map out from beside her seat and pushed it at Charles. "We're going to the Marriott, it's on North Gloster, should be an exit right up here."

"Yeah, there it is." He pointed out the exit and she followed the cloverleaf around and over the highway. "The Marriott, cool. At least it's not that Twilight Inn we stayed at in North Carolina. I knew we were in trouble when I saw all those rusted appliances out in front."

"That wasn't a very good experience all the way around. The cockroaches were as big as my fist." Laura shook her head, remembering her last Open. *Probably had a lot to do with walking away, didn't it?* "Well, I make a little better money now and we might as well be comfortable."

"How is the job? I know it isn't Dallas."

"It's good." She saw the sign for the hotel and put on her blinker, taking note of the restaurants clustered close by. "Rough couple of months, but everything seems to be working out." She turned into the parking lot and thoughtfully considered that two months ago it looked like her career had been flushed down the toilet.

"Good, 'cause you're a lot more relaxed than you were in Austin." Nothing stayed hidden from Charles for very long, Laura thought, and it was *always* better to beat him to the punch. *You're gonna have to tell him sometime...before Chris gets here.* She pulled in under the driveway cover and hopped out.

"I'll get the rooms, you wanna wait?"

"No, I'll come in." Laura looked back at him and smiled. He looked every inch the pro shop staffer in tan chinos and a striped polo shirt, and she felt a surge of fondness for her childhood friend. He held the door open for her and she slipped into the coolness of the lobby, briefly thinking that the abrupt changes in temperature from hot to cold over the next week were going to make her sick as a dog.

"I have reservations for Kasdan." She leaned on the counter as the clerk went about assembling the paperwork and plastic card keys.

"That's a suite and an adjoining room? Rooms 534 and 35, no smoking…sign here, enjoy your stay." Laura gathered up the receipt and keys and stuffed them in her cargo shorts. After grabbing a map of the hotel layout they went to move the Jeep. Their room was on the end of the building, so Laura parked by the side door and they unloaded the bags. "You want the clubs upstairs?" Charles asked.

"Yeah, I just have the duffel, we can do it in one trip." She hoisted the clubs on one shoulder and the bag on the other. Fortunately, the elevator was just inside the door and they shuffled on board to stand waiting until they were delivered to the fifth floor.

"This is definitely not the Twilight Inn," Charles said as Laura unlocked the door to the suite.

"This one's mine, yours is next door."

"Can I clean out the mini bar?

"I am *not* paying four dollars for a bag of peanuts."

Charles only laughed as Laura dropped her bags and gave him the key to his room. He left her alone for a moment and she inspected the spacious suite. *I can be happy here for a week…If I make the cut. No,* when *I make the cut.* She heard Charles tap on the adjoining door and she opened it. "I like traveling on your news director's salary, Kaz; we should do this more often." His teeth flashed as he beat her to the usual answer. "Someday, yeah I know. So, what's the plan?" He settled his tall frame down on the sofa and opened a bottle of water freshly liberated from his refrigerator.

Laura shrugged as she stopped and sat down in the chair opposite the caddy. "Nothing tonight, maybe some dinner. I'll register tomorrow, my tee time's at 2:50 for my practice round."

"It's gonna be miserable."

"I know, but it's better that we get used to it. You know I'm not allowed on the course without a caddy?" He nodded. "We can walk it tomorrow morning just to get a feel." She looked down at her hands and rubbed the calluses in her palms. "Thanks for doing this with me. I'm sorry that you're giving up vacation time and there's no money in it for you."

"Hey, none of that. The deal is room and board and airfare. I get to pass out business cards and make contacts. This is as good for me as it is for you."

*That word again.* Laura swallowed. *If I had a dime for all the deals I've made, I wouldn't be hanging around waiting to be vested in my stock plan.* "Okay then. We'll wait to see the course and get the packet before we talk about how I want to play this."

"It's a USGA course. You're going to play it very carefully." He regarded her evenly. "Seriously, one or two under could win this thing. You go in like a cowboy with that grip and rip and you'll spend two days hitting out of the weeds they call rough and going home Friday night."

"I don't play that way anymore."

He grinned. "Just checking. What else has changed, by the way?"

She was expecting it, but the question caught her off guard anyway. "Why does everyone keep asking that?" she muttered. "Changed?" *Stalling is not gonna help you out here.*

The soft brown eyes of her oldest friend probed gently but relentlessly. "What's happened since Austin? You could barely sit still two weeks ago, now you're not pacing, and you're not cracking your knuckles. What's changed?" he repeated.

She grimaced, looking for an escape route. "It's complicated." *Remember when you told Chris that you tried not to make assumptions about yourself, and you didn't have any family to speak of? You are such a damn liar.* "I'm…seeing someone." Charles's eyebrows raced up his forehead. "It's someone I work with, it could be real sticky."

"Little Kaz in love…never thought I'd see the day."

*Wait a minute!* Laura froze. "It's not that way." She crossed an arm against her chest and brought her fist up to her chin, her thoughts racing. *You never considered that, didja Kaz? Not an obsession, not a distraction, just love. Oh come on, I don't even know what love is.* Blindsided, her eyes were stricken when she looked at the caddy. "It's one of my anchors," she murmured, "Chris Hanson. You'll get to meet her later this week." There. It was out baldly on the table, and she tightened her jaw, waiting.

Charles didn't react in any way that Laura expected; he just smiled in his slow teasing way. "Like I said, I never thought I'd see the day."

The worry lifted slightly and she gave a half smile. "You're okay with this?"

"Well, I'm not telling Dad. That ball's in your court." His eyes clouded. "You're as close as a sister and the best friend I've ever had. I want you to be happy and I know you haven't been. Might be the best thing in the world that you had to leave Dallas." Charles knew it wasn't that simple, but judging by the look on Laura's face, she had other issues she needed to deal with, and sometimes she couldn't see past the nose on her face. He took a swig of water and stood up. "It's three o'clock; what are you gonna do this afternoon?"

"A shower, I think. Maybe a nap."

"Can I borrow the Jeep? I need some sunscreen and some other stuff. We can do dinner around six-thirty, seven." He caught the keys as she tossed them over. "Anything else I need to know?"

"I think we've about covered everything," she said dryly.

Charles stopped, his hand on the doorknob. "I haven't seen you this relaxed since you were a freshman. Whatever happens, it's been good for you. You're still too skinny, though." He closed the door as she threw a pillow at him and she could hear his laugh through the thin divider.

With a deep sigh, she stretched out on the sofa, wriggling to get comfortable, and promised herself that she'd only close her eyes for a minute. Unbidden, thoughts of the blonde reporter flooded in, filling every crevice of her mind and startling her with their intensity. *What's not to love? But real never let go, forever kind of love...am I even capable of that?* The idea was sobering. *Could Chris ever love me? I'm such a fucking prize.*

It hurt more to think about feelings that weren't reciprocated than the feelings themselves, and Laura growled at her own quirks. She pushed off the couch impatiently and almost reached for the phone. Instead, she stalked over to the mini fridge and began rummaging through its contents. Resisting the urge to break her vow of no Coke, she grabbed a bottle of juice, and without remorse for its five dollar price tag, gulped it down and wiped her mouth with the back of her hand. *As soon as this is over, I'm gonna drink a two liter bottle of Coke in one gulp and feel it burn all the way down. Probably belch for a week and a half.* With a sigh of resignation, she went over to where she had dropped her duffel and started to unpack.

She hung up all the shorts and shirts, hoping that she wouldn't have to iron too much, and then laid out the carefully polished and respiked golf shoes. The routine was reassuring, and by the time she was finished, a measure of calm had been restored.

But the phone still beckoned and, cursing her lack of willpower, she dug a card case out of a pocket and fished out her calling card. *Numbers, numbers, numbers. Too many numbers*. She waited impatiently, not wanting to hear the machine, then sighed in relief when she heard the receiver pick up. "'Lo." Chris's voice was thick with sleep.

"Caught you in bed on a Sunday afternoon?"

"Oh, hey. What time is it? S'almost four. Didn't get much sleep this weekend...but you'd know that. Played softball, took a shower, fell asleep."

"Who won?" Laura sat down on the floor next to the bed, wrapping an arm around her knees. She could almost see the tousled blonde hair and sleepy green eyes.

"We did. Keith hit a two run dinger in the bottom of the seventh." Chris yawned and stretched.

"Yes, but how did you do?"

"Double, single, double, and no errors. So you got there safe and sound."

"Yep. Picked up Charles and checked into the hotel. We're going out to dinner tonight and I start practice rounds tomorrow."

"Mmm. Bunch of people on vacation next week, it'll be strange."

Laura pushed her bangs away from her face. "So you'll be here Thursday?" *For someone who didn't want an entourage, you sure can't wait to see her.*

"I don't know, I need to check with my supervisor," Chris teased. "Keith found a hotel. Guess I should tell you that he's planning on coming if you're still playing on the weekend."

"Wish he'd stay home, I'd rather have him there in town while I'm here."

"Henry's on call," Chris said, referring to the Executive Producer and third in command. "And Keith wants to see you play."

"I don't think this is a very good idea. You…me…half the staff and hotel rooms…Do you see where I'm going here?

"I think you're worrying too much. I'll be there to do a job and I can certainly separate my private life from my professional responsibilities." Chris thought by saying it she could make it so, but she crossed her fingers just in case.

Laura rolled her eyes, recognizing that things with the blonde reporter rarely went according to plan, and wondered how she was going to handle damage control and still play decently. *Remember, it's just one distraction, right?* "This is repetitive, but *please* be careful."

"What could happen?"

"The mind reels," was the dry reply.

It was the most exquisitely manicured parcel of land that Chris had ever seen. The expanse of emerald green grass was broken only by darker trees, the white of the sand traps, and the silvery blue of the lake that led away from the white-columned clubhouse. Flowerbeds and shrubs were carefully mulched with woodchips in what must have been a landscape worker's nightmare. It was more like a painting than real life, a postcard of a playground for the rich and privileged.

Jody drove the station Taurus slowly, following the directions of the security guards to the media lot, and pulled into a space between a van and a Blazer, both marked with network logos. They both stepped out of the unit and Jody reached back to grab his photographer's vest, stuffing it with batteries and tape before looping his press ID around his neck. Chris waited by the trunk, patiently looking through the press packet for directions to the media tent while the cameraman assembled his equipment. "I'm not bringing the tripod just yet, I'll shoot off the shoulder," he told her.

"Okay, we need to check in with Media Relations, then we have to find the satellite truck corral to set up the live shots; Keith booked the sat time." Chris looked up at the sky, noting that dark gray clouds were gathering. "I'm supposed to get two interviews this afternoon, then maybe we can look for Kaz." It had been a last minute decision to come out on Wednesday rather than Thursday to take advantage of some of the players' availability, and Chris was a little apprehensive about seeing Laura. *Just a hunch, but I'm pretty sure that now is not the best time for surprises.*

Jody shouldered the camera and they started walking toward a cluster of tents, the asphalt radiating heat through the soles of their shoes, promising misery for those not used to the warmth and humidity of a Mississippi summer. Signs directed them to the check-in and they picked up their credentials with a minimum of fuss. Chris clipped hers on her belt next to the WBFC ID and asked directions to the sat truck corral. One of the workers offered to take them in an electric utility cart, so Chris rode up front and Jody sat in back with the camera. Shrubbery hid most of the course from the road, but occasionally they glimpsed a group of golfers making their way through the final practice round. "The course looks fabulous," Chris told the driver, guessing that this was the golfer's equivalent of a conversation starter concerning the weather.

"Been a little dry…rough's not as high as it should be." He nodded as they passed another cart. "Probably get some rain tonight but it's a little too late."

*Okay, low rough means the course isn't as dangerous, so the scores'll be lower.* Chris stored the information away in her newly acquired "all about golf" mental file as they pulled into a gravel lot filled with trucks emblazoned with network logos and with independent satellite operators. They found their network truck with no trouble and Chris confirmed their times with the operating engineer.

"Where to now?" the driver asked.

"Clubhouse…let's find some players." Chris grabbed the handle next to the seat as the cart jerked forward and they were whizzing back toward the plantation-style building that served as the centerpiece of Cypress Hill Golf Club.

A crowd was gathered around the pro shop where the driver let them off, most of them trying to get inside where the air-conditioning offered momentary relief from the ninety-five degree temperature. Across a small brick courtyard was the putting green, and golfers milled around underneath an ivy-covered arbor. As Chris and Jody crossed over to the practice green, they heard a burst of laughter and a smattering of applause, and then a clear tenor voice broke out in song. "*I got drunk the day my mama got out of prison….*" Chris looked at Jody and they pushed through the crowd to get a better look.

"*And I went to pick her up in the rain…*" There, standing on the steps leading to the clubhouse, was a tall black man singing at the top of his lungs with his arm thrown around their News Director's shoulders. As the reporter and photog watched in open-mouthed wonder, Laura added her rich voice to his. "*But before I could get to the station in my pickup truck, she got runned over by a damned old train*!"

"Are you rolling on this?" Chris asked Jody incredulously.

"You'd better believe it," he answered as a number of caddies, golfers and the crowd joined in the chorus.

Chris smiled broadly as clear blue eyes met hers and she felt a lurch in her chest.

*"Why don't you ever call me by my name?"*

The gallery applauded loudly and Laura hopped off the step blushing furiously and pulled her singing partner, still bowing and laughing, over to where Chris and Jody were standing. "You're early," she said, embarrassed at having been caught in an activity so out of character. "This is Chris Hanson and Jody Banks, two of my very best," she said to the tall man. "And this is my caddy, Charles Cryer, who is known to spontaneously break out in country-western songs on occasion."

Charles flashed even white teeth. "Little Kaz exaggerates; we always sing—she'd be disappointed if we didn't." For just an instant, Chris felt a twinge of jealousy at the closeness between Laura and her caddy, as though her lover wasn't entitled to an old friend who surely knew secrets she couldn't even guess at. Charles shook Jody's hand, then looked down at Chris and his warm eyes lit up. "It's a pleasure to meet you."

Jealous or not, Chris couldn't stop a lopsided grin. "She was *singing* with you. If I hadn't seen it myself, I wouldn't believe it."

"Yeah, well, don't tell anyone…it'll blow my image." Laura took off her hat and shook her hair loose, running her fingers through sweat-dampened bangs. "We just finished our round. Have you been here long?"

"Long enough to check in and catch the show," she teased. "I've got interviews set up for later, that's why we came early."

Laura nodded. "You okay, Jody?"

"Yeah, I'm going to get some B roll. Chris, I'll meet you back here in 'bout a half hour. And I got that on tape, Kaz." The photog winked as he turned to leave and was swallowed up by the crowd almost immediately.

"I wonder how much he wants for that," Laura muttered.

"What about you two, what's next?" Chris pushed her sunglasses to the top of her head as darkening clouds obscured the sun.

"Are you gonna hit the range?" Charles asked Laura.

"Think I'd better before it starts raining."

"I'll get the bag." Charles jogged off to pick up the clubs, and Chris followed Laura up the hill to the practice tee, surprised that, except for mild embarrassment, Laura was more relaxed and at ease than she expected in what should have been a high pressure situation. *Maybe it's just another game face. A solitary sport…Yeah, it suits.*

"So where are you staying?" Laura interrupted her thoughts as they bumped shoulders, the touch making Chris want more than just casual contact.

"We're at the Hampton Inn. It's a two-room suite thing with a bed and a sleeper sofa. Guess we'll toss for the bed."

"Well, you could…"

"Nope, I'm here to do a job and so are you." Green eyes laughed back at her and Laura smirked, reading the reporter's mind easily. "I wasn't going to offer, I was going to suggest that you get on a waiting list for cancellations."

"Oh."

Laura was still chuckling at Chris's chagrin when Charles caught up with them as they reached the range. There were already a number of golfers practicing, the bronze of their tans evidence of hours spent in the sun. "Hey Kaz, they've got the pairings posted. You go at 1:10 tomorrow." Charles held up a folded sheet of paper.

"Let me see." She moved beside him to look over the list. "Good. That means I'm playing in the morning on Friday." With a businesslike movement she pulled on her glove, flexing her hand as she fastened the Velcro and stepped around the ropes into the practice area proper. Charles followed Laura and handed her the driver, dropping the bag next to a pyramid of balls. Chris watched as the two of them conferred over something, then the caddy nodded and came over to where she was standing and stepped over the rope. "Come on, Chris, I want to get something to eat."

"Don't you need to stay here for this?" The reporter stood mesmerized as Laura swung the club a few times, all long limbs and easy grace.

"Nah, if she needs help she'll ask. Besides, she hates it when I watch." Chris turned away reluctantly and they walked back down the hill to the clubhouse. Charles ducked into a tent next to the pro shop and Chris followed curiously, then caught a bottle of water as it was tossed her way. "Turkey or ham?" Charles asked as he stood over stacks of boxed lunches.

"Turkey."

"Turkey for Kaz, too." He gathered up three boxes and two more bottles of water, nodded at the attendant and led her to a table set up by a portable cooling unit. "Only the players and caddies are allowed in the clubhouse restaurant," he explained as he sat down.

"This is fine, and free food is free food." Chris opened the box and lifted out a thick sandwich.

"Yeah, we'll eat pretty good for the next few days." He took a large bite and washed it down with the water and wiped his hands on a napkin. "This is the part where I play the big brother and ask you about your intentions."

Chris swallowed. "Excuse me?"

"You and Little Kaz…she didn't tell me much, so I figured I'd go to the next source. You're the reporter so you'd know about that, right?"

"I'm sorry, but I barely know you." Chris's natural inclination was to start her own interrogation.

"Look, I'm not…Let me start over." Charles took a deep breath. "When Kaz came to Austin two weeks ago she was wound tighter than a cheap watch and nothing but skin and bones. She shows up Sunday and it's like a whole other person, except she's still too thin."

Chris raised an eyebrow. "Does she know you're giving me the third degree?"

"Are you kidding?" Charles snorted. "She'd kill me. I'm invading her privacy, and if you know her at all, you'd know that." He shook his head impatiently, trying to make a point without betraying any confidences. "Kaz isn't…Oh hell, for someone who's run one of the busiest newsrooms in the country, she's not very…"

"Experienced? You're not telling me anything I don't already know," Chris said softly, touching him lightly on the hand.

"Why you? I'm not trying to be insulting." His mouth tightened. "It's just that no one's ever gotten close…She cried in Austin. I've never seen her cry before. I wasn't sure she could."

Chris bit her lip considering what the caddy said. *He's got the answers; do I know the right questions to ask?* "What happened in Dallas?"

Charles snorted again. "It didn't start in Dallas, that was just the explosion. It started with that stupid fucking deal she made with her dad."

"What deal?"

Charles blew out an exasperated breath. "Look, Chris, this isn't my story to tell. You're better off asking Kaz."

Asking Laura was out of the question; she stood a better chance with the caddy. "No, Charles, you started this." Chris nodded to herself as she came to a decision. "I love her, and nothing you say will change that." She gazed across the table at him, a smile playing across her lips. Saying it out loud made her realize there was no going back. "You asked me what my intentions are. I intend to be around for a long, long time. Now you can either help me out, or get out of the way." Chris calmly took a sip of water while she flexed her reporter's muscles. *Now answer the questions and tell me the story.* "What deal?"

For a moment Charles didn't answer, then he nodded grudgingly. "Ten years. She promised her dad ten years in the news business. She thought it would make him happy because it was the only thing he ever really asked for and she wanted his approval, I guess. He didn't give a rat's ass about the golf, that wasn't a way to make a living."

"But her Mom…"

"Was an amateur. Sarah never turned pro, and she was a snob about that. She was one of the USGA muckety-mucks. She wanted Little Kaz to play, but not necessarily as a pro. Then Kaz won her first U.S. Amateur in '95. That was great, 'cause that made them the first mother-daughter to ever win it. Then Sarah got sick and Kaz blew up at the Open…she just fell apart." Charles looked down his face creased in a frown remembering. "Sarah died right after that and Kaz won her second Amateur. She told me she was going to talk to her dad about the deal they'd made, but the son of a bitch went and got himself killed and after that she wouldn't go back on her word."

"Bosnia." *Don't make promises you can't keep. When did she tell me that?*

"Yeah. Kaz quit golf then. Came home one day and she was sitting on my steps. Told me to sell her clubs." Chris could feel her heart breaking for the woman who had packed up a part of her life and given it to a friend to discard, only to turn to a job where she was disliked and unappreciated. "They made her News Director," she whispered.

"Uh huh, I didn't see her for over a year. She just buried herself in work. We'd hear things but we never saw her. Then I came home one day and there she was sitting on my steps same as before. This time she wanted to know if I could get her on at Oak Hills, that's the club where I teach. She wanted to play a round." Charles's face lit up. "I couldn't get her on fast enough."

Chris played with a potato chip thoughtfully. "If she won the Amateur in '96, she had a two year exemption for the Open. Why didn't she play last year?"

"My dad didn't think she was ready, and both of them decided to take the chance on qualifying this year." Charles opened another bottle of water. "See, before when she played, her game was all power and pretty wild. She might hit a ton, but she didn't always know where the ball was going. She made it work by sheer determination. Now it's different. Her short game is fabulous and the rest of it is more controlled. Her swing was always beautiful, but now..." He shook his head in awe. "Really good athletes always have a special awareness of themselves. Their mind knows what every part of their body is doing at any given time, like a Michael Jordan or a Mark McGwire. They can make a tiny adjustment and it makes all the difference. Kaz is like that." He stopped, and his eyes fairly drilled into Chris. "But only about golf. Or news. Anything else and she'd be..." he searched for a word, and not finding one, Chris supplied it.

"Lost."

Charles looked down and nodded. "So you know." Chris pushed her food away and leaned back crossing her legs. She had her answers, and now things made sense. She was mulling over the information when the caddy stood up and interrupted her thoughts. "So I'm asking again, why you?"

She gave him a lopsided grin as she got to her feet. He was even taller than Laura was, so she had to look up quite a ways. The answer was already on the tip of her tongue, and she thanked whatever god it was who looked out for her charmed life and drawled, "Just lucky, I guess."

---

Lori Kendall was a good interview, and Chris thanked her for her time as Jody removed the mic from the front of her shirt. The young golfer was from Arizona State and she answered the questions with a lot of charm and told some humorous anecdotes. It was going to be a good story; two interviews had already provided the framework and Chris was counting on the Open to do the rest. So she was pleased and happy as they packed up the gear and left the media room to haul it all back to the Taurus. But a group of grumbling golfers, caddies, and tournament officials were gathered around the door, peering out as rain fell in a steady downpour.

"Aww great," Jody muttered, setting down the camera and light kit in the hall. "Might as well wait it out. We still have about an hour before we have to be at the sat corral." He took the tripod from Chris and laid it next to the wall and they both tried to get out of the way of the milling crowd.

A slender woman with dark curly hair tried to ease by and caught sight of Jody's ID and the logo on both their shirts. "Hey, are you guys from WBFC?" At their nods she stuck out her hand. "Jan Sheffield with the network, we were supposed to get with you some time tomorrow."

"Chris Hanson and Jody Banks," Chris supplied. "We've got some sat time booked with one of your trucks, what else did you need?"

"Your news director…" She checked a clipboard that marked her as some kind of producer. "…Laura Kasdan, is playing, and we want an interview."

Chris looked at Jody. "Um, you'll have to talk to her; this is her vacation, and she was pretty clear about staying out of her hair."

"Yeah, but she's one of ours so that makes it interesting. Do you know where she's staying?"

"No," Chris lied. "You'd better just go through media relations and set it up that way."

Instead of being insulted, the dark-haired woman laughed. "Protect your boss and your job, I get it. Okay, I'll do it the old-fashioned way. See you around, Chris Hanson."

They watched her continue down the hall then open an umbrella and scamper out into the rain. "Boy, I never thought of that," Chris reflected. "The network chasing her down. She'll freak." She glanced sideways at Jody. "Did you get some video of her practicing?"

Jody scratched his jaw. "Yeah, and it wasn't easy." He pointed down the hall where two dripping figures in rain ponchos were coming towards them. Chris couldn't help but smile. *Of course she was prepared, she plans for everything.*

Laura's hair was slicked back and damp from the rain. One more walking tour around the course and she finally admitted to Charles that there was nothing more they could do to prepare, so they wandered back. Laura had hoped she would stumble across the reporter and Charles had gamely followed, not once questioning her. "Hey. Get everything you needed today?"

"So far, so good. The network folks are looking for you, though." Chris swallowed as the difficulty of their forced distance hit her squarely when she looked into clear blue eyes.

"Mmm. Bet they gave you the 'She's one of ours' spiel."

Chris laughed. "How'd you know?"

"I have magic psychic news powers." She shrugged. "They sent an e-mail. Wanna get something to eat?" For the first time in weeks, Laura was starving.

"What happened to staying out of your hair?" Chris said it for Jody's benefit, hoping to be forgiven someday for deceiving a friend.

"I think she's tired of me." Charles's wry observation was perfect and the cameraman grinned and replied, "Okay, but you're buying."

"All right then. Go and do your uplink for the Six. Ah, thought I didn't know?" Laura clicked her tongue at the look on their faces. "Magic psychic news powers, remember? Tell Keith no horn blowing. Then we'll meet about seven at my hotel. The Marriott, room 534." People were leaving the hallway as the storm eased and Jody bent down to pick up the camera. Charles grabbed the light kit and Laura hoisted the tripod onto her shoulder. She and Chris hung back as the two men ducked out the door and jogged to the parking lot, the rain slowing to a light drizzle. "You were right," Chris murmured, "Maybe this wasn't such a good idea."

Laura didn't have an answer; she just gave a light squeeze to the smaller woman's shoulder before heading out. With a sigh, Chris followed, the weather matching her mood.

"You're really good, Chris. How long have you been in Burkett Falls?" Jan Sheffield was frankly admiring as Chris got the all clear and took the IFB earpiece off and wrapped the cord around her hand. It had been a smooth uplink and a fun live shot to do; now they were finished for the day.

"A little over two years, just started anchoring in prime, though," Chris answered as she rolled up the mic cord and handed it to Jody.

"Your first job?"

"No, I was in Atlanta for a while. Market sixty-one is not entry level, Jan."

The other woman smirked, "Neither is Atlanta, maybe you should have stayed."

"Ah, but I didn't want to."

"Well, at least let me give you a lift back to the media lot. If you see your boss, tell her we already put in a formal request for an interview and we'd really appreciate her time." Jan led them over to an electric cart on the edge of the corral and motioned for them to join her. Chris watched as Jody silently hopped on the back. The photog never said much around other people, but Chris knew she'd get his observations later and she was looking forward to them with some amusement. Jan dropped them off right next to the Taurus with a promise to see them later. With some relief, they got into the station vehicle and headed to the Marriott.

"She wants you." Jody's laconic statement jerked Chris out of her drifting thoughts and caused her to face him in alarm. "Excuse me?"

He chuckled softly. "Bet she tells you to send a tape to her boss and she'll put in a good word if you wanna make the jump to network."

"What makes you say that?" Jody was seldom wrong and Chris had learned to listen to the resourceful photog.

"The sat engineer was talking. Really, Chris, you oughta be flattered."

She was. A little. Network, she thought, *Wow.* Chris had never considered much past getting to the anchor desk, and the idea was attractive in an ego-building kind of way. She gave a half smile as she turned to look out at the landscape. *What would Laura say?* Then she shrugged; it wasn't even a possibility for three years.

Fifteen minutes later, they were standing outside room 534 and Chris couldn't keep from grinning as Laura jerked open the door and waved them in. Charles was sprawled on the couch channel surfing and Jody plopped down beside him. "God, this is huge, I was wondering where all your money went." Chris's comment caused Laura to raise an eyebrow.

"It goes to that fancy country club."

"Yeah, but you drive that old Jeep and you live..." Chris stopped short as she realized where her commentary was going and how personal it sounded. With a glance at Jody she muttered, "Sorry."

"S'okay. You ready for dinner? Come on guys, I'm hungry."

Charles clicked off the TV and tossed the remote down. "We're going to Vanelli's again, it's a Greek and Italian place," he said to Jody. "She likes it so I'd better get used to it."

"I'm paying so I get to choose," Laura smiled, surprised that she felt happy and relaxed and was looking forward to the dinner. Okay, so anything personal with Chris was strictly off limits, but things were going well. *I can handle this.* She looked over at the blonde reporter and green eyes almost took her breath away. *Oh sure, you can handle this. It's gonna be the longest four days of your life.*

Laura was nervous but doing her best not to show it. Sprawled in a chair next to the putting green, she sat like a cat at rest, deceptively at ease, but ready to pounce. A sleeveless white polo shirt was tucked into soft cotton olive green shorts and a logo-free tan baseball cap held her hair in a ponytail threaded through the opening in the back. Dark green and white saddle shoe spikes completed the outfit, nothing unusual or memorable about it except in the way it was worn. Laura almost jumped out of her skin when warm hands came down on her shoulders. "You okay?" Chris's voice was so welcome she almost laughed.

"Where's Jody?"

"He went with Charles somewhere. I think your caddy has decided to run interference for us. Your muscles are really tight." Laura turned to look at Chris, relaxing as she felt the reporter's hands gently knead the tension out of her neck.

"Good ol' Charles," she murmured. "Coach, confidant, and nag. You look nice."

"Thanks. I have a station shirt in every color imaginable, even my no-no colors." Chris crouched down next to Laura, clasping her hands in front of her. Dark green shorts complemented a paler green polo shirt. Sunglasses covered the eyes that Laura knew would be crinkling into a smile. "So just half an hour to go?"

"Yep. Then I see if all the work was worth it."

"Do you know the two women you're playing with?"

Laura nodded. "Barbara Nelson is British…big hitter, but she's got a case of the yips."

"Yips?" Chris balanced by laying a hand on Laura's arm.

"She's having trouble putting. Susan Fisher is a fortyish mother of two and she's *really* good. She beat my mother at the Amateur in…I guess it was '82; she won it three times in a row. Susan rebuilt her game last year and it's paying off."

"Like you did?"

"Yeah." Laura closed her eyes and focused her attention on the part of her forearm where Chris's hand lightly rested, centering on that one patch of skin. She could smell the floral perfume and the shampoo the blonde woman used. It was more than comforting, and she gave in to a light shiver despite the heat and blinked her eyes open only to see the sunglasses removed and a look of uncertainty in the eyes that devoured her face. "What?"

"You're not at work, you're playing golf at one of the finest courses in the country with the best golfers in the world. Has it ever occurred to you that you should just enjoy it?"

The breath caught in Laura's throat. "It couldn't possibly be that easy," she murmured.

"Kaz, it's time." Suddenly Charles was there, lifting the bag up and slinging a large white towel over his shoulder, the yellow USGA caddy vest in place with her name on the back. Laura tightened her jaw and swallowed as she rose to her feet. With no inhibition and disregarding the photographer standing behind the caddy, Chris threw her arms around Laura in a hug.

"Good luck," she mumbled into the taller woman's shoulder, then drew back and smiled shyly. "Sorry…I've always been a toucher." Then, to Laura's surprise, Jody did the same, thumping her on the back and grinning from ear to ear. For the second time in as many minutes, the News Director was speechless.

"Come on, Kaz." Charles nudged her toward the first tee and with one more backward look she was gone, the clacking of the metal spikes on concrete stopping as they stepped onto the grass and started up the hill.

"She'll be okay." Chris was firm in her belief. "Let's go."

Laura checked in with the starter and introduced herself to the crew that would be following their group for the day: two scorers and the young man who carried the sign with their scores posted. After pocketing a scorecard with her yardage book, she and Charles stepped up to the tee box where a pair of ornate brass geese served as markers. Laura touched one of the rounded heads absently, her nervous hands needing activity.

"Little Kaz! It's so good to see you again." Susan Fisher's greeting was sincere as she reached up to clap Laura on the shoulder. "Heard about the show yesterday…Charles, how's your dad? We were wondering when you'd come back and play."

"Susan, good to see you too. Barbara…"

"Kaz." The Englishwoman's voice was clipped and Laura could already see signs of her famous impatience. "It'll be slow today," she said dourly.

They posed for the obligatory photo, the three women representing five Amateur and two U.S. Open titles. Moving to stand with the caddies, Laura waited for her introduction. Charles stripped the Kazmanian devil head cover off the driver and handed the club to her with a grin.

"Teeing off at 1:10, two-time U.S. Amateur Champion from Dallas, Texas, Laura Kasdan."

Chris clapped with the rest of the crowd as Laura bent over to tee up the ball, barely even taking a practice swing. The marshals held up their hands for quiet and before the gallery had even settled, Laura was into her takeaway. Long arms swept the club back and powered through the ball, sending it straight down the center of the fairway. Chris could see a pleased smile before the game face was back in place.

The other two women were introduced and they both hit booming drives to the delight of their audience. Then the players, caddies, scorers and part of the crowd left the stage that was the first tee to head down the hill onto the course for their first round of the Open.

"She didn't even use a driver. That was a two-hundred and fifty-yard two iron." The man standing next to Chris couldn't say enough about the power displayed by Barbara Nelson. They were on the fourth hole and Laura had just birdied number 3. Now all three women were waiting for the green to clear.

Chris was absolutely fascinated by the crowd and the golfers. She stopped for a hole to observe the group behind Laura's since it contained last year's Open winner, Mi Ja Song, and Stacey Kim, the Amateur Champ, who had applied lipstick three times by the third hole. *Okay, it's a hundred degrees and you're playing in the U.S. Open. Maybe looking pretty shouldn't be your top priority.* She and Jody laughed at the absurdity and then at their own hypocrisy when Chris asked Jody if he had her makeup bag.

*God it's hot.* Chris looked over where Laura was leaning on a club talking softly to Charles and nodding. *She looks great, not sweating at all.* She was playing well and staying out of trouble. According to Charles, that was the game plan: nothing dangerous, and play the high percentage shots. It was all so much mumbo jumbo to Chris. *I just want to spend some time with her.*

The green finally cleared and all three women hit quickly. Jody left to get some B roll of the college students they were following and Chris fell in behind a group of women who had apparently decided they were going to stick with Laura for the rest of the round. "She's just gorgeous," one of them gushed, "and those eyes…" Chris groaned inwardly.

Another par for Laura and they were on their way to the fifth tee when the weather warning sounded just as lightning streaked across the sky. The safe house was just behind the tee box and the tournament officials started herding golfers in that direction. Chris was wondering what to do when the rope was lifted in front of her and Laura was gesturing for her to follow. "Come on. Where's Jody?"

"He went to get some video." Chris ducked under and trailed after Laura over to where Charles was waiting. "Did you know you have your own fan club? They were ooooing and aahhhing over your eyes."

"Don't tell her that, she already has a big head." Charles handed Laura a bottle of water. "Seen any good stuff?" They walked toward the house where a crowd was gathering.

"It's been interesting. How long do you have to wait here?"

"Depends on the weather," Charles answered. "Right now they're more worried about the lightning; I don't think we'll get any rain." He maneuvered his tall frame and the bag through a small opening onto a covered porch ringed with wooden benches.

"So do you just go in and raid the fridge?"

Laura chuckled, "Something like that." Laura always hated rain delays, especially if she was in a rhythm. But Chris was here, and that was something she'd never had before. After covering the clubs, Charles went inside to get some relief from the heat, but Laura stayed outside with Chris, not wanting to change her body's temperature too dramatically. She cleared her throat nervously, wondering how she could be so intimate with Chris and still be so awkward at times. "How was sharing a room with Jody?"

"Not much fun. He snores louder than you do. I closed the door and I could still hear him."

"I don't snore." Laura dropped her voice as another group of golfers came under the porch. Chris sat down on one of the benches and Laura joined her, offering the bottle of water.

"You keep telling yourself that."

"There you are, Chris. Figured I'd find you here. You must be Laura Kasdan…Jan Sheffield, I'm one of the producers for the network coverage." Jan was dressed impeccably and looked like the heat wasn't bothering her one bit. "Do you ever check the message board?" she asked Laura.

"No" was the frank reply.

Jan didn't blink and Laura got the idea she would be dealt with the same way the producer handled annoying talent. "We want to do a sitdown interview this afternoon, will that be a problem?"

"I'd rather do it tomorrow." Laura took the water back from Chris and took another sip. "I'm gonna be wiped when I'm finished here."

"Still, it would be better…"

"Look, I appreciate the difficulty, but tomorrow is better because I'm playing in the morning."

"Sure," the producer backed off. "I'll get someone to coordinate the time. We've got a set in the clubhouse, that's where we'll do it." She smiled down at Chris. "I'll see you at the sat trucks later."

Chris watched her leave, puzzled by Laura's reluctance to cooperate. "I'd think you'd be a little more understanding, you know what it's like when you can't get an interview."

Laura snorted. "But I'm just fluff…filler…a kicker. I'm not a story and I know that. She knows I know that. There is nothing unique or different about the people who make it to network Chris, they only pursued the opportunity. Now when the network does the chasing, that's a different story."

Chris frowned thoughtfully. "Didn't you ever want to work for one of them?"

"Nope. That was my dad. What about you? Any network aspirations?" Laura was curious, wondering for the first time how she would handle Chris's ambitions when her current contract ended.

"I hadn't really thought about it 'til yesterday," Chris admitted. "Something Jody said…It's a little far away isn't it? At least three years." *I'm supposed to want that…In three years I'll be twenty-eight, the same age you were when you took over at KDAL.*

Laura watched the idea flicker across the blonde reporter's face. "It'll go by before you know it." She turned to look out over the course without really seeing any of it. She'd been right from the beginning: Chris was too good to stay in a medium market forever. *Three years, that's all, then time's up...for both of us.* Laura passed the water bottle back to Chris and they sat there in silence, unable to do anything but wait for the game to resume.

There wasn't enough cold water in the world, Laura decided as she leaned on her elbows against the corner of the shower and waited for her body temperature to come down. After the forty-five minute weather delay, play had continued except that she, Barbara, and Susan had had to wait for practically every shot. That was the problem with playing with the two fastest women on tour, and Laura hadn't slowed them down at all.

But the heat was oppressive, and judging by the way the veins were standing out on her hands, she wasn't drinking enough.

She twisted her head under the spray, breathing through her mouth as the water streamed down her thick dark hair. Over and over, she replayed the round in her head, wincing at a few lost opportunities, but pleased overall. *Not bad, and even though scores were really low, 4 under is great.* Susan finished at 7 under and Barbara was at even par. The course was not playing like a typical Open, and unless an act of god caused the rough to grow an inch or two overnight, scoring records were going to be set.

After a while, Laura was chilled and she adjusted the taps to warm the water. By the time she had shampooed her hair and soaped her body she was starting to feel a little waterlogged and a lot better. Without drying off, she stepped out of the shower to put on a terry robe and left the bathroom dragging a brush through her hair as she went. The room was cold and she adjusted the thermostat before lying down on the bed. *Just a little nap, so tired.* Almost immediately she drifted off, dreaming of endless green fairways stretching as far as the eye could see.

Laura snapped awake, blinking and swallowing in confusion. Looking at the clock, she saw that she'd only been asleep for an hour, then the persistent knocking that had awakened her resumed its steady rhythm. She stumbled to her feet, groaning at the stiffness in her legs, and made her way to the door. She opened it without bothering to look through the peephole.

"I know I'm not supposed to be driving station vehicles, but it was only a few blocks and there were no cameras or stories involved, so I thought I was pretty safe."

Laura tried for a snappy comeback, but drew a complete blank. *Speechless again? This is starting to become a habit.* She shook her head, disoriented, before trying again. "You're here," she croaked, stating the obvious.

"Where else would I be?" Chris smiled gently. "I figured that you wouldn't feel much like going out so I brought some dinner." The heat seemingly had not affected the reporter; she looked as cool and relaxed as when she started the day. The only evidence of a day spent in the sauna that was Mississippi in June was the healthy gold tone of her skin, which contrasted nicely with a white T-shirt and denim shorts.

"Where's Jody?" Laura stood back as Chris came in balancing several bags and boxes of something that smelled wonderful.

"Asleep, dead to the world. I think hauling that equipment around in the heat did him in. Your name's up on the leader board, you know, big as life in a three-way tie for fourth." She pushed the door shut with her hip and crossed the room to set dinner on the round table next to the sofa.

"You can't win it on Thursday, Chris."

"I know, but you didn't lose it either. I brought enough if Charles wants to eat with us."

Laura ran a hand through her damp hair trying to restore it to some kind of order. "He was going out somewhere, he took the keys to the Jeep."

"Then it's just dinner for two, I guess."

"Yeah." Laura stood quietly as Chris opened the boxes and distributed pasta salad and marinated chicken. "I'm hungry," she observed in a mildly surprised tone.

"Good. I brought all kinds of things to drink since I wasn't sure what you had." She pulled out a chair for Laura, patting the back lightly. "Sit down and eat and I promise you'll feel better." The tall woman made no move to sit down, and Chris was getting a little concerned as she pulled several bottles of Gatorade and fruit juices out of the bag. "It's not a very good vintage but you need to drink it."

Laura gave herself a little shake and went over to the chair. "You're a good friend." Chris raised her eyebrows at her choice of words but said nothing as Laura sat down and exhaled. "I feel a little foggy right now."

"Hard day. What time did you get out there this morning?"

"A little after seven. Too early, I know." She took a bite of the pasta and hummed with pleasure, enjoying the different spices. "Vanelli's?"

"Yep."

"Hard to believe that I had to come all the way to Tupelo, Mississippi to find my favorite restaurant." Laura ate it all and most of the chicken before leaning back in her chair, stuffed to the gills. "How did your day go? I didn't see you after the 12th."

Chris wiped her mouth with a napkin and bobbed her head. "Good. We got some stuff on those two girls we're following, and the uplink for the Six went well." It was different and fun, and she'd enjoyed working with the folks from the network. "Jan Sheffield asked if I'd be interested in doing a little crowd interview filler piece for them to run on Saturday. Do you have any problem with that? They may not even use it, but I thought it would be good for Jody and me."

Laura swallowed. *So, it starts now.* "I don't think that's a problem, and you're right, the exposure would be good for you." She felt a little curl of hurt in her gut and tightened her jaw, determined not to show it. Standing up from the table, she gathered up the empty boxes. "I'm going to, uh, put on something to sleep in. There's about six movie channels on the TV if you want to take a look." She made her escape to the dressing area, dumping the boxes in the trash along the way, and Chris let out a sigh of exasperation, wondering where she had stepped wrong. It didn't take long for the reporter to decide on a course of action and after counting to one hundred she went to the door of the bathroom and tapped lightly. "Okay, what did I do?"

The door opened and Laura was drying her face with a towel as the faint scent of soap and toothpaste drifted out. The terry robe was missing, replaced with an oversized T-shirt and fleece shorts. "Nothing." She tossed the towel down on the vanity and snapped off the light. "I'm just worn."

"And?"

"And nothing. The heat just got to me and I'm worried about it." With an attempt at a casual shrug she tried to move past Chris without touching the blonde woman or meeting her eyes, but Chris stepped in front of her, not buying the excuse. "I'm sorry, Chris, but I'm really tired." Trying to hide her weakness was wringing out Laura's last bit of strength.

"Then come to bed." It was a simple request, spoken softly, and Chris gently took the taller woman's hands in hers and kissed them tenderly. Dazed, Laura offered little resistance as she was led across the room and when Chris pulled the covers back she sat on the edge of the bed. "Scoot over." Another simple entreaty and Laura complied, lifting her legs onto the bed and moving to the center. Chris sat up against the headboard placing a pillow behind her back before cradling Laura against her shoulder, her hand threading through the dark mass of hair.

"Sorry." Chris barely heard the mumbled apology.

"For what? Exhausting yourself?"

"For being a jerk." Laura wrapped an arm around Chris's waist. "Jody's gonna notice you're gone."

"Not for a while at least. What time do you want to get up?"

"Six." Chris looked to make sure the alarm was set then turned out the lamp. In the darkness, Laura moved closer and Chris brushed her lips across the top of her head. A murmured question caught her by surprise. "Did you always want to be a reporter?"

"Yes." The answer was immediate. "I was interested in print journalism at first, then I found out that in TV I could tell the story too. Ego, I guess." She gave a light squeeze. "All you news directors bitch about the talent's ego."

"Mmmm. Yours is pretty healthy."

"Ah, but we take all the risk. If the 'cast goes down the toilet, the viewer doesn't blame the producer, they say that Tom and Chris are idiots." Chris could feel Laura's chuckle and she smiled. "Oh, and you aren't the least bit conceited, Miss Four Under Par?"

"About some things. We always say whatever it is that makes you good on the air makes you hell to deal with off it. You do a good job, have I told you that?" Laura's speech was slurred and Chris knew she was almost asleep. With a sigh she closed her eyes, intending to stay for just a little while.

The thunder woke her after three and she swallowed, her mouth dry. Laura had moved and was lying on her side facing away from Chris, hands curled up under her chin. *Not much of a cuddler, but she's learning.* Carefully, Chris leaned over and kissed her temple, then eased out of the bed and slipped her sandals on. *Will she even miss me when she wakes up?* "Love you," Chris whispered, then felt her way to the door, closing it softly behind her.

The alarm went off at six and Laura slapped at it, managing to stop the buzzing without throwing the clock off the nightstand. Groggily, she hugged a pillow to her chest, inhaling a familiar floral fragrance. *Chris.* Laura scrambled to sit up, but her senses told her that she was alone in the suite and her shoulders sagged in disappointment. Still, it was more of Chris than she expected and she hadn't slept that peacefully in weeks.

Open.

Early tee time.

*Priorities.* The part of her brain that was discipline and determination forced her out of the bed and over to the adjoining door. "Charles," she knocked twice and turned the knob. "It's six, I want to be out of here by seven." She peeked around the edge of the door and saw his head lift up.

"S'morning already?"

"Yeah buddy, and it's gonna be hot." She left the door open a crack and went to the table where Chris had left one of the bottles of red Gatorade. It wasn't cold, but Laura cracked open the seal and downed half the bottle anyway. Wiping her mouth with the back of her hand she took stock of her body's condition. *Not too bad, drink more today or they'll be sticking IV needles in your arm.* The previous day's exhaustion was replaced with cautious optimism as she flexed her shoulders and heard the joints pop. She went to the closet and started laying her clothes for the day, choosing a blue shirt to go with khaki shorts. *Four under par. You'd think I knew what I was doing.*

A good night's sleep made all the difference. *Thanks, Chris.*

"Are you somebody?" A woman held out a hat and a sharpie pen to Laura in a plea for an autograph if she was in fact somebody.

"No..."

"Oh look, that's Mi Ja Song!" The woman turned to chase down the new object of her affection and Laura was immediately dismissed. Shaking her head, she continued up the path to the practice tee where Charles already waited, and she quickened her steps when she saw the slim figure standing next to the caddy.

"Morning. Did you get any sleep?" Laura surprised herself by draping her arm around the reporter's shoulders.

"Enough, I think." Chris let her eyes rove over Laura's face and smiled. "When we checked in they let us have a golf cart today. Did you have anything to do with that?"

"It seems I still have some influence."

"Kaz, you'd have some influence if you were a pig farmer in Abilene," Charles said as he zipped up a pocket on the side of the club bag. "Wanna hit a few?"

"No, I'm warm enough." She slid her arm off of Chris's shoulders with a pat. "What's on the agenda today?"

"That filler piece for the network. Don't forget the interview after your round."

Laura grimaced. "I know, but if I don't make the cut it'll all be moot."

"Don't even say that," Charles chided, "One shot at a time, one hole at a time, one day at a time."

"See what I have to put up with? Zen and the art of golf."

Chris grinned. "Just play like you did yesterday."

Laura unwrapped a new golf glove and slapped it on her thigh before tucking it in the waistband of her shorts. "Easier said than done," she muttered.

"It's just a golf cart, why can't I drive it?"

Jody only rolled his eyes and snorted derisively as he braked to allow some pedestrians to cross in front of them. They had caught Lori Kendall on 16 and followed her through the 18th. It looked like she was going to make the cut since she finished the day at even par, leaving her at 2 under for the tournament. Their other college student didn't fare as well; Terri Stockman was going to finish a dismal 17 over par, her first Open experience less than memorable.

"We should be able to catch Kaz at the turn. How does the cut work again?"

Chris held on as they flew around a corner dangerously close to some azalea bushes. "Really, I could do a better job of driving this thing." Obediently, Jody slowed down. "It's ten strokes within the leader, ties included, or the top sixty scores."

The name Kasdan was holding steady in the middle of the leader board and had moved to 6 under. Laura was also leading in the statistical category of most greens hit in regulation but when Chris mentioned that to Charles, the caddy shook his head. "We don't talk about that. It just means she's sticking to the game plan."

They pulled up close to the tee on the 9th hole and Chris hopped out. "I'm going to walk for a while, is that okay with you?" She picked up a bottle of water and made her way through the crowd, craning her neck to see who was on the tee box. Laura and Charles were easy to spot; both of them were much taller than the others on the elevated grass mound.

The routine was familiar to Chris now. She watched Laura spin the club, thump it down and look down the fairway. Half a practice swing, then a moment of stillness before the graceful power exploded. The gallery became more appreciative with every drive, and Chris recognized a few faces that had followed this group of golfers on the day before. Charles took the driver and Barbara teed off with no practice swing and then they were all striding down the fairway as the clubs rattled in the bags.

"You were with her yesterday, weren't you?" A tall tanned woman in Ray Bans fell into step beside Chris. "Laura Kasdan, I mean. We've been following her. She sure is fun to watch."

Chris nodded. "She's my boss."

"Really? I know she's an amateur, what does she do?"

"She's the News Director at a TV station."

"Cool, so you're in TV too?" Two other women joined them.

"Yeah. Are you from around here?" Chris slipped into reporter mode.

"No, we drove over from Pensacola. We try to do a couple of LPGA events every year and this was pretty close, so…" She shrugged. They came up parallel to Susan Fisher's ball and stopped when the course marshals held up their hands for quiet. A well-hit fairway wood left the ball short and right of the green and then Barbara Nelson hit hers to the edge of the green. Laura's ball was twenty yards further and the gallery moved forward. She was in the middle of the fairway, and Chris watched her nod at something Charles said before she took the club and waggled it as she set up.

Laura didn't wear sunglasses when she played, so her emotions were on display after she made contact with the ball. Concern first, then optimism, and finally a pleased grin as the ball bounced to the center of the green before her game face slid back into place.

Chris turned to the three women who were still standing next to her. "Would you mind doing a quick interview on who you're following? It'll only take a minute." She waved at Jody, who had parked the cart in the shade. He grabbed the camera and headed their way.

"Sure," she said, obviously flattered at being asked.

"Let me get your names." Chris had her notebook out and was scribbling away as Jody framed the shot. A few minutes later she was thanking them and jumping into the cart hoping to see Laura putt for eagle.

The putt didn't fall, but she made the birdie and the red "–3" for the day went up on the leader board. Now, at 7 under, Laura left the green passing by Chris and Jody. With a wink, she handed the ball she'd just pulled out of the cup to a girl standing outside the ropes and smiled when she squealed in delight. Then all three golfers and their caddies went across to the clubhouse to use the facilities before taking on the back nine.

The pars added up faster than the birdies and Laura found herself grinding her teeth at missed opportunities. Play had slowed considerably, and by the 15th tee she was pacing along with Barbara. After a look at Susan the three of them decided to duck under the ropes and go stand in the shade of some trees, mixing with the gallery and causing the security people to mutter into their walkie talkies.

"So how is life in the real world, Kaz?" Always friendly, Susan started the conversation.

"I'm not sure TV news qualifies as the real world," Laura responded dryly.

"Heard you ran into some trouble in Dallas." Susan asked the question but Barbara chuckled.

"Is there *anyone* who doesn't know about that?"

"Assume that if you keep playing like you are right now *everyone* is going to know," Barbara said in her droll British manner.

Laura resisted the urge to crack her knuckles and turned to scan the crowd that had moved away from them at the urging of the marshals. She spotted the camera and gave a brief wave, smiling as Jody's head popped up from behind the viewfinder. Her searching continued until she spotted the pale gold of Chris's hair. The reporter was chatting animatedly to a man and a woman, and Laura felt a smile shape her lips just from watching her. Chris looked over at that moment and their eyes met.

*Electric calm. Weird.* Laura felt a shiver and suppressed a laugh.

"We're up." Susan nudged Laura's shoulder and they walked back to the box. *Gotta find some strokes...somewhere.*

She found one on 15. The long par 5 almost spelled trouble when her second shot landed in the bunker on the left of the green, but a nice out left her a very makeable putt for birdie. Another par at 16 and a six-inch tapped in birdie on 17 left Laura breathing a little easier on the tee box at 18.

She drank some water and draped a cold towel around her neck as they waited for the group in front to move up. "Looking good, Kaz," Charles told her as he wiped off the ball and passed it over. "Finish up and I'll buy you a drink."

Laura yawned a little nervously and tossed the towel back to the attendant before pulling on her sweat-dampened glove again. The birdie on 17 gave her the honor of hitting first, and she rolled one of the orange tees between her fingers before teeing up the ball. The crowd completely surrounded the final hole and bleachers ringed the green as they waited expectantly for the drive. One twirl of the club as she pictured the flight of the ball, then the address. *Swing easy, all the way through.* She felt and heard the contact, already analyzing the motion before she ever lifted her head to follow the ball. It was a good, long, safe drive, and relief washed over her in waves.

After the others hit, she walked up the fairway with her head down. It wasn't a particularly tricky hole, but it could certainly make a golfer pay for a lack of concentration. Strokes could be made up and lost here and that's what made it a perfect finish.

Laura flipped out her orange yardage book then looked for the sprinkler head at 125 yards out. Finding it, she paced off the distance to her ball. She stepped out of the way, waiting for Susan to hit first since she was the furthest away. *115 to the front of the green...pin's ten yards back. No wind, should be a wedge.* She turned and Charles was already handing her the club.

Susan's shot landed safely on the green and then it was Laura's turn. She put a little more into it than she intended and winced as it rolled a good twenty feet past the hole. Impatiently, she stripped off her glove as she waited for Barbara to chip up. Then all three were striding to the green to the sound of applause from the gallery.

Two putts later and the round was history for Laura who escaped with a par, as did Susan. Barbara three-putted and fell to 1 over par. Since Susan was in the clubhouse at 10 under, the chance of the Englishwoman making the cut was slim.

*5 under today and 9 under for two days, you really couldn't ask for more, Kaz.* She signed her scorecard and left the scorers tent, only to be buttonholed by a USGA media rep and led to the media room. *And I still have to do that damned network interview. Crap.* All Laura wanted was a shower. She and Susan were ushered to a table and someone gave them bottled water before the questions started. Most of them were for Susan, since she was more recognizable, but a few went Laura's way. "How does it feel to be the low amateur?"

"Everyone isn't finished yet."

"Is the heat or the crowd bothering you?"

"No." *Like I'm gonna tell you it is?*

"What do you do for a living when you're not playing golf?"

*Oh boy, someone didn't do his research.* "I'm the News Director at WBFC in Burkett Falls." There was a moment of silence and Laura could feel Susan holding back a snicker.

"What are you hoping to accomplish here, Ms. Kasdan?"

"A top ten finish would be nice. Mostly I'm tuning up for the U.S. Amateur."

"If you're successful here, do you think it will influence you to turn pro?" The question came from the back of the room and Laura almost knocked over her water bottle when she heard the familiar voice.

*Chris. What is she doing?* "No. Not anytime soon." Puzzled, she looked into green eyes and tilted her head. *You could've just asked. Why here?*

The rest of the questions were for Susan, and Laura made her escape down the hall only to run into Jan Sheffield. "Just who I was looking for. You weren't going to skip out on me, were you?"

"The thought had crossed my mind."

"Uh huh. Let's get you wired up. Hey Chris, did you want to sit in on this?"

Laura smirked without turning around. *Didn't even have to look...knew she was there.* "I'd really like to, okay with you Laura?"

"Sure," she said with fake sincerity, but Chris just patted her back and chuckled.

The production assistant tried to help her with the mic, but she waved him away and did it herself, looping the wire expertly before clipping it to her shirt. Some other assistant powdered her face to kill the shine and she knew it would be paste in a matter of minutes. Robin Gardner, the network's host for women's golf coverage, came in and introduced herself before settling into the chair across from her. "When we first talked about doing this, we really had no idea you'd be so high on the leader board. You were more of an interesting sidebar. How would you judge the Open Championship so far?"

Laura opted for the cliché answers. "The course is in beautiful shape and everyone has been just great. It's been a fabulous experience."

"Laura…"

"Call me Kaz."

"Right. You won the '95 and '96 Amateurs, but you dropped out of the competitive spotlight. What have you been doing?"

*Hardball?Okay.* Laura shifted in her seat. "I concentrated on my career in television news. It took up a lot of my time."

"So why come back?"

"Things change. I wanted to play again and this seemed like a good opportunity."

"Okay, cut." Robin looked at Laura and raised a perfect eyebrow. "You're not giving me much here."

A tight smile crossed Laura's face. She knew she was being hostile, but couldn't seem to stop herself. "Robin," she leaned forward and spoke softly, "I am not going to tell twenty million viewers my reasons for quitting. I will tell you about rebuilding my game and how much work it took, how much time it takes to balance a career with amateur competition, or I will tell you what I think the USGA needs to do to get more people including women and minorities interested in golf, but don't ask me to explain why I walked away. That ain't gonna happen."

Robin nodded slowly. "So how did you go about rebuilding your game, and why did you think you had to?"

Laura chuckled, "I have a great coach, and I finally decided to listen to him. His son is my caddy…"

"Aahh," Laura groaned as the masseuse worked on the muscles of her lower back and clenched her teeth when he hit a particularly sore spot. She was in the trainer's room, where four massage tables had been set up, and all four were occupied.

"Hey. Interesting interview." Chris sat down on a chair next to the table where Laura was being worked on. "Certainly reminded me of why you're the news director and I'm not."

"Oww, how did you get in here?"

"Running away again? This isn't off limits to the press and besides, Charles told me where you were."

"Good ol' Charles, the rat fink." Laura jerked as the masseuse hit another tender area.

Chris leaned in. "Don't talk about your caddy that way, he and Jody are going bar hopping tonight."

"Really?"

"Really," Chris answered with a wiggle of her eyebrows. "Though I'm not sure how much bar hopping one can do in Tupelo. Should tie them up for a few hours anyway." As if a light switched on, Chris suddenly became aware of the vast expanse of naked flesh stretched out on the massage table. The sheet only covered Laura from her lower back to her knees, and the sight of the masseuse manipulating muscle that Chris had intimate knowledge of was…disturbing, distracting, and arousing all at the same time. She swallowed as her breaths started coming in shallow gasps. "I uh, when you're finished here…I'll wait outside. Right outside." She stood up and practically stumbled to the door.

Laura winced again and wondered what was going through the reporter's head.

They had dinner at a steakhouse that boasted the largest salad bar in Mississippi, Laura still managing to remain anonymous despite the fact that the town was crawling with golf fans. "You gotta wonder how many six-foot blue-eyed women wander through here on a regular basis," Chris observed as Laura unlocked her hotel room door. "No one's asked for your autograph yet?"

"Well, a couple have asked but they thought I was someone else." The room was clean again and she went to the fridge automatically and got out some water. "Want some?" she offered.

"No, I'm good." Chris walked over to the sofa and picked up the remote to turn on the TV. "Hey, you're on SportsCenter."

"No kidding." Laura grinned in childish delight as she watched herself birdie the 17$^{th}$ all over again and Chris smiled at her reaction. *She works in TV but this is still a thrill for her.* She sat down on the sofa and tugged on Laura's hand in an invitation to join her. "You were great today. All that hard work is paying off."

"Mmm." Laura exhaled and plopped down with an unusual lack of grace. "Not yet, we'll see."

"Is that all you're hoping for, a top ten finish?" Chris asked, one hand moving to play in dark hair.

Laura turned and regarded her lover as blue eyes darkened with emotion. "No, Chris, I'm playing to win. I *always* play to win."

*"But just in golf or news; anything else and she'd be…lost."* Chris frowned slightly as she moved her hand to the back of Laura's neck, pulling her closer until she could just barely feel their lips touching. Slowly, she traced the outline of Laura's lower lip with the tip of her tongue before kissing her in earnest. Then her hands were pushing the long lean body back against the cushions, wanting to reacquaint herself with the woman who dominated most of her waking thoughts.

Chris could feel Laura's hands against her abdomen unsnapping her shorts to pull her shirt free from the waistband and make contact with warm skin. She moved to bury her face in the fragrant mass of dark hair before nipping at the pulse point on Laura's neck. With a growl of frustration, she pulled at the front of the shirt keeping her from touching all of the flesh she wanted to. "Damn polo shirts." A brief snort of laughter vibrated the body underneath hers and Laura stopped what she was doing to yank the offending garment over her head. Chris claimed Laura's lips again as she ran two fingers around the edge of Laura's sports bra.

Breaking off the kiss she looked down. "No hooks…you're not helping me out here."

An eyebrow arched. "We could just stop and strip," Laura breathed with a smile.

"Where's the fun in that?"

Limbs tangled and clothes eventually came off so that skin slid on skin and Chris could touch and taste to her heart's content. Laura arched against her, and as always, she never made a sound as the shudders of her climax wracked her lean body.

Chris laid her head over Laura's heart, listening to the pounding slow and become steady and even again. She closed her eyes and stopped herself from saying the words that threatened to spill out. *How can I love someone so much and not say anything?* Chris swallowed the niggling fear that even if she said it, the feelings might never be returned. *And isn't part of her better than none of her?* It was a new feeling, this insecurity, and Chris thrust it back into a dark corner of her mind. "You okay?" The question rumbled under her ear and she pushed herself up, her arms supporting her weight.

"Fine," she grinned. "And you?"

"Considerably better than just fine." Laura moved quickly, reminding Chris about the power and grace of her body as she reversed their positions. "You got a little sun today." She bent down to kiss a shoulder and trace a line down the middle of the smaller woman's body.

The callused hands that gripped a golf club so confidently began to explore Chris's compact body, coaxing shivers and soft cries from the blonde woman. Again and again Laura brought Chris close to the brink, only to back off and start a new attack. Finally, she finished what she'd started and winced when Chris dug her nails into her shoulders as her hips bucked. "Kaz," she ground out, "you…are…a tease."

Laura waited for the smaller body under hers to calm, then smiled against Chris's throat. When the air conditioning kicked on she shivered lightly. "I'm a little cold, how 'bout you?"

"Uh, no. I have a blanket, you're the one who's exposed." Chris was hit with a blast of cool air as Laura left the sofa and she whimpered at the sudden loss of warmth. Laura was back a moment later, draping the blanket that she robbed from the bed over the two of them as she settled back on the sofa.

"How much time do we have?" Laura murmured as she pulled Chris closer.

"I told Charles to call first." Chris smoothed the hair on Laura's forehead. "Probably ten or eleven. This is harder than I thought." Laura didn't answer so Chris cleared her throat and went on, "I always thought that I'd meet someone while I was doing the things that I like to do. Like softball or running or something like that. But you know, I spend most of my time at work and I like my job, so why is it such a mistake to get involved with someone I work with?"

"Because I'm not just someone you work with, I'm your boss. And there are other considerations."

Chris sighed, "I know. It would just be nice if *something* in my life was simple."

"It would be nice, but it wouldn't be nearly as interesting."

* * * *

On Saturday after the cut, there were two in each playing group instead of three, so things moved along a little faster. Laura was in the second to last group and her partner was a Swede who was even taller than she was. Carin Andersen had an impressive list of tour victories to her credit and was a bit of a maverick on the course. With her long baggy cargo shorts, her skintight black sleeveless top and black golf shoes, she needed only a wallet on a chain to complete the biker chick image. Carin actually owned a Harley and she and Laura bickered over the merits of the American cruiser versus Laura's Triumph Thunderbird.

The most amazing thing about the Swede was her ability to get in and out of trouble. Hole after hole she landed in the rough, the sand, the tall fescue, and the woods, but somehow she managed to pull herself out of trouble with some miraculous shot. Carin finished at even par, which, given the extent of her errant shots, was pretty impressive. Even though Laura was disappointed with her 3 under, she enjoyed the round thoroughly and actually trudged from the scorer's tent to the network booth with a smile on her face.

Keith was there along with Chris and Lisa as they wired the mic and powdered her face again. This time, Robin Gardner was a little friendlier as she asked about the round and Laura was enthusiastic as well. After wishing her good luck, Robin dismissed Laura and she stripped off the mic before handing it back to the production assistant. "How'd it look?"

"Better than yesterday," Chris said dryly and Lisa laughed, "Still working on those social skills, huh Kaz?"

Laura rolled her eyes as they moved to the hall. "Who else is here?"

"Just us and Jody's wife. Trey couldn't make it." Keith led them down the hall to the media room. "This is going to be kind of tough for you. Don Farmer called yesterday and he said that we are to 'No Comment' anything about you in Dallas, so my guess is they're already asking questions."

Laura nodded, understanding how the game was going to be played; hell, it was her game. The media rep led her to the table and she faced the reporters. She wasn't a kid, she was one of them—but any hopes for professional courtesy vanished with the first question. "Miss Kasdan, why did you leave Dallas?"

"That is between me and my employers." Laura folded her hands and waited for the next shot.

"You had an exemption for last year's Open; why didn't you play?"

Laura really thought about answering truthfully. *Because I sucked.* "I wasn't prepared to play in the Open last year." *Don't ask, don't ask, don't ask.*

"Is it true that you struck an anchor in Dallas?"

*Godfuckingdamn.* It always came back to Dallas, the one professional failure that everyone could point to. Any serenity that might have been left from her night with Chris and a good round of golf vanished and left a bitter taste in her mouth. "I can't comment on that. I thought we were here to talk about golf?" Laura waited a beat. "No? Then I'm outta here." *You were right, Barbara; everybody's gonna know.*

She was out the door before the media rep knew what happened.

Laura headed for the locker room, but as luck would have it she ran into Chris and Jan Sheffield huddled together in the hall. *The golf has been great, it's just when the media gets involved it all goes to hell in a handbasket.* Laura caught the words "resume tape" and suddenly she was back in Dallas watching events spiral out of control. The dark machine took over and she was powerless to stop it.

"Excuse me, Jan, could I have a word with you?" Laura crooked her finger at the producer with a grim smile. "Just a second, Chris."

Laura turned and crossed her arms, using her patented glare to full effect on the network lackey, and lowered her voice. "Let me be a News Director for just a minute. Am I mistaken, or are you soliciting one of my contracted employees?"

Jan smirked, "Laura…"

"Kaz."

"Kaz, then. Contracts are broken all the time…or bought out. Any station could use some spare cash."

"I'd rather keep my talent. Just because you're network and we're an affiliate does not exempt you from a lawsuit for tampering."

"Oh, I don't think…"

Laura snarled, "Oh, I do. Chris, are you finished here?"

Chris jerked back in alarm. *What's going on with her?* "Sure," she said in a puzzled voice. She shrugged at Jan as she passed and it didn't go unnoticed by her boss.

Laura was still wearing her spikes and they clacked over the threshold when she pushed open the door and stepped outside. The crowds were thinning and Chris followed the taller woman out past the courtyard to the place where Charles had left the clubs. "What is wrong with you?"

Laura whirled around, her posture stiff and angry. "Do you want to pursue a network opportunity now?" *Please say no. Say 'of course not, I'm happy where I am.'*

"I was just asking…"

"Come on, Chris, a network seduction is about as subtle as a jackhammer." *Just say no, you weren't interested. Say you wouldn't leave.*

"I know that."

Laura reached for the only weapon she could think of and flung it out, mindless in her need to hurt as much as she was hurting. "And if you want to break that contract, Erica's the one you'll have to go up against."

Chris paled. "That's a rotten thing to say."

"Get your tape ready." Laura hoisted the bag over her shoulder and started walking to the parking lot.

The anger boiled up and Chris chased after her boss. "You can't just throw that at me and run away…Oh, wait, that's what you're really good at."

"No one twisted your arm, Chris, you chose." Laura opened the back of the Jeep and tossed the clubs in. "And like it or not, everyone pays for their choices." *Some things you never quit paying for.*

Chris exhaled angrily. "Lisa and Charles were right about you. You don't have a clue about anything outside golf or news."

"Charles was right, Lisa was right. Was there anyone who wasn't right about what I am?" Laura snapped.

"Yeah, me," Chris shot out bitterly. "I thought you could learn to care about something else. So what was I? A convenient diversion, just a body to pass the time with?" She could feel an ache in her chest that threatened to stay with her forever. *I will not cry.* "So that's it?"

"Tell Charles I took the Jeep." Laura jumped in and started the engine, squealing rubber on her way out of the lot. Chris turned and slammed into Keith's solid form. *Oh goddamn.* "Did you hear…?"

"Everything." He adjusted his glasses in what Chris knew was his all-purpose nervous gesture. "It certainly explains…a lot." He dropped his hands, not sure what he should do. "I suspected you were…I mean, it doesn't matter to me."

Chris sighed. "Who else knows?"

"That you're gay, or that you're sleeping with Kaz?"

Chris covered her eyes. "Both, I guess."

"No one's said anything about Kaz, but I can think of just a few people who've mentioned the possibility that you might be gay." He stuffed his hands in his pockets and shifted his weight from foot to foot. "Come on. I found three more hotel rooms. Kaz'll freak when she gets the bill. I'll just drop you off and you can have one by yourself to crash in."

She gave a short laugh to keep from crying. "Okay, but we'd better find Charles."

As she walked back to the clubhouse, Chris shook her head. *It's television. Everybody looks. Professional infidelity is nothing in this business.* She stopped as a thought suddenly occurred to her. *Unless you couldn't tell the difference between personal and professional infidelity.*

*Oh God.*

---

At one o'clock on Sunday, Laura shut down every thought that had nothing to do with golf and took the driver from Charles.

*"The last group on the last day of the U.S. Open. If you can walk down the 18th fairway with a chance to win it, you'll have done better than I ever did."* Laura remembered her mother saying the words as clearly as if she'd said them yesterday. Well, she was in the last group, but whether she would have a chance to win it remained to be seen.

Just you and me, Kaz." Susan Fisher smiled at Laura and briefly thought that Sarah Kasdan's daughter was more dangerous than anyone she was likely to play against on tour. "Your mother would have been pleased to see you with a chance to beat me."

"Yes, she would. But I'm not my mom."

"No, you're not."

Susan was introduced and teed off first since she was the leader at 15 under. Like a surgeon, Laura drove her ball precisely down the center of the fairway and started walking even before it finished rolling.

The course was stingy on that Sunday afternoon. Laura continued to play flawless golf with no bogeys, but she didn't find a stroke until she birdied number 7, a par 3 over water to an elevated green. Susan bogied number 8 to fall to 14 under. On the teebox at number 9, Laura took the time to study the leader board, noting that no one was within five strokes of her score. She tightened her jaw and looked up at Charles, who was regarding her with a worried look. *Waiting for me to fall apart? Not this time.*

The crowd was growing, gathering in more spectators as the final group finished each hole, and up at the 9th green the bleachers were overflowing. Laura flexed her shoulders before twirling her driver, then caught sight of a blonde head in the gallery just up from the tee box. *All the sun has made her hair even lighter.* Shaking her head at the break in her routine, she went back to where Charles was standing and wiped her hands on the towel slung over his shoulder.

"You okay?"

"Yeah," she sniffed. "Just lost it for a minute." Walking back, she re-teed the ball and swung, disappointed at the slight hook that put her in the rough on the left.

Again she purged her mind of anything that didn't relate to the course and her game and managed to get the ball out of the rough and onto the fairway to set up for another par. *At least I can still putt.*

She and Susan stopped at the turn and Laura strode quickly through the locker room to run cold water over her hands and face. She ran through the remaining holes in her mind, looking for opportunities, violating one of her cardinal rules in the process. *They're out there. I just have to find them.*

Back out into the heat and Laura was greeted by another long par 5. Susan birdied it to move back to 15 under and Laura settled for another par.

11 and 12 were adventures at the beach as Laura landed in the sand traps on both holes. Still, she managed to make par. Charles was starting to get nervous, his usual cheerful manner evaporating along with the opportunities to make up strokes, the only consolation being that Susan couldn't break the par wall either. Finally, on number 16, Laura's second shot landed just two feet from the hole and she had another birdie. She tossed her putter down and took off her hat to run her hands through her hair before heading to the 17th.

Laura was one stroke back with two holes to play, but the birdie had given her new optimism, and since she had birdied 17 on Thursday, Friday, and Saturday, her confidence was growing.

*183 yards, water on the left, sand around the green, a little wind from the right.* Laura asked Charles for the seven wood. She placed the ball on a tuft of grass without a tee and spun the club. After a half swing she set up and drew the club back smoothly, reversed the motion, and swept through, hitting slightly behind the ball.

Laura knew it was trouble as soon as it left the clubface and headed left, catching the edge of the green and rolling down into the sand and close to the water. *Shit!* She ground her teeth. "Am I wet?"

"I don't know, could be on the edge." Charles took the wood and slipped the cover on. "We'll look."

Susan landed hers in center of the green some twenty feet from the pin and they all started the walk to the green. The course marshals were gathered around the sandy area called the beach that led from the green to the water. As Laura approached, her heart sank, because apparently her ball had.

Well, not quite. Half of it was sticking out of the water and she and Charles stood staring down at what looked to be an insurmountable obstacle.

"What happens now?" Chris turned to Lisa, her eyes concerned.

"She can go back to the tee and hit another shot but she'll be hitting her third shot. Then it's pretty much all over 'cause she can't make up two strokes to tie, not really, and that's only if she finished with a four here."

"So it is over." Chris felt the disappointment welling up from underneath the hurt she was already sure she couldn't deal with.

"She could play it where it lies, but that's a big risk. She could lose a bunch of strokes just getting it out of the water."

"What will she do?"

Lisa snorted. "What she always does."

"Go back to the tee box and try for the 4. Hold your position." Charles was adamant.

Laura wiped her mouth. "Charles, I have no position. I am an amateur and I'm not playing for money. This could be my last best chance and I'm not throwing it away. If I go back to the tee, I've already lost." She smiled bitterly at the caddy and squeezed his shoulder. "My choice, remember?"

He looked down and nodded, then turned away to reach for the bag, pulling out the sand wedge and handing it to her. "Can't ground it."

Laura nodded and bent down to untie her shoes, pulling them off and tucking her socks inside before handing them to Charles. She cringed a little as she realized her ridiculous tan was on display for all the world to see, her white feet contrasting with the bronze of her legs as though they had been dipped in paint. Shouldering the club, she stepped into the water and set up behind the ball. She practiced the angle of the swing without touching the water before digging in and with one final calculating look at the green, Laura swung down as hard as she could.

She was drenched by the splash and the ball popped almost straight up. Her first thought was relief that she had at least gotten out of the water, but the ball landed above the hole and started rolling and Laura only needed to hear the roar from the crowd and see the look of incredulity on Charles's face to know what had happened. Scrambling out of the water, she made it to the green, bare feet coated with sand, and pulled the ball out of the cup. Awkwardly, she acknowledged the crowd with a wave and walked back to where Charles stood with her shoes.

"Aw, Kaz." He grabbed her in a bear hug. "It's always better to be good *and* lucky."

Laura took the shoes and the towel and sat down to clean her feet. She got them on and wiggled her toes to dislodge some of the remaining grit and stood up to see Susan make par. *So, you have your chance. Whatever else, you came through here.* She looked at the ball then searched the crowd as they all started to move to the 18th. *Stop looking, you won't find her.* But she did, and without knowing why, she walked over to the ropes where Chris stood, the plastic of her All Access ID card reflecting the late afternoon sun like a beacon. Laura swallowed as she got closer and wished that she were wearing sunglasses so she could be as shuttered as the reporter was with hers. She leaned over and pressed the ball into her hands, the crowd building and pushing around her. "Here, hold on to this." Then the marshals were moving her along to the next tee.

A solid 250-yard drive and Laura was halfway home. Susan's drive landed close by and they headed for the center point of the hole, the crowd applauding in waves as they passed. Susan hit first and placed it about ten feet from the hole. The gallery went wild, sensing a birdie opportunity and a possible playoff if there was a tie. Laura swept the club a couple of times across the grass before stepping up to her ball. *Easy, don't overswing.*

It made the green easily and rolled inside Susan's. She gave the club to Charles and he grinned. She walked up the fairway of the 18th hole in the last group, on the last day of the Open, for a chance to win. The applause and cheers were deafening, but Laura had never felt so empty in her life. *Because this isn't all there is.*

She marked her ball and tossed it to Charles to clean as Susan lined up her birdie putt. Stepping back, she watched the older woman stroke the ball with a firm touch. It never wavered from its path, and the ooooohs of the crowd exploded as it dove into the cup.

*Make this for a playoff tomorrow or miss and lose.* It was as simple as that. Laura walked around the ball, looking for any kind of break or clue that would tell her the right line. *Six feet, I've made a million of them.* She stood over it slightly longer than usual and that might have been what made the difference. The stroke was sure, but the line was wrong and it missed the hole by a scant inch.

Laura closed her eyes and shook her head ruefully as she walked up to tap in. Susan had won her first Open and Laura was the first to congratulate her. Turning, she looked for Charles but spotted Chris first instead, and Laura remembered everything she had lost.

Second place sucks. Don't let anyone tell you differently.

*"The deal's on."*



The silver medal was for second place; the gold pin was for low amateur. A lifetime of dedication was condensed into two shiny bits of metal and Laura rubbed a finger along one edge before snapping the boxes closed and dropping them into her tote bag.

The locker room was empty except for the clutter left behind by golfers eager to move on to the next stop where fortunes might be reversed on another course on another day. Laura tossed her damp towel into the laundry chute and gathered up the rest of her things. There was no next stop for her on tour, just another Monday in the newsroom, and since there would be hell to pay on so many levels, there was no comfort in that.

Anxious to avoid the crowds out in front, she went out the maintenance exit of the locker room and down the back hall to the service entrance of the kitchen. The Awards Dinner was in full swing and the staff was busy with trays of covered dishes waiting to be served as Laura slipped out the back and on to the loading dock. *No press, a nice clean getaway.*

"She choked. I coulda made that putt." Two men were standing at the foot of the stairs smoking, their shirts marking them as tournament volunteers. Laura's mouth tightened as she skipped down the steps and pushed her way past them, ignoring their stares and resisting the urge to comment. She crossed the pavement quickly and vaulted over a low wall into the main parking lot. She took one last look back at the antebellum-style clubhouse, trying to etch her last impression of Cypress Hill into memory, certain that she wouldn't be returning any time soon.

*Nothing like making your failures as public as possible. Dallas is out in the open, I* did *choke on that putt, and let's not forget that I tossed away the best thing in my life with both hands...in front of my Managing Editor.*

*Chris.* The pain was suffocating and the bitterness of regret choked off any excuse she might have offered in an effort to assuage the guilt. Swallowing back something suspiciously like a sob she turned away, realizing that she would never be whole again and wondering how one could endure half a life.

*He didn't; he gave up.* In that instant, Laura Kasdan understood her father.

Chris sat on the fender of the Jeep and waited. Dusk was still a couple of hours away and the day had yet to give up any of its sweltering heat. The ringing whine of the cicadas rose and fell in the typical soundtrack of a Mississippi summer. She was hot, tired, disappointed, and hurt. But she had all the patience in the world and the time to practice it. The scrape of footsteps was her first warning that her vigil was coming to an end and Chris looked up to see Laura slow warily as she approached the Jeep. *This is my version of waiting on the steps, can you tell?*

"Where's Charles?" It wasn't what Laura wanted to ask, but it would have to do. Whatever else, she swore to herself, she would hear Chris out. *I will not run.*

"Lisa took him to the airport on her way out of town. She offered." Chris kept her sunglasses on, knowing that if she took them off she'd be surrendering an advantage. Laura held no such edge. Her eyes were the blue-white of some barely contained emotion.

"Keith and Jody?"

"Already gone. I was hoping you could give me a lift." Chris held her breath.

Laura looked down at her feet. "You should... You should've gone back with one of them."

Chris slid off the Jeep and held out the keys that the caddy had left behind. "I wanted to go back with you. Just you." When Laura didn't take them, Chris closed her fingers around the keys and shook them like dice. "I told you that you'd never have a reason not to trust me. It was a while ago but you're usually pretty good at remembering things."

"I said don't make promises you can't keep," Laura muttered.

"I didn't." Chris moved closer. "I gave my word when I signed the contract. Before us, before I'd even worked with you for a week. There were no outs then, not for a top ten job and not for network."

Laura was silent but her hand tightened on the handle of the bag.

"You didn't trust me and that's what hurt the most." Chris's voice was gently accusing. "I like where I am, but that doesn't mean I don't appreciate being told I'm network caliber."

Laura breathed out a short laugh. *A huge ego wrapped in the thinnest of shells. You should have remembered that.* "You're anything you want to be."

"So what happened?" Chris asked.

"I…" Laura looked around the parking lot. "This isn't where I want to have this conversation, Chris."

"Tough. I have the keys and you really don't want to go back to the Clubhouse." Chris sealed off the avenues of escape and repeated the question. "What happened?"

"I was afraid you'd leave!" Laura snapped as she dropped the bag and stuffed her hands in her pockets. "That's all, afraid. Is that what you wanted to hear?" Frustration colored her tone as she started pacing. "If I'd known you existed when I was in Dallas, *I* would have made you an offer." Laura gave a brief grim laugh. "And Dallas. That's out now too. The only thing that saves me there is that there were no criminal or civil charges filed and if it's not on paper, it never happened—people can gossip all they want."

The floodgates were open now and Chris could only stand back and listen.

"…Corporate-wise they can sit back and deny everything since part of the deal was that Roger and I don't discuss it. Good ol' Roger. He's still grabbing my ass and I can't do a damned thing about it. Then that smug network bitch smiles and tells me that contracts are bought out all the time and any station could use some spare cash." Laura turned away and savagely slammed the heel of her hand against the Jeep. "And I know in my gut that if you wanted to go, Art would take that deal no matter what I said." The Jeep absorbed another blow. "Sell you off like you were cattle…for a nice price." Laura spun to face Chris. "Y'all are acting like you're best friends, and you don't say anything…you don't tell her you're not interested, you don't tell *me* you're not interested."

As abruptly as the anger appeared, it was gone, leaving confused hurt behind. "I didn't know you were just enjoying the stroke." Laura's voice dropped and she brought the argument full circle. "I was afraid that you'd go and I'd never…" She stopped, appalled at where her lack of control had led.

Chris waited for Laura to finish but all she got was a half shrug, the one that Chris knew dismissed whatever emotion the tall woman was feeling but didn't want to deal with. "You'd never what?"

Laura swallowed, aware that she'd given away too much and unwilling to back down for fear of never getting close again. She took a deep breath and brought both hands up to gently pull the sunglasses off Chris's face to expose green eyes flecked warmly with gold in the fading summer sun. *Will I be able to tell? Will I be able to see?*

Chris surrendered her advantage and she heard the Ray Bans click as they were folded closed. The face she looked into was open and vulnerable, blue eyes studying her with an intensity that made her heart dip in her chest.

"I'd never have the chance to tell you that I love you." She winced inwardly, it sounded so pathetic.

*Great, Kaz. In a parking lot. Your timing is impeccable and you certainly win points for style. Lisa would be proud.*

Chris gulped in astonishment. "Love me?" There was a rattle as the keys hit pavement. "You…" She blinked in wonder laced with doubt. "I didn't think you'd ever see it...much less *say* it."

Laura couldn't stand the disappointment and she twisted away. "That's pretty insulting." She bent to pick up the bag, wishing for numbness instead of throbbing hurt. The cool touch of Chris's hand on her arm made Laura jump and she schooled her expression into blankness.

"I didn't mean it that way." Chris stilled Laura's nervous hands with her own and brought them to her lips for a kiss before resting them against her heart. Breathing felt like such an effort but she reveled in the sensation anyway. "I can't believe you beat me to it."

Laura's jaw went slack. She had hope but little faith. "It wasn't a contest."

Chris couldn't stop the smile that spread across her face. "No, but I…You never cease to amaze me. Just when I think I couldn't possibly love you more, you go and do something like this."

"How long?" It came out as an astonished whisper.

"The live truck, I guess."

"Oh." Laura wished again for some skill in dealing with personal issues. *Never too late to learn.* "I'm just winging it, Chris. I have no idea what comes next. I'm so sorry for what happened yesterday. I can apologize a million times but I don't know how to ask you to forgive me."

"You just did." Chris wrapped her arms around Laura and buried her face in the hollow of the taller woman's shoulder. "About that network thing?"

"Hmm?" Laura swallowed against the sudden fear.

"You're not getting rid of me that easily."

Laura's breathing hitched as she rubbed her cheek against soft blonde hair. Relief that she hadn't spoiled everything seemed to be the only thing holding her up. That and the support of someone she knew was much stronger than she would ever be. "I want to go home. I'm so tired…please, let's just go home." Chris smiled at the childlike plea and rubbed the back under her hands before disentangling herself from Laura's body and bending down to pick up the keys.

"Home it is."

The Jeep was easier to drive than Chris thought and the hum of its tires on the interstate was only mildly annoying. She looked over to where Laura was dozing with her head against the rollbar and her jaw still clenched even in sleep. There were things that they still needed to work out, but for the time being, they were okay.

*She pushes too hard*. Chris rolled her shoulders to ease the stiffness, glad that they were almost home, and put on the blinker for their exit. No secrets, she vowed, and reached over to rub a hand along Laura's thigh. "Hey, we're almost there."

"Mmm." Laura rolled her head over and rubbed one eye. "Sorry I'm lousy company." She yawned and blinked. "You can go straight to your place, I'll take it from there."

"Or you could just stay at my house." Chris licked her lower lip uncertainly. *Sometimes we end up going back to the beginning.*

"I'm good with that," Laura answered softly.

They unloaded Chris's things and carried them into the house, dropping most of them just inside the bedroom door.

"I'm going to get a shower, I feel grungy." Chris slid an arm around Laura's waist and pressed a kiss to a tanned shoulder. She got a weary nod in response.

When she came out of the bathroom later Laura was already asleep on her stomach, the covers pushed down to her waist. Chris stretched out next to her, gently pulling the dark hair away from her face and touching the strong jawline with the tips of her fingers. Laura shifted into the caress and Chris smiled at the unconscious movement. For the first time in her life, she knew that everything she was and everything she wanted were about to collide. She wanted medium market, not too big, not too small, the high profile job, and Laura.

Chris lay awake and watched the other woman sleep. They hadn't talked about golf at all and somehow Chris knew that Laura would have to come to terms with that on her own. Sharing pain was not part of the News Director's nature but Chris would be patient. *You can't out-wait me, Kaz.*

Laura barely cleared the door of the newsroom before Janie was there thrusting a stack of faxes ands messages into her hands. "Thank god you're back. This place has been a madhouse and the phone hasn't stopped ringing. The next time you decide to take over the golf world, could you please give us some advance notice?"

"Glad to see you too." Laura kept walking to her office as Janie continued to hand over packages and letters.

"Elly is picking up the folks from Target Research at the airport, their presentation starts at nine…I don't envy you the two days of consultant hell. The book should be here tomorrow; Corporate won't pay for the advances so don't even ask. Anything else you need to know?"

"Where's Keith?" Laura was dreading that meeting most of all.

"Went to get some breakfast, do you want to see him?"

"As soon as he gets here." Her desk had been clean when she left a week ago and now it was covered again. She glanced quickly through the messages, shaking her head skeptically. Golf club manufacturers, agents, and requests for interviews dominated the pile, with a few congratulatory notes thrown in. *It wasn't supposed to happen this fast. Breakfast with the Mayor?* She tucked the invitation into the corner of her desk blotter and twitched a little at the thought of more privacy lost. *Well, if you do it right, they'll just think you're eccentric. How does Chris stand it?*

"I brought you a Coke. That's okay now, right?"

Laura looked up to see Keith standing awkwardly in the doorway. She smiled a little wryly. "Better than okay, thanks. Go ahead and close the door. What time did you get back last night?"

He pushed the door closed with his foot and brought the drink over to her desk. "About eleven. You were great, you know. I'm sorry the putt didn't fall but you were fabulous to watch." He took off his glasses and started cleaning them on his sleeve. "Where do you go from here?"

She regarded him somberly, knowing that he wasn't just referring to golf. "Nothing's changed Keith, but everything's different. I'm sorry that this will make things difficult here…we had some good chemistry in the newsroom and maybe that won't change. I'd like to think that it's not anybody's business but I'm not naïve. At this point I don't care what anyone says about me, but I will not tolerate gossip about Chris." Laura took a deep breath, willing to call in every favor she was owed to protect the blonde reporter. "I'm asking you to keep this to yourself. You're real close to becoming a news director somewhere, you might as well start learning to keep secrets now." She was uncomfortable with the request and the half-bribe.

"I can't believe you thought you had to ask," Keith said mildly. "I'll admit I'm not the most observant guy on the planet, or maybe I've just been selectively dense, but I knew something was going on." He rubbed his chin and quirked his eyebrow at Laura. "Are you two okay? I mean…" At Laura's slow nod he broke into a grin. "You're never anything but a pro in the newsroom Kaz. I don't expect that'll change. And Chris is…well, Chris."

Laura felt a surge of affection for the stocky young man and wondered what on earth she had done to inspire that kind of loyalty. "I don't know what's going to happen over the next few days. The research will tell us a lot, but the book's *got* to come in with some numbers or everything we've done over the last two months is going to be called into question." *If that happens, I'll put as much distance between us as possible. You shouldn't have to pay for my mistakes.* There was so much at stake now. Before, she'd only worried about herself or the station, never about the other fortunes that were tied to hers. She was wrong: everything *had* changed.

A tap on the door interrupted them and Elly stuck her head in. "They're here. Are you ready?"

"Yeah." Picking up a legal pad and her drink she moved to the door. "Thanks, Keith."

"It'll be good news. I have no doubts."

*That's good, because I have enough for both of us.*

"Kaz, good to see you. I watched you play over the weekend. That was a helluva shot on 17." Dave Franco was a slick producer-turned-consultant that she had known since she worked in Austin, and his ingratiating manner was more than a little irritating.

"Thanks. Art's going to be joining us for the research presentation. Hi Marti, still glad to be off the Anchor desk?" The redhead was Target Research's idea of the perfect on-air personality: bubbly and sincere, someone viewers didn't mind inviting into their homes every evening via the news. Laura couldn't stand her. "Well, Kaz, a week in Mississippi didn't hurt your marketability at all. If you're looking for an agent I could give you some names."

*With a healthy cut for you, I'm sure.* "No, I want to be a news director for a few more years." She met the numbers cruncher, Mark Jennings, and discussed a variety of topics as they waited for the GM to join them. Laura wasn't surprised when Dallas came up.

"Oh, come on," Dave said. "We all have a list of talent we'd like to pop. It's the nature of the business."

"Speak for yourself, Dave," Marti huffed.

"I can't even count 'em all on both hands," Elly said with a grin. The look the Talent Consultant shot at the Promotions Manager was pure venom.

Laura smirked but said nothing. It was easier to think about it now that the price for her lack of control didn't seem quite so high. Now it was time to see if things were really going to work out. "Sorry I'm late." Five pairs of eyes turned to greet the General Manager as he stepped into the conference room. "Let's get this show on the road."

Three-ring binders were passed out and the slide presentation began. First, Mark took them through the methodology of the research, then the market makeup, and finally the results from the survey itself.

"As you can see, the viewer preferences for Channel 4 have declined significantly and we have grown quite a bit." It was good news, but Mark's drone was making Laura sleepy. Art's eyes were narrowed and he seemed to be absorbing every detail. One bar graph after another went up on the screen and she kept pace, turning pages in the binder as they went along. A year ago she would have been ecstatic with results like these, but now she was chafing, anxious to get to the section on personalities. *It's like I can't think about anything else. Us... work... the lack of time. Nobody ever told me how difficult this was gonna be. Okay, no one told me anything, but that's not the point. How am I going to make this work when nothing is typical?*

"I don't have to tell you how important it is that this research remain confidential, especially this next section." Laura's wandering thoughts returned to the conference room with a jerk and she cleared her throat as she leaned forward. Dave started passing out a thin booklet, its cover declaring it the long awaited On Air Personality Study. "If this were to get out, your talent would have a significant advantage when it comes to salary negotiations." Laura rolled her eyes. The hush-hush business bothered her; talent had a right to know if they were any good, and, by the same token, they had the right to know if they stunk. "Marti, it's all yours."

"Thanks, Dave. Boy, do we have some interesting stuff here." The bar graph went up on the screen and Laura blinked at the amount of red climbing past the mark that read eighty percent.

"Oh my god," Elly murmured in awe.

"That's pretty much what we thought. Christine Hanson has eighty-four percent name recognition in this market, with only two percent reacting negatively. We've only seen that with weathermen, never with an anchor and certainly not one who just moved from daytime to prime. It seems you were right about her, Kaz."

*There's your insurance, Chris.* Laura nodded slightly. "What about the others?"

Another graph went up. "They're in the sixties with Michelle holding at fifty-nine. That's something you may want to look at later. Let me show you something else." The graph morphed into a chart. "Hanson hits over forty percent in viewer preference, and tops forty in the quality ranking as well. In short, you have a star. Give her lots of money and lock her in… or she's gone."

Laura felt the dread again for just a moment. "No. She's ours for three years." *Mine as long as I don't screw it up again.*

"Will she stay after that?"

"I don't know," Laura answered honestly. "Will those numbers hold?"

Marti frowned. "I don't see why not. This is phenomenal for someone just moving to prime; I can't emphasize that enough. I'd like to spend some time tomorrow with her, to get a little better feel of what we have here. She tests better than Kurt, your meteorologist; that's unheard of."

"And you were worried." Elly tossed a grin over at Laura. "Makes my job easier."

"Now this doesn't necessarily mean a successful ratings book…" Laura recognized the disclaimer portion of the program. "Sometimes it takes a little while to show up." Marti continued to click through a variety of charts and graphs stopping to point out some trend.

Laura had half of her answers and she was almost giddy with relief. *I was right. This is the payoff. Whatever else happens, Chris can fall back on these numbers and Target can get her a job in any market in the country. She did it…Chris made it work. Now, if we can come through with the book…*

The meeting lasted all day and then they watched the Five and Six. Their luck held and there were no serious glitches to be reported to Corporate as proof positive that WBFC still needed the services of Target Research. *It's not hard to keep a job if all you have to do is say that someone's not doing it right,* Laura thought. *Then you just skip away after you've wrecked a perfectly good news operation.* They all ate dinner at a popular restaurant and by the time the evening was over, she'd had her fill of Dave's and Marti's verbal sparring and Art egging them on. Worn out, she climbed into the Jeep, hating the fact that the consultants would be there for another day.

*Bet she's on the swing. Haven't seen her all day, unless you count watching her on the Six.* Without hesitating Laura drove down the quiet street and pulled in behind Chris's Volvo. For a second, she debated not bringing the report, then shook her head. No secrets, she decided, and opened the door of the Jeep.

"What do you talk about in those marathon meetings and is there any food?" The voice came from the darkened porch and Laura followed it, drawn irresistibly to the teasing sound; Chris was on the swing, barefoot in cutoffs and a T-shirt.

"Mostly we talk about our plans to take over the world using the media to manipulate the masses. Then we have really bad sandwiches and carrot cake for lunch."

Chris's peal of laughter was exactly what Laura needed to hear as she eased down on the swing tapping the rolled up booklet on her leg. "The Six looked good today. Glad to be back in the swim?"

"Mmm, yeah." Chris moved closer and rested her head on Laura's shoulder. "Are we okay here or is it a little too public?"

"Well, could you turn on the porch light for just a minute? There's something I want to show you." Laura waited while the blonde woman got up and reached inside the door to hit the switch.

"What's that?" Chris tilted her head to read the cover of the report before lowering herself to sit cross-legged on the swing.

"This is an On Air Personality Study. We pay Target Research a good deal of money to do these extensive market research projects. They do the surveys and it helps us to see what areas we're weak in and they make recommendations. Mostly what you and the rest of the station see are their little quarterly visits that make us all crazy." Laura looked up and Chris nodded in understanding. "We don't really talk to you about the research, we just try to shift the focus of our priorities."

"Who is we?" Chris asked.

"Management. Corporate, Art, Elly and me. What I'm trying to say is that y'all aren't privy to this information. I could lose my job by showing it to you."

"Do you know your Texas accent gets thicker when you're stressed? I don't want you to get into trouble over some report." Chris's tone was gently chiding.

Laura's mouth tightened. "No, I trust you and I want you to see it—professionally and personally—and you need to see it for your own peace of mind." She flipped open the cover and started turning pages until she got to the chart she wanted. "Here."

*Eighty-four percent name recognition?* "I don't get it," Chris said in a puzzled voice. "Only eighty-four percent of our viewers know who I am?"

"No, Chris. Eighty-four percent of the people in Burkett Falls and the surrounding areas know who you are. You test higher than any local anchor Target has ever seen. If we go through this," Laura turned to another graph, "you can see that you top forty percent in viewer preference. I've *never* seen that. Roger McNamara only hit thirty-six and he was the best I've ever had 'til now. And you've only been at this a month."

"So…" Realization was beginning to dawn on Chris.

"Here's your protection," Laura said softly. "I'm not saying that you're invincible, but regardless of how you choose to live your life, someone would have to think very long and hard before pulling you off the air." She hesitated for only a second before imparting one last bit of information. "By showing you this, I've given you the information you'd need if you ever had to file suit for discrimination. Now, past performance is not a guarantee of future success," Laura smirked at her own disclaimer, "but this is important, Chris; you have all the power here."

"But what about the book?" Green eyes looked earnestly into Laura's and the News Director smiled. "We'll know tomorrow, but trust me when I tell you that if you get a numbers kick like this in a research project, the ratings book is going to be fabulous. Elly about wet herself."

It was almost too much for Chris to absorb. It felt like a weight had been lifted from her shoulders. "Could you really get in trouble for telling me this?"

Laura snorted. "You could break us with the salary demand alone. This is what Jan Sheffield was seeing in Mississippi, Chris." She breathed out impatiently, "Aren't you listening to me at all when I tell you that you can be anything you want to be?"

Chris looked down as Laura's nervous hands played with the corner of the report. The news director had just given her a powerful weapon that she could turn on the station and launch a career that could go as far as she was willing to let it. But Laura had done it knowing that she was risking her job and without asking for anything in exchange. Chris couldn't decide which touched her more. "Okay."

"Okay, what?"

"Okay, thanks for telling me. I feel a lot better. Do I still get a ten percent raise next year?"

"Chris, don't you…"

"No." Chris placed her fingers softly over Laura's lips. "This couldn't have been easy for you to do. As far as I'm concerned that's it—subject dropped. I'm here for the duration of my contract at the salary we agreed on. Now in three years, you'll probably have to cough up some serious cash. As far as the rest of it's concerned, I still can't hold hands with you in public and that hurts. But I have you here and now. That's not too bad."

Laura felt the warmth spread from the center of her chest as Chris nestled into her shoulder. "Well, actually I can't stay. Hey!" The swing rocked abruptly when the smaller woman sat up. "I'm sorry, but I haven't been home in a week," she said apologetically. "I've got laundry to do and I have to iron."

Chris sighed. "I know, it's just we never have any time."

"Look, they're gone tomorrow. I'll take you to dinner after the Six. Your choice, then we'll go back to my place and you can plan to stay. That is, I'm asking you if you'll stay, even if it's a school night." Laura took one of Chris's smaller hands into her own, marveling at its strength and elegance compared to her tanned roughness.

"You're on. Anywhere I want?"

"We're gonna have Mexican again, aren't we?"

Laura was humming delightedly as she marked another line on the May Nielsen Ratings Book. The tiny print was making her eyes water, but that was the only bad news. Everything else about the book was a vindication of what she'd put the newsroom through over the last two months.

"Wouldja look at the men?"

"Hmm?" Laura looked up at the Promotions Manager who was pacing in front of her desk.

"Men are tuning in to the Six in *droves*…18 to 34, 35 to 54, all the demos we're looking for. We already had the women, but damn!" Elly quickly flipped to another page. "Could you work some magic for the Ten? It's not bad, but I want a twelve point turnaround next book there too."

"Everybody did a great job in May, your people too, Elly."

"We had a lot more to work with…made a huge difference. Ah, the woman of the hour." Elly looked at her watch. "Hey, Chris, how come you're not on the set?"

"Because I'm having the consultant day from hell!" Chris glowered as she tossed her briefcase down on a chair.

"She spent the day with Marti, so Tom's going solo," Laura supplied. "Are they gone?"

"Yes, I just dropped their interfering little asses at the airport. You were locked up with all three of them for nine hours yesterday? Why aren't you being held on an assault charge?"

"Because I'm learning to control my temper," she replied mildly.

"That's my cue to exit." Elly grinned at the blonde anchor. "Thanks for saving my job. Now I can go on vacation next week. Later, Kaz."

Chris frowned thoughtfully. "You weren't kidding about a management change if the numbers didn't come in."

"No, I wasn't."

"So how was it?" Chris gestured at the book in Laura's hand.

"It'll do." Laura couldn't keep the grin off her face. "Art is ecstatic, Corporate is thrilled, and Sales thinks we can make a buttload of money."

"So it's good?"

"Chris, we had a twelve point share turnaround at Six. That's worth about..." Laura shrugged as she calculated a figure. "...two million a year. We kicked their asses."

"Good, 'cause I'm really hungry and I deserve a big ol' dinner."

"Bad day?" Laura hid a smile.

Chris rubbed her forehead. "It didn't start out that badly. We did a makeup evaluation first, that was pretty easy. I look 'youthful and healthy'...those were Marti's words. I could stand to be more mature." Chris curled her lip. "Then we went on to hair. I am *not* going to try for a fuller look. If you want me to have that anchor helmet hair, you're gonna have to find another anchor."

Laura didn't say anything, and her face remained expressionless.

"Then she asked me about my eyebrows...did I tweeze or did I wax? I told her I tweezed. Wrong answer! And we're off to this beauty parlor to get my eyebrows waxed. Have you ever had your eyebrows waxed?"

"Uh, no."

"They paint on the hot wax with this little tiny brush, then they stick paper on it and rip it off, 'rip' being the operative word. It's a little painful...you could get good information out of a prisoner of war using that stuff. So I'm lying there stunned, and they rub this greasy stuff on my eyes and hand me a mirror. I looked like Rocky Balboa after the fight."

"They look pretty good now," Laura said in what she hoped was a soothing manner.

"Sure, *now* they do. Then we went shopping. Wait'll you see my expense report for this month. I got about eight new suits and a bunch of shoes. I *never* thought I'd say this, but I don't want to go shopping again anytime soon. That woman is merciless." Chris flopped down on one of the chairs gracelessly. "Screw the network seduction, Laura. There is nothing like a consultant who wants to take credit for talent that tests well. That's what she said. 'Chris, we're pleased with the way you were received by the viewing public.'" Her imitation of Marti's delivery was dead on and Laura laughed.

Chris ran her tongue across her teeth and grimaced. "We had a session on finding my 'comfort zone...'" Chris used her fingers to make quotation marks. "...and projecting it on air. The audience is supposed to join me in my 'comfort zone.' I'm not sure I want the audience to join me there, so if you don't mind, I'll just keep doing things the way I've been doing them."

Laura smirked. "Whatever makes you comfortable."

"Mmm." Chris pressed her lips together. "She asked me about my personal life. Do I have a boyfriend, am I living with anyone...I said no to both questions and she asked, 'Why? Good looking girl like you...are you gay?'" Laura's eyes snapped up to meet the anchor's. "I told her yes and asked her if she'd like to go out sometime. She laughed." Chris shook her head in faint amusement. "I didn't lie, it's not my fault she didn't believe me."

"You are incorrigible," Laura murmured, wondering how she would have told Chris to handle the situation.

"Yes, well, that's why I make the big money. Take me to dinner, Kaz. I'm starving."

"Why is it 'Little Kaz'?"

"Hmm?" Laura rumbled as her hand played in Chris's hair. She had almost fallen asleep with the smaller woman sprawled on top of her when she was nudged by the question.

"They called you that at the Open...Charles and Susan, some of the others. Was your mom Kaz too? 'Cause you're not little." Chris nuzzled Laura's neck and waited for an answer.

"No. Kaz was my dad." She shivered slightly at the touch. "When I was little and I hung around the course with my mom, I really hated my name so I'd tell everyone to call me Kaz, just like my dad. So they called me Little Kaz." She opened one eye and peered down at Chris. "You call me Laura when you're being serious or you're trying to tick me off. I'm Kaz when you're teasing, or when you're angry and I'm always, *always* Kaz right...before...you... Ah, don't stop."

Chris laughed and ran her fingertips across Laura's belly to her hipbone before kissing her roughly. Pulling away, she licked her lower lip where Laura's taste still lingered. "I'm going to make you yell this time...so loud they're going to evict you, then you'll have to move in with me and we can do this every night."

Laura couldn't suck in air fast enough. "That's always a possibility," she gasped.

She was awake before the alarm went off. The feeling of Chris naked and wrapped around her was erotically decadent in her limited experience and she shivered against the instant arousal. *Bless me, father, for I have sinned...It's been thirteen years since my last confession and you won't believe what I've been up to.* Laura pushed the guilt away and regarded the ceiling as the new day's light stole through the skinny blinds.

It was scary how easily Chris had slipped in, Laura thought. The blonde woman murmured in her sleep and burrowed closer, if that was possible. For what seemed like the hundredth time, she wondered why Chris would be interested in someone like her. *Interested, hell, she said she loved me...Or is that just the appropriate response when someone says 'I love you' first?* Laura sighed in frustration, sure she had missed some sign. *Still fumbling along.*

The phone rang and interrupted her musings, and with a grunt of irritation she grabbed the receiver and sat up, gently trying to dislodge Chris as the sheets pooled around her waist. "Hello?" She swallowed to clear her dry throat.

Chris sat up and rubbed her eyes, catching the first part of the one-sided conversation. "Oh good god, how?" She slid a hand up Laura's bare back to her shoulder and felt it stiffen with tension.

"Okay, what time? Wait a sec." Laura clicked on the bedside light and grabbed a pad and started writing. Chris was getting more concerned by the second. "That's 9:10, Delta flight 5927...I'll let Keith know. Sure, I'll tell 'em." Laura hung up the phone, her mouth set in a grim line.

"What's wrong?" A niggling fear was beginning to spread through Chris's belly.

Laura looked stunned and she pushed the bangs away from her face before she answered. "Roger McNamara died yesterday of an apparent heart attack. That was Don Farmer. They want me to come to Atlanta this morning."

"Roger is the guy you hit in Dallas."

"Yeah." Laura willed herself to calm before she looked at Chris. "I swear to god this was never supposed to happen...I was going to get out first, but I needed three years."

"What do you mean?" Chris was confused.

"The deal's on."

*"Ah, what the hell. Another day, another deal."*

"What deal?" Chris didn't panic often. Her experiences had blunted that response, but panic was an apt description of what was welling up and she swallowed it back.

Laura rolled out of bed, grabbing a T-shirt and shorts as though clothes would serve as protection from decisions made when her options were limited. As she pulled the shorts on and squirmed into the shirt, she was aware of green eyes burning a hole in her back. Still facing away from Chris, she rubbed her eyes. "You've never asked about what happened in Dallas. Why not? Lord knows you've asked about everything else."

"Everyone knows what happened in Dallas. It's on half a dozen news sites on the Internet." Chris imparted the information matter-of-factly. "Roger grabbed you and you punched him. Did you know that our insurance company paid about thirty thousand dollars to the plastic surgeon who fixed his nose?" She shook her head ruefully. "News people are the worst gossips. We couldn't keep a secret if our lives depended on it."

Laura groaned. "Which doesn't bode well for us."

"I thought we decided that I have a little protection. C'mere and tell me what you did in Dallas that has you tied up in knots now." Chris hoped that she at least sounded calm because she didn't know how long she could maintain the charade.

Laura turned to look at her lover. "You know," she murmured, "the most dangerous person in the world is the one who doesn't have anything to lose. I used to be very, very dangerous." She sat down slowly on the edge of the bed. "Not anymore."

Chris moved closer and laid a hand on Laura's back. "Tell me," she urged softly.

*It was never supposed to happen. Since when has anything in my life gone according to plan?* Laura put her hands together to crack her knuckles, then stopped herself. "I met with Don Farmer, the head of News Operations, right after it happened. They didn't want to lose me or let me run to the competition or sue Roger, so they sent me here. The deal was that when Roger retired in three years, I'd take over as GM at KDAL." She looked over her shoulder at Chris and took in the tousled blonde hair and bare shoulders. "I have a stock plan. In three years I'm vested and I could cash in for about half a million dollars if I left William-Simon. That's why I stayed with the company."

"So…you're going back to Dallas?"

"It looks that way." Laura replied tightly.

Chris felt her fear change to anger and grow until it broke free. "That's what all this was about? Money and getting back to Dallas? What the hell happened to making us better? Was all that just rah-rah bullshit? And the Network thing…that was pretty hypocritical, wasn't it?" She pushed away. "Silly me, I should've known you were meant for bigger and better things than a lowly sixty-one market." Chris put a fist against her mouth, appalled that she couldn't stop the tears. *Wrong again. Everyone* does *use everyone else.*

"No!" Laura faced Chris. "This was about survival and keeping my word. All I wanted was three years…that would give me ten years with Willy-Simon and ten years in news just like I promised." She tried to put a hand on Chris's arm but the reporter shook it off and Laura shrank back, smarting at the rejection. "I thought I could stand anything for three years…I didn't know that this was going to happen and nothing was ever going to be the same again." She swallowed, knowing that Chris would take this as one more sign that she wasn't capable of trusting anyone.

"You never told me…you expect me to figure everything out on my own." Chris let the sense of despair wash over her. "Didn't you think this would affect us?"

"No." Laura barely said it out loud. "We had three years. I thought I was never going back." She looked down at her feet, aware that she had miscalculated once again.

Chris looked at the dejected News Director. *I'm missing something here*. "You don't want to go?"

"No." Laura didn't look up.

"Why not? What do you need the money for—?" Suddenly all the pieces fell into place and Chris slapped her forehead almost comically. "You were gonna quit and play golf, keep your promise to your dad and walk away."

"Yeah. That's what was supposed to happen and who told you about my dad?"

"That's it?" Chris ignored the question and waited for Laura to say something, *anything*, that would make this emotional roller coaster ride stop.

Irritated blue eyes locked and held the reporter's, glittering with tears that threatened to spill over. "Didja think I'd just say 'I love you Chris,' then take off for Dallas?" Laura's voice was hoarse. "I may have the emotional maturity of a five year old, but I'm not an idiot!"

"You..." The roller coaster plunged again and Chris swallowed against the jerk of her heart.

Laura scooted closer and reached for Chris. Taking advantage of her momentary loss for words, she wrapped her arms around the smaller woman. "I love you. If you're still keeping score, I'm way ahead of you. I love you and I've gone as far in news as I want to go. I don't want to go back to Dallas, not to be a news director and not to be the general manager. I need the money to support myself on tour but that's still three years away." She buried her face in the pale gold hair and knew that she was crying. "You asked at the press conference and I didn't lie. I'm not turning pro any time soon."

"You planned it all." Chris murmured as she breathed in the clean smell of the T-shirt and the strong shoulder under it.

"I didn't plan this." *It would be easier if I was gone.*

"Don't even think about it."

"What?"

"Running away." Chris pulled back and took Laura's face gently between her hands. "As messy as this is, as dangerous as you think it is and no matter how much better off you think I'd be if you were in Dallas, don't you dare give up on us. You may have your reasons to leave, but I can think of at least a hundred more reasons for you to stay."

"It's not that easy."

"I'm not saying that it is. I'm saying that if you want to stay you can work it out somehow, some way. It's what you do." Blue eyes looked away uncertainly as Chris said softly, "Come back to me."

Laura focused again. The wanting was so intense she almost forgot to breathe. "I'll be back. I promise."

She checked for the exits automatically, counting the rows of seats so she would be certain to find a way out even in the dark. After adjusting the blower, Laura fastened the seatbelt and cinched it tight, paying heed to all the stories she'd seen, done, and read about in flight injuries. Finally she relaxed, closed her eyes and waited for takeoff. It wasn't long before the second-guessing began. *No, no, no. She never said she loved me, only that she couldn't believe I beat her to it. That's what I'm missing.*

They'd been in the air for about fifteen minutes and she'd finally gotten a tiny glass of Coke when the man sitting next to her politely inquired if she was Laura Kasdan, the golfer. She swallowed some of the beverage and grimaced at the burn. "That would be me," she replied.

"Oh this is *fabulous.* I watched you make that shot at 17 and I just *knew* you were going to win it all," he enthused. "Then that putt didn't go in." He left the comment hanging and Laura shifted uncomfortably as she looked out the window. *Get used to it.* "So when are you going to go on tour?"

"Not for a while." She really didn't have to answer since he just prattled on, oblivious to her disinterest. She was never so relieved in her life than when the announcement came that they were on final approach. After fending off an invitation for dinner, she escaped the cabin and made her way past the claustrophobic crowds at the gate and onto the concourse, scanning the faces briefly for the corporate representative sent to retrieve her.

She spotted him at the shoeshine stand a little way down the concourse. Shouldering her carryon bag, she threaded through the traffic and climbed up next to him, set her booted feet on the metal footrests, and gestured for a shine as well. "I'm surprised. They don't usually send corporate VPs to pick up errant news directors at the airport."

"You're not an errant news director anymore, Kaz." Don Farmer folded the newspaper he had been reading and looked down at his feet as the gnome-like shoeshine man gave a final flourish. "You can get the best shines in the world here. Bet you don't see many women, though."

"No sir." The man smiled. "Extra for the boots, ma'am."

Laura shrugged again. "That's okay, they need it." She watched as he applied the paste in quick efficient circles. *She implied it; she never really* said *it.*

"You did good, Kaz. Got their numbers back up, research looks great, and then there was the added benefit of the Open, which generated a whole lot of interest, even with the questions about Dallas. Since Roger's gone, we don't even have to worry about that anymore."

Laura swallowed, sickened by the dismissal of the anchor. "Jesus, Don, he's not even in the ground yet."

"Don't be a hypocrite, Kaz. You hated him." He adjusted the knot of his tie. "Time to move on, don't you think? We'll get you out of Bumfuck Egypt."

"It's a good station," she said carefully, still watching the hypnotic motion of the shoeshine man.

*She said to come back to her.*

"You'll meet with John Simon this morning," Don said, ignoring her comment. "We'll go over a few things and then your tenure in Burkett Falls is officially over."

*What if I don't want it to be over?* With one final pop of the rag, the shine was finished. "Good job." She twisted her foot to examine one boot and then the other. With a lopsided smile she hopped out of the chair and jerked her thumb at the executive. "He'll take care of it. Give him a good tip, Don." She stood and watched to make sure that he did. *It's not over 'til I say it is.* And with long strides she started down the concourse, forcing Don to hurry to catch up.

The newsroom was uneasy. Chris could feel it in the morning meeting and see it in the faces of her co-workers. Keith spilled his coffee twice and Janie snapped at Bobby, causing the photog to stomp out slamming the door to the edit bay, knocking over a stack of tapes.

She gathered her notepad and left the sounds of the scanners behind her as she pushed open the door and trod down the stairs to the news unit parking area. Jody was closing the trunk of the car they'd been assigned and Chris opened the passenger door, slipping on a pair of sunglasses as she sat down. "Let's get out of here."

"Med Center?"

"Yeah. Park by the Atrium." She fastened the seatbelt and fidgeted while Jody drove. The story was a no-brainer. Talk to the Assistant Chief Administrator about how state budget cuts were going to affect the hospital, the second largest employer in Burkett Falls, and package it for the Five. *Every time there's an election we go through this.* She wished fervently for a story that commanded all of her attention since this one gave her too much time to think about what was going on in Atlanta and the possible outcomes.

Begging. It was a concept offensive to Chris and she had to forcibly restrain herself from doing just that, begging Laura to stay. *Come on, it wouldn't be the end of the world, people have long distance relationships all the time.* Then she sneered at her own optimism. In her heart she was afraid that physical distance was all it would take for Laura to retreat back behind the walls forever. *Easily.*

With a start, she realized that they had reached their destination and she got out to help Jody with the gear. A lot of the reporters wouldn't help the photogs lift and tote, but Chris thought it was only fair to do her share. After all, the videographer had most of the responsibility of making her look good on air and a little consideration went a long way. Besides, the tripod wasn't *that* heavy. A man held open one of the glass doors to grant them entry and they stepped into the cool lobby. The bank of elevators was against one wall and Jody pushed the button. When the doors slid open they stepped inside. "Eighth floor?" Jody inquired.

"Mmm. Yeah. Interview first, then B roll." Chris crossed her arms. They were alone in the elevator, but it felt like it was straining as it started to move. They looked at each other in mild alarm, then the car seemed to pick up speed. Settling back against the wall she waited, brushing one hand down the front of her dark red jacket to straighten it.

A jarring lurch sent them both staggering and the folded tripod fell over with a crash. With one more jerk, the elevator ceased all movement, then the hollow quiet was broken by a clanging alarm. Looking across at the photog, Chris knew with the certainty of a clairvoyant that she wasn't going to be able to package her story for the Five O'Clock newscast.

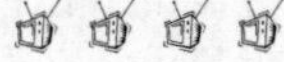

The corporate offices of William-Simon Communications took up the entire forty-seventh floor of the Sun Trust Plaza in the middle of downtown Atlanta. The opulence was a testimony to the high profit margin of a business that sold nothing but air. All marble, mahogany and brass, it gleamed with the power to intimidate. Laura was irrationally glad that she'd had her boots polished.

"This your first time here?" Don led her past the reception area to a wide hallway and the offices of the Vice Presidents.

"Yes, you were in the other building the last time I got the call." Laura frowned, remembering. Brian had wanted her to be News Director at KDAL but no one else had seemed to. The trip to Atlanta had been a test, one that she had passed with flying colors, but she never quite got over the feeling of being a specimen on display.

"You can leave your bag her in the conference room, no one will bother it." Laura complied, tightening her jaw in anticipation of the confrontation with the CEO. She hated power suits and had chosen to wear only a more formal version of her usual chinos, blouse and jacket. The black cowboy boots added even more height and should not have worked with the outfit. But they did. She and Don continued down the hall past cubicles and workstations until they reached a massive wooden door. Don pushed it open to reveal a desk set in a wide expanse of almost white carpet. "Ah, Mr. Farmer... It will be just a moment." The sleek, efficient-looking woman at the desk spun around to use the phone and announce their presence. After a moment, the door opened and an immaculately dressed middle-aged man was standing there, his beady eyes flickering over Laura behind gold wire-rimmed glasses. "So this is the great Laura Kasdan...although you prefer to be called Kaz, hmm?" He nodded them into his office and gestured to a chair as he moved behind his desk. "Your flight was good, I trust?"

Laura folded her hands. "Yes, it was fine."

"Good. Then on to the business at hand. As of yesterday morning, we have acquired an additional four stations: Phoenix, San Diego, San Antonio, and Portland, Oregon. That brings our total to thirty-eight, and now we need another regional manager. Brian Springmeyer is our prime candidate and that leaves us one General Manager short in Dallas. With Roger McNamara's untimely...demise," the beady eyes smirked and Laura was repulsed, "there is nothing to prevent your return to Dallas."

Laura took a deep breath and raised an eyebrow slightly. "There's just one tiny problem."

"And that is?" John Simon waited expectantly.

"I don't want to go back to Dallas."

*They don't need to cut the budget until they make sure the goddamn elevators are working*. "How much longer?" she called through the door. There was no answer from the workmen outside but at least the alarm had stopped ringing.

"Chris, it's gonna take as long as it takes." Jody slid down the wall opposite the door and stuck his legs out in front of him, crossing them at the ankles. "Can't do anything about it."

"Isn't there another way to get out of here? In movies they just climb out through the top." Chris looked up at the repair panel as she contemplated doing just that.

"Nope, you could lop your head off. Then Kaz and Keith would kill me for letting you."

Chris nodded sheepish acceptance and crouched down next to the cameraman. "You're always the reasonable one." *And Kaz is the practical one. Keith bullies me into doing it right and Kate puts it all together. How could I do it without any one of them?* She wasn't claustrophobic;

she just couldn't stand the inactivity. *She's there. I wonder what's happening. Will she call?*

"Did you send a tape to that Jan Sheffield?" Jody's question interrupted her thoughts.

"No." Chris bit her lip. "I can't go, Jody, and it'd be unfair for me to send it. In three years, who knows?"

"We were supposed to get out of here together," he reminded her softly. "You're my ticket out."

She gave a short laugh and looked at him fondly. "You are your own ticket out. You could work in any market you want or even go to network. Kaz told me something." Chris paused in concentration. "It was that there is nothing special or unique about the people who make it to network, they only pursued the opportunity. You just have to want it badly enough I guess."

"But you'll stay."

She looked down and nodded.

"For as long as she's here," he said slowly. Chris met Jody's eyes and there was nothing but understanding in them. "What if she doesn't come back?"

The blonde reporter had no answer for him or for herself. "I don't know," she said miserably.

"I see." The CEO's expression was unreadable. "Why not?"

Laura kept her gaze level. "I'd like to stay at WBFC."

"My understanding was that you wanted to return to Texas above all else." His eyes flicked over to where Don Farmer sat and the Director of News Operations gave a startled shrug.

"Kaz..." Don started, but John Simon held up a hand to keep him quiet. "You are a valuable commodity, Ms. Kasdan. Hiding you in a medium market is not the best use of our resources."

*Two months ago it was.* Her eyes narrowed as she considered what to do next. *He's never said that I get the GM's chair in Dallas, only that the way is clear for me to return...maybe as the News Director.* "Who replaced me in Dallas?" Laura asked, already knowing the answer.

"Roger McNamara was handling the News Director's duties. You know that," Don answered.

With that, Laura realized that the deal was busted. *Call him on it. Make him say News Director, not GM.* Tapping fingers were the only outward sign of her discomfort.

The CEO rolled a pen carefully between his hands. "Don Farmer has an affection for you and your work that I do not share. Of course, I cannot argue with results. Perhaps we should consider more than just returning to Dallas."

Laura's patience snapped. "Oh, for Christ's sakes, say it! I'm not ready to be the GM in Dallas, you're not gonna give it to me, and I don't want to go back as the News Director. So unless you've got something else up your sleeve, we're stuck."

The two corporate officers stared at Laura, almost comically gasping at the breach of protocol. Thrown off guard, the CEO cleared his throat. "You want to stay in Burkett Falls." It was a statement, not a question.

"Yes," Laura replied, tired of the double meanings and the games. John Simon regarded her coolly, his eyes never once wavering. "There is only one way that can happen."

Laura's lips twitched into a wry half smile. *Ah, what the hell. Another day, another deal.*

Chris and Jody went into the elevator at 10:37am. At 5:08pm, exactly four minutes after the story on the proposed budget cuts ran on the Five, the doors finally opened and Chris sprinted down the hall to the nearest restroom. Then it was back to the station to get ready to anchor the Six. Frustrated with a day of forced inactivity, she barely smiled as she pushed open the door of the newsroom to scattered applause and whistles. She spread her hands and gave a mock curtsy before digging her makeup bag out of her desk. "Any word?" she asked as Keith came up and handed her the scripts.

"Nothing. Nada. Zilch." He was nervous, as evidenced by his foot shifting. "Art's called a station meeting for tomorrow at ten. I guess we'll find out then if we don't hear something sooner."

"Great." She kneed the desk drawer closed.

Shift, shift. "Are you okay to do the Six? Tom can do it by himself."

Chris was irritated and tired of being coddled. "Could you let me do *something* today? Honestly, I'm about to go insane and I..." Swallowing, she pressed her lips together and closed her eyes briefly. "I'm okay, I just need to do this."

"Sure. You better hurry then."

Twenty minutes later she was on the set. *What a great way to make a living. I talk about death, destruction and human tragedy, and I get coached on how to look pretty doing it.* Chris shook herself out the bitterness and focused on the teleprompter as the show opener rolled.

It only got worse when Chris unlocked the door to her house. Left alone without his mistress for far too long, Biggio the cat had decided to remodel. Books, paper, framed photographs, and other odds and ends had been pushed from on whatever flat surfaces they had been resting to the floor. Chris berated herself for the neglect of her pet, and spent a long time stroking away hurt feline feelings. Her neighbor had fed and watered the cat while she was in Mississippi, but the normally easygoing animal was tired of being ignored. Amidst all the clutter, she never noticed that the phone had been knocked off the hook, its warning tone long silenced by the passage of several hours. Exhausted from her day and the stress of the night before, Chris crashed on the sofa, wondering why Laura hadn't called.

*No answer, no machine. What the hell is she doing?* Laura frowned as she dug her card case out of the front pocket of her bag, fanning out the various credit cards and ID looking for her laminated pager list. With a muttered curse she remembered seeing it on her desk next to the Rolodex.

She met with the other Vice Presidents and filled out reams of paperwork. Then there was dinner and hanging out with the boys. It wasn't what she wanted and she felt like she was signing her soul away, but it was the best she could do. Now all she had to do was get back home and wait for the explanations. *This is the last one, I swear.*

Laura looked around at the opulent hotel room and realized that everything had changed again. Picking up the phone, she dialed the newsroom's direct line, figuring that it was just before nine there. Henry, the Executive Producer and third in command, answered the phone. Surprised to hear her voice, he started with his usual list of complaints. The EP had uncanny news sense, but working with him was difficult to say the least.

"Well, Chris Hanson got herself stuck in an elevator today for some six hours, so we were shorthanded and the IFB in Live 2 is *still* acting up. I hope you're not holding us to two live shots per newscast until that little mess is straightened out, plus..."

"Henry," Laura interrupted, proud of herself for not voicing too much alarm, "Is Chris all right?"

"Of course she's fine. They didn't even singe her with the blowtorch."

"Henry..." Laura's voice growled in warning.

"Hey, I was kidding. Art scheduled a station meeting for ten o'clock tomorrow morning. Know anything about that?"

"No," Laura lied. She thought about asking for Chris's pager number and decided against it, still trying to maintain some semblance of discretion. "Just checking in. Tell Keith I called."

"Mmm hmm. I will." Laura could hear the clatter of his keyboard as he hung up, knowing that there was a fifty-fifty chance of the message being delivered. The aching need to talk to Chris was almost unbearable, so she played a game with her self-control and forced herself not to want. *I'm pressing. She has her own life...probably went out with Kate or something.* Miserable, Laura continued to brood. *I hope this works because I don't have any more cards left to play.*

Rust was supposed to be a good color for Chris, and certainly the new outfit was exquisitely made, but the heels on the new shoes were a little high for her taste and not really practical for a working reporter. Still, she couldn't fault Marti's clothes judgement. *It ought to be nice for what it cost.* She straightened the collar of the silk blouse and checked the mirror one last time. Still no word from Laura, and Chris was starting to get concerned. Rummaging through the jewelry box on her dresser for her favorite hoop earrings, her eye was caught by the golf ball that the News Director had pressed into her hands after the remarkable shot on 17. Picking it up, she looked at it as if seeing it for the first time. Laura had used a permanent black pen to mark it boldly as her own to ensure against hitting someone else's ball. From office memos and notes she recognized the familiar scrawl. *Just 'Kaz.' That's all.*

For a minute she rolled the ball between her thumb and middle finger, remembering the shot, the hurt, and the sudden elation when it went in. *It's what she always does...She makes the impossible possible and brings us all along for the ride. If they can't appreciate that in Dallas, they don't deserve to have her back.* Without really knowing why, she carried the ball with her like a talisman and dropped it into her briefcase. The earrings went on next and then she was out the door.

The darkened News Director's office cast a shadow over the newsroom and added to the fitful air. The morning meeting served its purpose of clearing the table of news issues as the entire staff waited for the station meeting. For a change, the newsroom was quiet except for the ceaseless crackle of the scanners. Chris hung up the phone; her contact on a city construction project that was in danger of a lawsuit refused to talk on camera and she was effectively back to square one. She heard a noise behind her and looked up as Keith rolled his chair closer. "Have you heard anything?" he asked softly.

"No, she didn't call." Chris tried to feign nonchalance but failed miserably.

"Henry said she called about nine last night but didn't leave a message." His eyes were worried as he glanced at the door to Laura's office. "This meeting…"

"I don't know. They could send her back. It's…complicated." Nervously, she tapped on the desk. "C'mon, they set up chairs in the studio. Let's get this over with."

Laura took a cab from the airport. Chris had dropped her off the day before, hugging the taller woman fiercely before releasing her into the crowded terminal, and although Laura had carried the memory with her to Atlanta, she was missing the real thing. *I could just bury my face in her neck and stay there forever. Ah, Chris. Not much longer.* She checked her watch; it was a little before ten. *Should be right on time.*

The taxi dropped her off and she entered the building through the front door for only the second time. Ever since the day of her interview she had used the back door. With new eyes, she looked around the attractive lobby with its potted plants and bank of talent portraits, settling on the photograph of the Six O'clock Anchor. *Doesn't even come close to the real thing.* The receptionist buzzed her through and she strode down the vacant hall and sales area to the double doors of the studio. She slipped inside noiselessly and took her place along the back wall with the rest of the department heads. Mark Wilson, the General Sales manager, looked over at her with open hostility. *He knows,* Laura thought, *and he's pissed.*

Art was saying something about the book and she listened with half an ear as she scanned the mass of employees looking for a pale blonde head. She felt an immediate sense of relief when Keith leaned forward and she saw Chris sitting beside the Managing Editor. *We're good to go now.* She let out the breath she'd been holding and dipped her hands in her pockets.

"Thanks to everyone's hard work, we are going to have a fourth quarter to remember." Art was on a roll now, his enthusiasm making him a better public speaker than Laura thought possible. "And this book is just what we need to establish ourselves as the dominant station in this market." At that point, Art's eyes met Laura's and she gave a brief nod. "I almost wish I was going to be here to see it." The GM smiled ruefully and waited for his comment to sink in. "I have an opportunity to take over as General Manager at KDAL in Dallas. It's something that I've wanted for a long time, and I'm really excited about it."

Chris and Keith looked at each other in disbelief, their thoughts identical. *He's taking Kaz with him.* It was real panic for Chris now and it was all she could do to keep from bolting. *No! She promised!*

"Which leaves us with the matter of my replacement." Art looked to the back of the room and gave a slight wave. "You have no idea how lucky you are." The entire staff turned to look as Laura made her way to the front.

"Kaz, It's all yours."

When things happen in television they happen very quickly. Art didn't have much to move out of his office, so the transition was slated to happen that afternoon. In keeping with the philosophy of being able to pack and run out of the station, his personal belongings filled a little over two boxes. Laura inherited his executive assistant, the dark cherry furniture, the white carpet, and the big leather chair. Laura looked around and wondered how long she had to graciously wait before she could change the décor. Art handed her the keys to the office and shook her hand briefly. "I start day after tomorrow. Everything okay back there?" He jerked his head in the direction of the newsroom.

"It will be. It's not like I'm gone."

Art looked around his office one last time and then turned back to the new GM. "I know we haven't always seen eye to eye, Kaz, but I wish you the very best."

"Right back at you." Laura smiled at the shorter GM. "Dallas won't be easy, you know. Brian had to fight every single day."

Art nodded. "I know, but I hope I'll be at least as successful as you were."

One eyebrow arched. "I wouldn't wish that kind of failure on myself if I were you."

"You didn't fail, Kaz. It got you here, didn't it?"

Laura didn't even need a box. Most everything she wanted to take with her went into her briefcase and she snapped the leather flap shut. *It's just another job in a familiar place. How hard can it be?*

"Am I ready for this?" Keith stood in the doorway watching as she packed up her career as a news director.

She looked at him, wishing that she could impart some knowledge that would make it easier and spare him some of the frustration that she had suffered through. "No one is ever ready for this. I wasn't." She picked up the key to the news director's office and handed it to him. "I was younger than you when I took over in Dallas. Now I'm the youngest GM in the country. It's gonna be hard for both of us…it always is when the number two guy takes over the number one spot. You'll be a good News Director. I have no doubts."

Keith looked at the brass key gleaming dully in his hand. "Thanks. I know you went to bat for me."

Laura smiled uncomfortably. "This is where I tell you that I've been a news director and I…can't be one anymore." She swallowed against a pain she never thought she'd feel. *It should be relief. I don't* want *to miss it.* "I'm going to have enough trouble learning everything I need to know to be a GM to…" *He looks so scared. Did I look like that? Do I look like that now?* "What I'm trying to say is that I'll help, but it's not my newsroom anymore."

Keith didn't say anything; he just nodded and didn't meet her eyes.

"I wouldn't set you up to fail, Keith," she said softly. "Is Chris around?"

"Ah, no," he swallowed. "Out on a story. Is that going to be an issue? My being her boss now?"

"Was it before?" Laura asked.

"No."

"Status quo, then. I'm taking the rest of the day. It's your show, enjoy it."

Chris knew she'd be there waiting on the swing instead of the steps, but the meaning was the same. Laura had changed into khaki shorts and was drinking Coke from a small glass bottle like the ones that came out of vending machines a long time ago.

"I met your neighbor. He was worried about the strange woman sitting on your porch. We talked about golf and his terrible hook. Is it okay if he comes out to play at my club sometime?"

Chris felt a hitch in her breathing and bit her lower lip to keep it from trembling before she answered. "You just take over the world and then show up at my house asking if my neighbor can come out and play?"

Uncertain, Laura blurted out the first thing that came to mind. "I called. No one answered, the machine didn't pick up, I should've paged you but I didn't want to seem…" She shook her head, searching for a single word that meant she'd given up all pretense of being a loner and was afraid of grabbing on to someone else. "Dependant," she finished lamely, then took it back. "I don't think that's what I meant."

"What did you mean?" Chris asked.

"I meant that I would have done anything to come back because you asked me. I can't imagine my life without you anymore and I'm scared because I really don't know...where we stand. I'm the GM now, it makes things easier…and harder. The golf makes me more public too, and it's going to get worse."

"What about the deal with your dad?"

"I guess I can thank Charles for shooting off his mouth again." Laura shrugged wryly. "He wanted me to make a difference in the way television news was done. I can do that from the big chair. It isn't breaking my word."

"And in three years?"

"I walk away."

Chris rummaged in her briefcase, retrieved something, and then dropped the leather case before sinking down on the swing. "Here." She held out the golf ball. "You left this with me."

"Oh that." Laura shook her head. "If the putt had gone in it might've been worth something." She took it from Chris and ran her thumb over the dimpled surface. "It was the one time in my life when I had to be perfect…" She breathed a short laugh. "And I was."

"You were perfect for four days. Not a single bogey."

"No, Chris, not perfect. It's kind of like the difference between a no-hitter and a perfect game. Flawless, maybe, but not perfect." The dark-haired woman looked away.

Chris closed her eyes. *The impossible become possible, and we all come along for the ride.*

"Have you ever known something to be true for so long you just took it for granted?" She asked the question in a voice a little louder than a whisper.

"I don't think so."

"Hmm." Chris reached for Laura's hand and laced their fingers together. "This is as much of a public display of affection that we can indulge in here, but I can tell you that I love you. I can say that a million times a day and it won't even come close to expressing how much I feel the actual fact…pardon the newspeak." She fastened on Laura's eyes and her lips turned up in a sweet lopsided smile. "I love you, and we don't need to keep score."

Laura could smell Chris's perfume and it was scrambling her senses. "I want us to have a life, and I don't know how. This is one thing I can't plan for."

"Did you ever think of just winging it?" Chris tucked one leg under her "It may come as a surprise to you, but I've been winging it since the first day I saw you with that wrecked news unit."

Chris chuckled as she looked out over her yard. "We could plant some big ol' privacy hedges here so we could neck on the swing."

"You are obsessed with necking."

"But it's such a nice neck." Chris sobered and looked down at their joined hands. "We can make this work, but no secrets, no re-thinking—and no running away."

"But what happens tomorrow?"

"We deal with it."

Laura rolled her eyes. "Yeah, but with your luck…"

Chris smiled. "Anything could happen."

The End...

***Of Drag Kings and the Wheel of Fate***, by Susan Smith

A sultry, mystical novel of love and destiny, of leather jackets and cigarettes, **Of Drag Kings and the Wheel of Fate** will draw you into its passion, power, and magic, leaving you spellbound.

Rosalind, a college professor, moves to Buffalo for her first job where she meets Taryn, a young butch tattoo artist, and they set the harsh upstate winter ablaze with their intense attraction, but find out it is so much more than that—all the world's their stage, and they must act on the demands of fate, or lose everything.

Smitty's eloquent prose lures you with its beauty and captivates you with its unashamed honesty; its intensity will overwhelm you and make you beg for more as the words burn into you. Rosalind and Taryn will reside in your heart and soul long after you've read this book for the 20th time. You will find the meaning of life, you will be entranced in the sublime, and you will be grateful for the moment.

And now for a special preview from the soon to be released JHP book by Susan Smith, ***Of Drag Kings and the Wheel of Fate***.

# Of Drag Kings and the Wheel of Fate

## Susan Smith

***

*An Excerpt*

It was in the cemetery that Rosalind Olchawski first received the word on love. She was walking in Forest Lawn, seeking beauty where it was rumored to be found. There weren't many places in Buffalo she'd found to be beautiful, but she'd only been a resident for a few months. It was Rosalind's nature to try and be generous, with places and with people, and to find pleasing what was presented as pleasing. So she walked, and her a*Tristaine* **preview by Cate Culpepper, another JHP offering***Tristaine* **preview by Cate Culpepper, another JHP offering**ccepting nature found the cemetery agreeable, the monuments somber and interesting, the trees stubbornly green against an early September sky.

Rosalind drew a hand through her hair, the strands mingling red and gold, the pale white of bleached bone, the yellow of saffron in a riot of color. Her eyes were a similar mingling, brown and gray and green, agate, like the edge of a mountain lake reflecting the changing leaves of autumn. Her face was that of an eternal youth, despite the fine lines that stress had started to carve near her mouth, around her eyes. At thirty-three, Rosalind Olchawski had the look of a perpetual teenager with the weariness of the aged.

Walking was an addiction, a time to put her seething brain on hold and let her body move without direction, a Zen exercise for a woman who lived too long and often in her head. In her own estimation, walking had saved her sanity during the writing of her dissertation. Having completed a doctorate, she was now convinced that no one went through the process and remained sane. She'd seen friends and colleagues succumb to their own brands of madness: fits of temper, drunken bouts, marriages thrown up on the rocks. Rosalind smiled, just a little, at that. Her marriage had already been shredded by the time she'd started writing, and over before she was halfway done. Poor Paul; he didn't even get the satisfaction of suffering grandly through her dissertation, claiming all the neglected spouse's privileges and sympathy. He'd been neglected long before, and taken his privileges elsewhere.

They had separated halfway through the first draft. The peaceful year that followed allowed her to write with a will, and only the awareness of how much she should have been suffering during the dissolution of her marriage kept her from speaking of it. A year of separation allowed him to dream of a reconciliation and allowed her to finish her doctorate in her maiden name. The degree and the divorce proceedings were born in the same month. By the time the divorce was final, she'd accepted a job teaching in Buffalo. The physical move from Ithaca over the summer was merely symbolic. She'd left long before.

Rosalind sighed and put her hands in the pockets of her jacket. It was an ungenerous memory, one that she didn't like to revisit. There was too much unfinished, too much inexplicable about the unraveling of her marriage for her to be settled with how it happened. Maybe no memory was easy until it was digested and reformed.

A car passed her on the cemetery path, moving at a stately pace. She stepped aside, wondering if they were visiting relatives, or were tourists. Rosalind ducked her head to acknowledge their potential grief, and hide the inappropriate thoughts she'd been thinking. She didn't know anyone who was buried here, but she could try and maintain a respectful air. A cemetery was a place for reflection, for communing with the divine. Her mind refused to get caught up in the rhythm of celestial time, and churned out thoughts that had no reflection of eternity. She held on to a hope that the beauty of the setting might change that.

An arrow of black tore across her vision, low and to the left. It took her mind a moment to recognize the shape. Rosalind watched as the crow back-winged and landed on a headstone some fifteen feet off the path. It arranged its feathers with a full body shake and turned, feet shuffling on the blue stone. One bright black marble of an eye found her. She had the oddest sensation that the crow was about to speak when it opened its yellow beak, but no sound came out. The silence was unnerving, as if she couldn't hear what was being said to her. The crow cocked its head, looked away, then was gone. The blue stone drew her eye. She walked off the path to get a better look.

*It was unfinished. On the front was a patch smooth as glass, with writing inscribed. Not the name and date that Rosalind expected, but a quotation.*

*Love is the emblem*
*of eternity; it confounds*
*all notion of time*
*effaces all memory*
*of a beginning, all fear*
*of an end.*

She reached in her pocket for a scrap of paper to copy it down. It was the kind of thing she'd love to recite, later, to a friend, to try and capture the moment of the crow and the gravestone. She wondered who slept under the stone, why they'd left no record of who they'd been, and when they had lived. A feeling of ineffable sadness gripped her, the weight of a grief she didn't possess. She interpreted the feeling as a stab of loneliness for Ithaca, for a familiar setting and familiar people. She was gentle with herself, letting the feeling pass. Loneliness was perfectly normal in a new town. She was starting a new job, which she had to admit she loved; she'd already made a friend.

Rosalind had had the impression, before she'd moved there, that Buffalo was a dying rust belt town, forlorn after the close of the steel mills, known only for chicken wings and bad football. She'd expected to find many sports bars, the truth behind all those snow jokes, and a monochrome city against a monochrome sky on the edge of a Great Lake. She'd consoled herself with thoughts of the two hour drive to Toronto, and all the theater to be had in that splendid Canadian metropolis. Ellie had shown her the way.

It was one of those getting-to-know-you department functions, the kind with nametags and plastic cups of juice. A chance, Rosalind thought very privately, for her to start practicing kissing ass. She remembered the very moment she met Ellie. She had to be from the Theater Department; her entrance was too perfect and too loud for her to be in English. The woman who entered wore black in celebration of mortuary finery. Black silk shirt, black leather jacket, black jeans over narrow black boots, all set against a curling array of ash blond hair. She sashayed into the room blowing kisses, just adoring everyone she came near in a manner too exaggerated to be real. Suddenly everyone else in the room was beige and wan. The woman poured herself a glass of juice, laughing with a mouth scarlet and brilliant.

Rosalind felt like she was back in high school. She wanted this woman to come talk to her, to laugh at her jokes, to turn the light of her attention her way. When the woman glanced at her and smiled, she nearly dropped her cup of juice. When the woman excused herself from an unfinished conversation and strolled over to her, Rosalind struggled to keep herself from looking over her shoulder to see whom she was approaching.

*The woman stopped right next to her and leaned in as if they were the oldest of friends sharing a secret. "You look like you have a sense of humor. It's my duty to preserve that." There was such amusement in her tone that Rosalind found herself smiling in return.*

*"I like to think that I do," she said. It was the start of a conversation that hadn't ended for hours.*

*Ellie would like the quotation*, she decided. The weight of grief she called loneliness shifted, she started walking faster. Maybe it was time to start unpacking her office.

"Dr. Olchawski?" The voice called from the partially open door, half shielding the office of the newest addition to the English Department at the University at Buffalo. The doctor in question, looking more like one of her students in faded jeans and a red t-shirt with a Shakespeare in Delaware Park logo, was lost behind a mountain of papers threatening to swamp her desk. She bravely held the trembling mass at bay, bracing an arm against it as she reached out with her foot, edging the door open.

"Incredible. I didn't think you were tall enough for that move, let alone limber enough. How can you have this much junk? The semester just started." Ellie's voice was rimmed with amusement. She sank into the empty chair at the corner of the desk, watching as the stack of papers started to teeter. The papers were given a firm shove back onto the desk, then a warning look.

"I'm still moving in," Rosalind commented to her reclining friend.

Ellie looked up at the picture over the desk, of Rosalind in Renaissance Festival wench's garb, a tankard in each hand, bosom straining against the low-cut gown. "You should put that thing away before your students start palpitating."

"This, from an actress. I thought you'd appreciate period costume," Rosalind said, sinking into her chair.

"Oh, I do. But you're lovely enough in your street drag. Put you in something low cut, and you're lethal," Ellie said with an appreciative look. Rosalind turned her agate eyes on her friend and narrowed them shrewdly.

"Thou dost protest too much. What's all the flattery for?"

Ellie's mobile face became the picture of innocence, a cherub out of Carravagio. "Can't I just appreciate my dear friend?"

"No."

"Oh. Well, Dr. Olchawski, I was wondering if I could trade sexual favors to get an A," Ellie said, brightly.

"Well, sure. I haven't had a date in months," Rosalind said immediately, putting her glasses on.

Ellie proceeded to look shocked and saddened. "Not my favors, unfortunately. I only wish I were gay; there are no heterosexual men in theater. More's the pity, Ros—you're a catch. No, I was thinking of a double date. Bill has a friend in Poetics, he'd be perfect for you."

Rosalind took her glasses back off, rubbing a hand across her eyes. "Oh, Ellie. No. School just started, I don't want to—"

"Ros. It's been final for nine months. You can stop mourning, it's the nineties. People do get divorced," Ellie said, taking the glasses away from her friend.

The truth was that Rosalind was not mourning, at least not her failed marriage. That she had expected from the moment Paul had proposed to her. There had been a warning voice in the back of her mind, saying *not a good idea.* She could never quite put her finger on why. He was a good man, pleasant to look at, good company, gentle in a fashion. They'd known one another forever, finally dating in their late twenties because everyone seemed to think they should. It wasn't regret she'd felt when he finally turned elsewhere to seek companionship, after she'd stopped sleeping with him. It was relief.

She hadn't even minded when he came home and told her about his affair. She'd accepted it with only a twinge of guilty pleasure, as if to say…*finally. We can admit that this was a mistake all along.* She hadn't chastised him for his infidelity, or turned down his offer of divorce.

It reduced him to tears that she didn't think enough of him to rage at him, strike out at him. *Why would I?* Rosalind wondered. She'd never hated him. That would require an intensity of emotion that didn't exist in her. She was a warm person, everyone said so, but hot, no. Not given to the fires of jealousy or rage, anger or revenge. Or, a small part of her admitted, love.

Paul had been good to her. She felt affection for his good heart, his simple masculine virtues and vanities, his dreams that seemed so manageable. All of this was coupled with a sense of superiority, a distance from the possessiveness he seemed to feel about her person. She really didn't care if he found someone else to make him happy, she just knew that she couldn't. It had broken his heart, finally, that she didn't love him enough to hate him.

"You're not normal, Ros. If I didn't know better, I'd say you were frigid. Or a dyke, but you never show any interest in girls either. You just don't get worked up over anybody."

She wanted to. In her heart, Rosalind yearned to be driven to distraction, to make every mistake a lover could, to lose herself in courtship's dance and retreat. To be out of control, to feel like there was nothing she wouldn't fight, wouldn't overcome to have…whoever.

That's where her imagination failed her. At thirty-three, nine months after her divorce from her old friend and erstwhile husband, she despaired of it ever happening.

*I must be missing a piece of my heart, damaged in some way, because I've never felt it*, she thought. *Shakespeare said that the poet, the lover, the madman are of imagination all compact…I'm not so sure.*

"Oh, Ellie. A poet. A blind date with a poet. Just what I need," Rosalind finally said.

"Look, I promise you it'll be fun. There's a drag show downtown at Club Marcella. I want to go check it out before I send my students to review it. You love that stuff—I've seen your notes for your Gender In Shakespeare seminars. You look like you need to have some fun, baby. Come out and play."

Hours later, in Rosalind's car on the way to the club, Ellie was still insisting that it would be a grand evening. Rosalind had insisted on taking her car as an escape valve. If the date went awry, Ellie could go home with Bill and she could slip away on her own.

"You remember my signal if he's boring the devil out of me?" she asked Ellie, not for the first time.

"You start choking on the little umbrella in your drink and fall off the chair. When you turn blue, I yell 'man overboard!' And drag you clear." She turned the rearview mirror so she could regard herself.

Rosalind turned the mirror back. "That's for driving, not looking at yourself. No, if I go like this, you meet me at the pay phone and we invent a sick relative."

Ellie nodded in a parody of comprehension. "The eagle flies at midnight. The crow is on the gravestone."

Rosalind looked sharply at her friend. After Ellie had surprised her with news of the double date, she'd forgotten about the quotation from the cemetery.

"Did I tell you about the crow?" she asked.

"You make this gesture…" Ellie said, demonstrating.

"No, not that. I spent the afternoon in Forest Lawn. I found this quote I wanted to read to you, something carved on one of the stones. I only noticed it because a crow flew down and landed on the stone." Rosalind left one hand on the wheel and reached in her pocket for the scrap of paper. She pulled it out, feeling a small thrill of triumph. "Read that."

Ellie did, squinting over Rosalind's handwriting. "How very Gothic and morbid. It's gorgeous. I didn't know you liked Madame de Staël. What had you haunting the cemetery this afternoon?"

"Just walking. I wanted to see Red Jacket's monument and the pond with the swans." Rosalind took the scrap of paper back and folded it neatly in half. "Do you believe in it?" she asked, casting a glance at Ellie. Ellie was fixing her lipstick, making obscene faces at herself in the mirror.

"Red Jacket, or the swans? I believe in swans, but they are a little suspect."

"Love." When Rosalind spoke the word, it took on the grandeur of Paris, the strangeness of Byzantium. She had added, without knowing it, a level of reverence that only those who had never visited could add to the name of a destination. "Love like that, that erases time."

Ellie stopped applying her makeup. "It's the blind date, isn't it. Look, I think he'll be a nice guy, Bill said he'd be perfect for you—"

"*Bill* said? You mean you haven't even met this guy?" Rosalind demanded, taking the corner sharply.

"I'm looking out for your best interests! Sweetie, you may not have noticed, but you are moping. I'm trying to get you out into the world."

"Ellie, I just moved here a couple of months ago. I'm starting a new job, getting to know the area, I don't have to start dating immediately," Rosalind said, indignant.

"Great excuse. I might even buy it, if I were an idiot," Ellie returned, smiling broadly.

It deflated Rosalind's small store of anger. She parked the car where Ellie indicated, sheepish. She picked up her purse, took a quick look at herself in the mirror, and saw the wary mix of despair and hope in her own eyes. She looked away, unable to face it. Life was much more bearable without the apparition of hope, whispering its sugared promises of paradise. That sort of thing happened to other people, people who were larger than life, like Ellie. She could see Ellie getting consumed with passion. Rosalind knew it was different for her. She'd been married, to a man she'd known most of her life. And wasn't friendship what all women's magazines recommended as the basis for a lasting relationship? She and Paul had been great friends.

There hadn't been the bodice-ripping lust, but surely that was fiction. Warm affection was the reality. "It's a crime that women grow up reading romance novels," Rosalind said, halfway to herself.

"It's a crime that love does exist, and we are reminded of its absence. If anybody ever told the truth about love, the pages would curl and burn," Ellie said.

"I should be so lucky," Rosalind said. Ellie linked her arm though Rosalind's.

"Your luck is changing. Trust me, I'm an actress. We're superstitious about these things. I see great change coming your way, starting tonight."

Ellie had included Marcella's on her tour of small theaters, coffeehouses, and gay bars. Rosalind knew that Marcella's was a drag bar downtown in the Theatre District, firmly planted between the two largest regional houses, Studio Area and Shea's Buffalo.

Both theaters Ellie advised her to take in small doses. "They cater to the white white suburban tourists from Orchard Park and Williamsville. They'll get touring companies doing *Phantom*, *Grease*, and for a real big thrill, *Rent.* If you like your musicals white bread, go to Shea's. If you want to find some good stuff being done, hit the Ujima Company, Buffalo Ensemble, Paul Robeson—any of the small houses. The tourists would drop dead of fright to see what's really being done in Buffalo," Ellie proclaimed like a priestess giving the mystery to an initiate.

The Theater District was largely a marketing ploy on behalf of a dying downtown trying to lure new blood and money in from the suburbs. Businesses were dying by the day and residents had long fled, but a small strip of bars and clubs aimed at young people were thriving on Chippewa Street. The Irish Classical Theatre on Chippewa drew a mixed crowd, suits and hipsters, students and old guard, suburbanites who wanted to feel very adventuresome. The bars on Chippewa had started a mini-revival, supporting a few restaurants, coffee shops and fast food joints mingled with the older businesses. The old shoe store was still there next to the new Atomic Cafe, the pizzeria still sat across from the porn shop that always had two huge cats sleeping in the window. Chippewa was alive with college students and yuppies.

An enterprising businessman from neighboring Rochester had

seen the market and found it good. He'd purchased the space next to Shea's box office, a club space that he transformed into Marcella's. He'd named the bar for his own drag queen persona and set about making a success of it. Local gay papers carried ads of buff, nearly naked men holding up text detailing drink specials. He held contests, special parties, events, and finally, the first regular drag nights in Buffalo. Model searches encouraged the young to show off their assets for the chance at a calendar or poster of their own.

The front room of Marcella's had a long curved aluminum and glass bar, a dance floor with a DJ booth, and an impressive light system. Handsome young men with soap star smiles and lifetime memberships to health clubs gyrated and enticed one another. Shined, oiled, sleek and sexy dancers hired for their looks performed on the bar, on the dance floor, as bar-backs and bouncers. Marcella had an eye for beautiful young men and included them in the decor. The bar was quickly adopted by a contingent of straight girls in full makeup and tight dresses enjoying the display of splendid male flesh, enjoying the chance to dance and flirt with the boys in an atmosphere oddly safe. They could dance salaciously with gorgeous men, who then went home with each other. When the crowd from Chippewa started drifting in, Marcella's became a gold mine.

Everyone had thought that Marcella's wouldn't last. A gay club in the middle of the straightest, most touristy part of downtown? Madness. Yet, a strange synergy took over. The Theatre District embraced Marcella's. The crowds from Amherst and Williamsville, some of them at least, loved it. It was like visiting a foreign country, where friendly, colorful natives are eager to perform their folk dances for you, take your money, then disparage you behind your back.

Straight people brought cash, so Marcella's catered to them. The drag shows proved to be immensely popular and became a fixture. Ellie had told her about the drag shows, told her that the level of performance could be exceptional. She wanted to send her first year acting students to see the show. "I'd send them to St. Catherine's to see the lap dancing if I could get away with it. Now that takes energy, working with enthusiasm night after night, but I don't think they're ready for that yet," Ellie said, breezing past the bouncer, a three hundred pound man in a security guard's uniform.

He nodded to Ellie affably, then held his arm up, blocking Rosalind from entering. Ellie turned around, and frowned at the guard. "Tony, come on. You know me. Would I bring the unworthy here?"

"She with you? Okay, Ellie, but keep an eye on that one. She looks like trouble." He pointed to Rosalind, who promptly blushed.

Ellie led them past the dance floor, past the gorgeous men displaying themselves for one another. Rosalind did her best not to stare like a tourist on her first trip to a gay bar. Ellie was a performance in herself, moving across the floor, greeting other regulars, blowing air kisses to the dancing men. One of the men turned, saw Ellie pass by, and threw a smile of appreciation at Rosalind. She realized that she was being congratulated, and felt a flush of warmth at the assumption. That someone would think she could land Ellie was flattering. Rosalind stood up a little straighter and smiled back, enjoying the moment of notoriety. She was still smiling as she followed Ellie into the back room. She started looking around, checking to see if anyone else made the same assumption. It was like trying on another identity for the night. Her mind skipped off, picturing what the night might be like if it were just she and Ellie there to see the show. People would see them sitting together, alone, laughing—they'd assume they were lovers. Rosalind pictured Ellie ordering wine, narrating the finer points of the drag show.

# Justice House Publishing

## Accidental Love

BL Miller

Rose Grayson, a destitute, friendless young woman, and Veronica "Ronnie" Cartwright, head of a vast family empire, are thrown together when Ronnie rescues Rose from certain ruin and nurses her back to health after a crippling, near fatal car accident. What happens when love is based on deception? Can it survive discovering the truth?

## The Deal

Maggie Ryan

In an inside look at television news, two dynamic women fall for each other behind the cameras, but there's a catch: one's the boss. Can Laura Kasdan and Christine Hanson fulfill both their contracts and their hearts? Details at eleven.

## Of Drag Kings and the Wheel of Fate

Susan Smith

A sultry, mystical novel of love and destiny, of leather jackets and cigarettes,

**Of Drag Kings and the Wheel of Fate** will draw you into its passion, power, and magic, leaving you spellbound.

Rosalind, a college professor, moves to Buffalo for her first job where she meets Taryn, a young butch tattoo artist, and they set the harsh upstate winter ablaze with their intense attraction, but find out it is so much more than that—all the world's their stage, and they must act on the demands of fate, or lose everything.

Smitty's eloquent prose lures you with its beauty and captivates you with its unashamed honesty; its intensity will overwhelm you and make you beg for more as the words burn into you. Rosalind and Taryn will reside in your heart and soul long after you've read this book for the 20th time. You will find the meaning of life, you will be entranced in the sublime, and you will be grateful for the moment.

## Several Devils

K. Simpson

What do you do when you live in the most boring city in America, you hate your job, and you're celibate? Invoke a demon to shake things up, of course. Join Devlin Kerry on her devilishly funny deconstructive tour of guilt, fear, caffeine, and suburbia.

## Above All, Honor

Radclyffe

Single-minded Secret Service Agent Cameron Roberts has one mission-to guard the daughter of the President of the United States at all cost. Her duty is her life, and is the only thing that keeps her from self-destructing under the unbearable weight of her own deep personal tragedy. She hasn't counted on the fact that Blair Powell, the beautiful, willful First Daughter, will do anything in her power to escape the watchful eyes of her protectors, including seducing the agent in charge. Both women struggle with long-hidden secrets and dark passions as they are forced to confront their growing attraction amidst the escalating danger drawing ever closer to Blair.

From the dark shadows of rough trade bars in Greenwich Village to the elite galleries of Soho, Cameron must balance duty with desire and, ultimately, she must chose between love and honor.

## Hurricane Watch

Melissa Good

In this sequel to Tropical Storm, Dar and Kerry are redefining themselves and their priorities to build a life and a family together. But with scheming colleagues and old flames trying to drive them apart and bring them down, the two women must overcome fear, prejudice, and their own pasts to protect the company and each other. Does their relationship have enough trust to survive the storm?

## Josie & Rebecca: The Western Chronicles

BL Miller & Vada Foster

At the center of this story are two women, one a deadly gunslinger bitter from the injustices of her past, the other a gentle dreamer trying to escape the horrors of the present.

Their destinies come together one fateful afternoon when the feared outlaw makes the choice to rescue a young woman in trouble. For her part, Josie Hunter considers the brief encounter at an end once the girl is safe, but Rebecca Cameron has other ideas....

## Lucifer Rising

Sharon Bowers

Lucifer Rising is a novel about love and fear. It is the story of fallen DEA angel Jude Lucien and the Miami Herald reporter determined to unearth Jude's secrets. When an apparently happenstance meeting introduces Jude to reporter Liz Gardener, the dark ex-agent is both intrigued and aroused by the young woman.

A sniper shot intended for Jude strikes Liz, and the two women are thrown together in a race to discover who is intent on killing her. As their lives become more and more intertwined, Jude finds herself unexpectedly falling for the reporter, and Liz discovers that the agent-turned-drug-dealer is both more and less than she seems. In eloquent and spare language, author Sharon Bowers paints a dazzling portrait of a woman driven to the darkest extremes of the human condition-and the journey she makes to cross to the other side.

## Redemption

Susanne Beck

Redemption is the story of a young woman who finds out that the best things in life are often found in the last place you'd look for them. Angel is a small-town girl who finds herself trapped within her worst nightmare-a state penitentiary. She finds inner strength, maturity, friendship, and love, while at the same time giving to others something she thought she'd lost within herself: hope. It is the story of how Angel rediscovers hope blazing within the piercing blue eyes of another inmate, Ice.

Ok, so where's the book? Right now its at the printer people's plant. Should be shipping to us for distribution soon. The suspense is suspenseful.

## Tristaine

Cate Culpepper

Tristaine focuses on the fierce love that develops among strong women facing a common evil. Jesstin is an Amazon from the village of Tristaine who has been imprisoned in the Clinic, a scientific research facility.

Brenna, the young medic assigned to monitor Jess's health, becomes increasingly disturbed by the savage punishments her patient endures at the hands of the ambitious scientist Caster, and a bond grows between the two women. The struggle Brenna and Jess face in escaping the Clinic and Caster's determined pursuit deepens the connection between them. When they unite with three of Jess's Amazon sisters, the simple beauty of Tristaine's women-centered culture weaves through the plot, which moves toward a violent confrontation with Caster's posse.

## Tropical Storm

Melissa Good

A corporate takeover pits mercenary IT executive Dar Roberts against soft-hearted manager Kerry Stuart. When Kerry comes up with a plan to save her employees' jobs and help Dar's company turn a profit, Dar discovers a new way to do business—and her heart. But when Kerry's father, a powerful Senator, gets wind, all hell breaks loose on the coast of Florida.

**A Year in Paris**

Malaurie Barber

When student Chloe Jones becomes an au pair, all she's looking for is an interesting year abroad in Paris, but she gets more than she bargained for in the mysterious Glairon family. While caring for sweet little Clement, Chloe begins to care a great deal for his beautiful but haunted half sister, Laurence, too. But not even the most romantic city in the world can help these two when the family's secrets threaten to destroy them all.